John Sinclair was born in England in 1962, and has lived in New Zealand since the age of seven. He studied literature at Otago University, is a graduate of Victoria University's creative writing masters programme, and has worked as a political speechwriter, a Treasury official, a roving public policy consultant and a yoga teacher. In 1995 he lived in Harbin, China, as a Visiting Fellow at the Heilongjiang Academy of Social Sciences, courtesy of the Asia Foundation of New Zealand. He lives in Wellington with his wife and son. This is his first novel.

THE PHOENIX SONG

JOHN SINCLAIR

VICTORIA UNIVERSITY PRESS

TE WHARE WĀNANGA O TE ŪPOKO O TE IKA A MĀUI

VICTORIA
UNIVERSITY OF WELLINGTON

VICTORIA UNIVERSITY PRESS
Victoria University of Wellington
PO Box 600 Wellington
vuw.ac.nz/vup

National Library of New Zealand Cataloguing-in-Publication Data

Sinclair, John, 1962-
The phoenix song / John Sinclair.
ISBN 978-0-86473-825-7
I. Title.
NZ823.3—dc 23

Printed by Printlink, Wellington

For Mai and Jack, and in memory of my father

Contents

Phoenix – *Feng-Huang*

The Chinese *feng-huang* has nothing to do with the phoenix of Egyptian and classical antiquity, apart from the fact that it too is mythological. It is mentioned in texts dating from as far back as the end of the second millennium BC; and in a commentary to the 'Spring and Autumn Annals' (4th century BC), we are told that the phoenix (along with the female unicorn, and the five magic beings – the white tiger, the tortoise, the green dragon, the red bird and the dark warrior) is a sign that the land is being ruled by a just king. Confucius is referring to the lack of such signs from heaven when he complains that the phoenix appears no more; presumably because the government is bad, and there is no prospect of improvement.

Chinese scholars consider it likely that the *feng-huang* was originally a god of the winds, as the written character is derived from the character for 'wind' (*feng*). Some think that the *feng* in the creature's name refers to the male, and the *huang* to the female phoenix: and that together the two words symbolise sexual union.

Wolfram Eberhard,
The Times Dictionary of Chinese Symbols

1. Door Mouth

When I was eight years old I taught my father how to walk through walls. It was the autumn of 1950, the year of our nation's first birthday, of my father's first stroke, and the first of my two solo performances for Mao Zedong. So young, they said, of all three of us: a young nation with all of its sacrifices ahead, a young man afflicted with an old man's disease, a young girl playing alone on the narrow stage of the unheated Palace Cinema in Harbin, in a circle of yellow light, while the Great Helmsman and his entourage sat somewhere in the darkness, their quilted coats unbuttoned, the flaps of their ushanka hats tied up, tendrils of mist seeping silently from mouths and nostrils. So young.

I had not met my father until I was four years old; indeed neither of us had known of the other's existence until, one day in August 1945, we were forced upon each another as father and daughter. And even then, during the ensuing four years of civil war, he was an infrequent visitor to the apartment where I lived with my mother and an elderly Jewish couple; so that whenever he walked through the door there was a moment of unease – a fraction of a second, no more – as when an actor steps on stage in a play and confronts the rest of the cast, and thinks:

This is the man who is my father.

This is the girl who is my daughter.

Now, in the autumn of 1950, with the war ended and my father returning to civilian life, we had moved as a family into our own house, but that unease stayed with me. So to be linked to my father in this way, for it to be whispered amongst strangers and friends, behind hands, over tea cups, that we shared this precociousness, this gift for doing things before our time, gave me a feeling of such warmth and happiness that, for a while at least, it overcame the worry of my father's illness and all that it meant for the times ahead.

The stroke stalked my father around his office in the China Eastern Railway building for several days. That is how he imagined it when, months later, he began to describe his affliction in his journal. Like a ghost it patiently observed his routines, he wrote, biding its time as he thumbed through a pile of requisition orders, as he received visitors, issued instructions, and asked for quiet as he signed the day's death warrants. It retreated into the shadows whenever Wen, his secretary, came in to replenish the tea in the battered metal flask; but then, late at night as my father unrolled the blueprints for the aircraft factory to be built on the edge of the city, it raised its shadowy talon over him and felled him swiftly before making its escape. It seemed like a mercury flare, he wrote, bursting behind his eyes or before him on the desk, he could not say exactly where, but it barely mattered, he concluded, for whatever the case he was blinded by some uncreated light. His head fell forward onto the desk and he felt the tissues of his brain go brittle, as if fused into shards of spun glass, or like saplings coated with hoar frost, tinkling tunelessly.

He lay slumped forward amongst his day-books and papers for several hours. Wen, aware that the Mayor and General Secretary of the Provincial Commissariat had no respect for the night or for sleep, dared not disturb him, until, deep into the night, having summoned the courage to ask permission to go home to his family, he found my father pitched forward on his desk, his cheek affixed to the glass top in a paste of congealed ink and saliva, his eyes flickering and a low moan, punctuated by clicking noises, sounding from the back of his throat. Wen brought my father home on the back of a bicycle rickshaw, swaddled in blankets, confused and mumbling. There being at that time no streetlights beyond the main city thoroughfares, and the night being moonless and clouded, Wen had to steer the rickshaw by the light of a hurricane lamp held in one hand, struggling to keep the handlebars straight and to propel my father's lolling weight around the corners and through the dark streets. As he pushed onwards a light rain began to fall, a welcome end to the summer drought and its dust storms, and so, when my mother and I opened the door to his urgent knocking and received our husband and father into our arms, Wen's face and hands shone with a ghostly glow. Towards dawn as we slept the rain became a downpour, thundering on the roof, overflowing the gutters and drains, flooding the central courtyard and sending dark muscular rivulets snaking under the doors and across the stone floors of the house like the black roots of an enchanted tree.

When he awoke my father found he had lost some strength on the left side of his body, and instead of cycling to work, as was his custom, he called for a car. My mother, who was a surgeon at the city's hospital, dispatched messengers around the county and within an hour had conjured up the only neurologist left in Heilongjiang Province, a White Russian, long ago retired. A droshky, borrowed along with its horse and driver from a Jewish family, made the trip out to his dacha outside of the city and brought the elderly gentleman (dressed for the occasion in an ancient three-piece suit, fob-watch chained to his waist-coat, black felt Homburg perched atop his white head) to the China Eastern Railway building for the consultation.

That night my father arrived home later than usual for our evening meal. The household was already eating: my mother and I, along with the Deputy Mayor's father and his two small children, who occupied the adjacent quarters in our compound. My father greeted the old man respectfully, nodded to everyone else and sat down to the bowl of noodles my mother put before him. She had kept aside for him some strips of dried pork and some tree fungus and added these to his bowl. He took up his chopsticks and instead of lifting the bowl to his mouth he left it on the table and, imitating the children, leaned forward amongst the rising steam and slurped the ends of the noodles through pursed lips. My mother put down her bowl and watched him. The little girl stared at him and her brother smirked into his soup until his grandfather tapped him sharply on the hand and then bustled both children out into the courtyard, drawing the door closed after him.

'He said it was probably just exhaustion,' my father announced immediately, without looking up.

'Do you take me for an idiot?' my mother said, and she reached across the table and took hold of his elbow and squeezed it fiercely. I watched my parents exchange glances like little slaps. Then both turned to look at me, and I cast my eyes down to my empty bowl, waiting to be dismissed, but neither spoke. My mother released my father's elbow and drew a long breath. 'If that is his diagnosis, then let's go to the mountains for a rest, all of us.'

'Perhaps,' my father responded, 'when we have time.' He smiled at my mother, but she turned away. 'Sometime, for sure,' he said once more, and then added, as a command rather than an appeal, 'Try not to worry.' He went on eating, and my mother watched him without saying any more, and everything seemed to have been decided.

The next week my father acquired a stick to steady himself when walking, but despite this he continued to cycle to work each day, winding between potholes or swerving suddenly to avoid patches of dappled sunlight in the road. He bought a new bell with a cheerful trill in the key of D, and used it liberally as he creaked down the street whistling old revolutionary songs and passages of Brahms, his favourite composer, all of them transposed, thanks to the bell, into the key of D, or D-minor.

At night he would return home, whistling 'The East is Red' to the citizenry as they walked home from the factories or sat on their stoops, and, whereas before he had said very little to us about his work, he now volunteered details about the tonnage of freight carried the previous month by the China Eastern Railway, the sterling achievements of the ball-bearing factory, the geological survey of the new oilfields in the north, or this year's roll at the school for steel workers' children in Mudanjiang.

He did not go to the mountains for a rest; but after a week or so he began to talk in an offhand way about 'my recent illness', as if it were a mildly retarded sibling who had come to stay and needed the occasional small indulgence. My mother seemed happier at this show of candour, and would politely point out small adjustments he might wish to make to accommodate the newcomer.

Then, after a month or so, my father's eyes began to play tricks on him. For a moment, he reported, everything before him appeared to be frozen, flattened onto a membrane inches from his face, like the elements in a child's painting – a house, a tree, a dog – with all sense of depth or perspective suddenly gone. The first few times it happened he flailed his hands in front of his face and cried out and grasped a wall or a desk to steady himself. But after a while he grew used to these attacks, enjoying them even, and trying his best to prolong them so that he could study the phenomenon more closely. Several times I saw him freeze and hold every muscle tightly in place, except for a smile that formed in the right corner of his mouth. Then after a few seconds he would relax his face and shoulders, turn to me and say, 'Fascinating,' and carry on what he was doing.

One evening I returned from my music lesson, violin strapped to my back, to discover my father standing motionless by the front gate gripping his bicycle tightly by the handlebars. I asked him why he did not go in. 'I have a little problem,' he replied, motioning to me to relieve him of his bicycle and taking his walking stick from the carrier. 'Our front door has disappeared.' He waved his stick at the battered lintel. 'See, someone has bricked over the door while we were out, and all that is left is a blank wall. Now who would have done that?'

I rested his bicycle against the wall, and stood by the open door. 'All you can see is a blank wall?' I said, pointing to the opening. My father nodded. I hopped across the threshold on one leg and spun around to face him. My father tilted his head and looked towards me, but not directly at me. 'Ah, just as I had hoped,' he said, nodding to himself. 'And quite amazing! She jumps into the wall, and simply vanishes. Are you still there?'

'Yes, here I am!' I said, and I stepped back through the doorway, pushing out my chest, unfurling one arm above me and raising my chin like the acrobats we had seen perform at Stalin Park. Just then, a cart passed by, loaded high with a dense knot of firewood and swaying with the progress of the donkey in harness. A peasant dressed in an oversized coat sat sideways amongst the firewood. 'Bravo!' he called out, clapping his hands with a dull whomping sound, and pulling his eyes and ruddy-brown cheeks into a leathery grin. The teeth were missing from one half of his lower jaw.

My father was unmoved. Dust from the cart blew around his ankles and settled on his shoes. 'What a trick!' he said. 'You sprang right out of the wall.'

'And if I stand half in the doorway?' I said, and I hopped on one leg across the threshold and extended first my hand and then my foot towards my father.

'Astounding,' my father said, turning his head on an angle. 'The wall has an arm and a leg, and . . . it's my daughter. Or at least, one half of my daughter. I think, like the great Lu Xun, that I will write all this down for the purposes of medical research.'

'So is this a game?' I said.

'One would like to think so.' My father shifted his weight again from his right leg to his walking cane, and back, and then looked down the street, which was empty except for an old woman out for a stroll, bent forward with hands clasped behind her back as if carrying her burden of years in an invisible sack. 'You must help me then.' He leaned towards me, twitching his eyebrow. 'Will you teach me to walk through walls?'

'Yes, of course,' I replied, and returned the conspiratorial twitch of the eye.

On several occasions we had played games like this, starting with some seemingly absurd task, ending in a lesson – a quotation from Lao Tzu or the Yellow Emperor or Karl Marx or Lu Xun, or a line of Tang poetry from the book he kept in a locked cabinet under the gramophone – which my father would flourish like an ancestral sword or a magician's rabbit. I told my father to stand as close to the door as he could, so that I could reach out from my side and pull him through. I extended my arm across the threshold. 'Take hold of my hand,' I said. He did so, his skin warm and dry and his grasp uncomfortably tight, and it occurred to me in that moment that this was the first time I had physically touched my father, that in the five years since we first met we had spoken many times, had sat at the same table, had ridden together on a bicycle and in the back of a car, but had never touched skin to skin. I began to pull him towards the door. He took a step forward and was about to enter the doorway when he jerked back, twisting my wrist and almost unbalancing me.

'I hurt you,' my father said, straightening himself.

'No, no, it doesn't hurt,' I replied, although the pain had burned my skin. I brought my other hand around and clasped his wrist. 'Close your eyes,' I said, and I edged his hand past the doorjamb. 'Now open them, and tell me what you see.'

'My elbow,' he said, '. . . but then the rest of my arm . . . gone . . . into the wall.'

'Your hand is safe on this side,' I replied, and pulled on one of his fingers to demonstrate. Then without warning him I bent my knees and pushed back on my heels as hard as I could. My father's body tensed and he pulled against my weight, and father and daughter formed an inverted triangle on the threshold, our strength counterbalanced for a moment before we relaxed and released our hands and stood facing each other on our respective sides of the imagined wall.

'Are you still there?' he called. 'If you are, stand away from the door. I will run at it so fast I can't stop myself.'

He retreated to the middle of the street, dropped his cane in the dust, and inhaling deeply through his nostrils clutched his fists to his torso, reminding me of a singer about to burst into song. He launched himself off his right foot, half running, half hopping towards the doorway, and then tripped over his feet and fell heavily against the door jamb, hitting it full force with his shoulder and his face. He crumpled in a heap at my feet, his jacket riding up over his shoulders and his shirt-tail escaping from his trousers.

I knelt down to help him up, but he shouted, 'Don't touch me! Leave me alone!' and hung there for a while, sucking in air through clenched teeth, clinging to the doorframe, his head below his hands, and blood seeping out between his fingers, tracing down his wrist onto the back of his neck and around onto his jaw. 'I am through,' he said. 'I am on your side.'

Slowly, he raised himself onto his knees, pulling himself hand over hand up the doorframe. He paused for breath, and let me prise his fingers from the jamb and clasp his right hand with both of mine. I pulled him to his feet and he stepped forward through the doorway, a shiny black string of blood clinging to his chin and his ruffled hair gleaming with drops of perspiration. As I released his hand I felt the slime of his blood on the palms of my hands and fingers, smooth and resinous, so that I felt I might be able to roll its substance into a ball between my fingertips. My father brushed the dust from his trousers and jacket, and then, pulling back his shoulders, he stepped out into the street once more, retrieved his cane and turned around to face me. 'Aha,' he said, 'just as I thought.' His tone of triumph, of vindication, puzzled me until I realised that the door had once more closed over for him, had become a wall again. He walked forward and stopped short, as before, but then reached out his bloodied hand and touched the doorframe. His face lit up, and he let out a triumphant 'pah', as if with that touch the thin membrane had curled itself away into nothingness, that the wall within his mind had become a doorway again. He walked through and

18

placed his hand on my shoulder. 'Thank you,' he said, and he shuffled off on his walking stick a few paces before stopping. I waited for him to announce the lesson, the maxim to be taken from what had just transpired; but he stood swaying slightly on his stick, and then without turning back said, 'After we have eaten, Little Magou, you will explain to me the significance of today's riddle. Take some time to consider it first.'

That night we gathered around the single light bulb that hung from the ceiling, my mother sitting cross-legged on the *kang*, the heated brick bed, making pencilled notes in a Russian medical journal, me and my father sharing the narrow table, he poring over papers while I practiced my characters, with the toe of one shoe hooked under the table leg to stop it wobbling. After a while my father rose and took a record from the cabinet under the gramophone. 'Tonight we will have Yuji Nomandi,' he announced to my mother, 'and the Brotherly Love Orchestra.'

'What are they playing?' the mother asked without looking up, as my father wound up the spring and set the needle to the spinning shellac disc. He said nothing, but as the opening chord sounded my mother nodded to herself. 'Si-bei-li-ya,' she said, 'Very good.'

As the music played my father took one of the thin paper forms from his pile, turned it over, and began to sketch something on it. Out of the corner of my eye I watched a geometrical figure – a dodecahedron – take shape on the page. Aside from the Party, music and mathematics were my father's passions. To his eye the universe in its vastness and its detail was one continuous feat of mathematical engineering, and music, he would often tell me, is merely a particularly beautiful branch of mathematics. His small library included translations of Euclid (the one the Emperor Kangxi commissioned from the Jesuits who were trying to convert him), Pascal's *Selected Works* and Bertrand Russell's *Principia Mathematica* (purchased during Russell's lecture tour of China in the 1920s). And throughout his daily sojourns he would see around him, either hidden or in plain sight, a world of geometrical forms, symmetries and series, combinations and proportions, progressions and regressions, so much mathematics on the world's surface there to be observed and understood. The curves of an arch as he passed beneath it, the gardens of frost that grew on a puddle by the roadside, the games that light and shadows played on factory chimneys as the sun set, the rising and falling pitch of train whistles, such things sent him into quiet, breathless contemplation, holding himself motionless as one may do when a tiny bird alights nearby, in the hope of prolonging the opportunity to view its plumage close up, before it flits away. What he was seeking in these moments, I learned, was some insight into the unseen numbers beneath the skin of things, beneath the world's skin, that substance which gives it shape and form, and he was confident that he would in time discern it, unless someone first tugged at his sleeve and brought him back into the world of appearances, into the world that mathematics sustained.

He told me once that as a youth he had been so mesmerised by watching the receding railway lines from the back of a train that he had packed his things into a bag, taken leave of his parents and siblings, and purchased a ticket to China's northernmost province, so as to resolve the question of whether parallel lines did in fact meet at infinity. This was fanciful, I knew, but the idea enchanted me. A young man riding a steam train from his home in Shanxi Province, seated up front in the engine, having bribed the driver with an offering of food, eyes fixed forward watching for a glimpse of infinity in the cold, blank wheat fields of Manchuria.

That night, as Sibelius played in the background, I put down my pen and watched my father complete his drawing, and when it was finished whispered to him, 'What are you thinking, Papa?'

'Thinking?' he said, and then smiled and reached into his shirt pocket for his cigarettes and match-book. 'Yes, Magou, I suppose you are right,' he said as he lit up. 'To the untrained eye I was merely drawing, but in fact I was thinking. I was thinking that all shapes are made up of intersecting planes and the spaces between, that planes are like walls, except you can pass through them easily, indeed' – and here he swept his hand across his body, dragging a trail of smoke – 'indeed, merely by doing this my hand passes through planes almost without number, *wan cheng wan*.'

'Ten thousand times ten thousand,' I said, screwing up my eyes. 'That makes one *yi*, is that right?'

He nodded. 'Yes, but you miss my point,' he went on, 'Each plane is only one particle thick, so you may witness me squeezing those planes, ten million, perhaps a hundred million of them, into a tiny space.' He raised both hands and mimed the compression of a span of air into an imaginary box, pressing it down onto the table, squaring its imaginary sides, and then holding up his thumb and forefinger with the smallest sliver of air between them. 'A particle is the smallest thing the mind can imagine; and that is all it is: an act of the imagination, an idea in the mind, a spider's web inside your head. That is why you can walk through a sheet of particles.' His hand began to shake, but I saw him clamp tight the tendons in his arm as he went on. He inclined his head towards me and lowered his voice, glancing quickly across at my mother, who was absorbed in her medical journal. 'You see, it is a simple thing, my little illness, my troublesome friend. At first I feared it was like a wolf roaming at large within the garden of my mind, but now I know it is merely a harmless spider. Yes, a spider has found a way into my head. I expect it crawled into my mouth when I was sleeping. So here is today's lesson: remember always to sleep with your mouth tightly shut so you do not acquire a little spider like mine, who spins his little webs behind my eyes when I am not looking, so that I see walls where there is only a doorway. When I touch them, the webs disappear, since each has only the strength of one thought. And, I ask you, how strong can a single thought be?'

I paused for a moment, and then an answer – the answer – came into my mind. 'Mao Zedong's thoughts are stronger than iron,' I recited.

'Indeed, that is true.' My father fell silent, and I felt a wave of embarrassment as I realised I had contradicted him. His eyes began to wander around the room as if following the flight of an insect. 'This shape worries me, however,' he said, stabbing at his drawing with his finger, 'as it once worried Pythagoras and Leibniz and Poincaré, so I am in good company. A dodecahedron is the largest of the perfect solids. You see, every face is a five-sided polygon, and at every corner three such polygons meet. What Pythagoras discovered, to his great consternation, is that no larger perfect solid is possible. Can you imagine that? Hexagons cannot fit together like this, you'd need to add a different shape – a square or a triangle – to complete the solid; and the same is true of octagons or anything larger. So this is as close as mathematics can get towards a perfect sphere using whole numbers, a shape made out of pentagons – close enough, you might think, but for a science as precise as mathematics it is an embarrassment, an offence. And that is what worried Pythagoras, and after him Leibniz and Poincaré.'

'What worried them?'

'That the sphere itself was inaccessible, that the largest of perfect solids was still so far away from a perfect sphere. They say it is what drove Pythagoras to madness.' He laughed and turned away. 'But this is not important for you. You have already learned today's lesson.' He touched my lips with his finger and told me to finish my page of characters quickly, as the electricity would soon go off for the night. And the moment the words left his lips, as if by his instruction, the darkness indeed closed around our little household with a faint thud. My mother reached for the book of matches at her side and one sparked into life and then described an arc towards the paraffin lamp on the shelf above the bed. She lit the wick and then brought the lamp to the table. Both of my parents returned to their reading, and gazing up at the ceiling I became aware of the yellow swatches of light flung up against the walls and ceiling, and then of our shadows between them, like flames in negative, three dark angels – our larger selves – suspended over us, shaking from side to side as the flame sputtered, mutely gesturing to one another, although I could not tell if it was with rage or laughter.

'When will you get us a generator?' my mother asked, without looking up. 'We have important work to do in the evenings, as does the Deputy Mayor across the courtyard. How does this darkness help achieve socialism?'

'Our work is no more important than that of any factory-hand,' my father replied. 'It shall not happen.'

My mother was silent, and she turned her face into the shadow so as to hold her medical journal up to the lamplight, while in the corner Yuji Nomandi and the Brotherly Love Orchestra played on.

*

When I first met him, my father and his comrades had newly liberated our city from the Japanese and their collaborators, and while the communist forces pressed south to liberate the rest of Manchuria my father was chosen to stay behind and became in the course of one day our mayor, party secretary, chief of police, judge, jailer – commissar, in fact, of everything. These duties left little time for family, so for months he would arrive infrequently, unannounced, at our apartment, shadowed by Wen who squatted on his haunches against the wall while my father perched on the edge of a chair, sipping loudly on a glass of tea, rapidly interrogating my mother on the progress of his daughter's studies and general well-being. If, when his questions finished, my mother had anything to ask him she did so immediately, because within seconds he would rise to his feet, summon his companion and resume city business as they descended the stairs.

It was during that time that he acquired the nickname *Tie Lu* – Iron Lu, the pun inevitable, as *tie lu* is Chinese for 'railway' or literally 'iron road' and my father, whose surname was Lu, had been before the war an engineer for the China Eastern Railway. But even so the title was deserved. My father refused to show either favour or mercy to the undeserving. Everyone knew that Iron Lu would calmly enforce upon others (as he did on himself) the duty to make personal sacrifices for the good of the masses.

Under his rule, food was rationed, entire neighbourhoods dragooned into building flood-banks, lazy officials demoted and humiliated, compradors and capitalists stripped of their wealth and sent to labour camps, curfew-breakers, criminals and traitors to the Party summarily executed. His impartiality, it was said, enabled his justice to be swift and brutal, if at times premature.

It soon became known in the neighbourhood that I was Iron Lu's daughter. On the street people would talk behind their hands as I passed, and when, at school, I would answer a question in class the other children would hold their breath until the teacher pronounced my answer satisfactory. I remember once uttering an angry remark, whereupon the room fell silent around me. A girl began to sob quietly, and I felt that, in that instant, I had grown taller and had acquired claws, that I had been transformed into a snow tiger from the forests of the north that had come to live in the city, playing in the streets and the schoolyard dressed as a small child. To be the daughter of Iron Lu meant that if I wanted I could reach out and tear a child's heart from its chest, and no one would stop me.

And yet, in those first summers together after the Civil War and after his stroke my father would return from his work and insist that I lie beside him on a bed of newspapers on the dusty flag-stones of our compound and study the night sky. He taught me the names of the planets and constellations, and explained that the universe was an infinite factory filled with every conceivable kind of machine, each with its celestial wheels and pistons, and that we observed its workings from a spinning platform on the edge of one of the smaller, less significant cogs. Then he would play scratchy music on the gramophone with his eyes tightly shut, or read aloud to me in an affected sing-song voice from his well-thumbed book of the Tang poets.

*

The morning after my father's encounter with the door frame my mother and I guided him out onto the street and anxiously

24

watched him get onto his bicycle. 'You have patients to attend to,' he said to my mother. 'I'll be fine. Go now.' And he was off, pushing hard with his right foot while his left foot rested unsurely on its pedal.

My mother pressed my schoolbag into my hands. 'Follow him,' she ordered. 'Make sure he gets there safely.'

I ran down the street after my father, keeping a safe distance in case he should turn around and notice me. His office was about a kilometre away from our house, on the third floor of the railway station, which temporarily housed the city government while a new town hall was being built. I arrived breathless at the grand entrance to the station and found that my father had already parked his bicycle, and made his way to the front steps where he now stood, like a stone amidst the stream of people flowing through the doorway. After several minutes he turned and, as if he had known I would be there, summoned me with a wave of his hand.

'So what am I thinking now?' he asked, nodding towards the station entrance.

'I don't know.'

'I will tell you,' he said.

He did not answer immediately, but after a moment took my hand and wrote two characters on my palm with his finger: the first an assembly of long verticals and short horizontals – *men*; the second a simple square – *kou*.

'*Men kou*,' I said. 'Door mouth.'

He pointed at the doorway. 'So now tell me what I am thinking.'

I turned my eyes to the building in front of us. The twin doors, at least twice the height of the tallest man, were set between two stone columns at the exact centre of the façade. Large arched windows spread out in both directions like the wings of an enormous cormorant, and high above on the cornice a great mast jutted out at an angle and on it the flag of the People's Republic was tugged this way and that by the morning breeze so that its four bright yellow stars, symbolising the four classes of Chinese society – the peasant, the worker, the bourgeoisie, and the capitalist – ascended and descended in turn amongst its vermilion folds.

I looked up to the flag, and then back down to the doorway through which flowed a stream of passengers, clerks, ticket-sellers, engineers, welfare officers, administrators, and cafeteria workers. 'What you see,' I said, 'is the mouth of the building.' I traced the arch of the entrance in the air with my finger.

'Go on,' he said.

'And the building is swallowing all these people,' I said, indicating them with a broad sweep of my hand, 'it is sucking them into its great big mouth.'

'Very good,' my father answered. 'Hungry for passengers and workers, the China Eastern Railway sucks in a string of people like one unbroken noodle, a sign, incidentally, of good fortune and longevity. And as they cross the threshold all of these people are eaten up, they are like numbers absorbed into the immense equation that is the China Eastern Railway, they become a part of the railway, just as a bolt or a screw or a lump of coal is a part of the railway.'

With that he squeezed my hand and turned me by the shoulders in the direction of my school. 'Never forget,' he whispered in my ear, 'you and I have learned to walk through walls. It is a gift few people have.' And he gave me a firm push to set me on my way. I took a few steps forward, but then turned around and watched him approach the doorway, holding out his hand to touch the doorframe. And I imagined – perhaps I saw – that the doorway was a solid wall until the moment he touched the surface of the stone, and that at his touch it opened to receive him and then closed up as he drew his foot across the threshold.

*

Years later it occurred to me that I took from that incident a lesson very different from what my father intended. I became convinced that things were there to be known, to be possessed by the mind so long as you pushed beyond their appearances;

that another, more real world lay beyond the walls that others saw, and that my father and I were singularly equipped to see into that secret heart of things. At one time my father – the engineer, the party boss, the amateur mathematician – might have agreed with me, but I now see that his passage through our front door that evening taught him a different lesson, a lesson about the eye's unsure attachment to the world of things, and the mind's unsure attachment to the eye. I understand now that for him it was the beginning of an education in doubt.

2. Harbin 1937

Imagine a cityscape, a far northern city crouched like a sleeping tramp beneath a yellow sky at dawn on a morning in early spring. The low sun picks out a jumble of shapes from amongst the rooftops – triangles, oblongs, rhombuses – harlequin lozenges of light and dark with edges ruled pencil-sharp. Towards the left, standing by itself, is the onion-shaped cupola of the cathedral of St Sofia. Migratory birds fly over it in formation heading north to the Arctic shores. A veil of sandy light covers the whole scene, somehow intensifying the extreme cold, making it crisp and astringent, minutely sharp, a vapour of tiny blades drawn through the nostrils onto the back of the throat. The city holds as still as it can to keep this cold at bay, making barely a shuffle under its blanket of silence, under a sky stretched tight like a threadbare awning against the vault of Heaven.

In the foreground the turning stretch of the riverbank is mostly in shadow. There are dim, blurred forms rising out of the gloom: the prows of lighters or flat-bottomed river-boats, the door of a boat-shed and, in the river itself, the last of the winter ice-floes. And along the front of the embankment there is a collection of twig-like shapes, a colony of the poor and indigent who, swaddled in rags and sacking, lie like musty foetuses in the shelter of the wharves and upturned boats.

Then the scene comes to life as a young man makes his way clumsily along Zhongyang Avenue. We move in closer. He is perhaps twenty-five years old, with untidy black hair, long Buddha-like ears and a scar that bisects one eyebrow, a fit man with a spare frame, whose clumsiness and panting breath are due entirely to the fact that he has for the last several kilometres been carrying a large gramophone of the kind now found only in antique shops, a varnished wooden box with a handle for winding up the internal spring, a heavy platen calibrated to turn at a constant seventy-eight revolutions per minute, a claw-like spindle and a brass cone shaped like an oversized iris-bloom which now addresses itself awkwardly towards the man's right ear. We pan out once more to the level of the rooftops and notice immediately that behind this man, beyond the dome of St Sofia's, a plume of charcoal grey smoke is now rising into the yellow sky and spreading out into a clump of stubby fingers like a harshly pruned rose or a disfigured hand, blackened and burnt.

The city is Harbin, on the banks of the Songhua River in Japanese-occupied Manchuria, a city of some half a million souls – Han Chinese, like my parents, Russian railway engineers, White Russian émigrés (marooned in the North of China after the October revolution almost two decades ago), and a battalion of Japanese soldiers, the enforcers of the Manchukuo puppet regime. The fleeing man is Lu Feng. In three years' time he will become my father, but on this day he has made his way through Daowai, the Chinese sector of the town, and is following the riverbank west towards Daoli, the city centre. He suspects (rightly as it turns out) that the agents of the puppet government who roused him before dawn are now searching for him, along with his comrades in the underground Communist Party committee. He fears that the safe-houses and rendezvous points have already been betrayed, and that he will be lucky to escape with his life.

*

The story of his flight from Harbin was one of the first my father told me. One Sunday morning, I recall, when my mother slept late, he roused me from my narrow cot and told me to get

29

dressed because he wanted us to go to the river to catch some fish. He waited for me in the courtyard of our house with a satchel over his shoulder and his hands grasping the handlebars of his bicycle. His fishing rod and tackle, along with a cone-shaped wire trap, were tied to the carrier, and he beckoned me to follow him through the gate onto the street. I climbed onto the crossbar and we set off. As we rumbled along the cobblestones I could feel my father's warm breath on my forehead, and several times I turned my face upwards towards his and watched his eyes as they flicked to and fro. The streets were quiet and we glided through the calm morning air for about twenty minutes, passing the railway station and the post office, and coasting down towards the centre of the city. We turned into Zhongyang Avenue, and came immediately upon a gang of men squatting on their heels in a circle in the middle of the road amidst wafts of dust. We swerved to avoid them and slowed to a walking pace as my father guided the front wheel of the bicycle around a litter of broken cobble-stones. Another group of men were working on the road some distance away. They were lightly dressed in grey cotton trousers and jackets, their feet bare and blackened with dust. One or two of them stared at us wordlessly as we passed, but most kept their eyes on the stones they were fitting into place in the road.

'Aha, my good comrades from Xiangfeng Prison,' my father said, and he bumped the bicycle onto the curb and turned into a gap between two buildings. 'Best not distract them from their work,' he said. We rode carefully along a narrow sunless alley, ducking under damp bedding hung out of windows. Wet gravel hissed softly beneath our tyres, and somewhere ahead of us a pair of hands emerged from a doorway to empty a pail of water into the alley. We soon encountered a dog with stumpy legs and a lolling pink tongue so thick and heavy it did not seem able to pull it back into its mouth. It stood square in the middle of the alley and panted up at us as my father edged the bicycle past it, and when we had gathered pace once more it ran after us, escorting us to the end of the alley before turning on its heels,

30

its duty discharged, and trotting back triumphantly to its post to await the next intruder. My father made to turn right and then stopped, extending his heels to the pavement and looking up at the surrounding buildings. 'Yes, this is the exact place,' he said. He gently pushed me from the crossbar, got off the bicycle and leant it against a lamp-post. He turned a full circle, registering the row of shops across the street, the factory gates further down towards the river and the old church to our left whose doors and forecourt now overflowed with used lumber. 'This is indeed the place,' he said to himself, and stroked his chin several times. 'That was the British Duck and Chicken Factory,' he said, pointing to an empty lot, 'and over there was the American Baptist Mission building.' Then he turned to me and said, 'On this corner, in 1937, I first met your mother.' I dutifully studied the uneven flagstones of the footpath where his finger was pointing. 'If you wish I will tell you the story of how this happened,' my father said, and he threw his leg over the bicycle and tapped the crossbar. I climbed back up and we pushed out into the street and rode down towards the river.

*

It was five a.m. on the morning of 15 April 1937. Lu Feng was asleep in his lodgings in the Daowai district of Harbin when he was awoken by voices in the street outside. He heard his landlord Tan go to the door, and then the commotion as a group of people rushed into the courtyard, asking, 'Are you Tan Yongshang? Are you? Are you?' Tan barely had time to answer them before they manhandled him out of the door. Moments later a car started up its engine and moved off down the street.

As Lu waited in the darkness he heard the intruders ransacking the house, emptying the contents of drawers and cupboards into the central courtyard. Agents of the puppet government, Lu thought, and his heart began to pound, for he was in a small room next to the *kang*, the heated brick bed where everyone slept in winter, and there was no way he could escape unnoticed. He fumbled in the darkness for his clothes to dress

31

himself, and slipped into the main room. He pushed his hands into his pockets and felt the folded piece of paper, remembering the three characters he had written on it, *Wang, Tong, San*, to remind himself: *Mr Wang. Tongfalong Store. Three o'clock.*

The agents were still searching outside, so he quickly opened the firebox of the *kang,* thrust the paper into the warm embers, and closed the iron hatch. In due course, the door opened and three agents wearing padded coats and carrying a kerosene lamp pushed his sister, Lu Min, and Tan's apprentice, An Libai, into the room. Lu sat quietly on the *kang* as his face was illuminated by the light of the lamp. He thought only of the paper in the firebox, willing it to catch fire and be consumed.

The agents pushed Lu Min and An Libai onto the *kang* and demanded to know their names. Lu Feng identified himself as a railway engineer, while Lu Min explained that she worked at the Tianxingfu No. 1 Flour Mill. They had recently moved into these lodgings after theirs had been requisitioned by the Japanese. An Libai had been living in the house for only a few days, he said, having been taken on by Tan as an apprentice carpenter. None of them knew much about their new landlord Tan, they said.

One of the agents produced a gramophone from Lu's room, unscrewed the back panel and began to search for suspect material inside. Another agent shuffled through Lu's collection of records. After half an hour they seemed to tire of their search and withdrew onto the street to talk amongst themselves. A car drew up to the gate and a minute later departed with a crunch of gears. Lu went to the doorway and noted that two of the men had remained outside the house, passing a cigarette between them.

Lu returned and checked the firebox, satisfying himself that the paper had burned. Then the three of them pressed their heads together in the darkness and planned their next move in whispers. They needed to warn the other party cells about Tan's arrest and the possibility that he had been betrayed, and they needed to contact Mr Wang, a senior cadre who was due to arrive in the city that afternoon from the Soviet Union, to tell him to stay in the countryside until they could assess how much the authorities knew. Their tasks agreed, they arranged to rendezvous by the river at dusk. Lu reassembled the gramophone, said farewells to his sister and his comrade and left the house. As he had anticipated, one of the agents stopped him and asked where he was going so early. 'You have damaged my gramophone,' he said, 'so before I go to work I need to take it to my friend on Anguo Street to get it repaired.' The agent shrugged his shoulders and let him pass.

It was the middle of April, but the temperature was still below freezing, and a heavy frost had formed overnight. Lu's leather-soled shoes slipped on the glazed surface of the cobblestones, and he had to twist his body so as to break the fall of the gramophone. Tightening his grip, he continued on towards Zhongyang Avenue, walking as fast as he could without breaking into a run.

Zhongyang Avenue was still in darkness, like the floor of a deep canyon, with falling light reflected weakly from the windows of the upper stories of the grand houses and *magasins*. Lu passed the foyer of the Hotel Moderne where the doorman was yawning as he idly brushed dust from his epaullettes. Lu tried to conceal the gramophone, shifting it from his left arm to his right, but its sharp corners cut into the top of his hip, so he shifted it back again.

As he passed the Palace Cinema, Lu peered into the darkened lobby. There were two billboards visible, one in Cyrillic script and the other in more familiar characters, but in a sequence that was unintelligible to Lu. A Japanese programme, Lu thought, and as he saw himself reflected in the glass doors of the cinema he caught a glimpse of a face at the window of the building behind him. He lowered his head and hurried on, sensing that all around him the people of the city were rising from their beds and pulling on their clothes and peering through their curtains at the new day. He had to hurry, for with his arms thrown around a gramophone he could not help being a memorable sight. Yet he did not break into a run for fear of falling on his face and attracting even more attention.

As Lu turned into Anguo Street he met a tide of workers tramping silently off to their shifts at the Flour Mill or the Soy Bean Oil Mill or the British Chicken and Duck Factory. He felt himself doubly conspicuous, travelling against the current and with a strange load held out in front of him. Stepping into an alley, he found the house where Feng Cean lived, and knocked several times on the heavy wooden door. No reply. Stepping back he looked up at the single high window, but it was obscured by a pull-down blind. Pinned to the door of the adjacent house was a poster: 'Glory to Russia!' it read in large Cyrillic print, and underneath, 'God. Nation. Labour.'

He made his way back to Anguo Street and to a small park where food stalls were set up each morning for breakfast. After looking without success for Feng Cean and Ai Fenglin amongst the customers, Lu bought a bowl of hot soy milk and a knobbled stick of dough-bread and found a space at one of the tables. He kept his eyes cast downwards, aware of the steamy breath of the other patrons, and the occasional dry smell of a cigarette. The man next to him read through a copy of the *Great Northern News*, folding and re-folding it. When he finished, he threw the paper on the table in front of Lu. 'Does it eat much?' the man asked, indicating the gramophone, and then left, chuckling to himself. Lu picked up the paper, but did not read it. He was already imagining that agents were spreading out amongst the morning workers asking after a man with a scarred eyebrow carrying a gramophone. He paid for his breakfast and returned to Feng Cean's house, where, not knowing what else to do, he sat on the doorstep and read the newspaper.

After half an hour, Lu felt a tap on his shoulder. It was Feng's landlord, an old Cossack whom Lu had met on several occasions, but whereas he remembered him as a tub of lard with stubby pink hands and a fleshy face lined with cold, velvety sweat, the man whose hand now rested on Lu's shoulder resembled a deflated balloon stretched over a skeleton. His eyes were yellowed, as if stained by dye, and his hand trembled on Lu's collar. Lu now recalled Feng telling him that his landlord had fallen on hard times, losing first the brothel he ran (the Japanese authorities had given the building to a brothel-keeper of their own) and then his wife, who had died suddenly from heart failure.

The pair spoke briefly in Russian with a sprinkling of Chinese and numerous hand gestures. Both Feng Cean and Ai Fenglin had been arrested, the landlord explained. He invited Lu in and showed him into their room. A drying frame was suspended from the ceiling and from it an old overcoat turned to and fro on a wooden coat-hanger like a hanged man. There were two upturned beds, and clothes, books and personal items were strewn about the floor.

'They are both good men and have done nothing wrong,' Lu told the Cossack, not sure if he could comprehend. 'I will go to the police and get them released.' The old man nodded vaguely, and moved about the ransacked room picking up and examining the scattered belongings of his tenants. Lu excused himself and left.

Back on the street, he gathered his thoughts. If both Tan and Feng had been betrayed the agents must have found a source from within the party. He must warn all party members to flee, but most importantly he needed to intercept Mr Wang before he walked into a trap. Wang was due in the city mid-afternoon, so Lu decided to pawn his gramophone first so as to put some money in his pocket for the journey ahead.

He turned the corner into Anguo Street and immediately collided with a young woman walking towards him at speed clutching a large book to her chest. The pair lurched together, as if in a drunken waltz, and the woman's book fell to the pavement while she instinctively grasped a corner of the tumbling gramophone. In a dance of hands and feet the weight of the gramophone passed from Lu to the woman and back again as they lowered it in a series of jolts towards the ground. Lu found himself on one knee with his hand beneath the box, holding on to the woman's ankle. She was sitting on the pavement clutching one side of the gramophone and with her other hand holding the sound cone into whose darkness she peered.

Lu apologised for his clumsiness, setting the gramophone to one side and offering his hand to help the woman to her feet. Her book had fallen open at a diagram of the human arm with annotations in Russian naming all the muscles and tendons. Lu handed the book back. '*Anatomiya?*' he said. The woman nodded and pointed at the gramophone at her feet. '*Muzyka?*' she said, almost laughing. Lu smiled quietly, picked up the gramophone, and continued on his way.

*

At this point my father's story stopped. We had arrived at the banks of the Songhua River and turned upstream onto the embankment. There were people scattered along the promenade enjoying the morning sun – old men ambling along with their rhythmic duck-like gait, a young Jewish man with a tall black hat and a monocle reading a book, a group practising *tai ji chuan*, small children in crotchless pants chasing each other like spinning dust-devils under the sleepy gaze of grandmothers.

'Is that the end of the story?' I asked, after a while.

'That is the story of how I first met your mother,' he said. 'Sadly it was not more romantic. We did not meet again for many years, and then the war separated us once more, as you know.'

'She was studying medicine,' I said. 'And you were taking our gramophone to the pawnshop.'

He nodded. 'From where I have now miraculously redeemed it,' he said. 'I was sure it would have been lost after all these years.'

I asked him to tell me more, but at that moment we encountered a team of young people singing a revolutionary song as they repaired a section of the flood bank with picks and shovels. 'There's Iron Lu,' one of them said, and hailed my father with a generous stiff-armed wave. The entire team crowded around us as we drew to a halt amongst them, and my father asked how the work was going and what their names were and where they were from, and the young people competed to answer his questions and laugh merrily at his jokes. 'Have you eaten?' one of the women asked me, and before I could answer she had reached into her pocket and produced a piece of dough-bread which she held out to me. 'No need, no need,' my father said, 'Comrade Lu's daughter must not get fat. Preserve your own strength.' And with that he began to sing the next verse of their song and pushed off again as they took their cue, bursting into song once more and reaching for their shovels.

We continued up river for a while. I clung to the handlebars and watched the birds skimming the surface of the water and the curling smoke of fishermen's fires on the opposite bank. Then without warning my father clutched the brakes and I lurched forward.

'We stop here,' he said. I hopped onto the ground and turned to face the river. He parked his bicycle against a linden tree and then we sat down together on a stone wall on the riverbank. He had not unhitched his fishing gear from the bicycle, and showed no interest in it. Instead, he cleared his throat and proceeded with his story.

*

Lu made his way back to Daoli. The rendezvous with Mr Wang was to take place outside the Tongfalong Department Store. All he had been told was that Old Mrs Chang – the only person who knew Mr Wang by sight – was to meet him and take him to the safe house near the cotton-fluffing factory. He did not know where she lived, so his only hope was to intercept her as she approached the rendezvous point. This would not be a simple matter, since the Tongfalong Store was at the intersection of four streets and there were numerous alleys by which someone could approach. The street was full of shoppers, Japanese soldiers and workers threading their way between cars and horse-drawn carts. Lu stopped next to a blind hawker who sat cross-legged on the footpath, plaintively calling out '*Guar zi, gua-aa-ar zi, guar zi*' as he measured handfuls of melon seeds into twists of paper. Lu bought a pack of seeds and surveyed the scene slowly as he cracked several in his front teeth. He spied the two men in padded coats standing by the entrance to the store, and another across the street squatting in a doorway pretending to consult a newspaper. He noted how the grinder on the corner held himself unnecessarily upright and alert as he pumped his treadle and called out, 'Knives, scissors, razors.'

Lu checked the clock on the stock exchange building. Ten minutes before Mr Wang was due, and no sign of Mrs Chang. He walked to and fro amongst the crowd looking for her, fearing that he was drawing attention to himself. He noticed an old Russian dwarf who was shining shoes in a doorway and slipped onto his stool. The Russian looked surprised to have a Chinese customer who was not obviously a comprador or official of the puppet government; nevertheless, he spat on Lu's modest leather shoes and began work. After five minutes there was still no sign of Mrs Chang. Lu entertained a vain hope that he might identify Mr Wang himself, but there were any number of men on the street who could have been him. The dwarf tapped Lu on the foot, told him he was finished and snapped his fingers. Without looking down Lu told him he wanted them to shine even brighter and promised to pay him double. The man shrugged his shoulders, summoned more spittle from the back of his mouth and started again.

Then Lu saw Mrs Chang come out of an alley across the street. She was carrying a string bag, had her head down and was walking directly towards the front door of the Tongfalong Store. Lu pressed some coins into the Russian's palm and strode briskly towards Mrs Chang, careful not to break into a run. He caught up with her just as she stepped onto the footpath, and took her by the arm as if she were his mother. 'We are betrayed, Auntie,' he whispered into her ear. 'There are agents everywhere.' Mrs Chang looked at Lu crossly at first, and then nodded and kept walking beside him. 'You must turn around immediately and go home,' Lu said, 'Mr Wang will know to leave the city if no one meets him. It is too dangerous even to talk to him. For all we know they may have followed you here.'

Suddenly Mrs Chang stopped and grasped Lu's sleeve. He looked up to find a man standing motionless on the footpath some twenty paces ahead of them. He had a battered suitcase in one hand, a thin coat unbuttoned, and a felt trilby pulled down over his ears. His eyes were hidden behind thick spectacles, but Lu could tell that he was looking directly at Mrs Chang. Lu felt Mrs Chang's body tense and he took her hand in his and pulled her around and headed for the entrance to the store, leaving the man standing by himself. Mrs Chang came without argument, but they had only gone a few paces when there was a commotion of shouts and whistles behind them. Mrs Chang pulled her hand away and spun around. Lu looked over his shoulder to see the man running away from them, his hat flying backwards and falling to the pavement. An agent was running after him with a pistol raised above his head, and out of the corner of his eye Lu sensed other agents in the crowd homing in on the fleeing figure. He seized Mrs Chang around the shoulders and pulled her towards the door of the department store. They watched as another agent stepped in front of the man and tried to tackle him. The man seized the agent's arm and swung him onto the road where he fell backwards hitting the side of a passing car and falling on his face on the cobblestones. Wang darted towards the entrance to the alleyway by which Lu had come, pushing the grinder from his barrow and seizing from his hand a pair of scissors he was grinding. But then he stumbled in front of the old melon-seed seller, and, scrambling to his feet, bent down to retrieve the scissors and then stepped back in alarm as the old man calmly produced a pistol from beneath his sack of seeds, steadied the long barrel on his left forearm and shot him once in the front of the thigh.

The impact sent Mr Wang sprawling backwards onto the pavement clutching his leg, and making loud gasping shouts, ah-aah-aaah, as if he were about to sneeze. The agents fell onto him and pinned him to the ground. He raised his head and shouted in pain as blood gushed in rhythmic spurts from his thigh. Even from a distance Lu could tell that the bullet had passed through a major artery. One of the agents removed the fallen man's belt and began to twist it around his bleeding thigh as a tourniquet.

Mrs Chang went rigid in Lu's arms. Her weight seemed to double as he dragged her into the rush of pedestrians fleeing the street into the Tongfalong Store. Inside the shopkeepers were peering out the narrow windows to see what was happening, and Lu was able to slip unnoticed through a storeroom into a back alley, keeping his arm firmly around Mrs Chang as they ran into the next street. They rested in a doorway while Lu checked that they were not being followed. Mrs Chang had not said a word all this time, but as Lu took her hand once more she turned her face up to him. Her eyes stared right through him. 'He is my son,' she said. 'I have not seen him in ten years. He has been in exile in Paris.' Her composure crumbled and she began to sob into her hands.

Lu tried to comfort Mrs Chang. 'There is nothing you can do,' he said. 'You must flee the city.' She went very quiet as Lu took a slip of paper and a pencil stub and wrote down the directions to a safe house in Jingxing County. She looked at it and shook her head. 'You leave the city,' she said, as she picked up her string bag and made to go. 'Don't worry about me. I will go to my brother's house and await news. Good luck.'

Lu made his way slowly to the river, cutting through the warehouses of the cotton fluffing plant and travelling back streets and alleys rather than risking the main boulevards. When he reached the embankment he felt his heart lighten. The spring sun was warm and birds shuttled amongst the trees on the riverbank. Old people ambled along the promenade. A group of schoolchildren marched past, holding hands in pairs ahead of their teacher. For a while Lu was merely another citizen taking an afternoon stroll.

He came to a solitary shed overhung by some dusty linden trees. It was here he had agreed to meet Lu Min and An Libai.

From the angle of the sun he reckoned he had three hours to wait until dusk, so he crawled under the shed and went to sleep. When he awoke the sun had dipped lower in the sky, and he scouted along the riverbank looking for a boatman who would take three people across the river at dusk. They could have tried to cross the railway bridge, but Lu knew that it would be a foolhardy option. He found a young man – little more than a boy – who agreed to make the journey and they agreed on a price. Then he returned to the shed to wait.

Darkness approached without any sign of Lu Min or An Libai. Lu could see the railway bridge in the distance, and could make out hurricane lamps moving along it and stopping at regular intervals. He heard his young boatman approach, calling out the name Lu had given him. Lu shushed him and told him he needed another half hour. 'But soon it will be too dark to cross the river,' the boy said, 'unless you are happy for me to carry a lantern.' Lu gave him a generous down payment and a cigarette, which the boy smoked in his cupped hands as he squatted by the shed.

The half hour passed. The boy rose to his feet, cleared his throat and spat on the ground. 'Time to go,' he said, 'or we wait until tomorrow.' Lu knew he had no choice. He could only hope Lu Min and An Libai had decided to flee to the southwest.

*

My father's narrative stopped again. We sat on the riverbank side by side, both of us hugging our knees to our chests. My father gazed into the water for several minutes, apparently mesmerised by its flow. Presently a steamboat with engines thrumming pushed its prow upstream, unzipping the marbled skin of the river to reveal a layer of troubled water beneath. Overhead a ribbon of birds hurtled northwards out onto the river, curled itself abruptly towards the east, then equally abruptly turned again to the north and skimmed across the water's surface. My father retraced their flight path with his eyes several times. It seemed an age before he spoke again.

'Those birds,' he said finally, 'you see how the leading bird flies wherever he wants, and another follows closely at each wingtip, and then another and another until there are a hundred or a thousand. It is a simple equation repeated many times over. That is how it must be for them, each following at the wing-tip of another and only the leader deciding where to go, otherwise it would be chaos, otherwise they would go nowhere and achieve nothing.'

He was silent for another age, shuffling his feet from time to time, and once or twice he picked up a stone and tossed it in a gentle arc into the river. Then, unprompted, he resumed his story.

'This is where the shed was, right here,' he said, pointing to the cluster of linden trees behind us. 'I boarded the boat right here and within half an hour I was on the other side of the river travelling through the fields in the direction of Qiqihar. When I looked back there were one or two fires burning out towards the east of the city. I never found out what caused them. If it was one of our cells putting up a fight then clearly no one survived.'

'What happened to everyone in the story?' I asked. 'To poor Mrs Chang?'

'She survived. She is still alive, I believe, although she is very old now.'

'And your sister?' I said. 'Did you ever see her again?'

'No, not yet,' he replied. 'But in this country people return from the land of the dead every day, do they not?' He brushed a stray hair from my brow, studied my face for a moment and then looked away again.

'And what about your comrades? Tan Yongshang? Feng Cean? An Libai? And Mr Wang?'

'All dead,' he said. 'I arrived in Qiqihar and found a cell of the party still intact. The *Binjiang Daily* was running an article about the crushing of the Communist Party organisation in Harbin, with a photograph of Tan Yongshang, An Libai and Feng Cean being executed in a courtyard behind the police station.'

'But not Mr Wang?' I said. 'Or should we call him Mr Chang?'

'Not Mr Wang, whom we should call by his name, Chang

Wei Li. You are very observant,' he said, 'And very persistent.' He felt in his shirt pocket and produced a cigarette and a book of matches. When he had lit it he drew hard on the cigarette and held his lungful of smoky air for ten seconds at least before releasing it slowly in two dragon-columns from his nostrils. 'Not Chang Wei Li,' he said, 'because he escaped from the hospital where they were treating him, and somehow made it to Qiqihar. One of the women found him sheltering in a warehouse on the edge of the town. He gave her instructions to find me and bring me to him at dusk, with food and clean bandages.'

'So you went to help him?'

'No,' he said. 'I had heard nothing from the party network in Jilin, nor from the comrades in Changchun and Mukden. Not a whisper, complete silence. So I had to assume the worst. I first gave orders for the members of the cell to flee into the countryside and hide in the villages.'

'And *then* you went to help him?' I insisted.

My father picked up a stone the size of a large egg, weighed it in the palm of his hand and then leaned back and threw it into the river. 'I had no choice but to go to him,' he said, 'It was my duty. But I did not wait for dusk. I went immediately. And not with food or bandages. All I took with me was a pistol and two bullets.'

My memory of the event stops at this point, like a scene that is held in the eye in the moments after a lamp is turned out. I can recall the burnished surface of the river flowing by, the rotations of birdsong from the trees behind us, and the imprint of my father's fingers on my forehead where he had brushed away my hair. But of my father I remember nothing save an impression of his lean body, perched on a rock, in white featureless silhouette as if his image had been carefully cut from a photograph. The image stays with me still.

'Do you understand?' the silhouette says.

I nod and say nothing.

3. The Bolshoi Prospekt

In the photograph a little girl, my mother, stands between the legs of a man and a woman, on floorboards that seem, because of the angle of the camera, to tilt towards us. She has large eyes, catchlit with silvery half-moons, which stare out at us, slightly crossed. Her straight black hair is pulled tightly into two bunches above her ears and tied with ribbons, and she wears a simple, cotton print dress. Her bare feet contrast with the pair of men's shoes to her right – a smart design, but weary and splitting – in which are planted two trousered legs. An arm hangs down limply, with the palm turned out. The little girl is holding fiercely to the man's index finger, as if she were a piece of string he had tied to it to remind him of something.

To the child's left are a pair of sturdy women's shoes, whose black leather is cracking and discoloured at the toes and badly worn. The woman's legs are covered in worsted stockings, with several tears sewn up with white thread so that they resemble the skeletons of small fish. She wears a thick black skirt and clasps her hands in front of her. The hands are beautiful: long, slender fingers, skin like dress fabric with gathers around the joints, nails pared in smooth arcs, shining with an olive sheen. The child has her arm around the woman's right leg, holding on as firmly as she holds the man's finger. With the tilting floor it seems that the girl would tumble forward into an abyss were it not for the weight of the two adults to whom she clings.

I now keep the photographs in a box under my bed, in the scarred leather album which arrived on my doorstep in a battered and sagging cardboard box in 1972, along with my mother's papers and personal effects, addressed to a woman called Margot Waterstone, who, I realised after a moment's reflection, was me. I had been informed of my mother's death by one of the diplomats who had dealt with my application to have her brought to New Zealand on compassionate grounds. 'To live out the last months of her life,' I assured them. 'She has cancer,' I explained, thinking that was all that needed to be said. But there were 'challenges' the diplomats had replied, meaning that New Zealand had no ambassador in China and still recognised the Nationalist regime in Taiwan as the legitimate government of the Chinese mainland. They would try their best; and after several months during which they assured me that representations were being made and channels explored, I received a letter telling me that, regrettably, the matter had been resolved by my mother's death.

At that time I had not seen the album for almost twenty years, not since 1955, when, on what was to be my last night in Harbin, it was my companion through a sleepless night in the apartment of Kasimir and Piroshka, the Russian Jewish musicians who had become my mother's guardians when she was a few weeks old.

*

Piroshka had met me at the school gate, explaining only that my parents had been called away to Mukden suddenly on party business, and that I was to stay the night at her apartment before catching the train to Beijing and then Shanghai early the next morning. Together we walked to my house, packed up my suitcase and violin, and with darkness falling around us walked the three kilometres across the railway lines and up the hill to the apartment block in Razyezhaya Street in the Bolshoi

Prospekt, stopping briefly at a blue-lanterned Muslim food stall to buy some dumplings.

By the time we arrived at the apartment the neighbourhood committee was already out in the streets calling the eight o'clock curfew. My train was to depart at five the next morning, so we ate quickly and set about retiring early. Piroshka had made a mattress of blankets for me on the parlour floor next to the piano, just as she had done for me during the first seven years of my life, when the apartment was my home. The city around us fell silent and I went to sleep almost immediately, but sometime around midnight I was woken by a brush of cool air against my cheek. The floorboards in the apartment had shrunk long ago so that they let in frozen knives of air in the winter and in summer admitted tiny river flies that would circle the high ceilings at night as we tried to sleep, invisible to the eye but menacingly audible like distant enemy aircraft. I lay quietly for a few minutes with the black façade of the piano looming over me like a mausoleum, then got to my feet and stretched my arms above my head. A faint wash of moonlight seeped through the curtain and in its dull gleam I could just make out on the table before me the silver knobs on Kasimir's camera. It was a rangefinder camera, an imitation Leica with a retractable lens and the name 'Zorki' engraved beside the eyepiece. He had brought it out of its box and placed it on the table to remind us in the morning to take one last photograph before I left.

I felt my way to the small cabinet beneath the window, found matches in the top drawer and lit the paraffin lamp on the table. The camera's shiny surfaces and facets glistened as if wet. Its narrow upper edge sprouted an outgrowth of silver dials and knobs and buttons which resembled gun-turrets on a tiny dreadnought. Indeed, for that reason it was known in the household as 'Battleship Zorki', and for several years it had been my job, when we went out to an afternoon concert or a weekend lunch, to fetch Battleship Zorki from its felt-lined box under the bed and, standing behind Kasimir, place its leather strap around his neck like a part of some ceremonial vestment.

I removed the photograph album from its drawer, set it on the table next to the lamp and opened it. The pages were of a heavy black paper, the photographs themselves fixed at the edges with gum that crackled as the pages were turned. Beside each frame a legend was inscribed in spidery Cyrillic script with a silvery grey ink – dates and places and names, and sometimes an explanatory detail ('the day the floods receded', 'casting of the breadcrumbs at Rosh Hashanah'). First were scenes from the St Petersburg days, posed black-and-white affairs – the couple in evening dress standing with other members of the St Petersburg Symphony Orchestra, Kasimir holding up his violin by the neck like a captured rabbit, and Piroshka, cradling her oboe, wearing a lace-shouldered black velvet dress that made her look like an armchair fitted with antimacassars. In others Piroshka was holding her fingers poised above a piano keyboard as she gazed up in stern admiration at some barrel-chested singer or asthenic violinist whose signature would be scrawled in the bottom corner, along with some words of demure affection. Then the scene changed, for Kasimir and Piroshka had fled St Petersburg after the Bolshevik Revolution, and, with their eighteen-year-old son, Vitja, found refuge for a while in the town of Samara on the Volga, the home of the short-lived White Russian parliament. Then the White armies crumbled and they moved on to Irkutsk. 'We were some fifty thousand exiles,' I remember Piroshka telling me. 'An entire city on the move; or at least an entire middle class. Watchmakers, attorneys, and haberdashers, stockbrokers, bookbinders, typesetters, gilders and silversmiths. There were some aristocrats, of course, and those with the means had their separate carriages – separate trains, even – equipped with silver samovars and with quarters for their maids and their cockaded footmen and for the boys who tended the Barbary falcons and the hunting dogs.'

In Irkutsk Vitja fell into a deep melancholy, disappearing for days to wander the shores of Lake Baikal, lamenting his abandoned studies and his lost friends, and dreading a future of stale obscurity amidst the retreating tide of Old Russia. There were arguments (muted since the family was lodging with relatives of an old friend), and then, as the Bolsheviks advanced on the city, a final parting on the railway station platform, three figures embracing each other violently as the second and then the third bell rang, muttering promises half in anger and hiding their tears from each other. Vitja loaded his parents' battered trunk onto the train bound for China, kissed them on the hands and the cheeks, and turned away as their carriage departed. Then he ran to catch the westbound train. Four decades would pass before they saw each other again.

In Harbin, after Battleship Zorki came into Kasimir's possession, the photographs in the album became more numerous and more candid: Piroshka sitting beside a great-coated rabbi in a droshky; my mother at age four or five in her best dress performing a curtsey in the foyer of the Opera House; Kasimir in a straw hat playing his violin to a group of picnickers reclining on cushions amidst the trees on Sun Island, mouths open from singing or laughing, while in the background two children and a small dog raid the food hamper.

For his first ten years in China, Kasimir led the first violins in the Harbin Symphony Orchestra and taught at the Harbin No. 1 Music School. He was short in stature, with a brown curly beard and china-blue eyes which, along with his nose and mouth, seemed to have settled into the lower half of his face, leaving a large expanse of bald forehead that was marked by three shallow creases running north to south. A mop of wispy hair stood on the apex of his head, and he would often run the fingers of one hand through it so that the strands stood dramatically on end like a line of tilting exclamation marks.

Kasimir was several years younger than his wife, and perhaps because of this was given to acts of virtuosity: reciting poetry or cracking jokes in French, Russian and Italian, mimicking voices and birdcalls, and humming the opening bars (and often much more) of any piece of music anyone could name. He appeared also to have done most of his ageing in his twenties, and thereafter hardly changed his appearance until his death at seventy-five. In photographs of the Harbin orchestra taken in the early 1920s one can instantly recognise the balding man with the long scrawny neck extending from his collar like a turtle's from its shell. But to identify in the photographs the other orchestra members, those who still visited our apartment in the 1940s, I had to scoop the flesh from cheeks that had since sunk or erase hair that had since been lost or, in one case, remove an eye and two fingers lost to a beating by the Fascists in the 1930s.

The most arresting photographs were those of Piroshka posing by herself. Like many of the Russian women I knew when I was a child, she was shaped like a pigeon – a *golubchik*, as Kasimir called her and her women friends, glancing over his shoulder to make sure she was out of earshot – with slender muscular legs holding up a rounded, top-heavy torso. What distinguished her was her face, severe and forbidding like an actor in heavy stage-makeup, a fortress atop the rounded escarpment of her bosom, with brows like a high parapet, dark eyes sunk into their orbits like gun-emplacements, and an assembly of cheekbones, nose and chin like angled plates of welded metal. Her voice was loud, though not deep, and she had a habit of speaking in complete sentences, without hesitation and with perfect grammar and measure, her arguments often emphasised by effortless rhymes and assonances, so that everything she said sounded eerily scripted, like pronouncements over a loudspeaker. Indeed, none of the couple's wide circle of acquaintances ever seemed quite at ease around her. She was an unshaded light, a magnesium flare they could not bear to look at face-on. Except, that is, for when she picked up her oboe to play, and the lines of her face would soften perceptively, and the company would breathe a quiet sigh and wait for her to begin. She would hold the instrument lightly in her long bony fingers and it would begin to dance around with the tempo of the music, slow circling adagios and vigorous flourishes during the faster passages, so that it seemed the instrument was leading and Piroshka merely holding on, submitting to something greater and softer than herself.

So too when she retreated to the kitchen to cook our evening meal her eyes would become bright and glassy as she examined the raw ingredients: mushrooms drying on threads over the stove, pickled turnips from glass jars on a high shelf, cabbages and potatoes summoned from the depths of a wooden bucket, a lump of salted fish. She would turn them in her fingers and make her selection as if they were jewels, and then murmur softly to the pots and, as the tempo of her work picked up, start to hum more loudly: chopping, pouring, crushing, the vigorous boiling in one pot playing against the gentle inspissations in another, the door of the tiny oven clanging open and shut. The meal would finally emerge from amidst this clatter and froth, with Piroshka delivering dishes to the table in a steaming fanfare, wiping stray locks of hair from her blushing forehead as aromatic vapours swirled around her clothing. Watching her on these occasions absorbed in her music or her work in the kitchen, I saw a crystalline quality, the unfolding of a luminous inner truth, in the harsh lines of her cheeks and eye-sockets, and at those moments I could imagine no one more beautiful than her.

Towards the end of the album were photographs from the 1950s in early colour emulsions that looked as if they had been touched up with watery paint. Many of those later images I remember taking myself, with Kasimir setting up the shot – usually an ensemble of their friends in winter furs, huddling together on a park bench on the esplanade or on the steps of the great ark-like synagogue on Artilleriskaya – while he barked commands to Piroshka, who assiduously turned the knobs and levers to their correct settings before seizing my hand and stretching my small fingers one by one into the correct places on the camera and stepping back to take her place amongst the group. Sometimes, at the last moment, my mother would arrive, dressed in her hospital clothes, fresh from her night shift, and the whole process would have to be repeated. And finally I would press my eye to the viewfinder, which split the scene into two halves which never quite matched, though I knew they were supposed to. 'Don't worry, and don't touch anything,' Kasimir would shout when I hesitated. 'Except the shutter, of course,' he would add. 'Just breathe in,' Piroshka would say. 'Hold still and press,' someone else would say. 'Pay attention to your depth of field,' another would say. 'Obey the rule of thirds,' someone would intone unhelpfully. I would tense my muscles until they began to shake and press the shutter out of desperation, merely to put an end to the ache in my fingers. Many of my early pictures were blurred as a result, but despite that they were faithfully put in the album and my skills called on again and again until I became more proficient. I remember thinking at the time how grown-up it was for me to record the lives of my elders, not as a child in their care, but as an outsider, one whose gaze gave them form and shape, holding them in the palms of my hands, making sure that not one of them was lost from the frame. Looking again at these images on that night it occurred to me that mine was the only reality that was affirmed by the photographs, even though I rarely featured in them. I was implied, rather than stated, but curiously that seemed the more permanent state of being. Undoubtedly my mind was occupied with the emotions of my imminent departure, but it seemed true nevertheless that everyone within the frame had the melancholy look of those being left behind at the platform of a train station. 'Fare forward, traveller,' they were saying, under their breaths.

As I studied the photographs in the lamplight I heard a purring noise from one of the two clocks that sat side by side on the mantelpiece. Both were family heirlooms and it was Kasimir's that was making the noise, a squat, brass-knobbed, brass-footed affair whose innards produced a sonorous, introspective hum, a kind of musical indigestion, every hour. Beside it sat Piroshka's clock, altogether more grand, a house-like structure in wood and beaten copper with two trapdoors above the face. The two clocks filled the room with their soft ticking, sometimes in strict ordinary time – tick *tick*, tock *tock*, tick *tick*, tock *tock* – but for the most part in an ever-changing syncopation – ticka ticka tock ticka tock tick ticka tock. I had grown so used to this noise that it had become part of my experience of silence. I rose and stepped up onto the brick hearth by the mantelpiece and waited for a moment. Sure enough the trapdoors of Piroshka's clock suddenly sprang open. In some distant past, gilded angels or stooped Germanic burghers had emerged from these doors to greet each other, but, as a result of some domestic disturbance during the July Putsch, I was told, all that now appeared were two matching metal levers which presented themselves, groped lewdly towards each other like crab-claws and then politely withdrew.

I turned around and surveyed the scene of my childhood from the slight elevation of the hearth. It seemed tiny, perhaps four metres square, and now I was leaving it. To my right was the door out into the landing and nailed to its back was the old mirror whose network of blind spots would spread a disconcerting lattice of black capillaries, a pox on vanity, across the face of anyone who peered into it. Beside the door was the curtained opening into the bedroom where Kasimir and Piroshka were sleeping, and next to it the piano, whose bulk filled one side of the room, so that one had to turn sideways at its far end to slip into the tiny kitchen. On the far wall the gramophone sat against a background of wallpaper, striped blue and green with a filigree of tiny roses – white for death, red for birth – winding in a helix like the interweaving motifs in a piece of music. Above the gramophone were three photographs in a descending diagonal: a daguerreotype of Piroshka's parents on their wedding day set in a carved frame with chipped gold paint, a photograph of Kasimir and Piroshka with their son Vitja, then aged ten or eleven and dressed in a blue-trimmed sailor suit and hat, and a photograph, which I had seen in the parlours of several of their Jewish friends, of three rocks set amidst smooth ribbed torrents of black water which, upon closer examination, revealed itself as a face, the rocks being in fact the bulbous nose and slightly crossed eyes of a smiling middle-aged man (whose name I never learned) surrounded by a contiguous mass of beard, moustache and hair.

My earliest memories were of accompanying Piroshka on her daily shopping expeditions. She would seize my hand and walk along Razyezhaya Street with a brisk high-stepping action, leaning far back on her heels, her shoulders pulled back, her bosom pressed to the sky, as if life for her were nothing but the long ascent of an interminable hill. I would sometimes have to run to keep up. During these excursions we would pass the Jewish cemetery (and next to it the old synagogue with its honeycomb friezes), or the marble-fronted building that once housed the Higher Music School, or the former offices of one of the Russian-language newspapers, and she would relate to me another episode in the history of her second city, the grand and now faded Harbin of the 1920s. 'We had fled the Venice of the North,' Piroshka told me, 'and came to the Paris of the East. At the time it didn't seem a bad swap.'

At the railway station we would often pause for a moment in the arrivals hall and look up at the old map of Manchuria painted on the wall above the ticket office. Harbin, represented by the dome of St Sofia's skirted by a cluster of houses, sat at the T-junction where the China Eastern Railway sent a spur to the south, and then carried on eastwards towards Vladivostok. Curving snakes' skeletons linked us to Mukden and Jilin to the west, leaving vast areas of blank plaster dotted with a few smaller towns, each marked by a clump of houses with a copse of trees to one side. The names of all the cities and towns were painted in Cyrillic script, alongside of which Chinese characters had later been added.

Beneath the map a collection of old photographs showed the first train to arrive in Harbin, when the city comprised little more than rows of workers' cottages made of rough-sawn timber, each with a number stencilled in large white letters on the side. Others showed the railway station under construction, and, on an elevated piece of land beyond the railway tracks and depots, the New Town, Novy Gorod, with its two-storeyed villas and smart apartment houses, its restaurants and baths, gentlemen's clubs and the Cathedral of St Sofia.

'We found this Russian garden growing on Chinese soil,' Piroskha explained. The boulevards were lined with linden trees and the horse-drawn droshkies of the wealthy clattered and swung around the cobblestoned shopping district. The hotels and restaurants bore the same French names that were then fashionable in St Petersburg and Moscow – Bel-Etage, Café de la Paix, le Véry. Barges and small craft plied the river, and lovers strolled along the promenade between May and September, when the temperature rose above freezing.

She explained how she and Kasimir had disembarked late on a winter's night so cold the temperature could not be measured. They had walked with their luggage past a dark mass of men sitting sullenly atop travel chests on the platform amidst a miasma of cigarette smoke and body steam, eyeing the newcomers with silent contempt. These, they were later told, were left-wing émigrés exiled over the years to the island of Sakhalin off the far eastern coast of Siberia and now making the return journey to take up arms for the Bolsheviks.

Inside the station the news spread quickly that there was no accommodation to be had in the city. The floor of the arrivals hall was filling up with families arranging trunks and pigskin suitcases as makeshift mattresses for sleeping children and laying piles of coats and blankets on the hard tiles. Piroshka showed me the niche behind a stone pillar where she and Kasimir waited out the long hours until daylight.

The following morning they were awakened by the discordant trilling of a military band warming up. A crush of people pushed through the doors from the arrivals hall onto the platform, swaying and over-balancing like a field of ripened wheat. They jostled the players who were installed on the edge of the platform, and were waved back by the band leader who brandished a quivering baton like a fencing foil. Then with a blast of steam and clanging bells a train pulled into the station, soldiers swinging from the sides of the boiler and the flags of Tsarist Russia streaming from poles stuck into crevices in the engine and lodged in the windows of the front carriages. Four soldiers leapt from the first carriage and cleared a space with their rifle butts. Then the doorway behind them darkened, the conductor's baton flinched and the band sputtered into the first bars of a jaunty anthem. A short, stocky man appeared on the top step of the carriage. He was dressed in black knee-length boots, a simple military tunic with a thin collar, and a flat cap with a shiny medallion bearing the double-eagle emblem of Imperial Russia. His face was round, his skin dark, and an oily black pennant moustache dangled from his thin nose. Cheers of *Zhivio!* echoed around the hall.

'Who is he?' Piroshka whispered into the ear of the man next to her.

'That,' the man said, leaning his head towards her, 'is Ataman Grigorii Mikhailovic Semenov, the hope of White Russia, and the man behind him is Baron Ungern-Sternberg, who served with him in the Carpathians.'

Piroshka now noticed in the shadows behind Ataman Semenov a thin man with a head the shape of an inverted pear and a closely-cropped V-shaped beard. A pair of wire-rimmed glasses had slipped down his long nose, and, like Semenov, he was kitted out in a starched uniform. As soon as the band finished its piece, and without waiting for the noise of the applause to die down, Semenov began to speak. His theme was the ancient and venerable brotherhood of Rus, the vile scourge of Bolshevism, the tragic exile of the Tsar, the desecration of the Mother Church, and the perversion of the peasantry and the peaceful way of life of the Russian countryside. Someone behind Piroshka burst into melodramatic sobs, and a woman in an embroidered *sarafan* attempted to push past the soldiers, holding aloft a silver plate with several small loaves of black bread and a pile of salt. She was thrust back into the crowd, shouting repeatedly over her shoulder, *God save the Tsar! And God preserve you, Ataman Semenov!* She stumbled in front of Piroshka and her plate fell to the platform, scattering the bread and salt at her feet.

Semenov stopped mid-sentence, dropped his head and clutched the hand-rail beside him as if he were about to faint. He roused himself and began once more, his voice now exploring the full register of the human larynx, from a whisper to a low operatic growl to a full-throated shout, now tearful, now vituperative and righteous, his sentences explosions of sound, of fury, pathos, and outrage, carrying through the hall and out into the street, and then finally a strangled cry of despair, his fist clenched in anger, rising to a shriek as he swore an oath on his mother's blood that with these two Russian eyes he would witness the Romanovs borne on the shoulders of loyal countrymen, trampling the bodies of the Red enemy in the streets of Moscow's holy city. With one voice the crowd roared, flags and banners snapped overhead, the band launched into another tune, and Semenov and his lieutenant descended quickly from the train to be propelled by a wedge of soldiers, like the charge in an artillery shell, through the crowd to a waiting carriage in the street outside.

Piroshka lost Kasimir in the crush and was sucked out of the station by the mass of bodies and dumped in the gutter. 'To St Sofia's!' a soldier shouted to the crowd from the roof of the carriage. 'Follow us to St Sofia's for the blessing of the Metropolitan!' She picked herself up and made her way back to their niche by the pillar.

Piroshka reserved her bitterest language for Ataman Grigorii Mikhailovic Semenov and Baron Ungern-Sternberg. Bandits, opportunists and thugs, she called them. Fools and strutting peacocks, Kasimir would add, at first without looking up from his newspaper, but then it seemed that the very thought of Semenov and Ungern-Sternberg unnerved him so much that he had to put aside the paper, rise to his feet and roam around the apartment for a while, flicking dust from shelves or rearranging books and papers, all the while repeating to himself under his breath foul epithets for the pair. For the next month Semenov and Ungern-Sternberg had occupied a suite at the Hotel Moderne, dining with displaced aristocrats, bankers and intellectuals, plotting the overthrow of the Bolshevik state. Meanwhile, outside in the streets and tea-houses, the talk of the city was how to finance an invasion, what route the armies should take, and which allies could be trusted.

Then news came through of the execution of the Romanov family in a cellar in Ekaterinburg. The streets fell silent. Semenov and Ungern-Sternberg fumed for days and then fell out with each other so badly that they fought a duel on the steps of the Hotel Moderne. It was said that neither man had aimed to kill, since they quickly made up and, without settling their accounts at the Moderne or several of the best restaurants, slipped out of Harbin on a river boat, heading for Khabarovsk and careers as minor warlords in the maritime provinces of eastern Siberia.

In time, all thoughts of opposition to the Bolsheviks lapsed. Buildings sprang up to house the newcomers; first cheap clapboard houses, and then – as the White Russians began to retrieve their money from bank accounts abroad – apartment buildings, mansions in Novy Gorod and dachas in the surrounding countryside. The Harbin Stock Exchange opened its doors again, and a new air of gentility descended upon the city, as money and trade flowed in from Paris, London and Amsterdam, and the White Russians settled in to wait out the Bolshevik ascendancy. Three new daily newspapers were established. Attendances at concerts swelled. The Jewish population, now grown to several thousand, built a new synagogue and a hospital. The streets filled with droshkies carrying gentlemen to houses of assignation, or smartly dressed families to dine at clubs and restaurants, or to theosophical coffee houses or parties on one of the riverboats, and in the hot summer of 1919 a new generation came down to the banks of the Songhua River and bathed themselves in the warm shallows, rowed out to Sun Island with picnic hampers and bottles of vodka and wine, and lay in the grass into the long summer evenings watching the sky slowly darken, and tracing with their fingers the necklaces of stars they had once traced on summer evenings in St Petersburg or Moscow, nestled like diamonds in the same blue velvet case.

It was around this time that a small Chinese girl began to appear in the photographs with Kasimir and Piroshka. My mother did not seem curious about her birth or about how a Chinese child came to be in the charge of two Russian Jews. Neither did I think to question it until I was six or seven, and on the few occasions when I raised the subject I was given a look of incomprehension, as if I had spoken in some foreign tongue. A fingertip would be placed benignly on my lips, and the matter was closed. Clearly our origins were part of a mystery so deep it could not even be formed into a question.

In any case the 1940s in Harbin was no time to be asking such questions. So many other things needed explaining – uprisings, occupation, famine, floods, plague, civil war, my own arrival and then, in 1945, my father's. To examine matters as remote in time as my mother's birth meant sending messengers on a long journey to a distant land, and I assume she no longer deemed it worth the effort.

Sometimes, lying beside me in bed at night, she would tell me that if you closed your eyes and looked carefully you would see pictures from your past imprinted on the back of your eyelids, and that one picture could be made to fade into the next, like a magic lantern show. She would help me compose pictures of my day while I lay on the bed, telling me to leave out any bad things I had remembered – a dead dog in the gutter, a cuff from a passing soldier, a bruised knee, a taunt from a school mate. It was many years before it occurred to me that this was how she might have dealt with her earliest memories, how, if she needed, she would deal with anything.

Kasimir and Piroshka treated my mother as a daughter in most respects. She accompanied them to the synagogue on Artilleriskaya on each of the High Holy Days and for *bar mitzvah*s and other special occasions, and she would often play with the children of other Russian Jewish families. However, there was an understanding that she was not Jewish, and would never be initiated into the faith. Instead, they would ask Wang Taitai, our concierge, to take her to the Temple of Extreme

58

Happiness every year at the time of the temple fair and to teach her to offer incense and prostrate herself and pray to the Buddha for the souls of her unknown and unknowable ancestors.

For the most part I accepted the mystery of my origins. After all it was not uncommon amongst my schoolmates for family trees to be mutilated and twisted out of shape by war, flood, disease, or by the temptation, always present in a railway town, to abandon one's ties and seek a fortune – or at least an unencumbered poverty – in one of the other boom-towns along the line: northeast to Khabarovsk; east to Vladivostok; west to Irkutsk; south to Port Arthur, and then by ship to Shanghai or Hong Kong.

I satisfied myself with fairy tales. Kasimir and his friends would often talk of the early days with the orchestra in Harbin, when, due to a fire in the opera house, concerts were moved to the arrival hall of the railway station. Sometimes trains would pull in during performances, filling the hall with steam and disgorging their passengers into the audience. At dinner parties, Piroshka often told a story of how, in the days when exiled Russians were still arriving in small numbers, among them artists, writers and musicians, she heard a rustle beside her in the middle of a performance and turned to find that another oboist (a young man from Minsk in a tattered fur coat) had slipped a chair beside hers, oboe in hand, and, quickly glancing at the sheet on Piroshka's music stand, had joined in. Similarly, she went on, Kasimir had been playing in a quartet which disappeared momentarily into the burst of steam from an arriving train, and emerged magically transformed into an octet, now overshadowed by a stack of luggage. I imagined one of these pieces of luggage – a hatbox, perhaps – unclaimed; and Kasimir opening it to find a small abandoned Chinese infant, my mother, and taking it home to Piroshka. Inside the box there would be a note from Guan-Yin, the Goddess of Compassion, with instructions – written by one of her thousand hands – to bring the child to the temple once a year so that the Goddess could renew her blessing.

From what I could tell, my mother's girlhood was happy and largely without incident. She grew up speaking Russian and Chinese, sleeping in a curtained-off section of the bedroom in the third storey apartment overlooking the Club of the Russian Student Society. It was a routine of school and piano lessons, of being taken to concerts and put in the care of old Russian matrons while Kasimir and Piroshka performed. In the spring time there were train journeys to the countryside, passing through fields of poppies and irises and villages where long strands of noodles dangled like giants' hair from large wooden drying frames, their ends stroking the dust in the breeze. There would be musician friends to visit or some touring soloist in a borrowed dacha, and my mother would roam the fields with the Jewish children and fall asleep on Kasimir's shoulder on the return journey.

Kasimir and Piroshka frequently entertained visitors – musicians, intellectuals, journalists, women with clothes that smelled of perfume and cigarettes, bearded men with deep bellowing voices, swinging their coat-tails and cigar smells around them as they entered the apartment – and on these occasions my mother was packed off to bed early, if only to make more room in the parlour. She would lie awake listening through the thin walls to every word spoken or sung in the adjacent room as clearly as if she had been lying curled up amidst the dishes and cutlery on the table.

The photographs of the time show a Chinese girl steadily growing taller surrounded on all sides by a revolving cast of Russians, slowly ageing, growing correspondingly smaller, so that her presence somehow explained why it was they had come thousands of kilometres from their homes – to pose with her and be vindicated by her unfolding.

Then in February of 1932 the world changed before my mother's eyes. Around noon one day a shell was lobbed across the river by a Japanese heavy artillery unit. It spun over Daowai on a gentle crescent, clipped a chimney on its descent to the street, and skittered along the cobblestones like a dog with its ears pinned back, before demolishing a cart filled with vegetables and coming to rest, spinning and steaming, in the middle of an intersection. It did not contain a charge, so there was no explosion. But it did contain a message: stating, simply, that no part of the city was safe for the forces of the Chinese general, Li Du, or for the citizens who harboured them.

My mother and a school friend were among those who rushed to extricate the terrified horse from a blood-stained tangle of broken wood and harness-leather. Li Du and his army had been quartered in the city for several months, holding back the collaborationist forces even after the rest of Manchuria had succumbed to Japanese occupation. So in February the Japanese committed their own troops, along with tanks, artillery and aircraft. In the days following that first shell, Li Du's forces fought and lost a few skirmishes and then quietly melted into the countryside.

The Japanese swaggered into the city in a procession led by their mounted officers and by a pair of tanks that seemed ridiculously small and squat, as if they were children's toys commandeered for the occasion, with grown men in uniform standing at attention in their tiny round turrets. The White Russians watched from their doorways, unsure whether to applaud politely, as if they were exotic performers arriving at a garden fête. To many of them the Japanese were the least of three evils, it being clear that the Nationalists would seize their businesses, while the Communists would hand over the Russian émigrés to the Red Army for repatriation.

The new occupiers quietly but firmly applied a tourniquet to the livelihood of Harbin's White Russians, Kasimir and Piroshka among them. New laws, concessions and monopolies eased most businesses into Japanese ownership or control. The Russians clung to the China Eastern Railway, which had been their first foothold; but the other foreigners, the British, the Americans, the Koreans, sold out and left.

My mother became aware of the changes in the city during the great flood later in the year. The spring had arrived early, and the rivers thawed quickly and then were filled with melting snow from the mountains to the south. The lower parts of the city soon disappeared beneath the flood water, and the population fled for the higher ground of Novy Gorod. The water rose even further, so that it was waist deep in the Bolshoi Prospekt. My mother had her fifteenth birthday as the waters began to recede. She was sent out on some errand, wading along a narrow street through water up to her thighs, when she encountered a Japanese officer paddling around in a barrel fixed with guy-ropes inside a square crate. The two oars were held in place with bent nails, and the craft was listing to one side and then the other as water sloshed around the bottom of the crate. The man had a thin, almost mournful face, a clipped moustache and round glasses through which portions of his eyes and cheeks were refracted. He was dressed in a linen shirt buttoned up to his chin and a long jacket with pockets down the front like a dresser full of small drawers. An oversized pistol was strapped to his chest. He was not making good progress, but was at least kept dry whereas everyone else was soaked from the waist down.

As she went to pass him, my mother dropped her head, not wanting to stare at the man and his ridiculous vessel. But he quickly manoeuvred in front of her, and blocked her way with an outstretched oar. My mother changed course, her skirt swirling around her thighs; but the man jockeyed his barrel to the left with jerky arm movements, and held out the other oar to block her passage. My mother retreated in fright, and stumbled backwards into a half submerged doorway. The man swung his makeshift craft to and fro across the doorway, fixing my mother with his gaze. When she moved to the left again he moved to block her way; when she moved right he parried, shuffling his crate through the water, leaning this way and that to maintain his balance.

My mother noticed some other people, further down the street, and considered crying out; but then realised that the man seemed to have no intention of harming her physically, only of taking full measure of her with his eyes. He kept her cornered for several minutes, watching her with a gentle mocking expression that my mother could not quite fathom – contempt? amusement? lust? curiosity? After a while, my mother told me, their eyes met and fixed for a while, and then the man abruptly spun his craft around and resumed his clumsy progress along the flooded street.

*

The following year, without warning, the Soviet Union sold the railway to the Manchurian government. Within months twenty thousand railway employees and their families were repatriated, and with this, many of the White Russians lost their employment. The orchestra folded, as did the opera, the music school, most of the restaurants and the newspapers. Many White Russians fled south to Port Arthur, where they queued on the dock for days awaiting steamers to Shanghai. Kasimir and Piroshka stayed on, finding work as music teachers amongst the dwindling Russian community. Perhaps they stayed because of my mother; but perhaps also because they could not contemplate uprooting themselves again. Better to have chosen the ground upon which fate would finally snare them.

The city settled into a weary decadence. Its tree-lined streets and dachas were still charming, and it was still the Paris of the East to its few White Russian inhabitants, but they now littered the boulevards at despondent leisure, congregating by day in family groups, their weekend best slowly fading on their backs: valetudinarians with white canes sniffing the breeze from behind tinted medical spectacles; double-chinned matrons stoic, with nothing better to do than fuss with their grandchildren's hair; young men dandyish and bored and lamenting the absence of cheap entertainment; old men phlegmatic, sitting by themselves smoking and not saying much. It was the younger women who seemed to suffer the most, enduring a slow, spiralling descent, cushioned at each step by the pawning of jewels or bibelots or a gold tooth relinquished to the brokers off Zhongyang Avenue.

It was known that some of them also pawned their virtue, and thereafter, step by step, let slip even that cloudy residue which virtue leaves behind when it is sacrificed to necessity.

My mother would see the White Russians on her way home from school, sitting on park benches like abandoned wreaths around a cenotaph, islands of old Russian torpor amidst rivers of cool Japanese efficiency and Chinese indifference. As the seasons turned their numbers slowly dwindled until the civil guard began to move them on (for their own good, it was explained, since the city's robber bands soon learned that there were banknotes sewn into the lining of their coats – which they wore even in summer – so as to effect, if necessary, a rapid departure).

The only segment of the Russian population that flourished under Japanese occupation was the Russian Fascist Party of Manchuria, which held its meetings at the Club of the Russian Student Society, across from our apartment on Razyezhaya Street. Posters invited the public to lectures by stern, whiskered gentlemen on 'The Role of Masonry in the Demise of Russia', 'The World Conspiracy of Judeo-Masons', and 'An Exposition of the Protocols of the Elders of Zion'. At the top of each poster ran the motto: 'God. Nation. Labour.'

The Party somehow acquired a three-storey building in the city centre, and the money to place on its roof an illuminated blue swastika which competed on the Harbin skyline with the dome of St Sofia's and the cross atop the American Baptist Mission. My mother told me she would often encounter small groups of young men on her way to school dressed entirely in black: black caps with a black peak, black tunics, shoulder belts, riding breeches and high boots. At first she took them for unemployed droshky drivers. Then she noticed that on their left arm they wore a band with a black swastika set on a bright orange circle, and above it the image of a double-headed eagle. As she passed they would salute each other by sharply throwing up one arm and shouting, 'Glory to Russia!'

When she told Kasimir of her first encounter with the Fascists, and asked him why they wore only black and used the same symbol as the one that appeared around the altar at the Temple of Extreme Happiness, he merely closed his eyes and joined his fingertips at the bridge of his nose. My mother waited in silence, and, thinking he was falling asleep, reached out to touch his shoulder. He opened his eyes slowly, and said, 'This has nothing to do with you.'

She asked the same question of Piroshka, who turned to face her, seemingly unaware that in doing so she was pointing a large knife at my mother's chest, and replied, 'Kasimir is right. It has nothing to do with you. What more do you need to know?'

One day several months later, soldiers cleared the main thoroughfare of the city to allow the Fascist Party to hold a parade, starting by the river bank and ending on the other side of the city where a new chapel had been consecrated to the memory of the two Crown-bearing martyrs, Nicholas II and Alexander Karageorgeovic. The Municipal Government decreed that school children should be given an hour's reprieve from their lessons to witness the spectacle. My mother stood with her school friends, outside the school gate on Kitaiskaya Street, and watched as a Japanese film crew set up their camera on the roof of a military van parked by the curb with its engine idling.

At the head of the column walked Metropolitan Archbishop Nestor, his long black robes swaying in time with his steps, and his face obscured beneath a grey patrician beard whose tendrils brushed against the three pendants that hung from his neck and clacked against each other amidst the folds of his tunic – one a small icon of Christ and his Mother, the second a large cross embedded with jewels, and the third the double-eagle emblem of imperial Russia. A round mitre of dazzling white linen was set on his head, and a short train of the same material hung down over his shoulder blades, with flaps at the front like spaniel ears. On the front of the mitre a jewelled cross glinted in the sunlight as the Archbishop marked each of his steps with an elaborate staff, itself covered in gold. In the Archbishop's wake a gaggle of priests in starched white vestments bore between them various emanations of the prelate's divine aura: a crucifix on a pole, icons attached to red velvet banners with gold tassels, a silver aspergillum, a censer also made of silver, its incense as yet unlit, and a large icon of the Virgin and Child set in ornate gold filigree and surrounded by an arrangement of flowers and greenery.

At a respectful distance a detachment of Cossacks, dressed in the uniforms of various regiments, nudged their horses forward, trailing three-coloured banners and flags, and these were followed in turn by a contingent of cadets in khaki uniforms, marching three abreast. The cadets were attempting a goose step, but kept losing their timing and having to regroup, hounded by a parade sergeant who hissed between his teeth the commands he clearly wished he could shout. He seemed uncomfortably aware of the calm orderliness of the Blackshirts that followed him, those sleek young men in riding breeches, shoulder belts and peaked caps, chins defiantly jutting, boot heels thudding into the ground, each primly restraining a smile.

From time to time, prompted by calls from onlookers, a Blackshirt would salute and cry out, 'Glory to Russia'. On their heels came a cloud of young people from the Avangard, the Union of Young Fascists; then a column of middle-aged women from the Women's Fascist League in black skirts, white blouses and swastika armbands; and at the rear a small group of visiting Fascists from various countries – the United States, Britain, Egypt, Korea – all wearing their national costumes under their swastika armbands. After the column had passed, the film crew quickly dismantled their tripod and stowed it in their van before racing off down a side street, apparently intending to loop around to another vantage point further along the route and capture the whole procession again.

The day after the parade the newspapers announced with banner headlines the return of Ataman Grigorii Mikhailovic Semenov from years of sojourning in the United States and Japan, and within a week he was officially declared by the Japanese authorities to be 'head of the Russian emigrants in Manchukuo'. There was a photograph of him in the newspaper meeting the new Emperor of Manchukuo, 'Henry' Pu Yi, also installed by the Japanese. 'Greetings to the Leaders of a New Mankind – Mussolini, Hitler, Semenov,' the Fascist newspaper announced.

On hearing the news, Kasimir and Piroshka closed the curtains of the apartment and sat in the gloom. My mother arrived home at the same time as a couple of family friends, and, after a murmured greeting, they ascended the stairs together. The adults sat around the edges of the darkened room, listening to the ticking of the clocks above the mantelpiece and saying little. Someone started to talk about Betar, the youth wing of the Zionist Revisionist Party, which was planning its own march through the city, and had set up vigilante protection squads to guard the Jewish community. 'More uniforms,' someone said. 'They put on uniforms. We put on uniforms. Where will this end?'

'It will end with the blatter of motorcycles,' someone replied. 'And then the blatter of other things.'

Six o'clock struck on Piroshka's clock. The company waited for Kasimir's to follow, but it remained silent. Piroshka immediately rose, and, as Kasimir looked on, swung open the round glass door of his clock, inserted the brass key and, with a few gentle words of encouragement, wound it on several rotations. The clock murmured its thanks and began to tock softly.

Unprompted, my mother took charge of the kitchen for the first time in her life, cooking a stew of vegetables – there being no meat to be had in the city – and some rice, all the time listening for, but not hearing, conversation in the adjacent room. She felt four sets of eyes upon her as she ceremoniously delivered the meal to the table, imitating the flourishes Piroshka made when she removed the lids of the serving dishes and announced what was inside. Silence hung in the room, as steam rose from the table. Then someone laughed and soon they were all laughing, and Kasimir said something my mother didn't understand – a proverb in a language that was not Russian – and they all descended upon my mother's first meal. 'Where did you get this roast lamb?' Piroshka asked her, filling her plate with my mother's simple vegetable stew. 'You must tell me. I have never found any lamb like that at the market.' One of her friends countered, 'She must have found it at the same stall that sold her these truffles.' 'And the quail eggs too,' someone added. 'Can it be the season for quail eggs?'

*

In my journey through the photograph album I came to a signed picture of Simon Kaspé, a promising young concert pianist and son of the owner of the Hotel Moderne on Central Avenue. In 1935, while home on holiday from a season playing in Paris, he was kidnapped and a large ransom was sought for his release. His body was eventually found, badly beaten around the head and torso, and with two inches of his tongue missing, in a disused warehouse by the rail depot. On the facing page was a newspaper clipping announcing that three members of the Russian Fascist Party had been arrested for the crime. I knew, however, that they had been released within days upon the intervention of the Japanese authorities for reasons that were never explained.

Many of Harbin's remaining Jews departed for Shanghai over the following months. Kasimir was asked to arrange for the sale of a small dacha in the countryside on behalf of a family who had left for the South. On a visit to check on the property he fell from the train and broke his left arm, snapping his elbow so badly that the arm lost most of its strength. From then on he could not raise his arm much higher than his waist, and it hung loosely, the hand involuntarily rotating outwards. It was the end of his playing days.

Now I felt a hand on my shoulder, Kasimir's good hand. 'Look at that,' he said, leaning over the photograph album. 'He is watching you, poor, sweet boy that he was. He is happy to see you go to Shanghai to join the Conservatory. He wishes you well.' I studied Simon Kaspé's young face, clean shaven, eyes bright with promise and with dedication to his art.

'How do you know?'

'It's obvious,' he said, 'Can't you see it too?' and he reached across and turned down the wick of the lamp until the flame went out, leaving only a line of tiny fibres glowing orange. 'Sleep,' he said from the darkness above me. 'You have an early start in the morning.' I put the album away and lay down again on my blanket, pulling another blanket over me. But I did not sleep again that night, and when Piroshka's clock struck four I rose and got dressed and closed my suitcase, and then sat by the window looking across the roof tops of the city, searching for the first light of day.

4. Love's Song

I was born in January of 1942, a war-child in a city under
military rule, with chaos and despair all around, food and
medicine in short supply, rats and sewage fouling the water. The
Japanese had pillaged the city's stores of soybeans and wheat
to feed the soldiers dug in around the periphery of the city. At
night their artillery lit up the sky, fired into the freezing mist at
blurred shapes on the surrounding plain, shapes that could have
been the Red Army, the Chinese Nationalists, or the Chinese
Communists, or perhaps just terrified peasants or other fauna.
In the week of my birth, coal and firewood doubled in price,
and then trebled. And the winter, as usual, froze everything:
the Songhua river, water pipes, spittle fresh from the mouth,
the whiskers and eyebrows of old men, the manes of horses and
donkeys, and the flesh of beggars or unfortunate citizens who
had lost their way in the dark during the blackout.

It also froze Yao Xijiu, my mother's first husband, who, as
I emerged into the grey half-light of a hospital ward, lay half a
kilometre away, dead, part of a snowdrift on the river, not to be
discovered until the spring thaw. The couple had been estranged
for most of a year. Indeed, my mother could not say exactly why
she had married him, and perhaps for that reason she did not
tell me about Yao until I was preparing to leave home at the age
of thirteen. It is never good to keep secrets from your children,
she admitted; but sharing them too soon can be worse. If you

leave things buried long enough some get absorbed into the soil, she added; others rise to the surface like stones in a field, but you never know which things will come back, or when.

'What else are you hiding from me?' I remember asking.

'Nothing,' she said, and smiled at me.

When she married him Yao was running away from his comprador family, from the gaggle of wives and concubines tiptoeing on bound feet about the family courtyard as if drunk, from the obligation to pay homage to the ancestral tablets on the family altar, from the elder brother whose duty and pleasure it had been to beat him, and who, from the day after his wedding, sat smoking at the dinner table waiting for his new wife to place his chopsticks in his hand. Yao had joined the Communist Party after reading Lu Xun's *Diary of a Madman*, a pamphlet which opened his eyes to the ceremony of cannibalism that was Confucian family life, each generation consuming and embittering the one that followed it.

He had changed his name, found a job, and forsworn the twin evils of opium and foreign commerce. My mother met him at a night class in political theory, and she was present at the ceremony when he swore allegiance to the Party. Then just months after they were married, he disappeared for several days and returned to inform her that he had inherited an opium den from his uncle, and planned to use its profits to fund the Party's publications. That night as he slept my mother walked out of the room they shared carrying all her belongings in a canvas bag. The party found her lodgings elsewhere, and since the opium trade was at that time monopolised by the Japanese, it was only with great difficulty that my mother convinced the local communist organisation – and in particular Lu Feng, the railway engineer from Shanxi Province – not to eliminate Yao as a traitor.

Yao did not betray the party to the Japanese opium bosses; but when he discovered that my mother was pregnant to Lu Feng, he cut a hole in the crust of ice that covered the river and tried to drown himself. Two schoolboys pulled him from the water – a lump of human jelly, flesh blackened with the cold – and he was resuscitated by diners on a table at the Delicious Overflow Dumpling House, which stood on the river bank by the promenade. As soon as he was well enough he tried again, this time climbing onto the railway bridge and throwing himself onto the ice. There were no witnesses, and a fall of snow covered his body. The next spring he floated to the shore suspended in the middle of an ice-floe, arms outstretched like a diver. My mother, holding me in her arms, identified his body in the mortuary.

When she married Yao, my mother had not long returned to Harbin from Beijing. Indeed, on the very day three years previously when she had collided with a young man carrying a gramophone outside the British Chicken and Duck Factory she had learned that the Harbin Medical School would close. The teaching staff had been reduced to only four professors, the others having left for the Soviet Union or Shanghai, and the Japanese had no interest in supporting the school. My mother managed, through one of her professors, to secure a place at a medical school in Beijing run by an American missionary with socialist leanings, and within a week was on the train heading south.

On her return to Harbin in 1940, she found her old neighbourhood in the possession of ladies in kimonos, their wooden sandals clopping on the pavement, shadowing their menfolk, performing their bird-like greeting ceremony whenever they met some acquaintance, with deep bows and high-pitched twittering. In the fashionable district of Uchaskovaja beige-clad Japanese soldiers, on leave from the war in China, lounged outside department stores whose balconies were draped with the white flag with the red central sun.

My mother found work in a Chinese mission hospital in Daowai, amongst the workers' tenements. Her patients now included many impoverished Russians, forced out of lodgings in Daoli. She slept on the floor of the apartment in the Bolshoi Prospekt, and used her irregular shifts to conceal from Kasimir and Piroshka that she was attending secret meetings of a Communist Party cell and courting Yao Xijiu. She knew that, to them, communism's sole virtue was that it was not fascism. Besides, to reveal her political convictions would have put them in danger, for in those years life for the communists of Harbin, and for anyone associated with them, was often brutish and short. The Party was dominated by young writers and poets who flirted with martyrdom by staging 'flying demonstrations' of street theatre, inviting identification, arrest, and, if not execution, at least a harsh beating in the police cells.

The cell to which my mother, Yao Xijiu and latterly my father belonged was in charge of the printing press, and thought itself the nerve centre of the Party. Yao had himself bought the press from a bankrupt Russian pamphleteer, dismantled it, and transferred it in small shipments to the back room of an abandoned dacha just outside the city. He tried to convince my mother that they should live in the dacha, and make use of its small vegetable plot to grow food. She refused, but pointed out that, were they married, she would be eligible for a cramped seventh-floor room with a shared kitchen and bathroom that was adjacent to the hospital and near Yao's workplace. Yao agreed, and after her next shift took her to the registry office.

She explained all this to me as we assembled a pile of clothes for me to take with me to Shanghai.

'So Kasimir and Piroshka didn't attend your wedding.'

'I didn't want to put them in danger,' she replied.

'From the police?'

'Or from the Party itself,' she said. And she explained that after the debacle of 1937 the local Party organisation would be seized by paranoia from time to time, and cells would purge suspected traitors in their midst with a bullet to the head or burial alive. Often family members met the same fate. Indeed, after the revolution was over my father, with his liking for statistics, had worked out to his chagrin that more party members had died in this way than had been killed by the Japanese or the Nationalists.

So my mother had arrived home and told Kasimir and Piroshka simply that she had got married and was leaving that night. They had sat speechless for an hour, she told me, sighing occasionally and patting each other on the hand while watching my mother pack her clothes and books. Finally, Kasimir had turned to Piroshka and said, 'In truth, my dear, did we at any time in the last twenty years think it could end any other way?' They rose and embraced my mother stiffly, and she went on her way.

Around the time of her wedding my mother was asked to treat a number of frostbite victims from a mental asylum run by the Japanese military on the outskirts of the city. Every few days an officer would bring in one or more inmates with severe frostbite to fingers, feet, toes, noses and ears. The inmates – Russians and Chinese – were delirious with pain and, my mother suspected, a dose of some powerful sedative. It was minus thirty degrees Celsius most days, but so many cases from one place seemed strange. After the second group of victims was brought in, my mother called a colleague who had some Japanese and together they tried to question the officer about why so many inmates were suffering frostbite. Were the asylum staff aware that the mentally ill often had impaired ability to feel pain? Did they allow the patients to spend time out of doors without supervision? The officer refused to respond, but instead smiled sweetly and made a sawing motion with his finger to indicate the treatment required. He stood watching as orderlies restrained the patients while my mother administered diluted opium as an analgesic, removed the affected limbs, digits and facial features, and cauterised the exposed flesh. None of the patients was allowed to stay at the hospital to recuperate, and the officer insisted on retrieving the pieces of blackened tissue and body parts, placing each of them in a separate canvas bag, one for each patient, and packing them into a small suitcase.

'Perhaps they are going to eat them,' my mother's colleague whispered to her. 'Perhaps it's some sort of Japanese delicacy.'

'Then surely they should fatten them up first,' my mother replied.

*

One night my mother arrived home from her shift to find Yao in animated conversation with a tall man whom he introduced as Lu Feng, an experienced party organiser just arrived from Yan'an. 'But he is originally from . . .'

'. . . from Harbin, yes I know,' my mother interjected. 'And your gramophone?' she asked the visitor, looking him full in the face, 'Do you still have your gramophone?'

Lu's brows tensed momentarily. 'No,' he replied slowly. 'I pawned it, and I haven't had time to go looking for it again. And you,' he continued, 'did you ever recall those lines of verse that you had forgotten?'

'Lines of verse?'

'Unless I am mistaken, you were the girl I met on Anguo Street,' Lu said.

'Yes. In 1937. You were carrying a gramophone.' She directed a smile at Yao, who was listening to the exchange, open-mouthed. 'And I had my medical textbooks.'

'But you were trying to remember some lines of verse,' he said, 'at least that is how it looked to me. You had a faraway look in your eyes.'

My mother laughed. 'I was probably memorising parts of the human skeleton . . . but have it your way, then; what poem was it, do you think?'

Lu pursed his lips, and, addressing himself to one of his hands in the manner of an actor, intoned:

May all your tears, wanderer,
fall into the Yangtze at its western source.

The room fell silent. It was Yao who eventually chuckled to himself and completed the verse:

Then the river will flow to the east,
bringing them here to my home.

Over the course of the evening, Lu explained that since

75

his flight from the city in 1937 he had travelled west to the Communist Party headquarters in Yan'an, where he had received further political training and made plans for the takeover of the railway network. He had returned to the north, recruiting cadres in villages near the Russian border, before being sent back to Harbin. He had retrieved his record collection from a comrade, but he had no money to redeem his gramophone. 'My cousin has a gramophone,' Yao said, 'so you must come back tomorrow night with your record collection. You must promise to do that.'

The next day Lu was there at dusk with his records, and strode up the seven flights of stairs two at a time to find only my mother there, puzzling at the failure of her husband to return from work. 'I don't know the cousin my husband refers to,' she explained, 'Perhaps he lives across the other side of the city.' An hour passed and Yao had not returned. She fed Lu Feng a small piece of pork, some greens and some noodles, eating little herself. Lu and my mother continued to talk about the music inscribed (for the time being uselessly) into the black shellac of his records, but then, as the curfew was called in the street below, Lu took my mother's hand and led her into the dark stairwell.

'The concierge will see us,' my mother protested as they descended the stairs, but on the second floor Lu opened the door to an apartment and without hesitation led her past the occupants at their evening meal, the husband silently acknowledging him with a glance as the wife and children averted their eyes. He led my mother through a small door onto a fire escape and down into a courtyard hung with laundry, and from there through a series of alleys and factory yards, avoiding the main thoroughfares, sometimes feeling his way along walls with his fingertips, until they arrived at a staircase at the back of a warehouse. This they climbed and slipped into a dimly lit room where several men sat or lay on the floor.

'Comrade Lu,' one of them said, rising to his feet.

'You must hurry, Peng,' Lu said, 'Comrade Yao is missing. Doctor Xiao says he did not return from work. That was three hours ago. Go at once to the police station. Ask for our friend Hui and get him to look for Yao in the cells.'

Peng disappeared and Lu motioned to my mother to take his space on a thin mattress. 'Wait here,' he said, 'and close the light. No need to take risks.' He slipped out into the night. The light was extinguished and my mother sat in total darkness, listening to the breathing of the men in the room with her.

After half an hour Lu returned with Peng. Yao was not at the police station, they reported.

'Is that good news?' my mother asked.

No one spoke, and it seemed as if the dark had swallowed her words. She repeated her question.

'No,' Lu said. 'It's bad news. They may have taken him out into the fields to deal with him.'

'Or to Unit 731,' one of the other men said.

'But we don't even know for sure that he's been detained,' said my mother.

'True,' Lu replied. 'We know nothing, but it is always dangerous when we know nothing about a Party member.'

'To know nothing is always to know something,' said a voice from a far corner of the room, an older man whose presence my mother had not so far registered. 'Go home, sister, and advise Comrade Lu as soon as you hear anything.'

Lu escorted my mother back to her building, entering via the fire escape, passing the sleeping forms of the family they had interrupted. He left her in the stairwell without a word.

Several days later, Yao returned with the borrowed gramophone and a new set of clothes. By way of explanation he told my mother the story of the young boy who stops to watch two old men playing a game of chess, unaware that they are in fact immortals. When he returns home to his family after the game he finds that many years have passed and his formerly middle-aged parents are now in their dotage, and they embrace him tearfully as their long lost son.

My mother did not even smile at this. Nor at his breathless explanation of how much he thought he could bring in from his opium den to support Party activities. She waited until he was asleep, then left for her shift at the hospital and did not return.

My mother told me nothing of the remaining moves of this particular chess game, except that I was conceived two months later and that, before my mother could contact him to tell him she was pregnant, Lu was arrested by the Japanese, identified as a worthy trade for Japanese soldiers captured by the communists and consigned to Xiangfeng Prison, some ten kilometres to the south of the city.

*

So I arrived; in the hospital where my mother worked, by candlelight because the electricity had failed, and in the surgery ward because the labour was premature and there was no room anywhere else. (My mother showed me the bed once, telling the story to its new occupant, a man dying of pulmonary emphysema who bestowed a benison upon my head with a shaking hand.)

Out of courtesy to her patients, my mother bit on a roll of cloth during the labour, to stifle her screams. Even so, most of the inhabitants of the ward lay awake through the night, occasionally passing on words of encouragement from their own darkened corners. A Christian woman intermittently prayed aloud for 'Jidu' to have mercy, and at dawn, auspiciously, I fell head first into the world, to be greeted by a circle of faces in the half-light.

It was my first audience, and my imagination has provided me with a memory of the scene, a large canvas by one of the Dutch masters in a carved antique frame. Beneath the high vaulted ceiling, a crowd gathers around the foot of the third bed on the left where a midwife holds up a child to their view. There is a man in a wheelchair missing both legs. A young girl with a patch over one eye. A nurse wearing a gauze mask. Light descends from high windows. The floor is strewn with sawdust and brown slicks of blood and other fluids. There are dark figures observing from the shadows, showing only the whites of their eyes. There is an open door to the right, through which can be seen the muted shapes of others, going about their business indifferent to something as ordinary as a nativity scene.

*

My birth forced a reconciliation between my mother and Kasimir and Piroshka. My mother suffered post-partum bleeding and became severely anaemic, and the wet nurse she had arranged for me had contracted a fever the day of my birth and was sweating it out on a blanket in the corner of an adjacent ward. So my mother arrived back at Razyezhaya Street one morning carrying me under her coat. Wang Taitai the concierge helped her up the stairs and let her into the apartment and put us both to bed, which is where Piroshka found us several hours later.

I spent my first eight years sleeping in the same tiny bed in the apartment on Razyezhaya Street – shared with my mother, when she was not on night shift – listening to the clocks chiming and the voices and laughter in the next room, just as my mother had as a child, except the talk was different now and where in the past there had been half a dozen guests there were now only one or two gathered around the table, faces lit by the buttery glow from the kerosene lamp which was pressed into service most nights when the electricity went off. Many of the voices my mother had overheard were by my time present only as names, their fates either illuminated by snippets of news or else the subject of speculation. The conversations would continue late into the night, punctuated by the clinking of bottle on glass and the hiss and gargle of a borrowed samovar, and then there would be awkward silences when no one spoke for a while, followed by quiet, relieved laughter as someone resumed the conversation rather than standing up to bring the evening to an end.

I tried repeatedly to stay awake to hear the guests leave, but never succeeded. I would drift off to sleep and be wakened by my mother returning from her shift in the early hours of the morning and releasing her weight slowly, reverently, into the

79

bed beside me. I would hear Piroshka gently snoring behind the curtain. At daybreak I would slip out of bed, leaving my three grown-ups to sleep on, and would sit in the parlour alone, marvelling at the fact that, despite the eating and drinking and singing of the night before, the room was spotlessly clean by morning. And from the freshly dusted mantelpiece the two clocks would shower the room with the crisp, white notes of ordinary time.

*

As with all war babies, the story of my infancy was the story of the war. My significant dates were the property of more momentous events. What, after all, were my cries alongside those of new widows and orphans? Or my first steps alongside the advance of an army of eighty thousand across a front a hundred kilometres long? Or my falls compared to the fall of cities? My three guardians worked tirelessly to provide for my needs and their own, but seemed inclined only to endure, rather than to mark, the passage of time. There were few photographs. And yet during that time I grew as any child would, learned the spoken rhythms of Russian and Chinese, slept curled against my mother's belly (as if I had never left it), played on the stairs, was blessed with 'aunties' on every floor, and every evening leaned my back against the panels of the piano, feeling them vibrate as Piroshka produced delicate dishes by Mozart, Schubert and Chopin – feathers on a breeze of notes, she said – to calm herself after her day's work was done.

When I was three years old I received my first violin. It was a miniature version of a full-sized instrument and was pieced together on an intricate metal frame by a maker and repairer of stringed instruments who worked out of a dimly lit basement workshop near our apartment. I had seen a similar instrument at a friend's place, and had picked it up and started running the bow over the strings. I forgot about it after that, but the incident was enough for Kasimir to take it into his head that I would play the violin rather than the piano or the oboe. (There

80

was never a question of me not playing anything.) In all the early family photographs I am holding the tiny instrument, sometimes cradled in my arms like a doll, sometimes held by the neck, and sometimes jutting outwards from beneath my chin like a spindly kind of goitre. My mother, Kasimir and Piroshka, and sometimes one or more of their friends – the cantor from the synagogue or the violin-maker and his wife – would be standing witness in the background.

By the time I knew them, Kasimir and Piroshka had time on their hands. The orchestra had folded, since its audience had been repatriated to the Soviet Republics, and most of its players – in particular those who were Jewish – had fled south to Shanghai. Those few who remained put on concerts for themselves and their families out of a sense of habit. I attended some of these, sitting in the cold of the unheated opera house before it was commandeered by the Japanese army for some unknown purpose. As the community dwindled so did the volume and texture of the applause, leaving sometimes no more than half a dozen family members or passers-by who would leap to their feet and, glancing reproachfully at the empty seats next to them, clap faster and louder in an attempt to give their applause a head start on the hollow echoes that quickly hunted it down and silenced it.

My first violin lessons are among my earliest memories. Kasimir would stand me on a chair facing him, position his own violin under his chin, and play the open strings with the bow in his right hand. Then he would motion to me to do the same, teaching me how to hold my elbow, how to find each string with my eyes closed, how to play short, staccato notes and long, languid ones, how to play two strings at once, and how to play pizzicato, plucking the strings with my index finger while still holding the bow in my little fist. I learned bowing technique using melodies with only four notes – G, D, A and E – and developed, for a child, particularly strong neck muscles.

I played simple duets with Piroshka on the piano, Russian folk tunes which Piroshka would speed up with successive rounds so that I learned to move my fingers across the strings faster and faster. On rare occasions, my mother would accompany me for my practice. I remember one occasion in particular when I was four and Piroshka suffered repeated bouts of vestibulitis that kept her confined to her bed for days at a time, groaning quietly while the world spun nauseatingly around her. My mother's performance was solid and error-free, but perhaps lacking in flair, and with constant appeals for advice to Piroshka, who lay inert on her side in the next room and replied in Italian, '*affettuoso, tesora*', '*piu saltando, tesora*', or, in a faint voice (when a fresh bout of nausea swept over her) '*a piacere*'.

I learned to read the lines of notes on a musical stave, and at night as I slept breves would bob around beyond my grasp like pork buns, and quavers would crack open like melon seeds. The treble clef would float by like a plucked chicken with its neck broken, before being drawn helplessly into the spinning vortex of the bass clef. And amongst it all would swim the Chinese characters and the Cyrillic and Hebrew script I was learning, alephs and tavs and the pictograms for man and child and mouth and bird, popping like soap bubbles when my dream hands grasped at them.

After my lessons, Kasimir would lose himself in the Chinese newspaper (the Russian language papers having ceased publication), mumbling to himself as he looked up unfamiliar characters in a dictionary whose disintegrating quires were sewn back together roughly with string. The exercise was a complicated one, as he only had the use of his right hand and needed to find the correct page and then hold it open while he read through the dictionary entry, and then scrawled the Russian translation with a pencil stub, word by word, in the narrow margins between the columns of the newspaper. His left hand served to hold the paper flat and keep his place on the page. Sometimes Piroshka and I talked for an hour or more while he worked his way meticulously through one page of news, declaring at the end that it was all untrue anyway and biased in favour of the Manchukuo Government.

'Untrue?' Piroshka would reply. 'How do you know it is not your translation that is untrue?'

'Would a dictionary lie?'

'For sure it would. Translate it again and maybe it will tell you different things.'

Kasimir would utter a soft 'Pah', and wander off to talk to one of the neighbours.

*

Throughout my early years my father lived barely ten kilometres away in Xiangfeng Prison, just outside the city. My mother was aware of this, but kept it to herself and made no attempt to contact him. Then one day in August 1945 he rose at dawn and began to sweep the courtyard, accompanied occasionally by monotone exchanges between the crows which sat like quavers along one side of the perimeter fence. After a few minutes he stopped suddenly. The silence had persisted too long. And the telegraph wires by the front gate, which would sing faintly as the morning's first cables passed through, were now dead. Squinting up into the sun's first rays he saw that there were no guards in the sentry towers. Some other prisoners stumbled, yawning, from their dormitories, and my father realised that the morning wake-up call was overdue. He tapped the guardhouse door lightly with his broom-handle. It swung open. There were no guards.

With the help of a swaying stack of furniture, my father and several other prisoners scaled the barbed wire and searched the guards' quarters and the prison administration building. The rooms were littered with the slurry of a sudden flight: discarded clothing and bedding, drawers and their contents upturned on mattresses, and a bouquet of black peonies, the charred remains of documents, nestled in a fireplace. A set of keys was found in the superintendent's office, and soon the thousand or so prisoners gathered in the exercise yard, where my father stood on a chair to address them. He had barely begun when, with shouts and jeers, several prisoners pushed a Japanese soldier into the dust before my father's chair. They had found him shivering with fear in the bottom of a cupboard, clutching a sweat-dampened pack of cigarettes, eyes rolling around his head, unable or unwilling to speak.

'It's all an act,' one of the prisoners said. 'He's feigning madness, appealing for mercy.'

'Get him out of my sight,' my father said, 'and whatever you do with him don't waste much time.'

An hour and a half later an undisciplined column of prisoners arrived at the outskirts of the city, shaking up a cloud of dust with their bare feet. The streets were deserted except for stray dogs. They roused a shopkeeper, who hissed at them from his door, 'The curfew is in force until nine!' The prisoners continued on towards the railway station, troubled only by an occasional car or horse and cart until they drew within a few blocks of the city centre, at which point they met a group of young men who were running from door to door spreading the word that the authorities had withdrawn overnight with the surrender of the Japanese puppet government.

At the railway station the column of prisoners assembled quietly, conversing with a group of communist partisans who were guarding the station. The streets were starting with fill with people who had set out for work, but were now talking in groups or watching as more partisans took possession of office buildings, throwing papers and furniture out of windows and doors, and occasionally frog-marching a captive towards the railway station. Someone announced that the railway tracks had been blown up to the east and the south.

'Comrade Lu,' someone called, and my father recognised Li Changching, one of the partisan leaders. Several years his senior, Li had been with my father during his training at Yan'an in the South. He was dressed in a baggy khaki uniform and boots laced with string. 'Good to see you are alive. We heard you were a prisoner. How many men do you have here?'

'About a thousand, comrade,' my father answered, 'but they are not my men. They are merely the other inmates from Xiangfeng. Only a few of them are members of the Party.'

'Everyone who is not a Nationalist is on the side of the party,' Li replied, 'at least for now. Come, we have work to do.' Li took my father to an office in the railway station. He produced some fresh steamed bread from a paper bag, and the two ate as they talked. 'The Japanese forces are gone,' Li began, 'and the collaborationists are in flight. Our main objective now is to secure the city before the Nationalists can get here. I have received a wire from Marshall Lin Biao who tells me that the Nationalists hold southern Manchuria, and can be expected to mount an attack on us within the month. His plan is to hold Harbin and supply it from the Soviet Union so that we can become one arm of a pincer movement. There are ten thousand Soviet troops waiting at Irkutsk, ready to be moved here by rail as soon as we can arrange it. And ten thousand of Lin Biao's troops will be in Qiqihar within a week, and can be picked up from there.

'There are three things I want you to do. First, arrange for the tracks to be repaired and for trains to bring in the troops and their supplies from Irkutsk. Cancel all civilian trains until further notice. Second, I want you to take charge of the Mayor's office, put reliable cadres in charge of all the municipal services, and in particular make sure there are preparations for the winter food supply. We must have a competent administration in place quickly. The Party has never been in control of a city before. Shacking up with the peasants in the countryside is one thing; but now we have to show that the Party can run a city. We don't want to give the Russians any reason to revive their claims to Manchuria.' My father nodded in agreement, his mouth full of steamed bread.

'And finally,' Li continued, 'there are still a hundred thousand Japanese civilians and perhaps twenty thousand Russians in the city. Confine them to their neighbourhoods, and then we need to decide what to do with them. We hand over the Russians to the Red Army once they arrive. As for the Japanese, I am told we will be dealing with the Americans, who will be governing Japan from now on.'

Li rose and summoned a young man whom he sent to find a pair of shoes to fit my father. My father stood too, and brushed the dust from his clothes.

'Comrade Li,' he said, 'I have one question. The party printing press, the one that was in the dacha outside the city. Do you know what happened to it, and to the cell that ran it? That was the cell I belonged to.'

Li screwed up his face. 'I think it was uncovered several years ago. The printing press was smashed. As for the members of the cell, if they didn't end up in prison with you, I would assume they are dead. But ask old Mrs Chang. She has been in the city throughout the occupation and may know more.'

*

One day in November of 1945 I was in the entrance hall to the apartment, under the charge of Wang Taitai, creating something with twigs on the stone floor. A shadow was cast over my tiny edifice, and I looked up to see a man standing beyond the glass door watching me. Through the panels of imperfect glass he looked like a mosaic of tiles that had not been properly aligned, and then, as he moved closer to the door, a bubble in the glass gave him a bulge on his cheek, as if he were suffering a massive toothache or a boil. The man stepped inside and crouched beside me. 'Is this the house of Doctor Xiao? Does Doctor Xiao live here?' he asked as he examined my house of sticks.

'This is a house of sticks,' I answered. 'Nobody lives in a house of sticks.'

'In this building, then,' he said. 'Does Doctor Xiao live in this building?'

'Yes, but Doctor Xiao is at the hospital with the other doctors.'

'Do you know when she will return?' the man asked.

'Doctor Xiao is not here,' I repeated.

'What is your name?' he said.

'I am Xiao Magou.'

'And everyone calls you Little Xiao, do they? *Xiao* Xiao.'

86

'Yes, they do, and they always laugh.'

'So, Little Xiao, Doctor Xiao must be your mother, then?' I looked back at my twigs for a while, rearranging some that would not sit properly. 'Is Doctor Xiao your mother?' the man repeated.

'Yes,' I said, 'she is my mother.'

'And your father? Where is he?' the man asked.

I made no reply.

The man crouched by me for several minutes. The sun emerged from behind a cloud and I found myself in a pool of darkness formed by the man's shadow, while the floor around me was brightly lit.

'I don't have a father,' I said. 'Only a mother, an auntie and an uncle.'

I could hear the man's breathing, and see his hand resting upon his knee. He was wearing thin cotton trousers, no socks, and canvas slippers with stitching that was coming loose and brown stains on the uppers. He reached down and picked up some twigs, and bent them into a small frame which he sat on top of my building.

'Shall we build a roof for your house?' he said, and together we stacked more twigs against the four sides of the frame until the roof was complete. When we were done he leaned back to examine our work. I kept my eyes down. And then, with a quick scrape of his canvas soles on the floor, he was gone. The door swung shut behind him, and our twig building was illuminated in dancing slivers of refracted sunlight.

*

I have no memory of a tearful reunion between my mother and my father, or of a ceremony of introduction where he and I shook hands like the representatives of a large kingdom and its tiny new colony. There was no formal agreement that hereafter we would be father and daughter. Instead, he started to appear at meals from time to time, bringing gifts of food, and he and my mother would go out for walks, despite the onset of winter. It would be another four years before the three of us moved into a house together and became a family.

I liked him well enough, as did Kasimir and Piroshka. They had set aside their scruples about communists for the time being, and were especially grateful after my father arranged a holiday for the three of us. I was woken by my mother before dawn one day, and told that I was going with Kasimir and Piroshka to live in the countryside for a while. My belongings were packed into a small suitcase, and I carried my violin in its case.

We took a train south for several hours, and then drew into a small village with muddy streets, sagging houses and a pair of dogs that ran at full tilt alongside the train as it pulled to a halt, and, as we disembarked with our bags, exploded like little bombs full of high pitched barking. A man with a horse-drawn cart was there to meet us, and he took us to our quarters in a group of houses built around a courtyard with a large dusty cypress tree at one end and at the other several wooden frames over which hung long skeins of cloth dyed in bright reds and blues and yellows.

We had a single room above the village store, and could look down on one side to the street and the houses opposite and the fields beyond, and on the other to the courtyard and the grass-tufted roof of the storekeeper's quarters and, further away, two swaying plane trees that hid from our view the simple flagstone platform where the train stopped.

For the first few days we kept to our room, and only occasionally ventured down the external staircase to the storeroom at the back of the shop, where the storekeeper served us our meals on a small card-table. We would sit on three wicker stools amidst sacks of rice and potatoes and dusty brown bottles of sulphuric acid and kerosene, and each time a bowl or a cup was placed on the table by the storekeeper's wife the legs of the table would sag and squeak at the hinges and sway so that we all had to keep one hand on the table top to steady it, as if we were holding a séance along with our meal.

After a week Kasimir and Piroshka took to spending the

daylight hours sitting in the shade in the courtyard while I played amongst broken, nail-infested frames and barrels of old creosote. Occasionally I ventured into the store itself where the storekeeper would look at me sternly and sit me down on a stool behind the leather-topped bench which divided his customers from the shelves of dry goods and the boxes of candles. When there was no one in the shop the storekeeper would ask me questions about our life in the city, and about 'the Russians', indicating the room upstairs with a lift of his head. Sometimes he would summon me to the locked medicine cabinet whose few lonely bottles were multiplied in its mirrored back panel, and he would bring out one of these bottles – of quinine or valerian drops or sleeping draughts – and ask me to translate the Japanese or Russian instructions printed on their sides. I answered as best I could, and then he would order me back to my stool and return to measuring out rice or dried beans, which would tumble with a harsh grating sound into the four-cornered tin cradle of the scales. This enormous gold-painted tombstone of metal dominated the leather-topped bench and its single eye would leer at me before embarking on its slow numerical ascent as the cradle was filled, its wandering eyeball progressing in a right-tending arc, fixing a malevolent gaze in turn on the candles, the dried fish, the preserved eggs, the brown wrapping paper, the dried chillies, the jars of Condy's fluid, and the medicine cabinet, and then, the moment the storekeeper suddenly lifted the cradle from its metal hand, rushing back to where it started and, with a malicious judder, fixing itself once more upon the fearful child sitting upright on the stool in the corner.

In time I ventured beyond the store and began to explore the village itself and to play with the local children, who spoke with a strong whirring accent and never seemed to wash their faces or hands or change their clothes. Soon I was roaming freely along the lanes between the fields of wheat and soy and down to the river, which was reduced in summer to an undulating field of gravel along which a trickle of water slipped quietly and invisibly. After a month or so we were moved into a small hut by this river, a hut which the storekeeper had fitted out for us with straw mattresses and our card-table and stools, and for the remainder of our stay Kasimir and Piroshka sat in the shade of the adjacent gingko tree, swept out our two rooms, and cooked simple meals of steamed bread, noodles and vegetables. Every night I would practice the violin, playing my favourite tunes from memory (in our haste we had left behind all of our music) or new tunes hummed to me by Kasimir, and the people of the village would gather around our small hut to listen to me standing beneath the drying frame playing melodies from Beethoven or Brahms, the children climbing into the branches of the gingko tree and sitting there like oversized fruit.

The village chief asked Piroshka if I would play at the mid-autumn festival. He arranged for the villagers to sit in rows on forms borrowed from the school house and set out in the village square. During the first piece the villagers came and went, talking to each other, eating moon cakes and shouting at their children. It was very distracting, but I persevered to the end of the piece. When I finished I waited for them to applaud. There was silence; or rather, a continuation of the domestic hurly-burly. I snorted with anger, and Piroshka rose to her feet and started to clap loudly. The village chief followed suit, and waved to the villagers to applaud.

I started the second piece, but at a pause they burst into applause. I stamped my foot, and shouted that they should wait until I had finished. It was no use. At the next pause they applauded again. I stopped and they stopped. I started and they began to applaud again. I raged once more, and stormed out and ran down to the river bank. Piroshka found me there half an hour later and sat with me, and we threw handfuls of gravel into the shallow stream.

'Don't think badly of these people,' she said. 'They are innocents, they lack the culture even to conceal their confusion. I have encountered much worse audiences, audiences that were better dressed and knew when to applaud, but understood little else.'

90

We walked hand in hand back to the hut, and stopped at the door and looked up at the gingko tree, which had grown dark within itself against the still-bright evening sky. Piroshka seemed to read my mind. 'Would you like to climb it?' she said softly. 'If I were a child again that's what I'd want to do. Why don't you go and sit up in the branches for a while?' I let go of her hand and stepped into the tree's shadowy interior, and it seemed to extend a limb down to me. Piroshka was behind me again, and she seized me by the armpits and hoisted me up to where I could get my foot onto the low branch. I made my way forward on all fours, allowing the tree to draw me into its midst. I turned around and found that Piroshka had gone inside the hut and left me.

I sat in the tree while the village around me sank into a silvery darkness. The moon was up, and I could see approaching from the south a solid front of cloud topped by billows that glowed in its light. I heard the rain before I saw it, heavy drops hitting the high leaves, like the sound of several people clicking their fingers at once. A cool gust swept through the branches and within a minute the noise of the rain was roaring around me and I could see the volleys of raindrops bouncing off roofs and hear the villagers calling to each other to close window shutters and doors. Then, another few minutes, and the rain was gone, and so too the wind, and the village fell silent. From my vantage point I could see the roofs and gravel streets shining white with moonwater, and I could hear the trickling of the runoff as it made its way by dozens of small rivulets down towards the river. I had watched it all happen without it happening to me. A dog bayed somewhere and then stopped. I closed my eyes and listened as the leaves around me began to shed their drops with a pocking sound, first to my left, then my right, behind, and before me. An irregular pattern, an attempt at music. When I opened my eyes Piroshka was waiting silently for me at the foot of the tree. She had brought a small, black umbrella, which she twirled jauntily behind her head as she watched me descend and held out her hand to take mine.

I learned some years afterwards that our sojourn in the countryside had been arranged by my father to prevent Kasimir and Piroshka from being repatriated to the Soviet Union. He got wind of Red Army plans to round up Harbin's remaining White Russians and move them to work camps, and quickly reactivated an old safe-house near the border with Korea. My mother, exhausted from sixteen-hour shifts at the hospital, suggested that I accompany Kasimir and Piroshka.

All talk of repatriation ended once the civil war with the Nationalists began in earnest in 1946, and the Chinese Communist Party in Harbin fell out with the Soviet Army. My father sent word that it was safe to return, and we assembled by the railway track and hailed the next train. We were surprised to find that the train was carrying a dozen American soldiers, wedged in amongst units from a battalion of communist troops. The Americans were fascinating creatures, hard muscles under tight uniforms, all smiles, laughter and chewing gum. One of them tried to speak to me, pointing to my violin case and indicating that I should play for them. I refused, thinking perhaps that beings as strange as these would surely clap in all the wrong places.

Both my parents were at the station to meet us; but although my father shook our hands warmly, he immediately turned his attention to the officer in charge of the American soldiers, exchanging greetings with him in Russian and taking him aside. My mother, Kasimir, Piroshka and I were taken back to the apartment in a military car, while my father supervised the loading of the Americans and their luggage into a truck, and then himself disappeared with their officer in a car.

I did not see him again until, several days later. He appeared at the apartment with the American officer and a young adjutant. My mother was roused from her sleep, and the four of them talked around the table. I overheard scraps of the conversation from the bedroom where I had been sent to read quietly. My mother was describing a number of patients with frostbite injuries, talking slowly in Russian, and repeating herself often so that the adjutant could take notes. The American's Russian was stilted, and he made grammatical errors I would never have made, but without being corrected the way Piroshka corrected my mistakes. He said he wanted to transport several 'suitcases' (which my father finally ascertained were filing cabinets) back to Japan. He also mentioned Marshall Lin Biao, and said he had asked for complete secrecy.

Although in later years I quizzed both my parents about the visit of the Americans, neither would say anything, nor even acknowledge that it had taken place. This mystery was not solved for many years, until the 1980s when both my parents were dead, and documents were released concerning Unit 731, a compound on the fringe of the city where Japanese doctors experimented on prisoners and lunatics. The frostbite experiments were perhaps the least brutal of their scientific endeavours. Other victims were spun in centrifuges or hung upside down until they died, had their stomachs or parts of their brains surgically removed, had flea-colonies lodged in their orifices, were used to test grenades or chemical weapons or had air injected into their arteries to study the onset of embolism. After the Japanese surrender, the Americans promised the doctors immunity from prosecution on condition that they release the meticulous records that were kept of each experiment. The Communist leadership in Harbin – including, I suppose, my father – were rewarded for their silence by a convoy of a dozen DC-3s, which landed at Harbin airport late one night, unloaded Japanese arms, ammunition and rations, and left before dawn the next day.

*

A few weeks after our return, I opened the door to my father and found him standing in the corridor, grinning from ear to ear, and holding a gramophone. 'I have brought a gift for your birthday,' he said, and manoeuvred awkwardly sideways into the room. 'This will help you with your study of music.' He greeted Kasimir, who was standing on a chair attempting to seal the windows in preparation for winter, and bent forward to place the gramophone on the table, gingerly, as if it were a sleeping child. It smelt of must and linseed oil. 'I found it in a pawn shop,' my father explained, running his fingers along the brass sound cone which was speckled with a patina of bluish verdigris. 'The pawnbroker gave me a good deal. It is yours now.'

Next he removed from his satchel a stack of records in tattered brown paper sleeves and placed them on the table. He sat me down next to him, picked up the first record and showed it to me, insisting that we read together the Chinese characters printed on the circle of red paper at the centre of the disk. I knew the first two characters, but not the third. 'Ba-la-mo,' my father read out. I was mystified.

'Ba-la-mo? What is that?' I said. I was not familiar with the names of the composers in Chinese. At that time, I assumed one only spoke of composers in Russian.

'Ba-la-mo,' my father repeated, somewhat deflated. 'He is my favourite composer. He is German.'

I turned to Kasimir, who was attempting to stuff a thin strip of cloth into the window frame, and asked, in Russian, 'Who is Ba-la-mo?' Kasimir knitted his brows, then ran the fingers of his right hand over the top of his head and seemed to be looking for inspiration in his armpit.

'Ba-la-mo,' Kasimir said. 'Brahms, of course. Ba-la-mo. Brahms.'

'Of course,' my father said, and picked up the next record. My father's finger poked the characters as he half sang the word: 'Tso-pin.'

'Chopin,' Kasimir said without looking away from his work.

'Tsai-kou-su,' my father read.

'Tchaikovsky, I imagine,' Kasimir said, and, pursing his lips, imitated the sound of a French horn and started to hum the march from the Fifth Symphony.

'Te-fou-jia.'

After glancing at the ceiling for a moment, Kasimir said, with a note of triumph, 'Ah yes, must be Dvořák .'

'Wa-gu-ne.'

.Kasimir was silent. My father and I looked up at him, and found that he had screwed up his face. 'Never heard of him,' Kasimir said. (The next day Wa-gu-ne was missing from the pile, and never reappeared.)

'Ge-lei-su,' my father went on.

'Ge-lei-su?' Kasimir said, his voice rising sharply. He came down from his chair, and studied the record. 'Ge-lei-su,' he repeated, 'I can't think who that is. Gluck, perhaps, or Glinka or Glazunov? Why not put it on and see?'

I watched as my father slipped the disk from its cover and balanced it on his thumb and fingertips. He placed it delicately on the platen, aimed the beaten brass cone at us like a blunderbuss, and wound the handle a dozen or so times, releasing a sound like throat-clearing. He released a catch and the record began to turn. 'Seventy-eight revolutions per minute,' he said, and placed the needle-arm at the edge of the record. There was a crackle, so loud that my father winced. Then a violin began to play in a far away room – a sweet, lilting tune, but with a spareness that conjured up a waif-like violinist with concave cheeks and sunken eyes, clutching his bow in bony fingers.

'Kreisler, of course,' Kasimir laughed. 'Ge-lei-su. It's Kreisler's *Liebesleid*.'

'This also is my favourite,' my father said.

'But you said Ba-la-mo is your favourite,' I objected. 'How can you have two favourites?'

'I am Iron Lu, so I can have as many favourites as I like,' my father answered indignantly. 'They are all my favourites.' And he placed his hand reverently on the pile of records.

*

It was three weeks before my father's next visit. He had been called away to meetings with Marshal Lin Biao to negotiate Harbin's 'voluntary contributions' to the war effort, he said. And in addition, his plan to register all citizens required special measures to deal with the illiterate itinerant workers and 'bad elements'. The night he visited again we ate a simple meal by

95

candle-light, the electricity having been diverted to the aircraft factory and the Harbin Railway Car Factory, which was now devoted to the assembly of small Soviet-model tanks. After the meal, Piroshka rose abruptly and sat down at the piano. She nodded to me and I produced my violin. Together we played the *Liebesleid* from a score that Kasimir and I had laboriously transcribed note by note from my father's record.

This was the first time my father had heard me play. He stared at me as if I were some kind of miniature god, watching every move of my bow, and following the fingers of my left hand as they crawled like a spider up and down the strings. And in response to his gaze I found myself emphasising the swooping and diving of the melody with the kind of theatrical movements I had seen Piroshka use when she played the oboe. I wanted not simply to play the music, but to send it forth to penetrate the skin of my father's chest and to lodge amongst his ribs, as a bird finds its home in a metal cage.

When we stopped, my mother leapt to her feet and clapped. Kasimir slapped his right thigh and smiled his satisfaction. But my father only clapped quietly, as if not wishing to disturb some fragile thing with raucous noise. He called me to his side and put his hand up to my cheek. 'Lu Feng's daughter is right,' he said, continuing our conversation of three weeks earlier. 'I am allowed only one favourite, and this Ge-lei-su, it is my favourite.'

5. Happiness

For the duration of the Civil War my father's duties meant
he was for the most part absent from my life. From time to
time, he would appear, unannounced, at the apartment, always
producing from his satchel some gift of food – a jar filled with
millet, a leathery knot of bean curd wrapped in cloth, three
or four potatoes or some greens in a bag – and would stay for
an hour or two. He would expect me to play for him whatever
music I was learning, and Piroshka and I would oblige. Her
hands would dance across the piano, and she would hiss
through her teeth whenever she struck B-flat above middle C
(for it had slipped out of tune and the only piano tuner she
trusted had left for Shanghai the year I was born). I would
stand at her shoulder and play, turning frequently to catch my
father's eye. He would listen with his eyes closed, nodding his
head with the music, and then would open one eye to make
sure we had finished, before clapping loudly. I learned quickly
that, although he loved to listen to music, and could hardly
believe his luck in having a child who was musically talented, he
himself was not capable of telling a good performance from one
that was merely competent. Several times I remember turning
to bask in his enthusiastic applause knowing in my heart that I
had neglected my phrasing, and slurred notes that should have
been sharp like pins. If Kasimir was present on these occasions
he would slap his thigh by way of applauding, but his eyebrows

would be raised and I knew to expect a meticulous critique as soon as my father left.

During one visit my father produced a length of string from his pocket, laid it along the top of my violin, then folded it in half and got me to place my finger on the violin string at the exact halfway point. 'Perhaps your Auntie has explained this to you,' he said, with a glance at Piroshka, 'but every string on a stringed instrument covers two octaves – that is an unalterable mathematical truth – and so the note that is produced if you play halfway along the string should be exactly one octave higher than the note that is produced if you play the string without touching it. Try it and see.' I plucked the string twice, and my father's theorem was proved.

'And if you divide the length of the string in half again you will find it plays a note that is in harmony with the first note. And if you continue to divide by half, every note made will be in harmony. And what is more, you will find the same happens if you divide the length of the string by three. You see, music is simply the mathematics of the ear. All notes on the scale rest in a precise mathematical relationship to each other. There is a name for this, but I do not remember it. Do you know what it is?'

I looked to Piroshka who was mending clothes by the fire. '*Garmonicheskiy ryad*,' she said, without looking up from her needle. 'But don't expect me to say it in Chinese.'

'*Garmonicheskiy ryad*,' I relayed. 'We don't know if there is a Chinese word too.'

'How could there not be,' my father assured me, 'when it was Confucius who discovered it, and taught it to the Greek, Pythagoras?' He took the violin from me and turned it over in his hands. 'With a few measuring tools and the right formulae I could describe in precise mathematical terms the sound waves this violin emits. The dimensions of the box, the way the strings vibrate, how the sound bounces around inside before it comes out, that is all I would need. I could give you a compound formula for it, although I am a busy man and it would take me a long time to work it out.'

'And a lot of paper to write it down,' muttered Piroshka, without looking up.

My father handed the violin back to me. 'Have you ever been up onto the roof at night? If you listen carefully you will hear the music of the stars and planets in their orbits. Confucius listened to it all the time, and I have heard it myself on rare occasions when I was at Yan'an with Marshall Lin Biao. You need a clear night with no enemy bombers about. Even then it takes a very good ear to hear it. Perhaps China will develop a machine for listening to this music.'

After my father had gone, Piroshka sat at the piano. 'Draw a stave,' she said, 'and write down this melody.' She struck a key. 'What note is that?' she asked.

'F,' I said.

'Close. It's E,' she said. 'Write it down. And what is this next note?'

'A-flat,' I said.

'Correct,' she said. 'Now I will play the melody slowly, and you write down what you hear.'

The melody was no more than a few bars long. When I had finished transcribing it Piroshka looked at my work, and turned a couple of quavers into semi-quavers, then drew a small tick at the end of the stave. 'Good. Now I want you to draw three more staves, and I want you to do three things that your father would approve of. First, I want you to turn the tune upside down, so that instead of going up a third at the start, you go down a third, then down to the fifth, and so on. Then I want you to take the original melody and write it backwards. And thirdly I want you to write the upside down version and the backwards version on the same stave. You have ten minutes.'

She returned to her mending while I worked. I found the exercise harder than I had thought. The clocks above the mantelpiece thudded mechanically, and I felt my ten minutes running down, tock by tock. When my time was up, Piroshka turned one eyebrow towards me and said, 'You are finished, are you?'

I nodded. But instead of checking my work, she went straight to the piano and sat down. 'Tell me if this is what you have written,' she said, and proceeded to play exactly what I had in front of me: the original melody, the inverted version, the melody reversed, and the combination of inverted and reversed melody which turned out to be in perfect counterpoint. I followed each note, and at the end laughed and clapped.

'How did you know?' I asked.

'It is by Bach, and when Bach was in a mathematical frame of mind this is how he wrote music,' she said, shrugging her shoulders. 'We should arrange for your father to meet Bach. I am sure they would have a lot to talk about. Now tell me, do you think the piece is more beautiful because you know how it was written? Because you understand its inner mathematics?'

'I don't know,' I said. 'Tell me the answer.'

'There is no answer,' she said. 'I only know this: to be a good musician you must not play only from your head, nor must you play only from your heart. This is what some people say, but it is an absurd romanticism. Like everyone else you play with your bones and your muscles and your nerves. You play from the base of your spine.' She touched my lower back with her hand. 'Here,' she said, 'This is where all of these meet: bones, muscles and nerves. This is where you play from. Is there any mathematics here? Perhaps we will ask your mother to bring home a scalpel some night and we can cut you open and see.'

*

On his next visit my father brought a rolled-up map of the city which he spread out on the table, holding down its curling edges with two small marrows, a roll of dried bean curd and a bag of beans. 'See?' he said. 'I have divided the city into six districts in the interests of public order and hygiene.' He indicated thick pencilled lines which made the city look something like the diagram on the back wall of the kosher butcher's shop – a carcass divided into various cuts of meat. 'Each district in turn has been divided into fifty-eight neighbourhoods, and each neighbourhood has around fourteen thousand people. And we have organised seventeen thousand citizens into night watch self-defence teams.' As he spoke he drew from his breast pocket a pencil stub and wrote each of the numbers on a blank area of the map. (My father already shared the Party's faith in the innate gravity of large numbers, especially those in excess of ten thousand, a 'myriad' in classical Chinese, the largest number that the ancient mathematicians thought could be contemplated.) 'Each neighbourhood can be sealed off so not even a mouse can escape,' he went on. 'Soon we will have registered every citizen. No one will be left out.'

Public hygiene provided my father with a wealth of numbers, and these he also added to his map as he spoke; numbers for the repatriation of Japanese civilians, for the disposal of night soil, the rationing of food, and the detention of carriers of syphilis and typhoid and cholera. Next, my father declared, indeed that very night – and here he drew a circle around the infamous Pingkangli neighbourhood – there would be a war on brothels and pimps. And so early the next morning an army of purgation fell upon Pingkangli. Police armed with whistles and truncheons, and nurses trained in the arts of dosing and restraint, descended upon the Virtuous Wind Inn, the Red Eagle Inn, the Peach Garden Bookhouse and the Heavenly Happiness Hall. The raid was a failure. There had been a tip off, and my father's net landed a meagre catch of ageing syphilitics and one surprised brothel-keeper who was convinced he had bought protection from a high official. Although the premises in Pingkangli were closed down the trade continued elsewhere. A municipal edict appeared on posters throughout the city, and rewards were offered for information leading to the arrest of pimps and prostitutes and their clients. My father – foolishly, he realised later – required each of the fifty-eight neighbourhoods to root out two brothels apiece. Within a week all of them had obliged. Flushed with success, he asked for two more; and that quota was also met. At first he was delighted; but when the tally of underground brothels reached five hundred, and the police petitioned him to expand Xiangfeng Prison, he called the campaign to a halt, and discovered to his dismay that the cells were filled not with whores, brothel-keepers and pimps, but with small-time gangsters, displaced Korean traders, alcoholics, imbeciles, neighbourhood misanthropes and homosexuals.

In spring the Nationalists mounted a massive counter-attack and all matters of hygiene were set aside. The Communist forces, more used to fighting as guerrillas than as a conventional army, were expelled from the city of Changchun and pushed back across the Songhua River. On my father's next visit he complained of back pain and would not sit. Instead, he leaned on the fireplace like a drooping flower, and admitted that there had been 'myriads' of dead. My mother was sent to work in a field hospital to the south of the city, once again performing amputations and, exhausting her supplies of ether, resorting to opium and then to the barely effective mandrake root. And when I did finally climb to the roof of the apartment building, on a hot night in summer, it was not to listen to the music of the spheres but to witness the distant flashes of artillery fire in the night sky and to feel the heavy thuds through my feet.

The siege continued for six months, and then Marshall Lin Biao made his famous counterattack, crossing the frozen Songhua and attacking the Nationalists in their winter quarters. The battle lines crawled south, each day another few metres, another few hundred dead, until the combatants reached the railway junction at Siping. My father described the attack by 40,000 of our troops. '*Si wan*,' he repeated, 'four myriads, and a myriad dead on the other side,' as he unloaded wizened mushrooms and tubers from his pockets onto our table. He had brought my mother back from the front. She was thinner than I had ever seen her, the bones protruding from her elbows and collarbone. I helped her to remove her clothing, which was encrusted with brown slime, and watched her burn it all in a brazier in the lot behind our apartment. Then I watched as Piroshka took a razor and a basin and shaved my mother's head, and gathered her hair in the basin and took it out to the brazier as well. By the time Piroshka returned my mother was lying on her side in bed, motionless, her eyes open, but saying nothing, dismissing me with a curt flick of her eyes when I attempted to speak to her,. When I returned with some food for her she was curled up like a foetus, so still that I had to hold my finger gingerly to her ribs to check that she was breathing. I undressed and got into bed beside her. For the whole of that night I felt I was sleeping with a ghost.

After the victory at Siping the war grew more distant. The night flashes and rumbling never returned. But by then my parents had another challenge to deal with: an outbreak of bubonic plague. Where it came from was a mystery at the time, but history now traces it to the rats and fleas raised by Japanese researchers in Unit 731 and then released, rather than destroyed, after the Japanese surrender. The disease had been incubating in sewers, basements and garbage dumps, and in the spring of 1947 it began to spread through the city, claiming first the labourers, hawkers, porters, and unemployed droshky drivers, and all those who wedged themselves and their belongings into the city's crevices and ruins. Neighbourhoods were sealed off immediately, and I saw neither of my parents for the duration of the outbreak. They toured the city together in face masks, overseeing the quarantine, distributing crates of Russian vaccines, supervising mass burials, and issuing ammunition to the neighbourhood watch committees who were manning the barricades around the infected areas of the city.

All road and rail traffic was controlled. School was closed, and we were urged to stay indoors despite the onset of warmer weather. The apartment building on Razyezhaya Street filled up with stray relatives and their children, many of them sleeping in the stairwells and filling our nights with arguing and singing and the bellowing of infants. The rabbi's widow and her nephew slept in our apartment and repaid us by foraging all day for food. I stayed at the apartment all day and practiced with Piroshka, and soon we gained an audience of plague exiles, who would enter our room without knocking and sit along the walls and the hearth or cluster by the doorway. One of these guests produced a viola, which she played (badly) and another brought out his uncle's euphonium and asked to join in. Piroshka rolled her eyes at first, but then relented and we improvised on a Bach fugue.

When our morning's session was over and my fingertips were red and aching and Piroshka closed the lid over the keyboard and called for the rabbi's widow to light the samovar, Kasimir would regale us with stories about old Harbin or the lives of the great composers and musicians. Perhaps because of the plague and its air of extremity, he decided not to spare us the details of Schubert's syphilis, or Chopin dying abandoned by his mistress, or Schumann's failed suicide and madness or Pyotr Tchaikovsky's troubled homosexuality. Sometimes Piroshka would join in, once she had a large cup of Russian tea in her hands, and she would talk about the great operatic divas she had met. I came to understand that all either died young and tragically or old and forgotten, in any case bereft of some great love (a tenor or conductor or junior prince without the courage to leave wife and children). 'Great music,' she declared to our gathering, 'is what great people make out of great suffering.' And added, with a laugh and a quick glance out of the window to the silent street, 'But particularly the suffering they bring upon themselves.'

One of our neighbours was an elderly Manchu woman with a long, noble face, watery dog-eyes, and a top lip which strayed upwards involuntarily as if she were yawning, or snarling, or curling her mouth around an oddly shaped fruit (a sure sign of childhood polio, my mother told me). She would arrive at the apartment at daybreak in order to secure her seat, and when she was finally obliged to leave she would approach me and cup my chin in her hand. 'Your music chases away the plague,' she said to me, 'so stay with us here in this building and play, and we will all be saved.' I was captivated by the thought, imagining that each time I put down my violin the sickness would begin to roll silently towards our building like a river mist and wash against the risers of the balustrade until I dispersed it with another tune.

The Manchu woman proved to be correct. No one in our building – or indeed within the Bolshoi Prospekt – was affected. However, when the plague was over we discovered that it had killed Wang Taitai, who had been stranded on a visit to her sister, isolated from the rest of the city by armed barricades. Rations were thrown over the barricade, along with chlorinated lime and boric acid to cover the bodies of the newly dead. Of Wang Taitai's family, only a ten-year-old child survived. My father delivered the news that Wang Taitai's name had appeared one morning on the list of the dead. The official tally: *san wan*, three myriads.

I felt secretly guilty. Although I knew Kasimir and Piroshka would never have allowed it, and my parents would never have approved, I felt that I could have walked through the city playing my violin, like the Pied Piper, and saved Wang Taitai and many others – could indeed have chased the plague into the river, where it would have been carried harmlessly to the sea. I could then have turned south to march with our troops, dispersing the Nationalist plague before us. I was simply born too late to save the city, but I promised myself that I would never again pass up an opportunity to serve the masses with my music.

I expressed this ambition to my mother, and instead of dismissing it she turned to me and surveyed me from head to foot, circling around me, lifting my chin with her fingers and squaring my shoulders and straightening my spine. 'I believe you may be ready,' she said. 'Do you agree, Uncle?' she asked Kasimir, who was nearby. 'Is she ready to begin performing?' He pursed his lips, but after a moment nodded in agreement. 'So you will arrange it?' she went on. 'You will prepare her?' He nodded again.

Shortly afterwards I began to play at the fortnightly meetings of the Harbin Musical Society, which were held in a hall attached to the (by that time defunct) American Baptist Church. My audiences were the regulars, a remnant weak and small, and something of a rogue's gallery: musty intellectuals and White Russians who had eluded repatriation, sitting on the edges of their chairs, smelling of makhorka tobacco and hair oil, sunk deep within themselves like tortoises, or listening intently, bright-eyed, even slightly manic, with a foot wrapped around the opposite calf or a chin resting on the back of an inwardly turned hand. I found myself at each performance fixing my attention on one of them – a man in a velvet smoking jacket, wearing a monocle; an orthodox priest with a coloured scarf wrapped tightly around his head to alleviate his neuralgia; a younger woman with glossy undulations of thick black hair, whose preferred outfit was pin-striped trousers and a tailored coat, beneath which one could see a waistcoat of green stuff, a silk blouse and a cravat; an old man with swaying jowls, wearing a fez, and holding a lighted cigarette upright between his fingers like a joss stick. I would narrow my eyes until only that person remained in focus, and then play to my chosen audience of one, blocking the others from my mind.

Then one night when Piroshka was not with us Kasimir took me, not to the Musical Society, as he had told her, but to an old working-class area, and down a series of unpaved streets and alleys, though a courtyard hung about with damp washing, to a tiny house with a light in the parlour window and the sound of a violin and a clarinet seeping through the walls. We stepped directly into a small parlour, warm with the smells of beer, sweat, sausage and tobacco, and found it filled with more than a dozen people, adults and children of all ages, sitting or standing around a group of musicians: a small boy playing a violin with only three strings; two older men, both wearing hats (the boy's father and grandfather, I was to learn), playing respectively a viola and a mandolin; a woman in a baggy dress occasionally contributing a bar or two with a clarinet; and, seated in their midst, a teenage girl with a surly expression on her face heaving a small octagonal concertina to and fro on her knee. They were playing some sort of reel, with an irregular rhythm and tempo, punctuated from time to time with what, to my ear, sounded

106

like false notes, although they were repeated again and again so must have been deliberate. I heard a clicking sound behind me and turned to find a man in a rough jerkin made of sheepskin holding two spoons between his fingers and rattling them in turn against one hip and then against his other hand, held just inches from my ear.

'Klezmer,' Kasimir said into my other ear, and any other words of explanation were lost as he was greeted with squeals and hugs and full-lipped kisses by several women. The men nodded to him, the musicians carried on, and despite the cramped conditions an old man and a young child began to dance, caracoling this way and that amongst the sawdust and spittle and beer-spills.

My violin case was taken from me, along with the Brahms I had practiced. I made several lunges to retrieve them, but was held back firmly by the shoulders. A woman opened the case, removed my violin and handed it to the boy in the centre of the room, who swapped it for his three-stringed instrument without hesitation and carried on with the tune, throwing me an appreciative glance. I smiled back, and then found his instrument being forced into my hands, and from across the room Kasimir called to me, 'Just forget everything I have taught you; forget major and minor, forget your keys and scales and progressions; forget it all and just play.'

And so I learned to play klezmer, with Kasimir shouting instructions for the first few tunes, then leaving me to it after being drawn into the dance by an old woman, who seized his deadened hand and planted it first on her waist and then around her neck and led him around the room. After a while one of the dancers, a tall man with a curled moustache, broke away and, without a word, relieved me of my violin. He started to play it himself, holding it in the crook of his elbow, and I found myself promoted to the dance, spun around in precise turns by the firm, warm hands of a young man whom I guessed to be no more than fourteen, although I was surprised, after several minutes, to find him displaced by a young woman who placed an infant in his arms, pushed him aside with some harsh words, and began to dance with me. 'His wife,' Kasimir mouthed to me. 'And a jealous one at that.'

After an hour or more the dancers began one by one to drop onto chairs. The old woman who had claimed Kasimir announced that she was finished for the evening, and grasped both of his hands and kissed each of his fingers on the second knuckle, before attempting to pass him on to another old woman. Kasimir escaped only by pressing his palm against his chest and feigning an angina attack.

Food began appearing on metal plates, and glasses of vodka and tea, and the noise in the room died down as these were consumed. One by one the band stopped playing until it consisted of just me (reunited with my own violin) and the girl on the concertina. We played on, and I managed, through whispers and nudges, to manoeuvre the tune around to a dance *alla zingarese* from the end of one of Brahms's piano quartets, which I played with accelerating tempo and adding in the false klezmer notes I had now learned, enticing the boy violinist, vodka glass in hand, into a solo dance, and drawing from Kasimir the widest of smiles and then a salute as he raised his glass to the ceiling in a silent toast.

Afterwards, as we walked through the cold, darkened streets, Kasimir made me promise not to tell Piroshka where we had been, but when we arrived home she seemed already to know. She sniffed at Kasimir's coat as she took it from him, her face screwing up in its clatter of lines and plates. '*Makhorka*,' she muttered to herself. I sensed Kasimir preparing to stage a retreat, but she merely eyed us strangely and gave out a long sigh. 'I gather you have been taken to meet the *klezmorim*,' she said to me, 'our Ashkenazi *heimish* at their most pure and free.'

'I made sure they didn't put vodka in her tea,' Kasimir protested.

'That's good, but I'm more concerned about what they put in her head,' Piroshka replied, and she squeezed both my temples between her palms and then hugged my head to her breast and added, '. . . or what they removed from it.' Then she began to laugh quietly, continuing to do so every few minutes as we prepared for bed.

*

Later that month I went with Kasimir and Piroshka to see the movie *Eight Thousand Li of Clouds and Moon*. It tells the story of Xian Xinghai, China's first great violinist and the composer of the National Liberation Symphony. In the most memorable scene he attempts to console an audience of soldiers and peasants hiding in a village after the defeat of the Guangzhou Commune, in which his own uncle has been killed. As he begins to play, Xian starts to rise above the earth and, as in a woodcut of some ancient fable, hovers over the startled crowd, making to fly away until one of the soldiers climbs onto the shoulders of a peasant and seizes him by the heel. So long as Xian continues to play he is lighter than air, and the crowd gathers into a circle, the soldiers balancing on the backs of the peasants and tethering him to the earth with their rough hands until he finishes his performance and regains his weight.

That night I dreamt I was flying over the city. My neighbours and schoolmates gathered in groups and pointed at me and called up to me as I hovered and swooped. Then I noticed to my horror that the body of my violin had become my left arm, that my fingers were the keys, and my veins and tendons the strings. I looked to my right and found my hand was gone, and in its place, growing out of the stump of my forearm, was my bow, articulated at the wrist like a single, elongated talon. I was at one with the instrument. And then there was a painful pressure in my foot and I looked down to find that my neighbours had formed a human pyramid whose topmost member had seized me by the ankle. They dragged me down to the ground and tied my foot to a tree and left me there.

*

The summer passed, then autumn, and winter approached again. The news from the front improved week by week. My father reopened the quarantined neighbourhoods, reducing their number by two to fifty-six to take account of the deaths. I arrived home from school one day in November to find both my parents at the apartment – an unusual event for the daytime – and wearing new clothes, made of a deep blue cloth, with sharp creases on the jacket sleeves and the trouser legs, so sharp, in fact, that I recall thinking how diminished my parents looked, as if they had no substance, like the air in the bellows of an accordion, and could now be folded up and inserted into these envelopes of blue.

My father sat forward on a chair, one leg crossed over the other, his foot tucked behind the opposite calf. He looked immensely happy with himself, unable to stop smiling. He was smoking a cigarette and he closed his eyes as he inhaled, with an expression not unlike the one he had when he listened to me play my violin. Then he opened them again, and looked at me, with quiet affection, but without speaking.

My mother stood behind him, her hands resting on his shoulders. 'The war is over,' she told me. 'Soon all of China will be liberated. We are flying to Beijing in an hour. Chairman Mao Zedong will address the people.' For the first time in years I became aware of the detail of my mother's appearance. Until now, she had been constantly in motion, always vacating the space she occupied, as her thoughts ran far ahead of her body, diagnosing and treating her next patient, serving the needs of the next person. When she was with me I sensed I only had part of her, a part that was following instructions, implementing plans, while the rest of her – the thinking, feeling spine of her – was engaged elsewhere. So I had not noticed until now that her hair had become thin and was starting to grey at the roots, that her shoulders had settled into a permanent sag, that the skin on her cheeks had become pallid and stained with red creases like a map that is repeatedly folded and unfolded.

My father sang softly to himself between puffs on his

cigarette as he waited for my mother to pack her things into a small case. 'I wish we could take you with us, but there are not enough seats on the plane,' he said. 'It is a military plane,' he said, as if that explained everything. And then, 'Be sure to practice hard while we are away. China will need violinists to strengthen the morale of the people. We will be away for a week or so. Then when we return we will all be a family at last. We will be happy. We will live in a house together. We will have enough food to eat. All of China will be happy. Everyone under heaven will be happy now.'

'I am already happy,' I said.

'Let me assure you,' my father said, wagging his index finger at the ceiling, 'once all of China is united under Mao Zedong thought the happiness you have now will seem in comparison like deepest sadness.'

While I was still pondering this statement my mother re-entered the room and announced that she was ready. She placed her hand on my head, and my father, awkwardly, shook my hand. I noticed a young man waiting by the open door. He took the suitcase from my mother, and the three of them smiled at each other smugly and clattered down the stairs and into a car and were gone.

They returned ten days later, bursting into the apartment in the evening when I was getting ready for bed. My father was carrying a reel of film in a large tin under his arm. My mother threw her suitcase onto the bed and took my hand. 'Come,' she said, 'we are going to watch the newsreel of Mao Zedong at Tiananmen, proclaiming the founding of the People's Republic.' I dressed quickly and followed my parents down the stairs into the waiting car, noticing that they sat together very close, clasping each other by the hand. During that journey my parents seemed impossibly happy. They laughed at everything the other said. They laughed at what I said, at what the driver said. They laughed until they had to wipe tears from their eyes. My father put his arm around me and crushed me to his ribs. 'Ah, what bliss to have not one girl, but two,' he said, and burst out laughing again. I felt a surge of pleasure at the warmth of his embrace, but realised, with a sense of something like fear, that things would never be the same again.

We drove down to the municipal offices, where a crowd of party members had gathered in a large meeting room. That year the *Da Leng*, the Great Cold, had arrived early, and since my father had refused to relent on his decree that there would be no heating in the city until the middle of November, the room was chilly despite the warmth of many bodies. My father held the reel of film above his head like a trophy as we entered the room and were greeted with cheers. He handed the metal box to the projectionist who quickly threaded the film, and shouted for the lights to be extinguished. The screen remained white for a time, and the wedge of light from the projector illuminated the tendrils of steam rising from our heads as if we were all gently smouldering. For a second a blurry infestation of worm-like stains wriggled in the top corner of the screen and then a series of descending numbers appeared at the centre of a kind of target. We counted them down: 'wu – si – san – er – yi.' The screen and the room went black momentarily, and then, with the sound of a strangled fanfare, white characters emerged out of the fog of a black background – 'Victory for the Masses! China awakes to a new dawn!'

Suddenly I was in Beijing. There was a crowd, the biggest I had ever seen, delirious with excitement, waving banners with big bold characters written on them. A woman's voice was describing the gathering – how many delegates there were from Gansu and from Liaoning, how many peasants, how many intellectuals, how many bourgeois – and reading out what was written on the banners:

'Celebrate the victory of Mao Zedong and Zhu De!'

'The nation says thankyou to the People's Liberation Army!'

'All of China's minorities welcome the victory of the Communist Party!'

'Workers of the world unite! You have nothing to lose but your chains!'

For each banner, a smiling face, and a wave to the camera. And then a roar of welcome as a company of the People's Liberation Army marched into the square, walking in time, but with the syncopated tempo of comrades dancing, rather than the unanimous, metronomic swing of the parade ground.

The troops turned to salute the line of figures on the top of Tiananmen, and the camera panned along the faces. I felt my mother's warm breath as she whispered the names into my ear: Liu Shaoqi, Mao Zedong, Peng Zhen, Zhu De, Zhou Enlai, Chen Yun. Mao stepped forward to a copse of microphones, shiny silver boxes balanced on the top of metal stands, sprouting hoops, springs and black wires. He held before him a sheet of paper with characters written in the old style, top to bottom. I was fascinated by his curtain of thick black hair, set far back on his skull as if fleeing the light of the intellect resting under the smooth expanse of his forehead.

Mao began to read from the paper, slurring the words in the broad Hunan provincial accent which made him unintelligible to most Chinese, in particular to the people of the Northeast with our perfectly standard pronunciation. There was a murmur of dismay in the crowd, and someone near me asked without irony if it was English that Mao was speaking. My father stood up, motioned to the projectionist to hold the film and produced from under his jacket a thick sheaf of papers. 'A transcript of Chairman Mao's address,' he explained, and began to pass the papers around to the eager hands extended to him from all angles. There was a rustle of papers and a round of coughing, and then the projector stirred into life again and the film continued, except now instead of a sea of heads in front of me all I could see was the bobbing transcripts held above the audience's heads so they could be read by the light of the projector. I recall nothing of the speech itself except for the last line, when Mao put down his paper and shouted, 'China has arisen!' The crowd at Tiananmen erupted with cheers – as did the audience packed into the room that night – and Mao retreated to the line of august faces.

*

After the Liberation I moved with my parents into a new house. It was in a traditional four-sided courtyard, and we found ourselves with the unimaginable luxury of four rooms – a kitchen, a living room, my parents' bedroom with a *kang*, where we could all sleep in winter, and a tiny bedroom where I slept when the weather was not too cold. We shared a bathroom and washhouse across the central courtyard with the other occupants: the Deputy Mayor, his two children and his elderly parents. We were joint owners of a small rat-catching dog and a succession of pigs purchased as yearlings for the purpose of transforming our collected food scraps into sizzling New Year's treats.

My father surveyed our small pile of possessions, which had been deposited on the *kang*, and toured our quarters several times before pronouncing himself satisfied. That night he slept soundly, so soundly in fact that we could not wake him in the morning. I shook his arm, at first gently and then more vigorously, but he snored softly and did not open his eyes. My mother checked his pulse and pulled back one eyelid and slapped his cheek several times, at which he muttered something I could not pick up and then slept on. 'Exhaustion,' my mother explained. He had not had any rest for a decade. But when I returned from school that night she told me he was in hospital.

So I found myself once again sleeping with my mother, having been ousted from her bed for only one night. She too was exhausted, and would often sleep through the weekends, rising only to accompany me on our daily visits to my father in hospital. During that time I would rise and dress myself and make breakfast, or take a small lidded pot to one of the stalls on the corner where a pair of elderly twins would fuss over me like beavers with a cub, and I would return with my pot brimming with hot soy milk and two dough sticks balanced on top.

After a month or so my father returned home, but for the first week he did no more than patter slowly around the house in between long sessions of corpse-like sleep. Day and night seemed to have no meaning for him, and he did not even seem interested in playing his records on the gramophone. Sometimes I would wake up in the middle of the night, and see him reading, or making tea with the medicinal herbs he kept in a glass jar. I would sit up on the old *kang* with my legs tucked beneath me and watch him measure out the contents of the jar into a shallow cone folded from a sheet of paper, and then tip them into another jar. The discoloured petals, crumbling leaf skeletons, and what looked like the transparent wings of insects collected like a bird's nest on the bottom of the jar. He would pour in the newly boiled water, releasing a foul stink of musty alleys, fish, and camphor. I would pull the covers over my head and around dawn would hear him returning to bed, where he would lie perfectly still for ten or twelve hours.

Eventually he took it into his head to use his time to supplement my education in mathematics. We covered sheets of thin rice paper – mostly the reverse sides of official Nationalist-era forms – with sequences of algebraic formulae, meandering strings of calculus, angles, curves, grids and geometrical figures, and I would find myself bursting out laughing as I observed the sleight of hand by which he brought an equation to resolution, like the tumblers falling into place within the metal innards of a lock.

'If you are patient,' he assured me, 'and attentive, then anything you encounter will open its secrets to you. If you scratch the surface of anything you will find that what lies beneath is a fine web of mathematics. Everything is number, and number is everything. Each atom has its own formula, each molecule, the metal of the table leg, the wood on its top, the stone on the floor.'

'And people?'

'Yes, people too, a formula for how they move in space and in relation to things and to each other, how they walk, the sounds they make, the way they take in food and drink – if we could see the minute web of things we would find an infinite number of formulae. Wait, no' – and here he jumped to his feet as best he could and raised his index finger emphatically – 'No, these formulae are not infinite. It is a finite number of formulae, and one day we will master them all, as they meet and merge and transform and resolve each other endlessly, day and night, throughout the world and throughout the universe. They are millions upon millions, but we too – the people of China – are millions upon millions.'

He went on to explain gravity to me, how the individual object is drawn inexorably towards a larger mass via a formula which he made me write out several times. And the universe too, at least, the universe as envisaged by Blaise Pascal: 'An infinite sphere,' he read from his book, 'whose centre is everywhere and whose circumference is nowhere.'

'Like China,' I said, 'the 'middle kingdom.'

He tilted his head for a moment, and then smiled happily and patted my head. 'If you like,' he said, 'but not many can see that. A socialist needs to be alert, for if we notice, upon traversing some territory or other – be it physical or intellectual, a territory of ideas, events, people, history – if we notice that lines that should be parallel are not quite so; if we observe and measure and connect, and do not allow ourselves simply to pass over these troubling facts as if they were aberrations with no significance; if instead we recognise that the aberrations *are* what is significant; then we will see that we are living, not on a flat, regular plane, but on the curved surface of a sphere. And if we have three settled points and measure them accurately, then we can locate the centre of the sphere, and however distant it may be, it is a fulcrum from which the world can be moved, hidden from the many, known only to the few.' I tried to look as if I understood, and my father seemed happy to accept this obvious fiction, for he extended his hand for me to shake. What exactly we were agreeing to I did not know.

*

As my father's strength returned he began to take me on his bicycle around the city, and to tell me stories from the early days of the Communist Party and the struggle against the Japanese. I could not help comparing his tours of the city, of the sites of street battles and safe houses and ambushes, with Piroshka's accounts of the lives of the White Russians, the Jews, and the Fascists. Each showed me a city that the other had never inhabited and only partly understood, although we traversed the same streets and gave the same directions to lost visitors. On one occasion my father took me down an alley and through large gates into a hall with a high vaulted ceiling. My nostrils were immediately filled with a syrupy confection of blood and offal, as if we were walking into the maw of a sleeping tiger after a kill. Thick shafts of light descended from a row of skylights, illuminating benches upon which the carcasses of pigs, chickens, sheep, and ducks lay disassembled. Stall keepers stood at attention behind piles of intestines and stomachs, lungs and kidneys, tripes, gizzards, Achilles tendons and pizzles, watching us as if waiting for us to give the signal to begin a competition to put the carcasses back together again.

On one table four pigs' heads, with eyes and tongues removed, were stacked neatly in a pyramid. On the next sat three large vats of congealed black liquid with dirty red froth around the rim, which handwritten signs identified as the blood of sheep, pigs and chickens respectively. My father whistled softly to himself as he pushed his bicycle through the braided rivulets of blood that traversed the floor. What struck me was how different this place was, with its displays of gleeful carnage, from the small kosher butcher shop, the one with the *menorah* painted in gold on the window, and the map of the quartered lamb on the back wall, where I used to go with Piroshka every week to collect small parcels of flesh wrapped respectfully in brown paper.

My father leant his bicycle against one stall and pointed to a pig's head. The stall owner patted the head affectionately, as if it were his child. Money changed hands and the head was hoisted into the basket on the front of my father's bicycle. It journeyed home with us like a ship's figurehead, casting its eyeless gaze this way and that as we steered around corners, proudly sniffing the air, and calling to our neighbours with its tongueless mouth, 'Look everyone, look at who has honoured me, has invited me to grace their family pot! None other than Iron Lu and his daughter, the violinist Xiao Magou!'

On weekends and summer evenings my father would spend time in the courtyard, attempting to practice *tai ji chuan*, or chatting with the neighbours. Sometimes I watched him as he stood for a long time in the middle of the courtyard, turning to a different point of the compass from time to time and staring at the angles of the roof, the paving stones and the pile of rubbish stacked against the back wall. I wondered if he was taking his own advice, looking for some lost mathematical principle, confident that if he was patient and stared for long enough it would eventually give itself up to him.

Then one day he showed my mother and me some plans he had drawn up for a fish pond he said he was going to build at the back of courtyard, where there was an old dried-up well. He would deepen the well, he said, and (provided he could restore the flow of water) build a large concrete trough about three metres long, in which he would keep river fish to be fattened up for the table. His plan included a small electric pump to draw the water from the trough and aerate it by cascading it down a miniature gorge of pebbles. There would be water lilies and orchids, and he would find some paint so that I could decorate the interior of the trough before it was filled.

'And in the winter?' my mother asked. 'What happens in the winter when it freezes?'

'We borrow a hammer and chisel,' my father said. 'And we eat frozen fish until there are no more. And then we start again in spring time, and put more young fish in the pond.'

*

The next day my father felt strong enough to return to work, and found that in his absence others had taken over the task of making the city hygienic and orderly, and were reluctant to give it back to him. He still had his office and his secretary, but his papers were stacked in neat piles in a locked cupboard and his desktop gleamed with new polish. It was Wen who told me this, years later, when I was about to leave Harbin. He also told me that for the following week my father travelled to every corner of the city to drink tea with Party officials of all ranks, that every day he had Wen place phone calls to Beijing and Shanghai, and that he even took a military aircraft fresh from the production line at the new aircraft factory and had a test pilot fly him to Jilin and Mukden in one day to visit old comrades, with Wen cowering beside him white with fear and suffering cold sweats and nausea.

At the end of that week my father told us that he had relinquished the position of Mayor and was to become Party Secretary at China Eastern Railways, and Commissar for Flood Control. He seemed very happy about this, although I recall going to school the next day fearful that, after his change of status, the special regard in which I was held as Iron Lu's daughter might have diminished. My fears were groundless.

That very night he came home and, with the Deputy Mayor at his side, announced that I had been selected to play a concert for Mao Zedong in a week's time. Mao was returning from a two-month sojourn in Moscow, my father explained. He was bringing back not only his first-hand observations of Soviet economic planning, but also a small red lacquer box containing the ashes of Xian Xinghai, China's great revolutionary composer, who had died in Moscow in 1945.

The day arrived. The records show that Mao toured the railway workshops, delivered a speech (written text placed under the chairs in advance), attended a concert in his honour and spent a night at the suite on the top floor of the Hotel Moderne. I took top billing at the concert, accompanied by a small ensemble from the conservatory in Mukden. The heating in the theatre was working only intermittently, and the audience – party secretaries, local dignitaries, workers from the ball-bearing factory, and a company of soldiers from the barracks – sat for an hour waiting for the great man to arrive, hunched in their greatcoats with fur hats over their ears, steaming like a herd of bison.

I played a short piece adapted from the first movement of Xian Xinghai's *National Liberation Symphony*, Massenet's *Élégie* (which Xian himself had made famous after the defeat of the Guangzhou Commune), and Kreisler's *Prelude and Allegro* (which my mother requested I play, as a surprise birthday present for my father). I was followed by a dance troupe, and a children's choir who sang 'The Three Main Rules of Discipline and the Eight Points for Attention'. And to finish, the Mukden ensemble and I played Nie Er's *March of the Volunteers* – newly confirmed as the national anthem – after which the choir joined in and sang the words: 'Arise! All those who would not be slaves! Let your flesh and blood forge our new Great Wall!' Mao tapped one hand lightly on his opposite palm by way of applause, and afterwards made a speech about there being many strings in the bow of the Party, these strings being the individual Party members and the Communist Youth League, which must be stretched together in tight formation, or else there would be no sound. The shaft of the bow was Marxist-Leninist thought; the body of the violin was the Middle Kingdom itself. (My father was very pleased with this metaphor, claiming that he himself had suggested it to the Great Leader.)

In spring the floods came as usual, and my father summoned the Party leaders to the floodplain outside the city and, stripping himself to the waist, swam out to a large tree marooned in the still waters, where he hoisted himself onto a branch and sat, torso glistening in the sun, to announce that that year's flood would be the last. The news spread quickly around the city that tens of thousands of peasants from the western provinces – where one of father's Yan'an colleagues was Party Secretary – would arrive in summer to work on new floodbanks, and that my father had explained all this as he swung joyfully on a rope attached to the tree, urging the senior Party officials to shed their clothes and join him in celebrating the event. Wen showed me the photographs that had been taken at the scene: my father addressing the crowd from the tree; my father swinging gaily to and fro as some of his comrades – including our housemate the Deputy Mayor – struggled with their clothes and threw themselves into the flood waters; those that had remained ashore applauding, with fixed grins; my father, back on dry land, wearing a bath robe with the monogram of the Hotel Moderne, laughing, with his head thrown back and his hands on his hips and the scar on his eyebrow somehow larger than I had ever noticed. Within a year, Wen told me, all of those who had remained on the embankment had been quietly demoted to clerical positions in dusty border towns. Two had died by their own hands. The Deputy Mayor was promoted to Mayor, despite which, Wen told me, he still made a daily visit to my father's office to receive orders.

For the time being all thought of deepening the well and building a fish pond was set aside. After school each day I made my way up to the corner of Razyezhaya Street and climbed the familiar staircase of the dark brick apartment building for my violin lesson. By this time the building that had housed the Club of the Russian Student Society was the headquarters of the neighbourhood committee, and advertised night classes in Marxist political theory, perinatal health, the piano accordion, and Mao Zedong thought.

One afternoon in early summer I arrived at the apartment and found that Kasimir and Piroshka were not there. In their place were a young Chinese woman and an older man, a Russian who, in spite of the fact that it was a moderately warm day, kept his hands thrust into the pockets of a long overcoat with a belt and buckle dangling from its sides and a detachable cape.

'Are you Xiao Magou?' the woman asked.

'Yes,' I said.

'Your violin teacher has sent us to collect you,' she said. 'You are to have your lesson today in the centre of the city. It is all arranged.'

I followed the two strangers downstairs and they drove me in a car to Central Avenue, where we drew up outside the Hotel

Moderne. 'Here we are,' the woman said. 'Mr Karpin will accompany you to your lesson.' She withdrew, and the Russian man took my violin case and strode ahead of me through the main door of the hotel, barely acknowledging the salute of the soldier who stood guard.

We passed the hotel reception desk and walked briskly across the chess-board floor of a high-ceilinged lounge, threading our way amongst padded leather chairs, drooping palms and stands of bamboo in large porcelain tubs. The lounge appeared empty save for a trio of army officers holding conclave in one corner around a hissing radiator. A pair of long boots stretched out from behind a rubber plant, heels resting upon a grey footstool that on second glance turned out to be an elephant's foot.

We stepped into the elevator, and I noticed Mr Karpin's surprise when he turned from the panel of buttons to find that I was almost as tall as him. (I was prematurely sprouting in the legs and arms.) 'You speak a little Russian?' he said. I corrected him, 'I speak a lot of Russian,' and smiled to myself. He said no more. When the elevator stopped with a bump he wrenched aside the squealing brass gate and pushed open the door with his foot. We walked through the gloom of the corridor, the dim lights illuminating patches of vermilion wallpaper decorated with a gold scroll pattern. At the end of the corridor Mr Karpin opened a door without knocking and led me into a large room.

'Wait here,' he whispered, and handed my violin case back to me. Then he left the room, taking great care to close the door soundlessly.

I put my violin on a low table by the door and turned to examine my new surroundings. As if on cue, a silver clock to my right, set in its own cabinet with tiny drawers, announced my arrival with a tinkling fanfare. And as if in response, the crystal chandelier that hung from the ceiling rattled discreetly, and with its myriad facets directed beams of milky white light onto the other occupants of the room: a sprawling divan with round tasselled cushions, a marble chess set on a circular table, and a polished bureau, on which sat a silver samovar in the shape of a turnip and a matching silver tray whose lip encircled a plate of cakes, an array of scimitar-shaped knives, a tea-cutter, a sugar-hammer, and a nest of gold-rimmed tea-glasses. Standing beside the tray on its own lace doily was a bottle of vodka.

I had had very little experience of beautiful objects. With very few exceptions – the mirror, the clocks, a couple of plates – the things in the apartment in the Bolshoi Prospekt and now in our new house in Daoli were servants dressed in plain brown or black, who did their job silently and then retreated into anonymity. Here in this room everything sought out the eye in its own right. Nothing here was plain. Every surface was carpeted or papered or moulded in relief with geometrical patterns that folded in on themselves and led my eyes along intricate mazes. I wandered around the room studying surfaces that were turned or carved with designs of vines or flowers, or inlaid with some luminous metal, or polished so smooth as to give the illusion of glowing coals encased in a sheet of thin ice.

And then I felt the polarity in the room change and found myself drawn to a table in front of the window, tucked behind a high-backed armchair. On it was a violin case wrapped in navy blue cloth. Without hesitation I opened it.

I do not know how much I took in during those first few minutes. Later on, when it came into my possession, I came to know the violin intimately, as one knows the body of a lover or a child. In my memory, however, I pull back the loose satin cover and lift the instrument into the windowlight. I study the neck, the backward-sloping peg-box, the scroll shaped like the inside of a child's ear, all carved from a single piece of maple. I hold the instrument up close to my eye like a telescope, registering the dull shine of the ebony fingerboard, oiled with finger-sweat, and allow my focus to travel slowly forwards along the parallel lines of the strings down to the bridge, a thin sliver of Balkan maple from which have been cut two ears flanking the inverted heart in the centre. I spin the instrument sideways and run my eyes along the elegant inlaid purfling around the rim and then across the contours of the upper body, the table, two symmetrical wedges of spruce whose feminine curves and sinuous f-shaped sound holes give the instrument the appearance of a pair of butterfly wings, varnished with walnut oil to give a rich red glow. My gaze rests finally on the black ebony tailpiece where the ends of the strings concentrate, like nerves at the base of the spine, and the loop of gut which gathers all the tension of the instrument and deposits it onto a simple hardwood peg attached to the base.

A voice behind me said softly, in Russian, 'Perhaps you will play it one day.' I turned and saw a tall man, who had entered silently by one of the doors in the suite. He had black hair and a receding hairline, and his mouth and jowls jutted forward so that they seemed of a piece with the well-padded armchairs by the window. His forehead resembled a large boulder that had slipped from its original position, compressing his features into the lower half of his face. Even so he was not unpleasant looking. He was wearing a finely-checked jacket, a black shirt without a tie, and dark trousers.

He motioned for me to sit on one of the chairs and sat opposite me. 'You understand Russian?' he asked.

'Of course.'

'My name is David,' he said, 'and I am from Odessa in the Ukraine. I am travelling with another musician from Russia, Comrade Richter, for some performances in Beijing and Shanghai, but since our train passes through Harbin I had the opportunity to meet with Kasimir and Piroshka and to deliver a parcel – to deliver this violin.'

'The violin is theirs?' I asked.

'It belongs to their son, Vitja. You have heard of Vitja, no? I myself have not met him.' David leaned forward in his chair. 'Now, please listen,' he said, inclining his head towards me. 'Vitja is now a very sick man – still passably well in his body, but very sick in his mind. It was my duty to inform his parents, and they are very distressed, as you would expect. It is so difficult to have . . . to have circumstances which keep you from doing what a parent would want to do for a son.' The man was silent for a while, as if inviting me to speak. I could think of nothing to say. I felt the edge of his warm breath on my face. It was laced with unfamiliar spices. As he shifted in his chair his clothing creaked.

'Where are they?' I asked. 'Piroshka? And Kasimir?'

'They are in Comrade Richter's suite. I asked what I could do for them, and they said I could give you your lesson for today. So you are here. Kasimir believes that soon he will have nothing more to teach you.' The man's face suddenly became animated and he slapped both knees with his hands and rose from his chair. 'Shall we begin, then? What piece have you learned for today?'

'Dvořák's *Slavonic Dances*,' I said, 'but we don't have a piano to accompany me.'

'You ask a lot of Comrade David and the Hotel Moderne,' he said. 'Play. I will supply piano accompaniment inside my head.'

I took out my violin, which seemed like a toy compared to the one lying in the case by the window, and arranged my music on the stand. I closed my eyes and, envisaging Piroshka addressing the piano, counted myself in and began to play. When I had finished Comrade David clapped three times, and said, 'Brava! Very good. You have a beautiful, natural, unforced tone. Brava!' He cleared his throat, and went on. 'Now let us get to work. First, your vibrato. Very good, very lyrical, but you must use it sparingly or your audience will become distracted by your skill and they will miss the point of the music. Do you understand?'

I nodded, and Comrade David continued, 'And you must not overdo the sighing and the glissandi. Yes, I know the violin is the natural instrument for melancholy; but it is also the natural instrument for intellectual joy. Understand?' I nodded again. 'Pathos, yes,' he went on, turning on his heel and circling around an armchair, 'but also greatness, power.' He clenched his fist and jerked it twice in front of his face.

I nodded a third time.

'Now this piece by the beloved Bohemian – it is too playful for you, too romantic. You are a tall girl, and angular. You must

125

try something more suited to your physique and temperament.'

He turned and left the room, returning a minute later with a score under one arm and a violin and bow in the other hand. 'Here,' he said, 'you must play some Bach. Do you know Bach? I know Kasimir likes his Romantics, but you must come to terms with Bach. He is inevitable. If he did not already exist, we would have to invent him. Ha!' He arranged the score on the music stand and started flicking through its pages. 'This piece is for two violins. I played it in Moscow with Menuhin in 1945, just after the war. Yehudi Menuhin, you know. It was a symbol of unity with the West, I believe. He is a fine, fine violinist, and, of course, a Jew like me. A Jew from the East and a Jew from the West. How rich a symbol is that? Now, I want you to play one of the parts of the slow movement. It is a simple melody so if you do not know it you can sight-read. Do you want me to play it through first?'

'No,' I said, 'I will try it by myself.'

'Then I will count you in,' he said. 'Play the top line.'

I began, haltingly in the first couple of bars, until I found the rhythm, and then more fluently. Comrade David tucked his violin under his arm and turned away from me to look out the window to the street below, calling out from time to time – but without turning his head – 'slower' and 'more round' and 'less vibrato' and 'now, build, build, build, and . . . release.'

When I had finished he turned to me and said, 'You see what I mean? Emotion. And intellect. I see the violin as a horse, all power, all emotion, with wild eyes and sweat coating its limbs and its great heart pounding in its great chest; but you, a mere child, with no more than your intellect, with the fine muscles of your mind, with the strings of your bow, you . . . are guiding it up and down narrow ridges, through dark valleys and forests, and . . . Oh, I speak in riddles. Do you understand what I am trying to say?'

'No,' I said. 'Well, yes; I think so.'

'You think so? Is that any way for a young socialist to talk? We deal with facts, with certainties, even if they are expressed by riddling old men. That is what Comrade Stalin and Chairman Mao teach us, is it not?'

'I suppose so,' I said, wondering for a moment if I had thereby called Stalin and Mao riddling old men.

'And every note on this page is a fact, is it not?' he tapped the score with the end of his bow, 'a single autonomous fact which, with all the other notes, adds up to the larger fact of the piece?'

'Yes.'

'I rest my case. Now, shall we play both parts together?' Without waiting for me to reply, he placed his violin under his chin and plucked each string to check that it was in tune. 'You take the first part again,' he said, 'and I will follow with the second.'

I began to play, and after the first two bars he joined in, his playing curling itself around my own like a snake. After a while I was aware only of the sound of his violin beside me: an even sound, rounded off, flowing and melodic, deep in the bass and crystalline in the higher tones. I felt that I was not playing at all, or rather that my playing was enveloped in his. Then as the music rose to its highest peak and began its long, winding descent I began to hear my own playing again, distinct from his, the vibrato proffered and then withdrawn, the notes simple: facts without any adornment.

We finished and the music echoed around the room for longer than I would have thought possible, as if the silver clock, the divan with its scrolled arm, the pieces of the chess set, and the distant landscapes in their frames had absorbed the sound and were humming it to themselves. I knew in that moment that what my father had said was right; that a moment of happiness can be so great that in comparison all earlier happiness could seem merely another form of sadness.

Before either of us could speak there was the sound of polite clapping. I turned and saw that Mr Karpin had entered the room. 'Comrade David Fiodorovich, we must go soon,' he said. 'The train leaves in less than an hour. I must return Miss Xiao to the apartment and you must finish packing your bags.'

'Very well,' Comrade David said, and turning to me he offered me his hand. 'It has been a pleasure, but of course I wish the circumstances were better. Perhaps we will meet again, since, like me, you have been marked out as a socialist artist. Kasimir has begged me to find you a place in a Conservatory somewhere – with Carl Flesch in London, he suggested, or with Ginette Neveu in Paris, and I did not have the heart to tell him that both are now dead. Nevertheless I will try my best. I hope we will meet again. Now you must go.'

I quickly returned my violin to its case, and stole another glance around the room as I walked to the door that Mr Karpin held open for me. As I turned to thank Comrade David, I found he was closing up the violin case by the window and turning the key in its small lock. 'You must take this with you,' he said, holding out the case and the key to Mr Karpin, but addressing himself to me. 'I will tell Kasimir and Piroshka that I have entrusted the violin to their pupil.' He shook my hand again, and moments later I was standing with Mr Karpin in the hallway.

*

Back at the empty apartment I put the violin case on the table, turned the key in the lock and gently picked up the instrument and placed it under my chin. The E-string was slightly flat, so I sat down at the piano and tuned each of the violin's strings in turn. I was about to pick up the bow and start to play when I felt a weight on my hand, as if another hand were resting on top of mine, and a question formed in my mind: 'But what would you play?' The question paralysed me. As I was about to place the violin back in its case I noticed that the velvet lining bulged in several places, as if the padding beneath it were uneven. When I pressed down on the bulges with my finger, I heard the crackle of thin sheets of paper beneath. I examined the edges of the lining to see if it could be peeled back. Down one side I found that it was held in place only by a few stitches. I took a knife and gingerly cut these stitches, and pulled out from beneath the lining several small envelopes stuffed with papers. I removed the papers and spread them out on the table, having first returned the violin to its case and snapped it shut.

They were letters, written in a neat hand in Cyrillic script, the ink a blue-black colour, the paper thin and crinkled. Except for one letter. This one was typed on the back of three sheets of manuscript paper which were half filled with handwritten notation – a series of arpeggios in the key of D-minor, and a long passage in 6/8 time – with wavy lines drawn contemptuously through them. The letter was dated October 1946. I began to read.

My beloved Papa and Mama,

It is my intention that this letter be sent to you only in the event that some tragedy, common or extraordinary, has overtaken me. I hope you will have some comfort at least in receiving news that my life, for the most part, has been happy and fulfilled.

I have enclosed with this letter all the letters I have written to you but did not send for fear of placing you in danger. Some of them are letters that I have kept in my head, memorising them, and have only recently written out. The poets here have adopted this practice. For periods during the last twenty years it has been too dangerous to commit one's serious work to paper, or to publish anything except hymns to the local gods. So we have learned to compose in our heads, and we carry around volumes of poetry up there, small libraries, each with its wizened librarian and its roaming silverfish and dark, forgotten corners, all of it encased in bone, so that if we are searched there is no possibility of being found in possession of erroneous sonnets.

In this way Akhmatova's 'Requiem' was carried out of the country in the head of one of her friends. I wonder if you have heard it recited. It concerns a mother waiting in line at a prison gate, hoping for a glimpse of her son.

After my return from Irkutsk I completed my studies and have made a passable career for myself teaching at a small institute in Kronstadt, writing scholarly articles on Pushkin, and lyric poetry about the happiness to be had in the cycle of the seasons. More latterly I have been writing songs and libretti for composers. These are all based on folk stories, because as we all know Russian folk traditions speak of the lives of solid, loam-footed people, and of the happiness to be had in the cycle of the seasons.

I have many other poems in my head, poems like Akhmatova's. I wish someone would carry mine to America too, and publish them there. (I realise that I do not even know if you have reached America. Perhaps you are in Shanghai – but then with the war, the Japanese occupation, the ghetto, surely not . . .)

Now to explain the violin. You should recognise it, Papa, since it is the one the young princess played when you taught her in the Aleksandr Palace at Tsarkoe Selo. It came into my possession in 1920, not long after I returned to St Petersburg (or Leningrad, as they have now renamed our city). I opened my door one night to a man who introduced himself as a former footman at the palace. He had the violin with him, wrapped in a sack. He said the Grand Duke himself had entrusted it to him in 1914, with instructions to wait until the turmoil had settled and then to deliver it into your hands, Papa, as a token of their appreciation for your tutelage of the princess. The man had stowed the violin in an attic for several years, and then began to make enquiries after your whereabouts. It took him several more years to find his way to my door. I explained that you were probably in America and promised to find a way to get the violin to you. I fed the man the dinner I had prepared for myself, and have not seen him since.

You may recall that the Tsarina believed the violin was made in the late 18th century by Giuseppe Guarneri del Gesú of Cremona, which would make it one of the most valuable in all of Russia. It is certainly a fine instrument, but I am afraid she was mistaken. I showed it recently to a violinist friend of Dmitri Dmitrievich – about whom more soon – who identified it as one of the imitation Guarneri instruments made by Jean-Baptiste Vuillaume around 1860. She told me that Vuillaume's *imitations were astoundingly accurate, right down to the worn varnish and patination, and that only a tone-deaf capitalist would care that it was not a genuine Guarneri. Fritz Kreisler owns a Vuillaume, she told me, which he has given on loan to the Pole, Josef Hassid.*

I have now entrusted the violin, and my letters, to Dmitri Dmitrievich, or Mitya, as he insists I call him. He has been unreasonably generous to me, as was his uncle, Boleslav, in putting us up in Irkutsk (but I hear Boleslav is now dead, have you heard this news?). Mitya has recommended my work to several operatic composers. He himself will not write any more operas for fear that they will attract the same condemnation as his last one, which was officially described as 'chaos instead of music' even after it had received acclaim from the most orthodox of critics and had been performed more than a hundred times to full houses.

I have already related this story in one of my letters. And I have also told the story of our life in Leningrad during the 1941 siege. You will see that it is true that music carried the citizens of Leningrad through the inferno. One remembers Oistrakh playing at the Bolshoi Theatre with a hole in the roof and a shell crater by the orchestra pit; and Klavdia Shulzhenko and her jazz band performing 'Blue Headscarf' and 'Companions in Arms' on the front lines; but most of all one remembers Mitya's Seventh Symphony, performed one sweltering August night by members of the Radio Orchestra supplemented by soldiers on loan from army units defending the city. O, the lyricism of that symphony! elevating our patriotism into – dare I say it – the Divine light of humanism. Who would not embrace even death for that cause? Afterwards it was said on the streets in all seriousness: 'Shostakovich is more powerful than Hitler. Berlin may have Beethoven's Ninth, but Leningrad has Shostakovich and his Seventh.'

But you can read this for yourselves. The war is over, but what victory have we secured? Our dignity, our composure, our pride are under threat again, and so too our lives. My situation is very fragile. To be a 'rootless cosmopolitan' is very difficult (even after the terrible, unbelievable events in Germany and Poland), and to be one who writes is even more difficult. I often dream that a large iron key has been inserted into my mouth and turned so that it scrapes against my gums and crushes my teeth and bloodies my tongue, making all speech impossible. Mitya is more secure. His fame affords him protection (though not as much as one might think) and he has the opportunity to travel out of the country, which few others have. What is more, it is not so suspicious that he should have such a fine violin in his possession.

I am sitting at his desk right now, typing this on his typewriter, drinking the cup of tea his wife has made for me. I have asked Mitya, in the event of my death, to find some way to get the violin and the letters to you. I told him you would be in one of three places: Harbin, Shanghai or New York, and he put his hand on my shoulder and assured me that he would find you, as if these places were not immense haystacks and the two of you not tiny pins. But what else can I do?

I must sign off this letter which I hope one day to retrieve and destroy. I kiss your hands, beloved Mama and Papa.

Your son,
Vitja

When I had finished reading I glanced up at the clock and found that it was already very late. I did not know where Kasimir and Piroshka were, or when they would return. I looked down at the street below, where workers were making for home on their bicycles and carts and a convoy of army trucks rumbled past the corner carrying mute rows of young soldiers, tossing from side to side in unison like bottles in a crate. I arranged the letters on the table in order, with the typed one on top, locked the violin in its case and placed the key by the letters, and made sure the latch clicked shut as I let myself out into the crisp, cool silence of the hallway.

6. Passacaglia

For several decades a large mural covered a wall in the foyer of the administration building of China Eastern Railways. It depicted Mao Zedong's arrival at the Harbin Railway Station in 1950. At its centre is the great man himself in a heavy swirling greatcoat and workers' cap, with the sun breaking from behind him and his feet not quite touching the ground, and gathered about him there are workers and children turning their faces to his light, like heliotropic flowers. I have never seen the original, since it was painted several years after I left Harbin. However, it was one of the full colour plates in a picture book I acquired in the 1960s, entitled *The People's Republic of China: The First Five Year Plan.* When my children were young I would show them the page, telling them, 'That's my mother, your Ama; and that's my father, your Agon,' and indicating a couple who did not look in the slightest like my parents. 'And that's me,' I told them, pointing to the little girl at their side with her hair in short pigtails and a red-rose bloom in her cheeks, holding a violin and bow under her arm.

Attached to the wall beside the mural, I was told, was a small outline sketch naming all the individuals present: the Party Secretary, the Mayor, the leader of the most productive unit in the Railway Workshops, the President of the Heilongjiang Branch of the All China League of Women, a Soviet engineer, a prominent Manchu peasant leader. In 1961 the names of my parents were removed, and after 1966 the reference to Xiao Magou, violinist, was also deleted.

My memory is curiously empty of impressions of Mao's visit, although my parents talked of little else for years to follow. There is a photograph of me shaking hands with Mao and Li Jiefu, Director of the Shenyang Conservatory, after my performance. My mother sent it to me with one of the last letters she posted to my Paris address. I am dressed in a blue trouser suit, and both the men seem somewhat taken aback by my height (I am taller than Li) and large-boned physique. In the flash of the camera my face is white except for my black butterfly lips and the dried-cherry eyes pressed into my skin like covered buttons.

Indeed for many years all I remembered of my encounter with the great man was that unbearable light, emanating not so much from the camera flash as from Mao himself, like the light depicted in portraits of saints and deities. However, as time passed I began to reclaim other impressions, which I must have suppressed at the time: the eye-watering stench of Mao's halitosis, his teeth like shards of jade set in resinous gums behind which prowled a tongue like a freshly shucked mollusc, and the curious sensation that he was a kind of optical illusion, a trick with mirrors, and that I was extending my hand not to a real person but to some aspect of myself, something universal; the real Mao, if he was indeed present at all, was standing behind my back, his hand reaching forward to poke me in the back of the ribcage.

*

On the day after my lesson with Comrade David I arrived at the apartment at the usual time and found Kasimir and Piroshka sitting waiting for me. Kasimir was at the table, reading a score, Piroshka beside him facing the open window, her chin sunk into the heel of an out-turned hand, and her face caressed from time to time by shifting grids of sunlight from the movements of the embroidered net curtain in the breeze. I had the sense that they had been sitting this way in silence for several hours. The violin

134

case was still on the table where I had left it, the cover open and the red satin cloth neatly folded, as if it were a small coffin open for a viewing. The pile of letters lay beside it, weighed down by a large river stone, and as the curtain shifted a rhomboid of intense sunlight would illuminate the crinkled papers and reveal as intense blue the ink that, when cast back into the shade, appeared black.

I pulled out a chair and sat opposite them.

'Welcome,' Kasimir said, and reached out his hand to touch Piroshka's shoulder.

'I found the letters in the lining of the case,' I said, thinking it best not to conceal anything. 'I have read only the top one.'

'That's all right,' Piroshka said. 'You are so young, and we would not expect you to understand such things.'

'But I do understand,' I insisted, and then added, 'What will you do with the violin?'

'Why, keep it, of course,' said Piroshka. 'It was a gift from the Grand Duke, as you now know.'

'And may I . . . play it?' I said. 'One day, I mean. Not now, of course.'

Kasimir and Piroshka looked at each other. 'Why not now?' Kasimir said. 'Clearly I cannot play it; so if anyone is to play it, that is likely to be you.'

'If . . . ?' I said.

'What violin is not meant to be played?' Kasimir went on. 'What is a violin if it is not played? A wooden box? The carcass of a beautiful insect? What is it if it is not played?' He turned back the velvet cover to reveal the body of the violin and put his mouth to the strings and blew so that the strings started to vibrate softly – G, D, A, E. 'It has not been played for many years; not since another girl your age played it.'

'Ach, but in her hands it was a mere toy,' Piroshka sniffed, and, wiping the moistness from her eyes with her fingertips, gave me a rare smile.

'She was a princess,' I said.

'Yes, she was a princess,' Kasimir said, 'a bright and happy girl. She would bring us sweets she had stolen from her mother's room, and lay her head on my knee and tell me about what she and her sisters had been doing on the estate. And then she would pick up the violin without tuning it and play . . .' Kasimir hesitated and looked across at his wife and I saw her eyes widen and an energy flowed between them, like a sheet of lightning. 'And play awfully!' he exclaimed, and then he let out an explosion of laughter. 'Just dreadful – was she not, Pipi? – so that the hairs on your neck would bristle with anguish, and I laboured like Hercules to teach her to play sweetly, because I had promised her father that I would make something of her.'

Piroshka had covered her eyes with a palisade of bony fingers and was giving out irregular honks of mirth. 'But you, fond idiot, you encouraged her! You would praise even her worst performances and call her *milachka* and *solnyshko*, and dance around and twirl on your heels as she played on and on, out of key, out of tempo, out of her depth. Idiot, foolish souls, the both of you!'

'You too were besotted with her!'

'Yes, Kuzma, we both were,' Piroshka said, slowly wiping the length of her index finger along her eye socket, 'but how we would laugh in the droshky on our way home afterwards, laugh at her terrible phrasing and the way she poked her tongue to one side as she played . . . oh, and her fearsome earnestness.'

Kasimir looked at me across the table. 'She was like the daughter we never had.'

'That is true,' Piroshka nodded. 'Well, the first such daughter. Your mother was the second . . . the second daughter we never had. Ach, that girl, that sweet, silly child. How much better for her had she in fact been our daughter. How we ached for her, did we not?'

'Yes indeed,' said Kasimir, and in a moment his laughter fell away, save for a quiet chuckle like the last wash of water into a drain.

Piroshka turned to face me. 'Since you have read the letter, you know that our son, Vitja, is ill,' she said. 'You know that this

136

violin was sent to us by a man called Dmitri, a composer who is the son of my late friend, Sofiya Vasilievna Kokoulina.' She took from under Kasimir's forearm some large sheets of handwritten music, and unfolded them in front of me. 'Dmitri has written some music for our son,' she said, softening her voice, as if in reverence to the sheets of paper. 'It is a piece to be played on the violin, on this violin. And we would like you to learn it.'

I studied the sheet Piroshka had set before me. It was headed with the Roman numeral III and a word I had never seen. 'Passacaglia,' Piroshka said, seeing my puzzled look. 'It means a series of variations over a repeated bass tune. Think of the finale to Brahms' Fourth Symphony.' The music was in 3/4 time, in the key of A minor, beginning with a low F to be played *forte-forte*.

'You will be only the second person to play this music,' Piroshka said, 'and the first to play it in public.'

'Where is the violin part?' I asked. Piroshka turned the first sheet over and pointed to a treble clef written above the piano part, beginning at the top of the page, where there was a single line of notes marked *piano espressivo*.

'Shall we begin?' Piroshka said.

I nodded, and glanced at the violin on the table, and then at Kasimir, whose eyes tightened slightly. Not yet, he mouthed. I opened my own violin case.

It was difficult music. The fanfare opening went on for several bars and then dropped into a series of quiet chords. The entry of the violin was timed so that it slipped in on the last beat of a bar, and it was scored to be so quiet that it was barely perceptible, but simply rose from amidst the lengthening notes of the accompaniment like a lonely seabird trailing a retreating storm. I had to repeat it twice before getting it right. And the timing problems continued: the numbers in the back of my head seemed wrong, so that the dancer within me instinctively turned left, as it were, only to find that the score had turned right. 'Seventeen,' Kasimir whispered to me, 'the measure of the theme is seventeen, so you must count in your head to seventeen.' We stumbled through the first dozen pages, and then through a long second section in which the violin plays with only the lightest of accompaniments, engaged in reveries of its own. Then, at the end of a page, and far from anything that might serve as a home, musically speaking, the score abruptly ended.

'There is a page missing,' I said.

'That is how it is written,' Piroshka said. 'Remember this piece is one movement in a concerto, and unfortunately we do not have the others.'

I said it sounded to me as if the music was ending with a question.

'Is it so strange to end with a question?' Piroshka said. 'In revolutionary Russia people are encouraged to ask questions.'

Kasimir, who had been listening silently, said from across the room, 'Your playing is good, but it is too sweet. This is not a sweet piece. It needs to be played with bile; it needs to be guttural.'

'What is bile?' I asked. 'And what is guttural?'

'Bile is the bad taste in your mouth after you have been sick,' Kasimir answered. 'And guttural is . . . is the hawking sound people make before they spit.'

Piroshka raised an eyebrow. 'Find a better way to explain it, Kasimir Alexandrovich,' she said. 'How can she spit with a violin?'

'I agree it is not a pleasant way of speaking, Piroshka Iakovlevicha,' he said, rising to his feet and tapping on the window with his fingertips, 'but it is what the piece requires.'

'There you are, my dear,' Piroshka said to me. 'You must attempt to play the piece so as to sound like a nauseous person clearing her throat of spittle. Simple, yes?'

'You make your point,' Kasimir conceded with a gesture from his good hand. 'Go home, now,' he said to me. 'Think about it overnight, and we can discuss it tomorrow. Surprise us with your maturity, perhaps.'

As I packed to leave I asked if it might help if I could play the violin in the case. 'As if the violin itself might be sick and angry?' Piroshka said as she retreated to the kitchen, and Kasimir smiled

138

at me and whispered, 'Perhaps tomorrow,' and bent his head towards the violin in the case.

*

The next day I tried to play the piece again, and again Kasimir complained that I had not found the right tone. I had tried to play in an ugly and strained fashion – loudly, roughening my bowing technique and slurring the notes. But he said I should not substitute imprecision and deliberate blemishes for genuine anger and desolation.

'Genuine anger!' Piroshka complained from the piano. 'She is a child. Her anger and desolation it is that of the playground. Is that what you want?'

Kasimir brushed aside her comment, and addressed me directly. 'Here is the challenge to you as the artist: to convey anger in your playing, and despair, and disgust, and courage. But how to do that? Does it help if you feign anger yourself? I say no. If anything, your own emotion is an obstacle. The emotion is here, in the notes the composer has written, and the job of the artist is not to feel the emotion, but, like a window, to transmit that emotion from the darkened room of the composer's mind to the world outside.'

I could not suppress a sigh of frustration, and Piroshka rolled her eyes and said, 'You are confusing the girl, Kasimir. Yesterday you asked her to be bilious and guttural; today you tell her she should feel nothing.'

The two of them argued back and forth. After a while I lost track of their arguments and started reading over the difficult passages once more, running through the complex rhythms in my head. Their voices merged into one another in the background, until I realised that they had abruptly stopped talking and that Kasimir had addressed me.

'I'm sorry,' I said. 'I was daydreaming.'

'I asked you if you were willing to keep a secret,' he repeated.

'Yes,' I said.

'We want to give you another letter to read,' he said. 'It

explains how this piece of music was written, what the composer was thinking and feeling, and what he was trying to convey. I have agreed to let you read the letter, and then I will say no more about how the piece should be played. It will be for you to decide.' Kasimir handed me an envelope containing several sheets of paper, and he and Piroshka sat quietly as I spread the pages out on the table.

Like the other letter, it was in Russian. 'Let us know if there are any words you don't understand,' Piroshka said. 'And you must also promise something.' She placed her hand over the letter. 'Promise that you will not tell your parents about this letter. I fear they may not appreciate that the things it says relate to what has happened in Russia, and have no bearing upon what happens here in China.' I did not understand what she meant, but promised not to tell my parents. The letter was written in long-hand, but with a steady, regular script that was easy to read once I became used to its repeated dashes and loops. It read:

June 1950
My dear Kasimir Alexandrovich and Piroshka Iakovlevicha,
My heart is heavy as a lump of lead in my chest as I sit down to write, and yet I feel a sense of light-headedness, of vertigo. After all these years of silence from my family, I have now to communicate bad news to you concerning your son, Vitja. Not the worst news, but bad enough.

I have a selfish hope that some other letter has reached you to advise you of his situation, and that mine will not be the first. Nevertheless, after a year trying to track you down, I have discovered you are still in Harbin, and now fortune has provided me with the most reliable of couriers, and I cannot pass up the opportunity to write.

But to Vitja – he is passably well in body, but has suffered torments of his mind and spirit that I fear have caused his soul to depart prematurely; where to, I do not know, and I do not believe it will ever return as we have known it. He was picked up by the police, huddled under a bridge by the Moscow River, calling out threats and oaths, and shivering from the cold because under his coat he was completely naked. They took him for a drunk at the start, and locked him in a cell overnight with only a thin blanket. The next morning they called in a doctor from the insane asylum, since Vitja had cried out without ceasing throughout the night. It was this doctor who told me the story. (She is a distant cousin of Vsevolod Frederiks, who is married to my sister Marusya – perhaps you received Marusya's letter regarding her marriage, since she sent it to Harbin.) The doctor tells me that his illness may one day be ameliorated, but that there is no treatment other than confinement to an asylum. I have done for him what I can, and found a place for him in an asylum outside Moscow that is run by people with some humanity, although meagre resources.

As to what precipitated Vitja's breakdown, where do I begin? His is the sickness that has been creeping upon us all for . . . how many years now, I do not know. Others are dead of the same sickness. And many more are made drowsy by it, or simply struck dumb. I suffer from it too, although, as you may have heard, fortune has smiled upon the small sparrow-like boy with the big spectacles whom you first knew at the Conservatoire as Musya's little brother. I have had some success as a composer, enough that I am now known as the 'Court Composer' of the Soviet Union. This is a blessing only in that my family and I live comfortably, and I have a room with two pianos and the use of a dacha at the artists' colony at Komarova during the summer.

Even so I still live in a house made of paper. We all do; those of us that remain. Indeed the world of which you and Glazunov and Akhmatova and Meyerhold were a part, that world which nurtured me as a child, that St Petersburg of poets, and thinkers, and artists, and musicians, which believed that it held the soul of Russia in its hands – it turned out to be a city of paper; with substance, yes, a beautiful city of marbled paper, but fragile and now mostly reduced to ash, blown about by the wind.

Do I begin in the winter of 1948? No, that is too late. I must begin in 1936 with my opera, 'Lady Macbeth of Mtensk'.

Pravda published an enthusiastic review. But then only two months later the same paper printed a second, anonymous review, describing the work as 'chaos instead of music', 'din, gnash and screech', 'cacophony', 'pornophany', and 'musical noise'. I do not believe these words, and will defend my opera as I would defend my children. But that was not the point. So I was found guilty of the sin of formalism, of writing music for the sake of music alone, of creating a cloud of notes that did not yield any rain, of failing once more to serve Soviet Man. I had suffered these accusations before, but this time there were legions ready to lay siege to our paper city the moment Pravda issued the war-cry.

For my part I cancelled all further performances of the opera, and withdrew my Fourth Symphony from rehearsal. I accepted without dissent a ban on performances of much of my work. I wrote my penitential Fifth Symphony, and made it grand because they wanted grandeur, and noble because they wanted nobility; gave it marching tunes because they wanted the people to march, and sweet harmonies because they wanted euphony. And I gave it a by-line: 'A Soviet artist's reply to just criticism'. At its first performance many in the audience wept openly during the slow movement, and the applause at the end lasted longer than the whole of the final movement. (These tears, this applause, were the greatest triumph of my life thus far. The apparatchiks still don't understand what kind of a 'reply' it was.)

But of course nothing could stop what had already been unleashed. I watched many who were dear to me suffer. Vsevolod Frederiks was imprisoned, and Musya herself was exiled to Frunze for a while. Also imprisoned were my mother-in-law (released before the war) and my uncle Maxim (an old Bolshevik, no less). And then there were my friends, many of them your friends too: the poet Mikhail Zoshchenko, my long time opponent at cards (a terribly inept bluffer, but a man whose work still makes me laugh despite the memory of his pauper's grave); the librettist Yevgeny Zamyatin (my own collaborator);

142

my dear patron, Vsevolod Meyerhold, who saved me from a life of playing piano in a darkened cinema; his wife Zinaida Raikh (brutally murdered); my dear friend Elena Konstantinovskaya; the poet Osip Mandelstam, who has now died in Vladivostok; poor Marina Tsvetaeva, who hanged herself in despair after her husband and daughter were taken ('To you, insane world, only one reply – I refuse'). My breath stops in my throat when I consider that some of these were perhaps chosen not for their own misdeeds, but to teach me a lesson, because I was myself too well known or too useful to imprison, but nevertheless in need of 'instruction'.

During that time it was not safe to be one who earned his keep by thinking. Nor was it safe to be Jewish, especially after the pact with Hitler. Many Jewish Communists have been liquidated, and all Yiddish schools and cultural associations have been closed. In my view the war saved the Russian Jews from a fate as extreme as that to which it condemned the Jews of Germany, the Ukraine and Poland. Indeed the war saved us all, since, at least for those years, there was an enemy outside the gate so terrifying as to make them forget about rat-catching within it.

I come now to 1948, for here your Vitja enters the picture. He had made a small contribution to the libretto for an opera by a Georgian composer, Vano Muradeli, an opera that was banned after its first performance. In January of that year we were all summoned by Andrei Zhdanov (the heir apparent to Stalin, and merciless persecutor of my friend, Zoschenko, and of Anna Akhmatova and Sergei Eisenstein, the film-maker) to attend the First Congress of the Union of Soviet Composers, at which Muradeli's opera and its errors would be discussed.

I myself attended with a great sense of foreboding, since in the previous October my 'Poem of the Motherland' – a perfunctory offering for the thirtieth anniversary of the Revolution – had been rejected as politically inadequate, and the film Simple Folk, for which I wrote the score, was banned. 'Un-Soviet, anti-patriotic and anti-People,' they said. We were subjected to the bullying vulgarity of Comrade Zhdanov for several days, during which it became apparent to me that the criticism of Muradeli's opera was simply the tiger's first lick of blood. We delegates behaved like nervous schoolboys, laughing at the jokes of our overbearing teacher. Perhaps this emboldened Zhdanov to come after me, and Prokofiev, and Myaskovsky, and Khachaturian, for our alleged leadership in deviations from the tenets of Socialist Realism.

I have learned in these situations that there is nothing to be done. They are prepared for all our familiar ways of being brave, so one must be brave in ways that are too subtle for them. I took Vitja aside one day and explained this to him. He was walking around the Congress white as a sheet, his hands trembling. So I took him to a cafeteria and fed him cabbage and vodka and meat pies that were like stones. I was barely keeping my own nerves under control, but I sat him down and told him how I survive. 'I always carry one end of the banner in the processions,' I said. 'I always look cheerful, and if any task is given to me I do not shirk it. Instead, I do it with all my heart. When the crowd yells, I yell. When they turn, I turn. It is the only way to be safe.'

He was shaking his head from side to side, and I could not tell if it was just nerves or if he was disagreeing with me. In the end I had to take hold of his chin, and catch his eye and tell him, 'Vitja, remember that we are sparrows. All of us. We rise, we fall, we are crushed by the side of the road. But we have one thing. We have talent. I compose. You write. If they crush us, that talent is gone. If we endure, it endures. If there is a vindication, so be it. If not, so be it.'

He gave me no answer, but I was encouraged by the fact that he ate some pie and drank some vodka. I made him sit beside me during the next session, at which a young man trampled on the scores of my Eighth and Ninth Symphonies. I then rose to speak and thanked Comrade Zhdanov for his criticism. I reproached Muradeli for his blindness to his failures. I called upon our musical organisations to engage in

144

rigorous self-criticism, and I acknowledged that much of my own work had been in error – though I had striven throughout my compositional career to make my music accessible to the people – and begged the Congress for instruction so that I could do better in the future.

Throughout my speech I kept my eyes fixed upon Vitja. I made the speech directly to him, as if there was no one else in the hall. I sat back down beside him afterwards and glanced across at him. He was looking at his hands in astonishment, as if he had noticed for the first time what a miracle they were; the architecture of bones and sinews and skin that we carry with us in our pockets and use to write and to eat and to make music and love. At that moment I had hope for him, thinking to myself what better thing to do at such a moment than to marvel at one's own being.

As we stood to leave, a note was slipped into my hand. It said simply: 'Solomon Mikhoels murdered. Please come.' It was signed by Moishe Weinberg, the composer, who is Mikhoels' son-in-law. Another sparrow falls, I thought.

I had been friends with Mikhoels even before he founded the Moscow Jewish Theatre. Vitja knew him too. He was at that time the chairman of the Jewish Anti-Fascist Committee, and had publicly supported my Eighth Symphony (to no avail) against charges of recidivism and pessimism. Immediately I took Vitja to visit the grieving family, and we arrived at the same time as the body, which had been carried to Moscow that day on the train from Minsk, where the murder had occurred. We all stood shoulder to shoulder in a small room – at least twenty family and friends – as the men put the coffin on the table and unscrewed the lid. You can imagine the scene as we uncovered this great man, naked, tufts of his beard cut off for some reason, his rib-cage pierced, and his legs bent, Christ-like, to fit him into the cheap coffin. Someone quickly placed a black hat over his bloated testicles, and this made him look even more ridiculous, reduced by a couple of incisions to a jumble of limbs in a box, like a marionette laid aside after a performance. Vitja whispered in my ear, 'Don't you envy him?' 'Yes,' I replied, louder than I had intended, 'I envy him.'

The last I saw of Vitja was when I dropped him at his apartment. He seemed well. That is all I can say, and I believe that is something; to be well, if only for an instant. I myself went home, kissed my wife and my children, ate my supper with a smile, and started work on the third movement of my violin concerto. What else can one do? What else should one do? This concerto is a first for me. I have written string quartets, but nothing with a violin as the solo instrument. For the time being I have no more symphonies in me, and of course no more operas. The concerto is a companion to a set of short songs based on Jewish folk-tunes. I began these in response to the instruction to the Composers' Union to write new works celebrating the ethnic cultures of the Soviet Union so that they would feel included within Soviet Man.

I chose to celebrate the music of the Russian Jews. This music has made a most powerful impression on me. It can appear to be happy while it is tragic. It is always the laughter of desperation. All of man's defencelessness is concentrated in that brittle musical cloth. This quality of Jewish folk music is close to my ideas of what music should be. There should always be these two layers in music. This is music that has passed through music, and cannot find its way back. It is a spectator upon itself. It presses its nose to the window and watches its own happier self, dancing in the parlour, waiting for the soldiers to come.

The first movement of the concerto is a nocturne – an insomniac one. It is a soliloquy of foreboding and then of panic, as unknown fears play across the mind's dark curtain. The second movement is a scherzo, based upon a lively Jewish folk dance, one of those ones that are played faster and faster until the dancers begin to fly out of the doors and windows. And the third, which I worked on through that night, is a passacaglia andante, which, if I have any talent, mourns the dead of the Patriotic War and scourges the leaders who rewarded their sacrifice with a return to repression. But more than that, it

146

mourns Vitja and all the others, for I started work on the violin part for that movement after I heard the news of Vitja's illness and as I applied what influence I could to secure his care.

As soon as I finished the concerto I called my friend Dodik (who carries this letter and Vitja's violin and letters to you) and I sat at the piano and we played the entire piece through without stopping. At the end he was weeping and advised me that it was another one 'for the drawer', as we say here. I can only agree with him. And so it may never be heard, at least not in my lifetime.

I send to you as a gift the original manuscript of the third movement, in the version for piano and violin. I hope the two of you can some day sit down, as Dodik and I did, and play it for each other. (But put aside your measured tones when you play it, Kasimir, for my mother always said your playing was the most delicate and harmonious she had ever heard. This piece requires playing that is at times strained and guttural, with a barely concealed taste of bile.)

You may if you wish listen for Vitja in the music. He is there, most definitely. He is imprisoned in the opening bars, the first rotation of the passacaglia – play these bars fortissimo on the piano, for in the full score they belong to the kettle drum and the brass and the double basses – but then as the violin begins to play his soul slips through his chest with a sob. It rises above the earth, surprised to find itself capable of flight. In the orchestrated version I have inserted a line for the cor anglais (for your English horn, Piroshka). It twines itself around the violin, and they dance their grief together for several bars; but then the violin flies off, and although the oboe pursues it, calling to it, the violin can no longer hear, for it is engrossed in its own rage and its tears, and it plays on alone until it finds eventually a refuge in music of quiet and fragile purity.

I have imagined the violin like a soul from Greek antiquity, from Ovid's Metamorphoses. She dies and then awakens to discover herself immortal. She is hesitant at first, because she is naked; but then she begins to marvel at herself because she *realises that in death she is more beautiful than she ever thought possible in life. This new goddess awakens in turn to her form, to her power, and then to her memories and her anger.*

Look also for my little signature, my secret code: DSCH (in the German notation D – E-flat – C – B). It is a piece of myself that I put into my music whenever I can. If you tear aside the skin of this piece you will find it too; you will see me, a crazy, bespectacled old man playing the organ at the cinema, working the levers of my grand sound machine, the great war machine that is my music. I have buried it very deeply in this piece; elsewhere it is more prominent. One day they will notice it, but by then I will have another coded message, and another and another, until I am dead, and I am resolved that my death will be a code they will never unravel.

I must close soon. My hand is shaking as I write, and I have once more that sense of vertigo, for if this letter should fall into hands other than yours . . . well, I cannot contemplate it. Thank God for my great friend, the pianist Sviatoslav Richter, who will be here shortly to uplift this small package for you. He and Dodik leave for China tonight. (Richter is a brilliant young man, and is married to Nina Dorliak, the soprano for whom I wrote the cycle of Jewish folk songs, also destined 'for the drawer'. Her mother was the soprano Xenia Dorliak, who remembers travelling with you on the train from St Petersburg to Irinovka to visit my family. It must have been the summer of 1915. Vitja was such a handsome young man, she recalls.)

My wife Nina says there is a knock at the door. I convey to you the love of my sister, Musya, and of course my own. I clasp your hands.

D.D.S.

When I had finished the letter, I handed it to Piroshka, who carefully folded it into a small square, the paper emitting crackles that echoed around the room. 'It is late,' she said. 'It is time for you to go.' I gathered up my things and, as I was leaving, caught Kasimir's eye. He smiled and nodded, but said nothing.

*

The performance of Shostakovich's passacaglia took place in the parlour of an old dacha by the Technological Institute. I remember the crunch of the gravel on the empty road and the diagonal fall of aspen leaves as I walked to the dacha with Kasimir and Piroshka, and with Vitja's violin in its case held to my chest. The air was still and cool, and the sky was the washed out blue of late autumn, hazy with long parallel streaks of high cloud like the wispy beards of celestial sages.

Inside the house there were kisses from our host – the widow of a former rabbi – and her hand lay across my shoulder as she guided me into the warmth of the parlour. There were perhaps twenty people there, former members of the orchestra, the remnants of the Jewish community and the old violin maker whose body was bent almost shut with arthritis. Tea was brewing in a large china samovar by the door. Full cups of the hot black liquid, rattling on their saucers, passed precariously from hand to hand, guided over shoulders and around elbows, until they reached their intended recipients. There was a brief silence as we appeared in the doorway, then everyone came forward to greet us. I was kissed on the cheek, the forehead, the top of the head and – by a dapper old man with a stiff, military bearing – on the back of the hand. A cup of tea veered towards me, and someone took Vitja's violin from my grasp so I could take the saucer with both hands. It was Russian tea, sharply scented, spiced and sweet.

After a while Piroshka summoned me to her side by the piano at the far end of the room. As we arranged our music and tuned our instruments, Kasimir called for silence and invited the older members of the audience to take what seats were available. He explained that we were about to play a new piece by the contemporary Russian composer Dmitri Dmitrievich Shostakovich, and that it was a single movement from a larger work, a concerto for violin. As he spoke a woman in a wheelchair, whom I had seen from afar many times at concerts, was pushed forward so close that she was under my nose. I

149

could now see from her eyes, rolling independently in puckered sockets, that she was blind, and, since she paid no attention to what Kasimir was saying, it occurred to me that she might perhaps be deaf as well.

The piece was inspired by the composer's study of Jewish folk music, Kasimir went on. And today's performance, he said, was the first ever outside of Russia, and, if it were not for the fact that we had only one movement and had a piano rather than an orchestra, it would constitute the premiere performance. The audience looked suitably impressed. One young woman, with wavy hair and a studious look, began to scribble notes in a tiny leather-bound notebook, like a physician noting down symptoms or a policeman recording evidence. Kasimir did not explain how the score came to be in his hands, but he did mention his and Piroshka's connection to the Shostakovich family, and his memories of the young Dmitri and his sister Marusya. He said nothing about the origins of the violin I was playing. (On the way to the dacha he had warned me not to tell anyone of its history either. It was our secret, he said.)

The room fell silent, and I stood to play, nestling the violin into the hollow above my collarbone. I cannot say that I felt at one with the instrument, or that the soul of Jean-Baptiste Vuillaume or of the lunatic Vitja flowed into mine. It did not happen. I felt only that the instrument I was holding was, like Kasimir had said, the strange carcass of a beautiful insect, until I brought it to life. Piroshka played the opening chords – louder and sharper than she had ever played them before, and I felt the audience take a sudden breath. Then the energy of the fanfare was spent, and the piano sounded more sombre tones, enclosing itself in its dance of seventeen steps, pointing beyond itself, clearing the ground for my entry. My cue arrived. I raised my bow and the edge of the taut horsehair touched the first string, a long, sustained note that I felt would never end, and then more notes followed, tumbling from the violin, gathering at my feet and then spreading out into the room.

I remember little about my performance on that day, except

that it seemed only partly mine. Each phrase grasped me firmly as a partner in a dance so that I felt I was being led effortlessly from hand to hand, from note to note. I heard the music, of course; but it seemed to come, not from my bow, nor from within me, but from within itself, confident and fierce and implacable in its own steady unfolding. I was conscious of time – the insistent steam-hammer march of passacaglia time – but as if it were merely the filling out of a pattern, or the synchronous resolution of all the terms in one of my father's mathematical problems, solving and resolving itself, step by logical step. As I came to the end of the piece, there again was that question mark that had first puzzled me; that note begging for completion, that unfinished sequence of numbers, remaining alone and exposed, flailing in the wind like a prayer flag on a lonely mountainside. I lowered my violin and bow, and I remember only the sudden awareness of a trickle of sweat travelling down my back, between my shoulder blades, edging its way towards the base of my spine.

It took a long time for the audience to respond. When it came at last, the applause was warm and generous, restrained at first, and then more energetic, goaded by the old man who had kissed my hand, who rose to his feet and shouted 'Brava!' several times and waved his arms in an upwards motion. The audience rose to their feet. But I knew that that last note, that lack of resolution, had troubled them, even hurt them. They were used to music that was sad, and even angry. What they were not used to was the desolation of that rootless note, which forced upon them the knowledge that they too were alone and exposed, rootless and far from the homes to which they would never return.

Then the room came alive again with the rattle of tea cups, the clearing of throats, the shuffling of long skirts and the creaking of chairs. We drank more tea, and ate slices of something sweet made out of nuts and dried fruit. The audience started to slip away, some of them greeting Kasimir and Piroshka, while I myself sat alone with a cup and saucer on my lap. The rabbi's widow finally came to me, took my head in her hands and planted a kiss on the crown of my head. 'A voice, my girl,' she said. 'You are a voice from across the hills and the plains, and if you were not here to play to us I fear the sky would fall in upon us.' Then she kissed me again, and moved away.

I returned to the apartment with Kasimir and Piroshka walking silently either side of me. I did not mind that none of us spoke for the first kilometre or so. Then the silence grew oppressive. 'Did you like it?' I asked finally, not directing my question to either of them in particular.

'It concerns my son and his suffering,' Kasimir replied. 'How could I possibly like it? It seizes me by the back of the neck and pushes my face towards a dark abyss.' He could tell I was hurt by his words, and went on: 'But your playing – that I liked. Yes. I liked your playing. It was very fine.'

'And did you feel the emotion while you were playing?' Piroshka asked. Kasimir looked sternly at his wife, and received a stern look in response. I pondered the matter for a while. What had I felt? Nothing? All of the contents of the letter? The private grief of a man living far from me in a strange city? I did not know. I had felt the music take over, take responsibility for itself.

'I felt . . . nothing,' I said. 'Just the music. That is all.'

Kasimir laughed gently. 'Let that be the final answer,' he said, and held my hand tighter as we walked on.

*

It was only a few weeks later that my father suffered his stroke, and shortly afterwards developed his problem with doors, which in time became a larger problem with all surfaces and distances. He began to drop things and knock over cups of tea and bowls at the table; not often, but enough so that he could no longer rely on his sense of distance and depth, and the position of his own body. He wrote in his notebook that it was as if the light around him were refracted by one or two degrees, enough to disturb his ability to navigate the space around him. Or like the experience of standing between two parallel mirrors, he went on, unable to see what it is you really want to see, trying to outsmart your own reflection, but always failing.

At the start, my father tried hard to maintain his good humour, perhaps mainly for the sake of my mother and me. He would often make a game out of his misfortunes, deciding to be amused, even enchanted, by them. He would retrace his steps after walking into the wall, or replay some clumsy move of his hand, observing the exact point at which his perceptions had been misled, toying with it like a child playing with a mysterious object. For the first few months, he was scrupulous about apologising for his errors. He would mutter *dui bu qi*, 'sorry', whenever he upset anything or stumbled, and his eyes would seek out mine or my mother's gently imploring a pardon, which we readily gave. He would even apologise when he was alone, and I would sometimes be woken by the sound of him moving around the house at night apologising to a chair, a door, a cup – *dui bu qi, dui bu qi . . . dui bu qi.* But he soon grew depressed at his illness, and refused to talk about it, except obliquely. He stopped apologising, and sometimes I suspected that he dropped items (especially clattering metallic ones) deliberately, out of frustration and anger.

One day while out walking he told me the story of the sage, Chuang Tzu, who dreamed he was a butterfly and then realised that the butterfly was dreaming it was Chuang Tzu. When he awoke he was no longer sure which he was: dreaming butterfly or dreaming man. At the time I thought the story was silly, and told my father so. He seemed disappointed. He was trying to tell me something, and needed me to understand. But he could not say it to me directly. The conversation ended abruptly, and we completed our walk in silence. Now of course I know that he was referring to the slow horror of losing his confidence even in what he thought he saw and thought he knew.

Is this the girl who is my daughter?

Is this the hand that is my hand?

The face that is my face?

The thoughts that are my thoughts?

*

We passed the final months of 1950 in a kind of dull trance. My mother began to work a night shift, so we rarely occupied the house as a threesome. I did my school work, attended music lessons, and played at the Harbin Musical Society and for visiting Party bosses and delegations of Russian and Czech technical advisors. My father divided his time between his work and the heated *kang*. Indeed the bed became the centre of our lives. One of us was always asleep on it, or huddling beneath its blankets and quilts trying to read or to eat. We shared an unspoken pact to keep the fire alight, and our connection to each other as a family became, for a while, simply this repeated act of stoking its burner with kindling or lumps of coal. We rarely talked, like passengers forced to share a sleeping compartment on a train, speaking only to explain our actions, when that was necessary, and never sharing our thoughts.

In the spring, my father came out of his depression and resurrected his plan to build a fish pond. His own strength was clearly not up to the physical labours involved, so he enlisted the help of Zhu Shaozen, a former colleague with whom he had shared a small hut in the forest during his years attempting to rebuild the Harbin Communist Party. Zhu was still a young man – in his early thirties – but he had a damaged exterior. He had lost one ear and most of his front teeth. One eye had been punctured by a sliver of shrapnel and it now wandered at liberty around his eye socket. And years of malnutrition and its attendant diseases had left him with wisps of hair like a morning mist around his skull and a permanently sallow complexion which added another ten years to his appearance and put beyond him any hope of marriage or family, despite the redeeming effect of the rather smart black suit which he wore day in day out (acquired, he admitted unashamedly, from the wardrobe of a deceased Jewish businessman).

Zhu explained that he had unwisely forfeited his rights to his ear in a card game with the commanding officer of a POW camp, and that it had been removed using the bayonet of a Nationalist guard. 'I was so sure of my hand that I bet my tongue as well,' he said, 'but I was losing so much blood from my ear they decided to stop.'

'Tell me the name of the officer,' my father said. 'I will get Party headquarters to track him down so you can pay the other half of the wager.'

Every morning for several weeks during the spring of 1951, Zhu arrived at our house, along with his nephew, a boy of around ten. In contrast to his sharply dressed uncle, the boy wore, above his bare, stubby feet, a pair of heavy gabardine trousers that had been inexpertly taken in along the seams and crotch, and two woollen jerseys sewn together with string to form a single, moth-eaten garment. Zhu would immediately strip off his suit jacket, shirt and trousers, roll them into a tight cylinder, which he entrusted to his nephew, and descend with a small shovel into a hole of ever increasing depth, from time to time winching up a bucketload of earth for the boy to tip into a corner of the courtyard. Sometimes, when my father was too sick to go to work, he watched the excavation, dressed in an old pair of pyjamas and smoking his way through his ration of Party-issue cigarettes, giving some to the boy to ease his cough. He and Zhu carried on an unceasing conversation, shouted to and from the bottom of the well. The topic was always the same: the hardships and the triumphs of the military campaigns against Japan and the Nationalists; the history that had delivered them both (unlike many of their colleagues) into the present moment with their lives intact.

The work progressed slowly. Some days Zhu was too sick to work, and some days his nephew, whose chest, at the best of times, gave off a high-pitched sound not unlike a badly tuned radio. Another day was lost to a dust storm that billowed through the streets of the city on its way south, and the next to a thunderstorm that followed in the wake of the dust and filled the bottom third of the well with red-stained water. The well eventually connected with the water table and proved viable, whereupon Zhu brought in several bags of cement on the back of a mule-cart and began to shape the walls of the trough. My father and I took a bus to the river bank and collected smooth stones which we embedded in the top of the walls. My mother acquired some leftover paint from the hospital; a pale blue-green colour we all agreed was perfect, but it only covered the bottom of the trough and two sides, so we left it at that.

Where the pond abutted the well, Zhu constructed the small water-race my father had designed, with a shallow cistern at the top fed by an electric pump which recycled water from the bottom of the trough, and a slope piled with more river stones through which the falling water trickled. I was charged with checking the water level every day, and replenishing it from the well if it fell much below the lip of the trough.

Once he was satisfied that the system worked, my father hired a small row-boat and he, Zhu and I spent a day on the river catching fish in a net and storing them in jars of milky river water on the floor of the boat. Zhu claimed to be knowledgeable about the different species, and told us which ones to keep and which to discard. We caught baby pike, loach, whitefish, grass carp, and a catfish, which leapt around in the bottom of the boat snapping at our feet, so that we jumped about and almost capsized the boat. At dusk we landed the boat and rattled home on the bus with about forty captive fingerlings and a few larger fish, and released them into their new home. 'Grow fat,' my father whispered to them as he tipped them into the pond. 'I promise ten thousand years of good luck to whichever of you first graces our table.'

That night my father and Zhu sat by the pond late into the night, drinking and smoking and listening to our classical records and a recording of massed choirs singing revolutionary songs. I sat with them for a while, and played some tunes for them on my violin, and when my mother arrived home our neighbours joined us all by the pond. They produced an early-season watermelon and we sat in the moonlight enveloped in the smells of tobacco, red melon flesh and spring pollen, and we dipped our hands into the pond, hoping to stroke the glistening scales of our new charges.

*

As time went on my father's panic attacks continued, and he decided to deflect his sense of embarrassment by turning it into data 'for the advancement of science and the good of the people'. He revealed the diary he had kept since his illness began, and would ask my mother or me – or a work colleague, if an attack occurred there – to help him write down his experiences as accurately as possible.

My mother gave me the diary after he died, when I was in Shanghai. I read it often during the years that followed. It described the day he discovered that someone had filled the fish pond with cement, and the difficulty he had in accepting my assurances that this was not in fact the case. It recorded his astonishment when he discovered that my playing restored to him the transparent surface of the fish pond, so that he could once again select a fish for dinner. He put the gramophone beside the pond to see if recorded music had the same effect. But this did not work; the healing music had to be performed live, he concluded. He discovered eventually that if he sat by the pond and closed his eyes and then whistled a familiar tune until he was lost in the music, he could sometimes open one eye and slip his hand into the water to catch a fish.

He told everyone that the diary had already been accepted for publication by the *China Journal of Medicine*, who were merely awaiting its completion. One of my favourite entries read:

On March 27th Comrade Lu rides his bicycle to work, but finds he cannot stop at the railway station, and instead continues cycling around the city, unable despite all efforts to instruct his legs to cease pedalling. This continues for another hour, only ceasing when he finally faints with exhaustion. He speculates on why his mind would not allow him to interrupt the rhythmic movement of his legs on the pedals. This automaton behaviour

157

is something the Party should investigate further. As for Comrade Lu, applying scientifically his technique of touching door-posts, he finds that he can stop his bicycle if he touches a tree branch or some other item fixed to the ground. This also is worthy of investigation.

A week later he wrote:

Comrade Lu forms the hypothesis that he might ride with his daughter sitting on the crossbar playing her violin. Perhaps, he thinks, the completion of a piece of music would provide the opportunity for his mind to override the automaton response and to successfully stop his bicycle. This hypothesis remains at the testing stage, as, for the time being, regardless of how she is seated on the crossbar, Comrade Lu's daughter pokes him in the face with her bow.

And the following day:

An alternative must be found to carrying his daughter and her violin on his bicycle. The crossbar position leads to injuries to his face and chest from her bow, and if she sits on the carrier behind him this produces such a bumpy ride as to make playing music impossible. Comrade Lu is therefore experimenting with whistling familiar tunes to himself while riding, hoping that he will be able to stop himself at the moment the tune reaches its conclusion. To his surprise this has worked passably well, and he has now assembled a repertoire that takes him to the door of the China Eastern Railway at his normal leisurely pace, and a shorter repertoire for those days when, due to pressing affairs or a shower of rain, he has to hurry.

One thing the notebook did not record was the conversation my father and I had at dusk one evening by the fish pond. 'Did you know,' he began, 'that the ancients believed that the sky was a vast water-drop clinging to the edge of heaven?'

He withdrew his hand from the pond and held it up to his face, waiting for the water to drain from his fingers, except for one drop which rolled to the end of his index finger. He gazed intently at the drop of water. 'And they believed, with some justification, that it was held in place, like this drop on my finger, by a thin membrane, which let rain through small holes. They believed that the membrane could be burst by the misdeeds of evil or foolish princes, and that this was what caused the great floods.'

He noticed an insect perched on a stone at the edge of the pond, and held his finger over it. The water drop wobbled around underneath his finger, but would not break, until finally my father touched the insect with the drop, rupturing its surface and releasing a tiny deluge over the creature. 'I have become something of an expert on the origin of floods,' he said, 'and the remedies for them. Floods are wonderful mathematical phenomena, and they have a strange and terrifying beauty.'

'Surely it was not true,' I said. 'What they said about the sky was not true.'

'It was not true, no,' he said, 'but what a beautiful thought! The ancients had many beautiful thoughts, and when I reflect I realise I have spent my life amongst people with beautiful thoughts, who are convinced that what is beautiful must also be true – not that they would ever use those words. And in the years to come what great works may result from this mad pursuit of beauty?

'As for the sky, Mao Zedong has said that women hold up half the sky. Do you believe that? Mao is hardly being scientific. And who holds up the other half? Men, perhaps? I am not so sure. Men are too busy with other matters, so perhaps the other half of the sky is held up by all these fragile things, like virtue and duty and music.

'Do you recall our conversation about mathematics and music? How Confucius taught that mathematics is the foundation of music? Well, it has just occurred to me that while the two are linked he may have got the order wrong, that music may in fact be the foundation of mathematics. Now think about that!'

I must have looked puzzled, for my father broke into a gentle laugh and said, 'You must forgive me. How can I be of any use to the masses unless I express my thoughts more plainly?'

7. Shanghai 1955

In 1955, when I was thirteen years old, I left Harbin to study at the Shanghai Conservatory of Music. The Conservatory was housed in a clump of grand brick buildings with stone trim in the midst of one of the old foreign concessions. It was surrounded by similar examples of mercantile splendour, Georgian and Edwardian houses where, in the days when Shanghai was the gorgeous painted nipple on China's breast (before the Japanese occupation brought an end to their party), traders from the French and British middle classes had played at being members of the upper classes. The Conservatory had all but disappeared during the civil war and the early years of the People's Republic, but our Soviet brother had now sent a consignment of Russian teachers, part of an army of five thousand 'technical advisors' sent to build laboratories and teach at universities, and the call had gone out for young musicians from the whole of China to form the musical vanguard of the next generation. Somehow my name was on the list – I suspect that Comrade David had something to do with it – and a letter arrived at Communist Party headquarters in Harbin, inviting Xiao Magou, member of the Communist Youth League, to study at the Conservatory.

In case I harboured any doubts about going, one by one those around me whispered reasons why I should take up the opportunity. Now that Stalin was dead, Piroshka told me, there was a possibility that she and Kasimir might return to Russia to care for Vitja, and if so they would depart suddenly and without warning, and would never return. My father said simply that it would be a great honour to him and to my mother if I were to go. But it was my mother, late one night, who got me out of bed, poured me a cup of tea and took me into the courtyard by the fish pond, where she whispered to me that she and my father were coming under suspicion in the Anti-Rightist Campaign. When I asked how this could possibly be, she told me for the first time the story of her marriage to Yao Xijiu, the son of a capitalist and member of the landlord class.

'But that was many years ago,' I said, 'before I was born.'

'And then there are my links to the Russian community,' she said.

'But the Russians are our friends,' I said, 'our older brother.'

'Not the White Russians,' she corrected me, 'and soon the Red Russians will perhaps not be our friends anymore. The times are very confusing.'

I asked her why my father was under suspicion. He was a Party member of long standing, had fought in the war of liberation, had served the people tirelessly, and was still a Party Secretary. My mother looked into her tea cup for a while, at the slow circling dance of the tea leaves on the surface. 'I don't know why,' she said at last. 'Simply to be in his position means you must have enemies.'

I confronted my father on his alleged misdeeds the next morning as he was leaving the house. He put his finger to my lips and turned to get his bicycle. I ran after him and seized the handlebars so he could not leave. We struggled for a while, and I was surprised to find that he was no longer strong enough to wrest the handlebars from my grasp. He relaxed, and took one of my hands and started to write characters on my palm with his finger. They were the six characters of a proverb he had taught me years before:

When crows find a dying snake, they become like eagles.

'Now you have made me late for work,' he said sharply. 'Give me a push off.' He lifted his leg awkwardly over the bicycle, and I pushed him along the street until he gathered momentum. As I turned away I heard him ring his bell several times, and, thinking he was summoning me, I turned back. I was mistaken. He was ringing the bell so that he could find his note and begin to whistle once more, in D-minor, the jaunty, happy-sad melody of Ge-lei-su's *Liebesleid*.

*

I left Harbin during the harvest time. There had been an especially good crop of leeks. Truckloads had been brought into the city the day before and more or less given away. The Party newspaper advised – perhaps, ordered – that the vegetables be preserved for the winter by twisting them into a knot and leaving them outside to dry in the late autumn sun for at least a week, and as a result the morning I walked to the railway station with Kasimir and Piroshka, carrying a small suitcase and my violin, every flat surface in the neighbourhood – every window ledge and lintel, every stone balustrade, the sides of every doorstep, the roof of every coal shed and bicycle shelter – was covered in a layer of these drying vegetables. Tired from a night with little sleep, I was soon lulled into a doze by the motion of the train as we made our way south towards Beijing, and I dreamt that I was sitting in the train carriage by myself, looking out the window. My violin and bow were once again incorporated into my arms. And everywhere – outside on the ground and the ledges of the buildings, far away on the twisted onion-dome of St Sofia's Cathedral, and inside the carriage as well, on the seat next to me, the netted luggage-rack above my head, and the floor beneath my feet – lay a carpet of these green vegetables, each tied into a crisp knot: an overnight snowfall of tiny strangled corpses.

*

And so late one night at the end of September of 1955 my train shuffled slowly into Shanghai. I had instructions to wait in the arrival hall for a woman called Madame Huang who was to

163

take me to my lodgings. As it happened she was standing behind me as I manoeuvred myself and my luggage down the steps of the carriage. She was a small, round woman with wiry grey hair and a permanent smile that I would soon discover was an accident of her facial bones, rather than a sign of her disposition. She had been born with a smile, and could not shake it. She shook my hand and in the same instant took my suitcase from the platform between us. She led me through the crowd to the station entrance, tossed my suitcase into a bicycle-rickshaw, ordered me to climb in and barked instructions to the driver. She followed in another rickshaw, shouting out directions when my driver appeared about to take a wrong turn.

We swayed for half an hour along wide thoroughfares lit with ornate streetlights, and then down narrow unlit streets where two rickshaws could hardly pass each other, and where the sounds and smells of family life spilled out of open windows. It was late, so most of the apartments and shops we passed were in darkness, but there were still signs of life – loud conversations from above, clusters of people taking a walk in the hot clammy air, and men sitting by windows smoking or quietly ruminating. An old man lounged on a doorstep, dressed in shorts and a singlet he had pulled up over his belly so that he could cool his skin with a fan. In his other hand he held a folded newspaper, squinting to read it in the light of a single bulb above the doorway.

I had just fallen into a kind of tossing sleep when we arrived at the entrance of the Foreign Teachers' Building. Madame Huang paid the rickshaw drivers, carried my suitcase to the entrance and greeted the concierge roughly in a dialect I did not understand. Then she took my violin case from me, muttering something about bricks in my suitcase and pain in her back, and disappeared up a damp stairwell into complete darkness. I dragged my suitcase after her, feeling along the cold concrete walls with my fingertips, stumbling on the irregularly pitched steps. Up ahead Madame Huang began to talk to me, but faintly, as if she thought I was by her side. I sped up and bumped my head into her bony buttock, at which she grunted. These would be only temporary lodgings for me, she was saying. There was no room at the dormitory where most of the Conservatory students lived. This was where the Russian teachers were to stay. They would each have a small suite of rooms to themselves – bedroom, kitchen, bathroom, and sitting room – whereas I was to share a small room on the top floor with another student. I would be moved, she said, as soon as space was available elsewhere.

I had lost count of the landings when Madame Huang announced that we had arrived on the seventh floor. Some starlight filtered in from a window, but otherwise we were in complete darkness. Madame Huang knocked once on a door and pulled me into a room. I felt the greasy aromatic warmth of a sleeping body. 'Ling Ling,' Madame Huang called. 'Where are you?'

There was a rustling of sheets on a mattress, and a sigh of irritation. 'Over here,' a girl's voice came out of the darkness to our left.

'Miss Xiao is here,' Madame Huang said. 'Where is her bunk?'

'Come towards the window,' Ling Ling said. 'It's to your right – the bottom bunk.'

'Here,' Madame Huang said to me, and clutched for my hand. 'Put your things here and get some sleep. Ling Ling will show you where to go in the morning. Remember the instruction session at eight o'clock sharp. Don't be late.' With that Madame Huang put my violin case on the floor and retreated to the door. Soon the sounds of her descent died away. I sat in the darkness on my mattress, and after a while Ling Ling whispered from above me, 'There's a bucket with a lid outside the door if you want to go. It's too late to wash yourself. The water is shut off at nine. I can light you a candle if you really want one.'

I declined the candle and thanked her, and partly undressed before swinging myself onto the lumpy mattress and pulling the single sheet over me. It was a strange feeling, but not an unpleasant one – being alone in the dark in a strange city,

165

surrounded by people my age, musicians too, with the promise of a new life to begin in the morning. I fell asleep quickly, my face licked by gushes of wet warm air from the open window adjacent to my head.

The next morning I was woken by Ling Ling's hand on my shoulder. 'It's late,' she said, 'I have slept in. We need to go now or we'll get nothing to eat.' Ling Ling showed me the tap in the hall way where hot water was available for two hours in the morning and two at night. I noticed that our floor of the building was in fact a recent addition, a makeshift extra storey built of brick and plaster.

After I had dressed, Ling Ling led me downstairs and introduced me to the concierge before taking my hand and pulling me quickly along the street and around the corner to the Conservatory. She explained on the way that she was a pianist from the city of Suzhou, and that this was her second year at the Conservatory. She was several years older than me, although when I stood beside her she only came up to the level of my cheekbones.

The refectory doubled as a meeting hall, and when we arrived the tables were being cleared and forms were being arranged in rows. The room had large double casement windows along one wall through which bright sunlight shone in angled shafts, disturbed by the flickering shadows of the foliage in the courtyard outside. The food counter was at the back of the room, and the other two walls were covered in revolutionary banners, an array of large framed photographs, and big character posters, all of which I attempted to read as Ling Ling pulled me towards the food: *Follow the Leadership of the Party of Lenin, Marxism in One Sentence: Revolution is Justified, Celebrate Paul Robeson's Birthday, Welcome Comrade Tikhon Khrennikhov.* Ling Ling implored the cook to give us some breakfast despite our lateness, talking sweetly first in Mandarin, and then switching to the Shanghai dialect. The cook refused to meet her gaze until she started to point to me, seizing me by the upper arm in an attempt to demonstrate my urgent need for feeding. The cook looked at me as if I were a wounded bird, knitted her brows in concern and began making coo-ing noises. She then disappeared to an adjacent store-room and returned with a small billy in one hand, half full of cold thin soup, and in the other hand some rubbery bread stuffed with bean paste.

'What did you say to her?' I asked Ling Ling as we sat on one of the forms and ate.

'That you were from the Northeast, and arrived late last night,' she said. 'And in case that wasn't enough, I said that there has been a famine where you lived and that your father was a hero in the Korean War and was killed in a plane crash last week.'

'Thank you,' I said. 'But what do I do if my father comes to visit?'

Ling Ling smiled and did not answer because she had caught the attention of a friend who had just entered the room, and was waving sweetly, her hand circling around as if she were washing a window. I felt a surge of envy for her delicate, knowing beauty, *jiao mei*, as we say, 'peach pretty': her oval face with its sharp chin, her double-lidded eyes the shape of almonds, her complexion the colour and texture of an under-ripe stone-fruit. But suddenly she pulled her bottom lip to one side in consternation at something she had seen over my shoulder, and the whole effect vanished, slid into discord, like a hairline crack in a porcelain vase that is only visible when a gentle pressure is applied.

As the room began to fill up, Ling Ling explained to me that normal classes had been suspended during the Anti-Rightist Campaign. 'Today is the second day of the anti-Debussy campaign,' she said. 'They are going to criticise Debussy's music as bourgeois spiritual pollution.' Ling Ling could not say exactly why Debussy was being criticised, except that it had to do with being bourgeois. 'It's a shame,' she said, furrowing her perfect brows. 'I used to play Debussy all the time. My mother taught it to me. Then they found out how bad his music was.'

'Couldn't you tell that it was bad music when you played it?' I asked.

'Of course not. Badness can be very subtle,' Ling Ling said. 'Without political instruction it's easy to miss it.'

Ling Ling's last words were whispered to me, as a young man was standing on the podium at the front of the room calling everyone to attention. He had a pile of posters at his feet bearing slogans painted in large, red characters, and asked for volunteers to attach them to the walls of the room. Those in the front rows immediately stood and rushed at the pile of posters, and began to attach them to the wall, obscuring the posters that were already there. The new posters decried Debussy's music and political errors, as did many of those they now covered over.

Ling Ling noticed me looking around the room and the two hundred or so people. 'These are all the students and faculty of the Conservatory,' she said. 'And those are the first of the Russian advisors, who arrived two days ago.' She pointed to three men and one woman sitting together at the front of the room, and then identified the faculty members, although she could not see the Director, Professor Ho Luting. The young man who had brought the posters was Yu Huiyong, a new professor who specialised in Chinese opera. Once the posters were hung around the walls, it was Yu Huiyong who called the room to order, and began to speak. Claude Debussy was an effete aristocrat, he said, a landlord, a comprador, a bourgeois reactionary, and not a friend of the French people. Weren't all composers enemies of the people? Certainly not! By comparison, Mozart was a musical nationalist who pioneered the use of the German language in opera, and, by his famous departure from Salzburg, rebelled against the feudal order controlling music. He pointed to one of the posters on the back wall, and got us all to repeat what it said several times: 'Celebrate January 1956 – the 200th anniversary of Mozart's birth.'

'Debussy's music is like French pastry,' Yu went on, 'all sugar and fat, but no substance. When the poor people of France had come to Claude Debussy's door complaining that they had run out of bread, Debussy had said to his servant, "But why don't they eat pastry?"' Yu paused, and there was silence for a moment before the room erupted into laughter in response to some cue I had not picked up.

Yu continued detailing the sins of Debussy for another half hour, pausing every few sentences to allow us to rise to our feet and demand that his music be burned and his memory erased. I recalled Piroshka's frank histories of the lives of the great composers, and wondered whether any of them could survive such scrutiny. But Professor Yu obliged with a list of Western composers and artists who, although not necessarily Marxist, nevertheless demonstrated a correct approach to life and music. Beethoven, Mozart, Schubert, Paul Robeson, Brahms, Glinka, Dvořák, Massenet, Liszt, Chopin, Scriabin. It seemed to me a strange list, lacking Bach, Haydn, Tchaikovsky and Paganini, not to mention my father's beloved Fritz Kreisler; and including Schubert, the brilliant but dissolute syphilitic. And who, I thought, was Paul Robeson? I was heartened to see one of the Russian advisors wince at the list, and others – who did not appear to have good Chinese – look puzzled and bend their heads to one of their colleagues for a translation.

After Professor Yu finished speaking, he invited a young man from the audience to join him on the podium. I heard Ling Ling emit a quiet gasp beside me as a slender, handsome man in shirtsleeves stood up before the crowd. 'Who is he?' I asked.

'That is Tian Mei Yun,' she said. 'He is a pianist and a cellist, from my home town.' Tian began to speak; he had a fluty voice, nasal, but always resolving itself to softness, like a warm mist spreading across a lake, or the 'beautiful cloud' of his given name. He spoke of his upbringing in a middle-class intellectual family in Suzhou, and his early introduction to the piano. His uncle had taught him to play Bach, Mozart, and Beethoven, he said, but had not been alert to musical error and had one day brought home some Debussy, and required Tian to play it. This had been a disaster for the family, Tian said. His uncle made him learn the entire book of Debussy's music and perform pieces to guests. The children of the household had been unable to concentrate on their studies. The adults had begun to act selfishly, to neglect their civic duties, and squabble amongst themselves. Marriages dissolved, generations fell into bickering, and two of his cousins died of a fever.

It was only after his uncle was killed in a road accident, along with an unknown young woman whose relatives never claimed her body, that the family began to perform its duties and salvage some dignity. 'Down with Debussy!' he shouted. 'Down with spiritual pollution!' And he sat down amidst more applause. Ling Ling turned to me with tears in her eyes and made as if to say something, but the words did not come.

The session continued all morning, with speaker after speaker getting up to match or better Tian's story, as the heat grew intense and the air hung heavy with the smell of perspiration, pressed back down upon us by the ceiling fans which swung precariously to and fro above our heads. A young man rose and opened the windows to let out the rank air, and a cooler breeze entered the room, and with it the sound of birds singing in the courtyard outside. He slunk back to his seat, shielding his eyes with his hand as if fearful of having committed an error. The windows stayed open.

At midday the doors on the kitchen counter scraped open noisily, spilling the smell of burnt rice and cabbage into the room. The meeting was adjourned, and the Russians rose to their feet as one, some of them stretching and yawning. Ling Ling stood up on the form and scanned the crowd. 'I want you to meet Tian Mei Yun,' she said. 'I can't see where he has gone.'

I felt a hand grasp my elbow and turned to find Madame Huang beside me. 'You must come now,' she said, her eyes distant and suspicious behind that automatic smile. 'The Director wants to speak to you.' I left Ling Ling, and followed Madame Huang through the corridors and up one flight of stairs to a large office dominated by a desk, a piano and a padded leather couch.

Madame Huang sat on the couch and indicated to me to sit beside her. A young girl appeared in the doorway and was dispatched to get some tea. We sat in silence as the girl arranged three cups on the table and poured tea from a metal flask. The door burst open and Director Ho entered. He had a flat moonish face, round glasses and silver-grey hair interspersed with black locks that, from a distance, bore some resemblance to a piano keyboard. He shook my hand enthusiastically while losing his grip on a pile of books and papers in his other arm. 'Welcome, welcome,' he said, and spilled his burden onto the desk before drawing up a chair opposite the couch and taking a sip of tea. 'We are very pleased to have you at the Conservatory,' he started, removing his glasses, blinking at me cross-eyed several times, and then putting his glasses back on. 'The syllabus includes vocal theory, musical history, composition, piano, conducting and the study of symphonic style. The study of Chinese folk and classical music is compulsory, as is political instruction and a general education in the humanities and sciences. Your specialisation will be violin performance, of course. Comrade Meretrenko will be your teacher. Madame Huang here is the Party Secretary and all matters not relating to your studies can be referred to her at any time.'

Madame Huang leaned forward impatiently, her mouth opening to reveal a crumbling parapet of tiny irregular teeth. 'Now for another matter,' she said, and the Director relaxed back into his chair. 'You have been housed in the Foreign Teachers' Building. There is a reason for this.' Madame Huang drew a file from a stack of papers on the table. It had my name on it.

'We are aware that you are fluent in Russian, and that your parents are loyal Party members,' she went on, ending each phrase with a rising inflection. 'However, it is very important that you do not converse in Russian with the teachers in your building, and you are not to let anyone know that you understand their language. You are to make whatever efforts you can to overhear their conversation, so long as you act discreetly and do not make them suspicious.' Here Madame Huang softened her voice to a breathy whisper and her eyes widened as if she were speaking of ghosts. 'Our friends, the Soviet people's government, have told us that amongst these advisors there may be some revisionist sentiment. Of course, we are happy to assist our big brother the Soviet Union to root out bad elements, just as we would expect them to do for us. So we are asking you to report on their topics of conversation, and particularly on anything you hear concerning the Party and their views on China.'

'Do you understand what Comrade Huang is saying?' the Director asked. I nodded. 'She has a list of names for you, and I advise you to get to know them all as best you can. You are to report to her every day for the first week, and then as she instructs you. Do not say anything about this to your roommate. It is none of her business. She is living in the building merely for appearances.' Director Ho turned to look at the pile of papers on his desk. 'Now I have work to do,' he said. 'I am sure your time here will be very successful, and that you will bring honour to China and to the Party and your parents.' He shook my hand once more and Madame Huang ushered me out of the room. She gave me a sheet of paper with a column of Russian names and apartment numbers, telling me to commit it to memory and then destroy the paper.

Ling Ling was waiting for me in the hall, having been summoned to collect me. She linked her arm with mine and took me back to the refectory where, with a squeal of delight, she spied Tian Mei Yun at a table in the far corner. She gave a little jump, did her circular wave again and led me to the table where she introduced us, before going off to the counter to collect some food.

Tian was a striking man, like a small lion in his powerful shoulders and the flow of his movements, and in the protruding cheekbones that pulled his eyes into a look of feline intrigue. His lips were large and girlish, and shiny black hair swirled like water in a whirlpool around his crown, which he always presented to you, looking away with a boyish grin as if you were applauding him. He was dressed in pleated grey trousers, black leather shoes and a shirt with a slight billow in the sleeves and a hint of silk in the weave. I would soon learn that he was the son of a wealthy and somewhat dissolute family, indeed he made no secret of his bourgeois background and told me he had grown up in a street where every house had a grand piano, so that music wafted from every window to greet evening strollers. Looking back now it seems a miracle that his family had survived the revolution and that he had been admitted to the Conservatory under the Communist administration. It must have been his talent (he had been performing since the age of five) and his supreme confidence in it that made him both irresistible and, for the moment at least, untouchable.

Ling Ling returned with some bowls of rice and a plate of greasy vegetables topped with some thin scraps of pork fat, and immediately she was competing with Tian to tell me about their childhood. Their mothers were second cousins, she said, and they had performed duets together from a young age. They had been in demand at party functions, Tian said, had entertained visiting dignitaries sitting beside each other at the piano, Tian in a miniature tuxedo, Ling Ling in a lace gown, feet not quite touching the ground, playing Chopin with four tiny hands. Tian appeared to accept Ling Ling's constant presence and attention with the casual grace of a demi-god.

I mentioned that I had been practicing a piece by Alexander Glazunov and asked if anyone knew whether his music was good or bad according to socialist principles. The others looked at me flatly and remained silent, holding their breath, until finally Tian said, 'On matters of socialist principle, we must always defer to a senior member of the Party.' I nodded as if I had understood, and the conversation resumed as before.

During the afternoon session I manoeuvred myself closer to the Russians in order to get a better look at my subjects. The speeches resumed, repeating criticisms that had been made during the morning. Not a breath of wind stirred outside the building and the room soon became a furnace, the audience squirming inside their damp clothing. There was snoring from a far corner of the room, and the sound of someone being shaken, then a ripple of suppressed laughter through the crowd. One of the Russians muttered under his breath, 'This is absurd,' and the woman at his side squeezed his leg with her hand, digging her thumb hard into his knee.

When I thought no one could possibly have anything new to say on the topic, Director Ho bustled his way to the front and took the stand. He looked up and beamed at the assembly, but then, suddenly remembering himself, assumed an angry scowl. In one so talented as Debussy, he began, such errors were tragic. How could a man born into the age of science and in the land of Curie and Laplace have failed to understand what science makes clear: that music, like all the other arts, is political? 'We at the Shanghai Conservatory resist error in music, as in politics,' he said. 'Our music is science for the ears and science for the heart. Ours is the generation of composers and musicians who will create the music of socialist realism.'

We applauded enthusiastically. Even the Russians clapped with some energy, in an effort, I thought, to speed the session to its end. Professor Yu stood and approached the platform, but Director Ho stopped him with an outstretched palm. 'And now it is time to return to our teaching and study.' Yu turned back towards his seat, his face impassive, but his eyes black with anger.

That evening Ling Ling and I practiced together in one of five adjacent practice rooms. They were like long closets, with a piano and room for one or two standing musicians. A booking sheet was pasted to each door, and a queue of students milled around clutching sheet music and instruments to their chests and glowering at the clock, willing it to tick faster towards their allotted practice times.

Back in our room, I was relieved when, after the lights went out, Ling Ling fell asleep quickly. I lay on my back for a while, staring at the bulge she made in the mattress above me, then levered myself out of bed and padded softly into the stairwell, edging my way down the clammy walls to the sixth floor where I put my ear to the door. I tried to recall from my list whose apartment this was: Mitrofan Tretyakov, I thought, or perhaps Nikolai Golden. I could hear nothing, so I continued to the fifth and the fourth floors, where the result was the same, except for some snoring. On the third floor, however, there was an open door and a shaft of yellow light from a lamp, and voices in Russian speaking over the clinking of glasses. I glanced inside the door, but there was a thin curtain separating a small vestibule from the rest of the apartment. I leaned my back against the wall and listened.

There were three voices, a woman and two men. The conversation concerned the struggles that a son was having with his studies at a university in Kiev. 'Was it laziness at the heart of the matter?' one of the men said – a high voice, but smooth like a steady trickle of warm fluid. 'Take my own son, for example: I gave him Tolstoy and Nekrasov and Pushkin to carry with him on his military service, and he brought them back with the pages uncut, and now he makes a show of studying engineering, but in reality he spends his time at coffee houses. This is sad. This should not be.'

'In our son's case I suspect it is poor breeding,' the woman suggested, drawing a protest from the first man and slow, mirthless laughter from the second. Her voice was deep and breathy, but it had above it a faint, high-registered echo, like a tiny shriek.

At that moment I heard someone approach from below, and soon the stairwell was lit by a blush of yellow light. I retreated to the floor above and watched as a large man arrived holding a leather suitcase in one hand and two large boxes under the other arm. The concierge followed at his heels holding a Tilley lamp. The man dropped his parcels at the open door, muttered thanks to the concierge and knocked loudly on the open door. As the concierge retreated down the stairs her lamp threw an elongated shadow of the man, a tree shape, thick and bulky, onto the wall opposite.

'*Raduysya lyud!*' the man boomed tunefully, and then he sang in a deep bass, '*Raduysya veselisya lyud!*' before picking up the smaller box and entering the apartment.

'Ah, Mitrofan!' a voice shouted from within, and there were

the sounds of chairs scraping and backslapping as the newcomer was welcomed and provided with vodka and water. 'You have them, then? You have retrieved your suitcases?'

'I have only the larger one, alas,' the newcomer said, 'the other is still missing, and that is the one with the vodka in it, so I am afraid this bottle must last us for a while. But look . . . look what I have instead.'

'My God,' said the woman, 'See this, Pavel! Wherever did you get that, Mitrofan?'

'What is it? What is it?' The second man's voice. 'A beef tongue! Look, Kolya. Can it be? Do the cows here still have tongues?'

'Some vodka, Mitrofan.' The first man's voice, Kolya, I thought. 'And I will light another candle for you, and you will tell us how you smuggled a beef tongue across the continent.'

'Across the continent indeed! Across the river – that's where I found it,' Mitrofan said. 'Believe it or not, in a Jewish butcher's shop down a side alley. A White Russian and his niece living quietly amongst the good people of Shanghai. He tells me there are several hundred of them, Russians, some of them Jews, but not all.'

'They never told us that at the briefing,' the woman said.

'Perhaps they didn't know.' The second man, Pavel, I deduced. 'But how did you find this shop, Mitrofan?'

'Let the man drink, Pavel,' the woman said. 'And he will want some of our soup. Look, Mitrofan, they have given us a pot of cabbage soup that could almost pass for cold red borsch.'

'In the dark, perhaps; and if you eat it hot, and if you hold your nose as you eat,' Pavel said.

'You have had three helpings, you hypocrite!'

'I jest, my sweet darling. It is fine soup we are drinking, Mitrofan, and Raya will give you some, although the bread here lacks something; what does it lack, Kolya?'

'Yeast. Wheat.'

'So eat up, and tell us how you found these contraband cow parts.'

'I was at the station,' Mitrofan began, 'and they said my suitcases had gone to the wrong address and that a boy had been sent for them, but that he would be an hour at least. This soup is quite passable, Pavel. So I asked my guide – that young wind-player, you know, who looks like a hare – I asked him to show me around, and we crossed a stream into the oldest part of the city and he showed me the neighbourhood where he had grown up, and as I bent in a doorway to tie my boot lace I found myself looking at a very fine pair of ankles in worsted stockings, and, to cut a long story short . . .'

'You fell in love with a pair of ankles!' Kolya said.

'In worsted stockings!' added Raya.

'I suspect you fell in love more with what was inside the stockings,' Pavel said.

'I am a married man, and happily so! I was crouching in a doorway of a house tying my boot lace as the Jewish girl was leaving it.'

'What was she doing at the house?' Kolya said.

'How would I know?'

'Did you ask?' Kolya again.

'Why should I? It was a house like any other.'

'But not *her* house.'

'Obviously not, as she led me to her uncle's shop and the family seemed to live in rooms above it.'

'Unlike the three of you,' Kolya continued, 'I *was* briefed about the White Russians who still live here, and about how they make their living.'

'Selling beef tongue to errant musicologists.'

'What could be more satisfying?'

'So, Kolya, what were you told about the White Russians?'

'That they are tolerated here. That they put up a memorial to Pushkin somewhere in the city to commemorate his death.'

'To Pushkin?!'

'Yes, to Pushkin. And I am told that after the war the Jews among them were offered passage to Palestine, but have refused.'

'And no doubt that they should all be avoided,' Pavel added.

'But not their beef tongue,' Mitrofan said, 'And the old man tells me he can get much more; not just offal of various kinds, but as many pigeons as we want, and vodka, and *kvass* and *nalivka* made of something that could pass for ashberries, and Troika cigarettes, and decent coffee . . .'

'Decent coffee! Indeed!'

'. . . and, if we wish, his niece . . .'

'Is she made of ashberries too?'

'. . . she can make us *pelmeni* and cod liver salad.'

'You're salivating on the tablecloth, Mitrofan. Here, wipe your mouth on this.'

'They are to be avoided. The Whites.'

'Don't be such a *mudak*, Pavel,' Raya said.

'Don't call me a *mudak*!' Pavel snarled. 'But we have responsibilities, do we not, Comrade Nikolai Sergeyevich?'

'We do indeed, Comrade Pavel Mudakovich, and I . . .'

'See what you have started, Raya. Now everyone will call me Mudakovich! I am marked for life!'

'. . . and I . . . be quiet! I must make sure those responsibilities are met.'

'Very sober, Kolya. You do us proud.'

'And our first responsibility . . . listen!' Kolya's voice rose in pitch and gathered strength and unexpected volume. 'Our first responsibility is to our host, not to cause trouble or embarrassment. So you, dear Mitrofan, you must take care over any excursions into White Russian territory.'

'You see, he does not exactly forbid me.'

'I do not forbid you. These people are living in this city, and the authorities know about them. They are as much guests as we are. But you must tread carefully.'

'But not as carefully as Pavel insists,' Mitrofan said. 'They are not to be shunned, as he says.'

'Which is where I come to our second responsibility. More vodka, please. Our second responsibility is to this tongue.'

'What do you mean?'

'I mean how shall we cook it? I hate raw tongue. As a matter of socialist principle I refuse to eat it raw!'

'Kolya, you devil!'

'I have the very thing,' Mitrofan said. After more scraping of chairs, the apartment fell silent for a moment and Mitrofan appeared at the door and seized the larger box. 'Look here! I have . . .'

'What? Why . . . a samovar!'

'Where did that come from?'

'The ankles, of course, those worsted stockings! Who knows that song . . . *and she boiled her stockings in a silver samovar.* It gets rude after that.'

'Thank you for sparing us that, Pavel,' said Raya.

'What did she charge you for that?'

'It was the uncle, and it is a gift.'

'A gift? From a Jew? Surely not!'

'Pavel! You're overstepping the mark, Pavel. I have cousins . . .'

'Yes, you do, and I withdraw and apologise unreservedly. But this is not a gift, surely. It is an investment.'

'That is entirely a matter for me to decide,' protested Mitrofan. 'I was there.'

'You are wrong, my dear Mitrofan. It is for me to decide if it is a gift. It is part of the burden of my authority.'

'So, my dear Kolya, our great bearer of burdens,' Pavel said, 'what do you decide? Should he return it whence it came?'

'Let me think about it for a day or two.'

'Hah! See!'

'Take as long as you like to think about it,' Raya said, 'and while you do, find me a match . . .'

'Can one really cook a beef tongue in a samovar?' Pavel asked. 'My mother would turn in her grave at the thought. What will the tea taste like afterwards?'

'That is the problem with you men, always limited by your mothers!'

'You too have a mother. I can vouch for it; I have even met her.'

'And eaten her beef tongue?' Mitrofan asked.

'Which, I assure you, my mother would cook in whatever implement came to hand, and little Pavlik here would eat it with pickled vegetables and vodka until all hours of the night, sucking the jelly from his fingers up to the knuckle. Yes, exactly like that! Look, everyone! Disgusting, isn't it! No, Pavel, let me go! You have drunk too much! Now, give me that water jug, Kolya. And give *me* another glass of vodka, before you drink the lot. Thank you. Don't pull that face at me! You know what Chekhov says about women drinking: always vodka or brandy and always the best. Now how do we light this thing? Who has a match?'

'I am going to bed,' Pavel groaned. 'I have to teach my first class in the morning.'

'Ah, no you don't, Pavel,' Kolya sighed. 'It's Criticise Debussy Day again.'

'Who told you that?'

'Director Ho told me.'

'Christ! I thought we'd banished poor Claude to the tenth circle of Hades. Do they want to push him even further down, to the realm of the pederasts and traitors? Well, I might stay up then, if only to make sure nobody eats my share. How long will this thing take to cook?'

'About three hours, I'd say.'

'Christ Almighty!'

'And all his angels!' added Mitrofan.

'Profane tonight, aren't we! Find those matches or it will be four hours.'

'But we don't have enough vodka to last four hours.'

'I am named for Mitrofan the Blessed of Voronezh, Patron Saint of Blasphemy. I can blaspheme all I want!'

'We can water it down,' Raya said.

'The tongue or the vodka?'

'Or the blasphemy?'

'There! It is lit. Now unwrap the tongue. Don't drop it, Pavel, you idiot!'

'I can't help it. It's slippery!'

'Aha, a case of *lingua lapsis*!'

'Very funny, Kolya,' Pavel's voice.

'What?'

'A slip of the tongue, Raya! Where is your Latin? Ha!'

'Did you hear that everyone?' Pavel said. 'A comic genius at our helm. That's auspicious.'

'Are you sure it's fresh, Mitrofan? That slime worries me and it looks green in this light. Let me smell it. Pah! You did bring this across the continent in your suitcase, didn't you!'

'Of course it's fresh. My friend the Jew assured me it is.'

'Here we are!' Raya said. 'The burner is lit, and tongue is cooking, the lid is back on – our ship is launched! More vodka for a toast!'

'The bottle is finished.' Pavel's voice, followed by a collective sigh.

'Well then, beloved comrades,' Kolya's voice now, 'my duty lies heavy upon me. I will show some leadership here. I have another bottle of vodka in my room. I will get it.'

'It is you who are the saint, Kolya.'

'Give me that candle then.'

Moments later Kolya burst from the room into the stairwell, shielding a candle with his hand, and walked towards me. I had time to do nothing more than rise to my feet and give the appearance that I was descending the stairs. As I passed close to him I noted his tightly clipped beard and half-moon spectacles and a shirt that opened at the collar to reveal a burr of greying chest hair. He swayed slightly and muttered '*ni hao*' to me. I descended to the floor below and waited for him to return with his bottle of vodka, but after ten minutes standing in complete darkness I decided to retrace my steps. The door of the apartment was still open, and candlelight flickered across the vestibule curtain like a display of the northern lights, but the voices within were stilled. A warm, meaty smell wafted into the stairwell. I waited a while before climbing to the next floor and then two more floors, until I found the door of an apartment open, but all inside was darkness. I bent my head to the doorframe and heard a faint sound of heavy breathing.

*

The next morning on my way downstairs I noted the name plates beside the apartments: Nikolai Golden on the sixth floor, Mitrofan Tretyakov on the fifth, Fyodor Meretrenko and his wife Ksenia on the fourth, and on the third, Pavel Gachev and Raya Vishinsky. All the names were printed in Russian, with a clumsy transliteration into Chinese characters.

As instructed I reported the night's events to Madame Huang, who noted down the details, and asked me to repeat my story at several points. A tongue? Pushkin? Who is he? How much vodka? She said she would have a stern talk to the student who was assigned to guide Mitrofan, and I pointed out that it was the Russian, and not his guide, who had sought out the White Russian's shop. Madame Huang nodded several times and made to write something down, but then stopped herself. 'Perhaps you're right,' she said. 'Indeed you are. I think we will leave things alone and simply observe. No, to the contrary,' and she pressed her teeth forwards into her grand smile, 'I shall commend him for his initiative in taking Comrade Tretyakov to see his countrymen across the river. This could be very useful indeed!' She thanked me and told me to continue.

Nikolai Golden, or Kolya, had been correct, I was dismayed to find. That day's classes were indeed cancelled once more to allow the anti-Debussy campaign to continue. Students and faculty sat meekly in the refectory hall as a series of rainstorms brought some relief from the heat, rattling on the windows in a kind of angry counterpoint to the morning's sessions of criticism, led once more, and with particular passion, by Professor Yu.

Early in the afternoon session, after we had chanted slogans against Debussy for half an hour, Director Ho rose to make another speech. He had been sitting quietly near the front for the entire morning, placidly attentive to each speaker. Then, as the rain gave way to sticky heat and those around him began

182

to tug on their shirt fronts and fan their faces with spare anti-Debussy pamphlets, I noticed him take up a pencil and start to scribble some notes on a sheet of paper. When he finished he made his way to the podium, gave us his stern face with a hint of theatricality, and began: 'Now that the errors of Claude Debussy are beyond doubt, what is our duty as musicians and composers? What instruction should we take from the bad example of Debussy? Do bourgeois characteristics lie hidden in our music?'

Director Ho dropped his head and allowed his questions to hang in the air. I was not sure if he was waiting for someone in the audience to volunteer a response, and I started to formulate an answer in case I was called upon. There were several stifled coughs and some barely perceptible whispering; but then Director Ho looked up again.

'In China we have always known that to make music is a political act. The ancients believed that music affected both Heaven and Earth. Music was aligned with Heaven, with light, with the male principle, and with the *Yang*; while the sacred rites were linked to the Earth, to obscurity, the female principle, and the *Yin*.

'Mao Zedong expressed the truth more succinctly, when he said, "All culture belongs to a definite class and party, and has a definite political line." Our brothers in the Soviet Union have recognised the same thing. One of their composers, Dmitri Shostakovich, has said, "There can be no music without ideology. We, as revolutionaries, have a different conception of music from the composers of other countries. Lenin himself said that music is a means of unifying people, and eliminating the differences that hold them apart." Concerning his own composition, Shostakovich says, "I always try to make myself understood as widely as possible, and if I do not succeed, I consider it my own fault."'

Director Ho's round glasses flashed moonbeams around the room. 'So, for a socialist,' he continued, 'bad music is not simply an aesthetic problem; it is a moral and political problem.

Bad music harms its listeners and their society. Confucius recorded the story of King Zhou of Shang who commissioned a salacious work, "The Mulberry Grove above the Pu River". After the performance, the administration of the kingdom became dissolute; the people wandered about haplessly, vilified their superiors, and neglected their work. As a result the state collapsed, and the composer, seeing the people ruined, threw himself into a river and drowned.

'We read also in the ancient annals of Duke Ling of Wei, who, when visiting Duke Ping of Qin, urged his friend to order his music master to play tunes that were spiritually too potent for the unperfected virtues of young dukes and a pleasure-soaked court. Even during the performance, dark cranes appeared over the palace as an omen. The musicians and the court soothsayers became distressed, and many guests and courtiers fled; but the dukes persisted. As the last note was struck, a torrent of rain unleashed itself upon the lands of Wei and Qin, and all was lost in the floods that followed.

'We must not repeat these mistakes!' he shouted, looking down at his notes first, and then looking up and surveying the room over the top of his glasses. He paused and his eyes searched the room again, and I heard a metallic rattling from the corridor and turned, with everyone else, to watch two students manoeuvre a three-legged iron brazier through the door and up the aisle to the podium. Director Ho watched as they set it down on the floor, after which one of them handed him a sheaf of papers tied up in string. 'We will not repeat these mistakes, comrades.' And with that he tore the string from the papers and held up the top one for us to see. 'The *Préludes*,' he announced. 'Debussy's *Préludes*.' He tucked the score under his arm and produced a book of matches, struggling with them at his chest until he produced, like a conjuror, a sputtering flame. There was a gasp from amongst the Russians as Director Ho dangled the *Préludes* over the flame until one corner of it ignited and began to burn brightly, sending black ribbons of smoke up to the ceiling. The room fell silent, not a whisper or a breath, and we listened only to the soft, efficient roar of the flames as the paper curled and writhed, and Debussy's quavers and breves melted and blackened and turned to grey dust. I glanced across at Tian and noticed his Adam's apple quiver, then at Ling Ling and saw her eyes wide and her lip pulled unattractively to one side.

Director Ho held the score until the flame began to lick his fingers. He dropped it into the brazier and then produced another score from his pile. '"The Happy Island",' he announced, and dropped it into the flames. He held out the next score and the next, announcing the title of each piece in turn before dropping it into the brazier: announcing them brightly, as if they were being performed rather than summoned for execution. The fire hissed and spat, and ghost-birds of blackened paper rose with the heat and sought out the ceiling. Some were caught and savaged by the fans, falling upon our heads in a shower of tiny black snowflakes. Several rows in front of me I saw the only woman amongst the Russians, Raya I assumed, touch her lips with her fingers. The others, the men, observed impassively, barely blinking. Along the row from me a charred butterfly settled gracefully onto the outstretched palms of a student, weightless and crimped, lines of arpeggios still legible as silver threads embroidered on a black field. He stared at it for a moment, as if committing the notes to memory, before closing his hands over it and mashing it into dust.

Over the next half-hour, five, ten, twenty scores disappeared into the brazier. Director Ho's forehead and neck became red with his work, and although I studied his face carefully throughout his performance it never once showed anything but anger and indignation against the foreign spiritual pollution printed onto the pages that passed through his fingers. Finally he wound the string that had held the scores neatly around two fingers and put it away in his pocket. Yu Huiyong sat quietly by the podium, his chin in his hands. Outside the rain started up again. Gusts of wind came in through the windows and, with a flurry of light and smoke, conjured from the brazier a half-burned page – a firebird which danced jerkily over our heads, flapping its blackened wings, making a desperate bid for freedom before falling to the floor, scattering sparks along the floorboards and making several hissing lurches towards the door. A student made a move towards it, to stamp it out, but his neighbour held him back, and we all kept our seats and watched the fugitive creature as it was carried along another metre by a gust of wind before coming to rest and, in a final act of defiance and resignation, immolating itself in a burst of flame which burned deep scorch marks into the floor boards and then falling in on itself, a mess of blackness and writhing orange maggots.

Director Ho moved back to the podium, his cheeks flushed and sweat glistening on his brow. 'Now that we have dealt with Debussy, let us continue,' he said. 'Many of you will know the story of how the Yellow Emperor – the first and greatest of all the emperors – established a standard pitch, based upon the song of the phoenix that he had heard while on retreat in the mountains; of how, as he slept under one of the sacred dryandera trees by a dew-fed pond where the phoenix birds were resting on their journey from the South Sea to the North Sea, he heard the phoenix song, not knowing whether he was awake or dreaming. Immediately he tuned the strings of his lyre to the notes of the bird's song, and when he returned to the Palace he named this the 'yellow bell' pitch, made it the foundation for a series of twelve tones, and ordered that in his Palace night and day without ceasing he would hear music tuned to this 'yellow bell' pitch. The nation prospered under his rule as never before or since, with abundant water supply, a dependable crop cycle, and many advances in science, law and government.'

The Director's voice broke and he fumbled under the lectern for a glass of water. Tian leaned towards me and whispered, 'Where is this fairy story taking us?' I shrugged, and someone behind us hissed quietly at us.

The Director flourished a large handkerchief, formed it into a floppy mushroom, wiped his brow and went on. 'The death of the Yellow Emperor plunged the court into chaos, and the pitch taken from the song of the phoenix was lost. Many years later Confucius himself heard the phoenix song while in the mountains, whereupon he lost his desire to eat for three months, yet did not starve because the perfect music was resonating within his body. That led him to study the marriage between music and mathematics, and thus between music, life and society. He reasoned that, if that lost music of the golden age could be regained it would bring harmony and decorum to human affairs and to nature more quickly than ten thousand words of wise teaching.

'Year after year the disciples of Confucius would retreat to the mountains in spring, taking with them the finest of stringed instruments, to search for the sacred resting places of the phoenix and to listen for its song. None were successful. Some claimed to have heard the phoenix song and to have tuned their instruments to it, but on the way down the mountain they tripped and dropped their instruments, or encountered a sudden shower of rain, or were ambushed by bandits (or, it has been said, by envious rivals), and the yellow bell pitch was lost once more.'

Tian turned to me once more, his eyes rolled up into his forehead. Professor Yu continued to stare at his feet, seemingly in a trance. By this time the fire had burnt itself out and the column of smoke from the brazier had been reduced to irregular puffs that were sliced and dissipated by the ceiling fans.

'That was two thousand years ago. There have been thirty-five pitch reforms since the late Zhou period: thirty-five occasions when all the Court musicians of China were required to re-tune their instruments to a new scale in an attempt to bless the nation with peace and prosperity. Was all this effort wasted? Was it merely a folly of Confucianism and feudalism? Was the Yellow Emperor drunk when he hung his *qin* in the branches of the dryandera tree? Was he dreaming when he heard the sound of the wind vibrating the lowest string, and called that the phoenix song?

187

'We now know that the phoenix bird is a fable. But Mao Zedong has said, "Make the past serve the present. Make foreign things serve China." We have learned from foreigners the scientific method for achieving equal temperament in music. And although China invented the *qin* at least two thousand years ago, foreigners have introduced us to the piano, the *gang-qin*, the steel *qin*. Science has now given us an industrial instrument, made of the same material as guns and tanks, with a frame made of steel and machine-drawn wires which carry two-hundred pounds of pressure.'

Director Ho at this point produced a piece of paper from his pocket, unfolded it and shook it towards us. 'Here is the proof! We have made these foreign things serve China. This telegram arrived in my office this morning! Even though the foreigners have had three-hundred years' head start, we have quickly mastered the steel *qin*. Yesterday the pianist Fu Cong, a graduate of this conservatory, was awarded third prize in the Chopin Competition in Vienna, the first Chinese musician to be honoured in an international competition.'

There was a moment of silence. 'Long live Fu Cong!' the Director shouted, and he shook the telegram in front of us again and it rattled loudly like a snare drum. 'Fu Cong is a true patriot!' he shouted, and immediately the room exploded into applause. First one, then another, then a dozen students sprang to their feet, stabbing the air with their fists. 'Long live Fu Cong!' we chanted, leaping to our feet and then standing on our chairs. 'Fu Cong is a true patriot!'

The Director folded the telegram and waved us down. 'Of course, some of the credit must also go to the Soviet Union, where Fu Cong studied at the Moscow Conservatory.' More applause, and cries of 'Long live the Soviet Union!', and Director Ho approached the Russian advisors and pulled them to their feet and shook hands vigorously with each of them, as if desperately trying a series of locked doors to find one which was open. From the back of the room a photographer strode forward with a camera and a large shining reflector-dish. A magnesium flash momentarily fixed the Director and Nikolai Golden, clearly fearful of having his arm dislocated by the Director's aggressive pumping, in an impossible, god-like whiteness.

Director Ho resumed the podium and raised his clasped hands in victory. Another flash popped. 'I declare the Campaign against Debussy a complete success. Normal classes will resume tomorrow. And now I will now present a big character poster written in my own hand.' He nodded to someone behind us, and two women brought forward a large framed sheet of paper on which was written in bold strokes, 'Mao Zedong thought is a glittering light. Mao Zedong thought is the phoenix song'. As we continued to applaud, like a rolling series of rainbursts, the poster was hung on the wall beside the portraits of Mao himself and Zhou Enlai and Lenin, where it remained for the rest of my years at the Conservatory.

*

The evening after the anti-Debussy campaign ended I had my first lesson with Comrade Meretrenko, my new violin teacher. He was a withdrawn and melancholy man of about fifty, a wearer of corduroy trousers and a ribbed woollen jersey with leather patches on the elbows and shoulders, a man given to long sighs that could mean variously criticism or resignation or admiration, or, I began to suspect, some entirely unrelated thought or memory that had come to his mind during my playing, which he would never divulge. At his insistence our lesson took place in his apartment. His wife Ksenia served us tea brewed downstairs in Mitrofan's samovar, which seemed to have been installed more or less permanently in Pavel and Raya's apartment. She was a stout-legged woman with a pin-cushion face and yellowy blond hair pulled back aggressively into a bun, secured by a complicated set of brass callipers and a wooden clasp that, had it been several hundred times larger, could have served to hold the hawsers on a suspension bridge. Ksenia sat solidly at the table, one meaty hand clutching her teacup, watching us with cool green eyes, nodding at the things her husband was saying despite it being clear she had little or no Chinese.

Comrade Meretrenko was the only one of the advisors who spoke Chinese with any confidence, although his vocabulary began to fall away sharply once the conversation moved beyond music. He was of medium build and starting to loosen around the jowls, and he had tufts of black hair like miniature gardens planted at odd places – his ears, his nose, his wrists and along the backs of his fingers. His most prominent feature, however, was a pair of enormous black eyebrows, which would lie flat like obedient dogs when he played the violin, but at other times writhed around like caterpillars beyond his conscious control. They were immensely distracting: their arrangement and movement would seem either to reinforce or to undermine the point he was trying to make, like a pair of unruly court jesters, or they would quiver stiffly, giving me the impression that unnameable forces lurked within him which might burst out at any moment. Only after I learned to ignore his eyebrows completely did I begin to feel comfortable in his presence, and to benefit from his uncompromising exactitude and his enormous reservoir of patience.

Comrade Meretrenko explained the programme of music he wanted me to work on: works by Mozart, Beethoven, Schubert, Bach, Mendelssohn, Brahms, Chausson and Szymanowski. I asked him if I could learn some Russian music, and he gave one of his sighs and started to count off composers on the long bony fingers of one hand. 'Sadly Tchaikovsky has fallen from favour. There is some Glazunov and Taneyev, if I can get hold of the scores, and I suppose Prokofiev, but one can never be sure of their reputation from day to day. Khachaturian has a violin concerto, but it has little merit, in my opinion. So too Myaskovsky's concerto, which I can hardly listen to. And of course Stravinsky . . . ah, Stravinsky, he has placed himself beyond our reach.' I asked about Shostakovich, making sure that I pronounced the name clumsily with a thick Chinese accent. He frowned and said, 'I have little enthusiasm for the modernists. They have done nothing for the violin, in my opinion. Their main interest seems to be the tuba and the glockenspiel. Besides I know of nothing Shostakovich has written for solo violin. He is a writer of symphonies and motion picture scores. A symphony for every five-year plan – you can see it listed there in the official records: steel – five million tonnes; symphonies – one Shostakovich; table-tennis balls – one hundred thousand. And he will compose extra ones, if required, to mark military victories or a death in the Presidium.'

Before I left, Comrade Meretrenko commented on my accommodation on the top floor of the building. He warned me that it seemed to lack insulation and would be extremely cold in winter. I asked him whether I was likely to be taught by any of the other advisors, and he said I surely would be, and reeled off names and areas of expertise and one or two personal traits, which I scrupulously committed to memory.

That night I practiced with Ling Ling and Tian Mei Yun, and again lingered in the dark stairwell of my building listening for scraps of Russian conversation. I heard Pavel and Raya argue briefly over their son, and learned that he was studying physics, but faltering, either due to a romance with an unsuitable young woman who happened to be a cousin on his mother's side (Pavel's interpretation) or due to his having inherited his father's aptitude for self-discipline (Raya's interpretation). The argument flared briefly, like dry leaves thrown into a fire, and I expected at any moment to hear the sound of a slap or breaking glass; but it quickly subsided into silence. Raya came to the door and leant her shoulder against the frame. She was still wearing the clothes she had worn at the Criticise Debussy campaign, and I reflected on how dissimilar they were to what the Russian women in Harbin would wear, the flowing French styles they had copied from magazines and patterns that had found their way north from the old concessions of Shanghai. Instead, Raya was all faceted and bevelled and pleated and tucked; a skirt of tight broadcloth, colourless in the yellow light from the apartment, and a white blouse ornately-stitched with tight lines of small thread beads, that was tucked into her skirt and billowed outwards generously before tapering into a narrow neck and a scalloped collar with a line of embroidered circles along its edges. Whether by design or not, she was wearing a Criticise Debussy ensemble.

She produced from her closed palm a match-book and a cigarette which she lit, quickly blowing several smoke kisses towards the ceiling. From the shadows I studied one half of her face: high Slavic cheekbones, a protruding brow that was starting to slip forward over her large, round eyes, a large but shapely nose, and wide lips which she pulled tightly over her teeth and poked at repeatedly with the tip of her little finger. She held the cigarette in front of her face, pointed straight up like a little burning extension of one finger. She flexed one knee and rested her heel on the doorframe behind her, and I noticed that her legs were stockinged but that she had dispensed with her plain brown leather shoes and that while her toes were long and tapered, her ankles were beginning to thicken. Beauty – physical beauty – had visited her during her youth, I thought to myself, had lingered for some time, but had then been called away before its work was complete, promising one day to return before ordinariness engulfed her. And at the time she had not cared whether it came or went, for she had believed in beauty that lay elsewhere.

'Where are you?' Pavel called from within the apartment. Raya's brows tightened and she opened her mouth in a wide yawn.

'I am out by the door, it is cooler here,' Raya replied. Her voice resonated in the dark cavity of the stairwell around me, the tiny shriek still there like a slash across a piece of rich fabric. She took another long puff on her cigarette, hollowing her cheeks as she did so, and then she propelled herself forward, stabbed the cigarette into the opposite doorframe and retreated inside, leaving the door ajar. I stayed in the stairwell another half hour, but heard nothing more save the noise of the pair moving around, avoiding each other as much as was possible in the tiny apartment.

This became my daily routine over the weeks that followed. School in the morning. Musical education in the afternoon. A lesson with Comrade Meretrenko three times a week in the early evening, alternating with practice with Ling Ling and sometimes with Tian on cello. And then afterwards haunting the stairwell until the Foreign Teachers' Building settled into silence. Pavel and Raya were by far the most productive of my subjects, due to their hospitable nature, their habit of leaving their door ajar, and the grating tension in their marriage which they made little attempt to conceal. I reported to Madame Huang on snatches of conversation from other rooms and from brief exchanges overheard in the stairwell: some anger at Director Ho over the allocation of offices; grumbling about the food in the faculty dining hall; tears on receiving the news of the death of a sister; plans to return to the Soviet Union; and suspicion of an affair between one of the advisors and a senior student (which Madame Huang, after some discreet investigation, decided was unfounded).

My nocturnal duties and my studies left me little time to explore the city. On a few occasions the whole student body walked to the People's Park for mass demonstrations, and on Sunday afternoons Ling Ling and I would sometimes walk arm in arm along the Bund and admire the façades of the colonial buildings – former banks, headquarters of trading houses, and the former Customs House whose bells still chimed the same tune as Big Ben every hour (until, a year after I arrived, the tune was changed – at great expense – to 'The East is Red'). Occasionally, we would stray across the bridge into Hong Chew, the traditional 'Chinese area' of the old colonial city, now home to the remnants of other communities: the White Russians, the Arabs, and the Sikhs (former employees of colonial trading houses). I was tempted to seek out the Jewish butcher shop, but since I was always in the company of a classmate I dared not.

I also reported to Madame Huang on the excursions made by Mitrofan into the old parts of the city and the spoils he brought back from its Jewish traders. On one occasion, when

Raya had closed the door of the apartment on the third floor, perhaps in anticipation of having particularly sharp words with her husband, I had retreated only a few steps upwards when I heard Mitrofan ascending from below, calling loudly to Pavel and, upon reaching the third floor, pounding on the door until he was admitted.

'Look, my friend,' he called, and held out a cloth bag to Pavel as he opened the door. 'I have *knydl* for you! Ukrainian *knydl*! As fresh as our girl can make them.'

Pavel stood sleepily in the doorway and after Mitrofan had strode past him, he carefully placed a boot against the door to keep it open and retreated inside. 'It is stuffy in here, Raya, so I have opened the door,' he called.

'Voilà!' Mitrofan was saying, 'Look, Raya, pickled cabbage, *prianik medoviy* made with Siberian honey, I am told, and sorry, no *karavay* this time, but I have this Jewish bread I have never heard of: *mandelakh*!'

'You have never heard of *mandelakh*!' Raya said. 'Have you lived your entire life out on the steppes? Have you never been to the Pale of Settlement? Come, Mitrofan, hero of the revolution. See, I was just laying out the cards for a game of patience, but if Pavel agrees we can play a game of three-handed fool and eat *knydl* and drink tongue-flavoured tea from the samovar.'

'Please, no, I have reading to do,' complained Pavel. 'But a thousand thanks for your efforts, Mitrofan. These look like they are straight from the Besarabsky Market. Thank heaven for the Jews, eh Raya? We should summon Fyodor and Ksenia down from above.'

'If not cards, then chess,' Raya said. 'Let us have a game of chess. I haven't played since we arrived in Shanghai. Pavel refuses to play, and besides I always beat him. Here, you set up the pieces and I will pour your tea.'

'Come, Pavel, come, eat the *knydl*. They are still warm. Take two, Pavel.'

Pavel muttered his thanks and his shadow on the curtain grew larger until he parted it with his hand and stepped into the vestibule, cradling his food in his palm.

'Hey!' Mitrofan called from within. 'I have no queen. Where is the black queen?'

'Pavel,' Raya shouted. 'Pavel, where is the queen, the black queen? Don't tell me . . .'

'Yes,' Pavel called back, without turning his head. 'Remember it went missing last summer, when we were in Feodosia at your uncle's place. He thought he had dropped it in the mud bath. That shows how long it is since we played.'

'We will have to improvise,' Raya said. 'What can serve as a black queen? Here, use this! . . . And I will begin with pawn to king four.'

'You expect me to touch that thing? I will catch a disease. Here, I will open on the king's side.'

'Touch what?' Pavel called.

'A duck's foot! Your wife has given me a duck's foot for a queen. Surely this is bad luck!'

'It's all we have,' Raya replied. 'If I had a rabbit's tail I would give it to you. Good luck is hard to come by. Bad luck is better than no luck at all.'

'What kind of proverb is that?' Mitrofan laughed. 'Let me see what I have in my pockets. Here, let's try this.'

'My God! What could be worse luck than that? Pavel, he wants to use a bullet as a queen.'

'Is it live?'

'Indeed it is,' Mitrofan said. 'And it's not a bullet, it's a shotgun cartridge.'

'You have brought a shotgun with you?'

'No, only this cartridge. It's a stowaway; I found it tucked into one of my spare boots.'

'You must explain these strange trans-Caucasian customs,' said Raya. 'Keeping bullets in your boots? Whatever for? Check!'

'You can't fool me with that opening. That's a Latvian Gambit, isn't it?'

'I can't tell you. Pavel! Come here and tell me if I am playing a Latvian Gambit.'

Pavel snorted loudly, but did not move from where he stood in the doorway.

'Pavel!'

'Kolya is coming,' Pavel said, and out of the half-light I saw Nikolai Golden ascending the stairs. He laboured up the final few steps and stood for a moment face to face with Pavel, and then produced a folded paper from his breast pocket.

'Is it true, then?' Pavel asked softly, with a chuckle of resignation.

'I have the telegram here. My congratulations, Comrade.' He embraced Pavel around his shoulders. Pavel was unmoved. 'Come now, Pavel,' Kolya said. 'It is an honour. I don't have one of these. I will tell your wife.'

'No, don't tell her,' Pavel said without conviction. Then he grabbed Kolya's arm and said, without much urgency, 'Don't!'

'You are being foolish. It is an honour.'

'You know better than that.'

'Don't be a fool. Play along with it. What else can you do?'

There was a shuffle on the stairs behind them, and Comrade Meretrenko and his wife emerged from the darkness. 'Come in, come in,' Kolya said, 'I have an announcement.' He herded Pavel and the two newcomers into the apartment, and greeted Raya and Mitrofan. 'Where is Maria Ivanovna?' I heard him ask. 'Teaching still? And Sasha? Curled up in bed with her migraine, is she? Then let us begin. I will pass around this telegram that I received today. You see, our friend and colleague has been awarded the Order of the Red Banner of Labour for his services to music!'

For the next half hour the apartment was filled with cheers, rounds of applause, songs, toasts, and the clinking of glasses and bottles and teacups. Mitrofan's offering of food was devoured quickly, and gusts of laughter resounded into the stairwell every few minutes. I sat in the shadows and was soon overcome with a bout of yawning, but felt I should stay until the party broke up. I could not keep my eyes open, however, and woke with a start as two shapes walked past me on the steps only inches from me. It was Meretrenko and his wife, and if they noticed me neither said anything.

'Second class,' Ksenia said softly. 'Did you notice that?'

'Everyone did,' Meretrenko answered. 'To be awarded in absentia.'

'So that is where we are, that is where you have brought me: to the Land of Absentia.'

'Don't say that,' Meretrenko tutted, but then added, 'But I like that, Ksenia: the Land of Absentia. Very droll.'

Hours later, after the party had broken up and the building had gone silent, and I had ascended to the seventh floor and slipped into bed, I was awakened by the noise of voices nearby. I rose and went to the door and had already opened it a crack when I realised that two people were sitting on the top step, no more than a couple of metres away. I froze, and leant my ear against the door jamb.

'Tell me then, what do *I* do now?' It was Raya.

'Do nothing. Carry on as before.' A man's voice. Kolya. 'At least you don't have to attend any ceremony of presentation. That would be excruciating for you, I'm sure.'

'I can't do nothing. I am not the kind of person who can do nothing.'

'Learn.'

'I can't.'

There was silence for a minute, during which Raya sighed to herself twice.

'I'm going to bed,' said Kolya.

'No, don't,' said Raya. 'Please, don't. Say something else to me. Say anything to me.'

Kolya was quiet for some time, and then cleared his throat softly.

'Well?' said Raya.

'You know in Russia today – let me be more precise – in the Soviet Union today, we are on a ladder, all of us, every member of the intelligentsia, a ladder like something out of Dante or the Holy Scripture. And the intelligentsia forms itself into two groups, you see, those who are trying to get to Moscow and those who are being forced out of Moscow into exile in the provinces. Ascent and descent. Whether it is the real city of Moscow I refer to or a Moscow of the mind does not matter.'

'What is your point, Kolya?'

'I suppose, if you insist, there is a third group, of those who are attempting to leave Moscow of their own accord, fools and weaklings who believe that somewhere in Russia's provinces Nature still protects the weak, like all of those good and weak men in Chekhov.'

'Again, what is your point, Kolya?'

'Let me come to my point, then. We all of us live each day on the same ladder, some of us thrusting ourselves upwards towards Moscow, others just holding on to the rung we are on, trying to keep our balance, others losing our grip and falling from rung to rung, from Moscow to Leningrad or Kharkov or Smolensk and then further, and taking others with us as we fall (so of course on each rung there are many kicks and bruises and much banging of heads against bony arses and desperate clutching and stepping on toes and out-and-out fist-fights for position); but the secret of each struggle – the struggle for an inch of room on each rung of the ladder, the struggle of any two people who seek to occupy the same space on the footpath, the same seat in a train, the same flat, the same job, the same marriage – is to know if we are in a contest with someone travelling in the opposite direction to us or someone travelling in the same direction, and if the latter, are we travelling up or down the ladder, and if down, are we travelling willingly or unwillingly. You see?'

'You have merely confused me. What is there to see?'

'Your husband has reached the top of his arc. That is what I am saying. Perhaps he reached it some time ago, when Zhdanov died, or last year when he stepped down from the Standing Committee of the Composers' Union. Twenty years is a long time to be on a committee. Tikhon Khrennikov now has the ear of Mikoyan and Bulgarin and, it is said, even of Khrushchev, so he has no need of Pavel. You, on the other hand, are still ascending, I am sure of it.'

The two shapes sat side by side for several minutes without talking. In the distance I heard the clock on the Bund strike the hour and play 'The East is Red'.

'*And even in the distant taiga we hear the Kremlin tower clock*,' Raya mused. 'Do you know that song, Kolya?'

'Of course, I do. We all know that song. Dreadful piece of shit. We know it by heart.'

One of the shapes rose and began to descend the stairs.

'Thank you, Kolya,' the other shape said. 'You are very kind, and you have answered none of my questions and given me no comfort whatsoever. But thank you all the same.'

'A pleasure.'

After they had gone, I stepped into the stairwell and took from the top of the window casement the candle, pencil and paper I had hidden there. I lit the candle and by its light wrote down all the new secrets of which I was now custodian. Then I slipped back into my room to be greeted by the soft music of Ling Ling's breathing. I thought I saw the glistening of her eye watching me as I closed the door and tiptoed to my bed, but Ling Ling did not stir and said nothing.

*

A month after my arrival in Shanghai, a letter arrived from my mother, thanking me for notifying her that I had arrived safely, and giving news from home – my father, happily busy at work and as well as could be expected; Kasimir and Piroshka, waiting to hear about prospects for their return to the Soviet Union to visit their son; and my mother herself, shouldering additional duties at the hospital due to a shortage of doctors. It would be several years before I learned the truth: that both of my parents were coming under increasing criticism as 'rightist elements,' and that Kasimir and Piroshka were eager to leave Harbin so as to dispel the perception that my parents were harbouring two enemies of socialism.

The winter came, and although I easily tolerated the icy cold outside in my padded winter clothes, I shivered with my classmates in the Conservatory buildings where there was no heating system at all except for the faculty offices. At night I shivered with Ling Ling in our draughty annex.

And then on December fifteenth, as happened each year on exactly that date, all the windows in the apartment building were sealed shut with thick masking tape, and the radiators sprang to life with clanging and hissing and a furious knocking that made me think some plumber's assistant had been trapped inside the pipes and was slowly succumbing to the boiling water. There was no radiator on our floor, but gusts of warmth were released into the stairwell and rose to our room above. Indeed, the heating system was so fierce that the apartments became intolerably hot for the Russian advisors, and most of them left their doors open when they were at home to give them respite from the clammy heat. This created ideal conditions for espionage.

One day in January 1956 – when there was a spell of unseasonably warm weather, and some of the Soviet advisors broke the sealing on the windows to escape the relentless billows from the radiators – Comrade Meretrenko told me in passing that he had been mistaken, that a Shostakovich violin concerto had been performed in Leningrad by David Oistrakh in October of the previous year. The musical community in the Soviet Union had been enthusiastic and there was talk of it being played in Amsterdam and New York. But the performance had received some indifferent reviews, in particular in *Pravda*. 'Their reviewers are more orthodox,' he explained, 'and are less likely to get carried away by modernism.'

That night I overheard him expressing the same views in Kolya's apartment. Pavel and Raya were also there, Mitrofan arrived bringing vodka, and I heard the deep, unfamiliar gong-like voice of a visitor, a man who I assumed was new to the city from the comments he made about the interesting sights he had seen that day. They had left the door open, and I sat for at least an hour while several bottles of vodka were consumed. The Shostakovich concerto was discussed, and Comrade Meretrenko, fortified with drink, railed against modernism as if it were an occupying force in possession of his homeland. The others laughed, politely at first, as if not wanting to give their visitor the impression that they argued amongst themselves often. Mitrofan began to protest on behalf of modernity, but Kolya quieted him: 'Let Fyodor say his piece, Mitrofan.'

When Meretrenko's complaint subsided, it was the visitor who spoke first. 'As one with no knowledge of music, I feel it is my duty to lead the defence of this new concerto,' he said, 'so that I can express naïve and inane sentiments in favour of modernism and you can politely shoot me down.'

'We have no guns, Comrade,' Pavel chuckled. 'And even if we did, we have no bullets, we have only an explosive black queen.'

'Let me say, comrades,' the visitor continued, 'this concerto is important, not merely for its musical merits, which you may debate, but as a sign that the times are changing: the era of Georgian ascendancy is passing, and the torch has passed to the Ukraine.'

'Stalin is dead! Long live Nikita Sergeyevich Khrushchev! Saviour of the Khokol race!' shouted Pavel, and was immediately shushed by his colleagues.

'*Pravda* damns the concerto with faint praise,' Raya said, 'which must surely be due to its Zionist sympathies.'

'They say it's full of klezmer tunes,' said Mitrofan, and he began performing a folk tune, first with a bird-like whistle and then a whining violin sound, accompanied by the rapping of spoons on the table edge.

'Shostakovich is our finest composer,' Pavel said. 'Finer even than Tikhon Khrennikov.'

'Surely you jest, Pavel,' Mitrofan wailed. 'Your views on Shostakovich are well known.'

'Do not confuse Pavel's views with those of his colleagues in the Composers' Union,' Kolya said.

'Former colleagues,' said Raya. 'Former colleagues.'

'Farting!' Pavel announced. 'Brilliant farting! Shostakovich is our finest composer, I say, and no one can match him in writing music to be played on the lower bowel!'

'Be quiet, Pavel,' hissed Kolya. 'Before our friend here is obliged to arrest us all.'

'On what charge, pray tell? Blasphemy?'

'Bad taste,' said Kolya. 'Speaking of which, have another round of Mitrofan's third-rate vodka.'

'Next time let me provide the vodka,' the visitor said. 'But let me rescue you all by changing the subject. I have not brought enough handcuffs for you all, so let us steer away from controversy. Tell me about you work here. Tell me about the Chinese taste in music.'

'Execrable, I'm afraid,' said Meretrenko. 'We have our work cut out for us.'

'Old symphonic warhorses,' Pavel said. 'That's all they want to play. Oh yes, and romantic piano music, like the second concerto of Brahms . . .'

'Ba-la-mo, you mean,' Mitrofan interjected.

'Yes, and, what's the other one? La-ker . . .'

'La-ker-man-yi-nou-fu!' Mitrofan announced triumphantly. 'The last great luo-man-ti-ker!'

'Anything, in other words, that inspires deep and imprecise feelings,' Pavel said.

'It is sad, but true,' Raya joined in. 'I have tried to interest the faculty and the better students in something more sophisticated,' she said over more clinking of bottles and glasses, 'Scriabin' – clink – 'Prokofiev' – clink – 'More, Kirill?' – clink – 'even Mahler . . .'

'Or Bartók, or Khrennikov . . .' Pavel added.

'Ha!' Mitrofan barked.

'Khrennikov writes perfectly serviceable socialist realism,' Pavel said. 'Like a well-oiled tractor.'

'But all to no avail,' Raya continued. 'They are fixed on this grand plan they have to perform Beethoven's Ninth with all-

Chinese musicians, as if it were a kind of musical Everest they must climb.'

'God knows what they would see from the top,' Mitrofan said. 'Clouds. Frozen Englishmen.'

'The English have succeeded,' Kolya said. 'Didn't you know?'

'I played some Mahler to several of the faculty on the gramophone in my office,' Raya went on. 'I played them the Eighth Symphony, the choral one, and I even quoted to them Mahler's claim that he had captured the music of the spheres . . .'

'He claimed that?!' Pavel interjected. 'What an imposter that man was!'

'These are no longer human voices, but coursing planets and suns,' Mitrofan intoned. 'Isn't that how it goes, Raya?'

'That's it exactly; but it was as if they could not absorb it, like water from a duck's feathers. They had nothing to say about it.'

'I think I understand their reaction,' Pavel said, sounding more sober. 'I suspect that in some way they simply do not hear it; it is pure white for them, their ears are not attuned to it and it slides off them.'

'Their ears have walls, you mean?' said Mitrofan.

'Oh, I like that,' Raya said. 'Their ears have walls; that is well said.'

'At the faculty meeting last week,' Pavel continued, 'I mentioned in passing that Beethoven's Ninth was Hitler's favourite piece of music, and that he had it played at his birthday parties.'

'And the response?'

'Dead silence.'

'Ah, yes,' said the visitor, 'but that is understandable. They feel the need of grandeur in their music to match the grandeur in their souls.'

'But what about suffering in their music to match the suffering in their souls?' Pavel said.

'Spoken like a true European,' said Raya. 'You Europeans want music to accompany you in your depression. This does

203

not occur to those of us from the North, and certainly not to the Chinese, for whom music is about liberation, not suffering.'

I heard the visitor's voice again, but it was hushed all of sudden, and for several minutes they continued to speak in murmurs I could not pick up. Gradually the alcohol began to reassert itself and their voices were raised. I realised that they were talking about Yu Huiyong, and the Campaign against Debussy. Raya said she had heard that Yu had links to Mao Zedong's wife, Jiang Qing, who, she explained to her guest, had been a film actress and opera producer in Shanghai, and still had many close friends in the city. The real purpose of the Campaign, Raya understood, was to destabilise Ho Luting, who was regarded by Jiang Qing as too bourgeois. 'It is well known that he admires Debussy,' she said, 'and that at heart he looks down upon traditional Chinese music. It is rumoured that he invites students to his house to listen to records, and corrupts them with these Frenchmen – not Debussy, of course, but Ravel, Fauré, Poulenc, Franck . . .'

'Belgian,' Pavel interjected, 'Franck was Belgian.'

'So was the campaign successful?' the visitor asked. 'Will the Director leave in disgrace?'

'It is too early to say, but it seems to me the campaign has been a failure,' Kolya said. 'The Director put up a good fight, and may have postponed his downfall. The burning of the scores was the purest theatre, a ritual self-immolation from which he emerged unscathed. And in the meantime all that he has lost is Debussy. This no doubt irritates him, but he is not undermined.'

'He is a friend of Zhou Enlai's, I understand,' the visitor said.

'That may be overstating it,' Raya said. 'Surely, Kirill, you would know that everyone who has ever met Zhou Enlai believes he is a friend.'

'But he has better reason than most to believe so,' said Kolya. 'Have you not seen the photographs he has in his office? Conducting his little orchestra in the caves at Yan'an, with Mao and Zhou and Deng Xiao Ping listening; playing Schubert and Mozart to the cadres while the Kuomintang fly their bombers overhead? I believe Zhou still consults him on cultural policy, which he regards as very important for matters of state.'

'But this does not mean Zhou will defend him,' Pavel said. 'One cannot take loyalty too far, you know.'

'Shut up, Pavel!' Raya hissed. 'You are drunk again.'

There was a shuffling noise from the apartment, and Fyodor Meretrenko bade good night to everyone. I stepped into the deep shadows as he passed me and descended the stairs.

'It is late,' said Pavel. 'We should go too. But first, Mitrofan, show us what you have in that bag. Comrade Mitrofan is our scavenger. He scouts out food and other oddities in the city. You know he even found . . .'

'Be quiet, Pavel!' Kolya snapped. 'Be quiet and let Mitrofan show us what he has.'

'Wonders will never cease!'

'What is it?'

'A bird, of course.'

'Yes, but what kind of bird?'

'Dead, for a start.'

'A seagull, Kolya, a mascot for our little Chekhovian band!'

'But we have no gun,' Raya said, 'only a shotgun cartridge.'

'Kirill could get us a gun, I'll bet.' Pavel's voice. 'What do you say, Comrade? Can you bring us a gun on your next visit?'

'We are diplomats now, remember,' the visitor said. 'But I will check the drawers in my new desk in case there is a spare.'

'It is not a seagull,' Mitrofan said. 'It's a sea bird alright, but that beak is too long. When I first saw it in the pawn shop, in the shadows under a pile of old hats, I thought it might be a dodo. It isn't, sadly, but the shopkeeper couldn't tell me what it is, and it has no label other than this on the base. Does anyone read English?'

'I do, a little,' the visitor said. 'Let me see: "Christ Church".'

'That narrows it down. It's a religious bird, then. Some kind of dove, perhaps? Although it's far too big for that.'

'It is a fine specimen,' Kolya said. 'I like the tapering of the beak, and these eyes.'

'They are fake, Kolya, you idiot!'

'Christ Church is a college at Oxford University in England,' said the visitor, 'so I imagine our little friend is from the collection of some British ornithologist, one who ran out of money for his expeditions and contracted a disease and died in Shanghai.'

'Of course, that's it! A phoenix! It's Director Ho's phoenix!'

'What is that?'

'What it is, Kirill my friend, is a very long story,' Kolya said. 'Perhaps some other time.'

'I will put it in my room and wait for it to sing, and when it does I will tune my hurdy-gurdy to it,' said Mitrofan.

'You are right, perhaps some other time,' the visitor said. 'No more vodka, thank you. I must go now. The car has been waiting for me half an hour already.'

I retreated up the stairwell as the sounds of farewell emerged from the apartment. The visitor, still arranging his coat around his shoulders, came out onto the landing, where he was joined by Kolya.

'What a pleasant surprise to meet up with you again,' Kolya said. 'And here, of all places. You have done well for yourself, Kirill.'

'You think so? You thought I would come to nothing, did you not?'

'I was drunk, my friend, and that was many years ago. How is your family? Your wife? Your children?'

'The children are well, I believe; I barely get to see them now. My wife . . . well, she has her life, her circle of friends and family.'

'And some time you must tell me what exactly brings you here,' Kolya said.

'It is simple: the Seventh Fleet brought me here,' Kirill said.

'I didn't know we had a Seventh Fleet.'

'We don't.' Kirill clasped Kolya's shoulders quickly and made his way down the stairs.

*

I related this conversation to Madame Huang the next morning, but withheld from her Raya's explanation of the anti-Debussy campaign and the arrival of the phoenix bird. I am not sure why I did this. Perhaps I thought the former was idle speculation and the latter no more than harmless mockery. Even so, she was less interested in the disparaging comments about Chinese musical tastes than she was in the visitor Kirill's reference to his car and the seventh fleet. I asked her if she knew anything about Kirill. 'He must be the new defence attaché at the consulate,' she said. 'He is responsible for liaison with the Southern Command of the People's Liberation Army. We are very interested in him.'

The phoenix did not sing to Mitrofan, but it did aggravate his asthma and it was passed around the various apartments until it settled on Pavel and Raya's sideboard. Kirill from the consulate returned once a week, bringing a bottle of vodka which he consumed over the course of the evening either on the fourth or the sixth floor, most often in the company of Kolya, Pavel and Raya, and sometimes also Mitrofan and Sasha, a garlicky young woman who taught French horn and complained constantly of the twin afflictions of migraines and ladders in her stockings. Fyodor and Ksenia were occasionally present, but always excused themselves early to go to bed. The door was usually left open, but the talk seemed to me unremarkable: world events, new books that had arrived at the consulate, life after Stalin, the difficulties of living in Shanghai, and the growing pains of Pavel and Raya's son. Months passed, and then a year. A simple routine of music and espionage. Kirill disappeared for weeks at a time, and then altogether. There was an occasional titbit of information about another of the Russian advisors, or a reflection upon a Chinese member of the faculty or the activities of Chen Yun, Liu Shaoqi or (very occasionally) Mao himself. Madame Huang received my briefings impassively, and after a while suggested we meet only once a fortnight, and then not at all, except if anything came up that sounded particularly important.

8. Flowers

In May of 1957, the *Shanghai Liberation Daily* – like every other newspaper in China – published Mao Zedong's essay 'On the Correct Handling of Contradictions among the People'. When I arrived at the Conservatory that morning it was pinned to the front door for all to read. Diversity of thought was a constructive thing, Mao wrote, and now that China had successfully emerged as a socialist nation in the years since the Civil War such diversity could be encouraged. The essay contained the sentence that was to be on everyone's lips for the next two months, and then locked away inside the deepest cavern of our thoughts for the next decade:

Let a hundred flowers bloom and a hundred schools of thought contend.

At the time I was taken up with watching two particular flowers bloom. First, I had been invited to join the second violins in the Shanghai Symphony Orchestra for their upcoming all-Chinese performance of Beethoven's Ninth Symphony. The practice rooms were down by the river, in a large warehouse upstairs from a fish market. Rehearsals began in late May, and coincided with the arrival of the *huang-mei*, a month of rain named after the yellow plum that ripens at that time of year. The rain itself, which came daily in gushing downpours, brought a temporary respite from the humidity and the heat. During that month, green mould formed on stored clothes, and we made jokes about our bed sheets yielding a crop of fresh mushrooms every morning. At night in the orchestra practice rooms, the smell of the day's commerce of fish gained in strength, until rehearsals were like a two-hour bath in a bowl of stale fish soup. I got Ling Ling to leave me a bucket of warm water in the hallway, so that I could wash the smell off my skin when I returned home.

The other flower bloomed in mid-June. Pavel Gachev had returned to Russia for the summer, and Raya Vishinsky was to stay on for a couple of weeks to finish some research before joining him. The night after Pavel left Kirill visited again, bringing a bottle of vodka and talking quietly with Raya for an hour before leaving in his car. It was the first occasion he had visited in Pavel's absence. This time they kept the door closed in spite of the humidity, and so I stood in the dark with my ear pressed to the keyhole, picking up the occasional phrase but nothing more.

The following night Kirill arrived again, this time carrying a large bag in his arms. Raya closed the door again, but after a couple of minutes opened it and waved a cloud of cigarette smoke into the corridor. I shrank into a corner as she stood in the doorway for a moment and took a long pull on her cigarette, turning it in her fingers and studying it while she breathed out through her nose and mouth simultaneously. She returned to her guest, but left the door ajar. I positioned myself by the door, amidst the slowly sinking drifts of hazy blue. Kirill was explaining that he had to go away the following week on consulate business. 'To Beijing?' Raya asked.

'No,' Kirill replied. 'To Moscow first. Marshall Peng De Huai the Defence Minister will be there for talks with Khrushchev. So I must be there also. And then afterwards I go to Paris and London and Washington.'

'Washington? Why Washington?'

'Some senior members of the Central Committee wish to go on a journey. It is my job to check out the accommodation and to ensure they receive a warm welcome.'

'So you are a travel agent, Kirill? Another string to your bow.'

'This is very special travel. Many, many people must independently cover great distances, and arrive simultaneously at new destinations.'

'Perhaps I should not have asked the question, and perhaps I would not understand the answer even if you told me.'

There was the clink of bottle on glass.

At that moment I heard the rustle of feet on the stairs above me, and the sound of several voices, including Comrade Meretrenko's. I sprang to my feet. With the light from the open door there was nowhere for me to hide. I took a few steps forward, heading down to the next floor, but then heard more voices and footsteps approaching from below. I was caught, and in my panic I slipped through the open door into the vestibule of Raya's apartment, hoping to hide there until the ascending and descending parties had crossed. Beyond the thin curtain, Raya and her guest continued to talk; but when they heard the commotion as Comrade Meretrenko greeted his neighbours in the corridor, Raya said, 'I should close that door now,' and came towards me. I quickly stepped in the coat cupboard, whose entrance was covered by another thin curtain, and found myself awkwardly positioned amidst padded winter jackets, women's knee-length boots, a broom and a floor mop. Raya closed the apartment door, and the chain-lock rattled into place.

For several minutes I stood perfectly still, waiting for the thumping in my chest to subside and for my breathing to return to normal. Raya and her guest were talking quietly about Raya's plans to visit her mother in Leningrad the following month. Then they were silent for a long time, so long in fact that I began to wonder if they had fallen into a drunken sleep. Then I heard the man's voice again. 'I have brought you a new record. Viktor brought it back from Paris for me.'

'A corrupting French composer?' Raya asked.

'What else?' Kirill said. 'It is Maurice Ravel. Let me play you my favourite piece. It is a kind of gypsy tune called *Tzigane*. Perhaps you know it.'

After a moment the music began: a dramatic solo piece on the violin, full of double-stopping, a difficult technique in which two notes are played simultaneously on separate strings. The music brought to my mind a Uighur dance I had once seen in Harbin, when a caravan of traders came to the edge of the city to sell pelts and knives and roots of ginseng (which, my mother pointed out to me, bore a striking resemblance to boiled children). The dancers – two men, one young, the other old – were tied together at the wrists, as if engaged in a ritual fight to the death, and flung each other around a circular earthen pit. Here too, in this music, there were bursts of energy followed by vertiginous pauses on single notes; and then the melody and the harmony, and with them my imaginary dancers, would swoop once again, twisting and turning around their locked wrists, centrifuge and pivot, planet and moon, matching limb to limb, muscle to muscle, flank to flank, face to face. It was like nothing I had heard before.

The piece lasted a good ten minutes, and when it finished there was silence once more, except for the repeated clicking of the stylus as the record spun beneath it. I waited for someone to raise the arm of the record player and for the clicking to end, but it did not. After several minutes I stole a glance from my hiding place into the vestibule, and then, hearing nothing at all from Raya and her guest, I tiptoed across the floor and put my face to the curtain, trying to catch a glimpse of what lay beyond. I could see only a sliver of the scene between the two halves of the curtain. I saw a portion of Kirill's bare shoulder, peppered with black hairs, and the back of his head; and lodged in the crook of his neck I saw the sole of Raya's foot, still clothed in a dark stocking, but with a large hole at the heel. Behind her heel I saw Raya's face. She was supporting herself on her elbows, her lips oddly pursed, her eyes flicking up and down, her brows flinching as if she were receiving treatment from some rough doctor. She tried without success to blow away a strand of hair that had fallen across her face, and then smiled and mouthed '*spasiba*' as Kirill's hand brushed it back. Then she brought

211

her arms forward and hoisted herself towards Kirill and her face appeared by his elbow, her eyes clenched tightly shut for a moment before they opened in a wide blank stare. I turned aside quickly for fear she would see me, and all I heard from then on was the sound of their breathing, gasps of laughter or surprise or disappointment, audible beneath the gentle clicking from the record player.

I retreated to the coat cupboard. My heart was beating fast and my temples hurt. The music was playing again in my head, and although I tried to I could not halt its progress. And this time I saw in my mind's eye, not the beautiful dance I had imagined previously, but the clasping of bodies, the clammy smell of warm breath, and the release of folds of flesh from sweat-moistened clothing.

After a while the apartment fell silent. I contemplated letting myself out, but realised that it would involve releasing the chain-lock. Even if the noise did not disturb the lovers within, the unattached chain might alert Raya to the fact that someone else had been in the apartment with them. I decided I would have to take my chances in the morning, and tried to make myself comfortable and to formulate what I would say in the event that I was discovered. An hour passed, and I was drifting in and out of sleep when I heard a noise next to me. Someone was standing outside the door of the apartment, and whoever it was began to knock on the door, gently at first and then more loudly. It must have been the driver from the consulate, impatient to retrieve his charge and return home to his bed. Within minutes I heard Kirill unhook the chain and let himself out, leaving the chain swinging free. I seized the moment and slipped from my hiding place into the vestibule and then out into the stairwell.

Back in my room I found my own bed, and as I lay waiting for sleep I heard the distant bells of the old Custom House, playing 'The East is Red' followed by two long tones.

*

Madame Huang carefully noted down the events of the previous night. I explained how I had ended up inside the apartment, and what Raya and her friend Kirill had said. 'Her foot was where?' Madame Huang asked, and as she wrote she tried several times to banish the smile that crept like a kitten across her face. She was most pleased with the revelation that Kirill was going to London and Washington. 'Now this is very important, and we need to know more. But it poses a problem for us,' she said. 'We cannot rely upon the door being left open.' Madame Huang pondered the question for a while, tapping her chin with end of a pencil. 'When did Comrade Vishinsky say she was leaving for the Soviet Union?' she asked. I told her I thought it was within the next couple of weeks. 'Good,' she said, and dismissed me.

In the weeks that followed, the Hundred Flowers Movement gathered momentum. There were protests against the Party and its elitism. 'Party members enjoy many privileges which make them a race apart,' complained one opinion piece in the *Shanghai Liberation Daily*. There were reports of the establishment of a Democracy Wall at Beijing University, covered with posters critical of the Party. Art and culture was suddenly in vogue. The papers published poetry by poets whose voices had not been heard for years. The Shanghai Symphony Orchestra was given new quarters, and we found ourselves rehearsing in the reception hall of a former embassy on Bubbling Well Road in the old International Settlement.

Meanwhile Director Ho published an article praising the prize-winning pianist Fu Cong, and the inspiration he had received from his father, Fu Lei, the translator of bourgeois French novels, who had received no mention in the initial enthusiasm over Fu Cong's success. Ho expressed regret that China had not passed through a capitalist phase, since he believed that would have inspired a more adventurous musical culture and produced many more performers like Fu Cong, not to mention works by Chinese composers that could have ranked alongside Beethoven's Ninth Symphony. He urged Chinese parents to encourage any signs of musical talent in their children, and to hold out to them the prospect of competing in international competitions, and winning accolades for their country.

Things also improved in the Foreign Teachers' Building. It was announced that the plumbing system would be completely modernised, and that work on the project would begin immediately. Although they had not complained about the plumbing system in the building, the Russian advisors were happy to go along with the idea. Asked why the haste, it was made clear that funds had been freed up from elsewhere and workmen were available. Besides, several of the Russian advisors were returning to visit their families during the summer, so June and July would be the least disruptive time to do the work. Raya Vishinsky brought forward her travel plans, packed her suitcase and was gone within days.

*

In September 1957 I received another letter from my mother. The Hundred Flowers were blooming in Harbin too, she wrote, and in the food stalls by the riverbank people met to talk late into the night about their hopes and their frustrations. *Everywhere there is argument*, she wrote. *In the streets, the markets, in factories, in the alleyways, in the hospital. It is as if life is our adversary, and every step forward must be won by belligerence and contention.* Kasimir and Piroshka had returned to Moscow, she added, matter-of-factly, to look after their son. And my father's health was not good, she went on. He had stopped riding his bicycle after several bad falls, one of which had led to a broken finger. But he continued to go to work most days, she assured me, and, she added, I should not even think of returning home. She and my father had discussed the possibility and agreed I should wait until the end of my studies.

I sat on my bed reading the letter over and over until I knew every stroke of every character that had flowed from my mother's pen, and as I read they released into my mind a flood of tiny, half-formed thoughts, like unresolved chords. That was where Ling Ling found me some time afterwards, sitting motionless with the letter in my lap. 'Where were you?' she said. 'We had a booking for a practice room, but you never turned up, so we lost it. Tian is mad with you.' When I didn't respond she sat down beside me on the bed quietly, and, placing her chin on my shoulder, began to read the letter. 'Bad news?' she asked.

'My father is sick,' I said. 'My mother is protecting me from the truth. She won't tell me how sick he is.'

'Then you must go to him,' she said, 'despite what your mother says.' And she sprang to her feet, and then crouched down beside me and pulled her suitcase from beneath the bed. She opened it, thrust her hand amongst her clothes and produced a small cloth pouch. From this she took a roll of bank notes and peeled off several. 'Here,' she said, folding the notes and pressing them into my palm. 'You'll need this to pay for your ticket. We can go the station right away and buy it.'

I looked up at her without speaking, and in response she closed my fingers over the money and squeezed my hand shut. 'But of course you'll need permission from the Director,' she said. 'We'll go to his office first.' And with that she pulled me to my feet, threaded her arm through mine, and guided me downstairs to the street and around the corner to the Conservatory.

We sat in Director Ho's office waiting for him to appear, while his secretary roamed about rustling papers and sighing at us. After an hour Director Ho bustled in, trailing a line a smoke from the freshly-lit cigarette in his hand. He made for his desk, and then stopped short when he saw us perched on the edge of his low sofa. The secretary appeared at his side. 'I'll tell them to come back later,' he said to Director Ho.

'No, no, no,' Director Ho said. 'We all have work to do. Better to deal with things when we can.' He sat down opposite us and drew on his cigarette, sucking as much out of it as he could before stamping it into an ashtray on the table between us. 'Please,' he said, 'tell me your business.'

I found my voice and began to explain the letter from my mother, the news of my father's illness, the reasons why I should ignore their plea that I remain in Shanghai. Ho listened intently,

215

muttering short affirmations at the end of each of my statements and from time to time rubbing his cheeks and eyebrows with his fingers, as if trying to wipe something from his skin.

'Show me the letter,' he said. I gave it to him and watched the top of his head as he smoothed out the pages on his knee and read it. 'You are right,' he said as he folded the letter and returned it to me. 'You must go to see your father. His condition appears serious.' He leaned back in his chair, and turned his face towards the window and the trees in the courtyard shedding their blossom. Ling Ling squeezed my hand tight. Without turning back to me, Director Ho went on, 'But first there is something you must do – a small detour, you might say.'

He paused. 'A detour?' I said.

He turned back to face me. 'I want you to pack your things and be ready to leave immediately. It may be tonight or tomorrow morning,' he said.

'Leave for Harbin?' I said.

'No,' he said. 'For Moscow or Bucharest. As of yet I can't tell you which one. In both cities there is an international competition. Our friend Comrade Meretrenko tells me your playing is of a very high standard, and that you are ready for such things.'

I began to protest my unworthiness, but Director Ho rose to his feet and summoned his secretary. 'I have no time for shows of false modesty,' he said, turning back to me. 'You would not be at this Conservatory if you did not have talent. Now leave me. I have to find seats on an aeroplane going west.' He ushered us from his office and shut the door behind us.

Before dawn the next morning I was woken by Madame Huang and bundled into a military car purring quietly at the entrance to our building. She handed me a small booklet. It was a passport, with a photograph of me that had been taken when I first arrived at the Conservatory at the age of thirteen. 'You are flying to Bucharest this morning with Director Ho and Tian Mei Yun,' she told me. 'There is an international competition. We have instructions to send our best performers. There was a military plane available, and we could not pass up the opportunity.'

She sat beside me as we drove through the quiet streets towards the outskirts of the city. 'There is something else you should know,' she said after a while. 'Our great pianist, Fu Cong, has defected to the West.'

'Why?' I said.

'It is said he has fallen in love with the daughter of Yehudi Menuhin,' she replied. 'No doubt he has also fallen in love with the life of ease his father enjoyed, and fallen out of love with China and its people.'

'And Director Ho . . .'

'Director Ho sees one of the stars on our country's flag trembling, and wants Tian and you to reach out your hands to steady it.'

'What do you mean?' I asked. 'Which one of the stars? The one that represents the bourgeois?'

She turned away from me and looked out of the opposite window and was quiet for so long that I thought she would not reply to my question. 'I am a simple person,' she said eventually. 'I know a lot about the struggle of our people, but I know very little about music. So my advice to you is the same advice I gave to my brother's son when he left for the war in Korea.'

'And what was that?'

'Do not fail.'

I wanted to ask if her brother's son had failed; but by the way she turned her face from me once more and put her hand to the window I knew immediately what her answer would be. We rode on in silence, and after half an hour arrived at an airfield behind a row of low-slung barracks. Our car passed two check-points, and was then ushered onto the tarmac where a squat silver-grey aeroplane was being refuelled. Director Ho and Tian Mei Yun were waiting for me at the foot of the steps. 'Hurry up,' Director Ho said. 'The pilot wants to leave as soon as possible.' He took my suitcase from me and carried it up the steps on his head, like a coolie. Inside we were ordered to strap ourselves into the hard seats for take off. Apart from the three of us, the plane was filled with soldiers, young officers going to Bucharest for training, we were told. They seemed to have orders to speak to no one. Director Ho leaned over to me. 'I have discussed this with Comrade Meretrenko,' he said. 'He has recommended the pieces you are to play. The scores are in my satchel.'

It was my first flight, and had I not been wedged beside a large soldier who smoked incessantly and then fell into a fitful snoring sleep, I might have enjoyed it. After three or four hours we were all jolted into alertness as the plane lurched forward into a steep dive. The engines began to whine and the fuselage rattled and juddered. The soldier next to me woke up, blinking rapidly, and seized the armrest tightly. A hot water flask tumbled down the aisle and came to rest against the door to the cockpit. Pressure began to build up in my ears, dulling the strained sound of the engines. I looked behind me and saw Director Ho and Tian, eyes tight shut, backs pushed into their seats, cheeks taut and drained of colour.

After several minutes, the plane came out of its dive, and moments later dropped its undercarriage and drifted in to land. I heard Tian vomit into a bag in the seat behind me, and I realised that I had grabbed hold of the hand of the soldier next to me and had sunk my nails into his skin. He held up his hand and looked at the tiny white crescent-shaped marks on the back of his hand. 'Air force pilots,' he said. 'They say it's a perfectly safe way to land, but I can never get used to it.' We had arrived at an airstrip in what seemed to be an endless plain marked by scuffs of dry grass and thorny shrubs. We filed out of the plane and wandered around the airstrip rubbing our eyes and shaking life back into our limbs. The temperature was near freezing, but the air was dry and fresh. After the roar of the aircraft engine it seemed unnaturally silent, as if the cold desert air around us was absorbing all sound.

I walked to the edge of the airstrip, enjoying while I could the crunch of gravel beneath my shoes, and noticed for the first time that the plain was not flat, but was dotted with small gently-sloping mounds of earth, of a uniform height, about half a metre. Like burial mounds, I thought, but immediately dismissed the idea, since there were so many of them, and they were spaced irregularly across so wide and expansive an area. Turning back to the plane, I watched Director Ho help Tian Mei Yun down the steps, whereupon our most promising young pianist spread out his padded coat on the tarmac and lay down on his back. Director Ho stood over Tian and appeared to exchange a few words with him. Tian flailed an arm around, like an insect that had been crushed under a bicycle tyre. The sound of their conversation died before it reached me.

Director Ho left Tian and joined me at the edge of the runway. He held out to me a thin parcel of musical scores, tied with blue ribbon. 'Bach,' he said – the word seemed loud and harsh – and then, 'Brahms and Mozart too,' each composer's name bringing forth a puff of steam from his mouth. I took the parcel from him. There was a note attached to the top score with a paper clip. *Wan shi ru yi*, it said, in Comrade Meretrenko's uneven and trembling characters. May ten thousand good things fall into your hands. 'He's rather late for Chinese New Year,' Director Ho commented.

In the distance a gearbox chuckled, followed by the low complaint of an engine. We searched the horizon until Director Ho pointed out some low roofs in the distance, and a truck crawling across the desert towards us carrying a large tank. He returned to the prostrate figure of Tian Mei Yun and crouched down on one knee beside him. I turned away from the plane and read through my scores, filling the emptiness around me with the sound of an imaginary violin.

Refuelling took half an hour, after which I helped Director Ho carry Tian, clammy with sweat despite the cold, back to his seat. We took off again, and in the course of the next ten hours our plane hopped across the continent, chasing the retreating sun and performing its dive-bomb landing at airfields in Uzbekistan and Azerbaijan to refuel. Towards evening we floated over the Black Sea – sparkling like a sheet of hammered gold – and landed into the setting sun at Bucharest airport.

A squat military truck backed up to our plane in the twilight as we disembarked, and wordlessly the soldiers and the pilots swung their bags into it and climbed aboard. The truck disappeared into the darkness, and the three of us walked to the arrivals hall, where a solitary official studied our passports, holding mine upside down until he found the photograph page, and sighed to himself as if we were some unfortunate fact of life, then raised a heavy blank telephone receiver and spoke softly into it for a minute before stamping our documents and waving us through a pair of solid wooden doors.

We found ourselves alone in a draughty hall with a high vaulted ceiling from which two rows of bare light bulbs hung on long cords, casting about a grainy blue luminance. Tian lowered himself into a corner by a pillar and hung his head between his knees. Director Ho and I stood in the centre of the hall and watched the only other occupant of the place, a fat-cheeked woman who was washing the floor and who punctuated the rhythmic sway of her mop with loud wet sniffing. She made her way directly towards us from the far end of the hall, not acknowledging our presence until her mop brushed Director Ho's shoes. She stopped her work, straightened her back, sniffed loudly and studied us for a moment, tilting her head to take us in. Then she resumed her mopping, making a detour around us so as to leave us standing on a dry semicircle of floor surrounded by wet slick.

A man dressed in a Mao suit stepped through the main entrance, blinking as his eyes adjusted to the light. When he spied us at the far end of the hall he turned quickly on his heels and strode towards us calling out apologies and clapping his hands repeatedly just beneath his chin. We pulled Tian to his feet, and the man introduced himself as an official from the Embassy of the People's Republic of China, before gathering up as much of our luggage as he could fit beneath his arms and leading us into dark night, where a car waited. I sat in the front, wedged between the official and the driver, while in the back Tian slumped across Director Ho's lap, breathing heavily.

Director Ho wiped his brow with a large handkerchief and whispered to him.

'The Triumphal Arch!' called our driver, raising a stubby finger in front of my face and wagging it at a floodlit edifice. He proceeded to point out the Great Hall of the Palace, various darkened castles and monasteries, and orthodox churches whose curved turrets reminded me of those dotted around Harbin. I was straining to hear what Director Ho was saying to Tian in the back seat: I caught only a repeated assurance that he would feel better in the morning, and a reminder that all of China's hopes were resting upon his shoulders.

At the embassy I was shown to a small high-ceilinged room whose single light bulb succumbed with a soft pop after a second of life. In the brief flash of light I registered a narrow cot, a threadbare rug beside it and a small chair and table beneath a window. There was a sheet of notepaper on the table and I picked it up and studied it in the dim moonlight from the window. Something was written on it, but try as I might I could not make it out. I set it down, stowed my case and violin in a corner, and went immediately to bed.

The note turned out to be a set of instructions to the dining hall in the basement, and at first light I made my way through the damp corridors of the building, guided at the last few turns by the smell of cooked cabbage. Director Ho was already there, in his characteristic white cotton shirt with the sleeves loosely rolled, talking with a sallow-faced man wearing a high-collared jacket. They were hunched over a table arrayed with small plates of food and a porcelain tea pot. Director Ho was pouring tea into two glasses and, upon seeing me in the doorway, summoned me and reached for a third glass. The other man reached his hand across the table as I sat down and introduced himself as the ambassador. 'Welcome to Bucharest,' he said, his voice thin, with a rising cat-like inflexion. 'I hope your journey was not too exhausting, and that you slept well.'

Before I could reply, Director Ho had started explaining the schedule for the four days of the George Enescu International

Competition: at ten in the morning, formal registration at the Romanian Athenaeum; an hour each day to practice with the accompanist; then the drawing of lots to decide playing order, and then hours of waiting until my turn. Every evening there would be a reception. Tonight's would be at the Cantacuzino Palace hosted by the Composers' Union of Romania. He slurped at his glass of tea, and I quickly asked how Tian was. 'We found a doctor for him at midnight,' Director Ho said. 'It is not serious. A bad case of airsickness, that's all.'

'Made worse by nerves, perhaps?' said the ambassador.

'He has no nerves,' said Ho. 'At least, not of that kind.'

At that Tian himself arrived at the door, briefly steadied himself and walked gingerly towards us before lowering himself into a chair. He seemed exhausted by the effort and mumbled a greeting before dropping his head onto his forearms. Director Ho, the ambassador and I exchanged glances. Tian drew breath in long gasps.

It was the ambassador who broke the silence: 'How do you feel, Comrade?' He smiled hopefully at me across the table.

'Not bad,' said Tian, without raising his head, and then he muttered something I could not hear.

'What did you say?' Director Ho asked, placing a hand on Tian's shoulder. Tian repeated himself, his words again lost beneath his breath, and when none of us responded he raised his head with great effort and looked at each of us in turn, his eyes puffy and his lips cracked and dry.

'I think I'll play the Schubert,' he said, and then dropped his head onto his forearms once more and was silent.

Director Ho covered his face with his hands and drew breath noisily through the gap in his fingers. Then he spread two fingers to one side and looked down with one watery eye at the back of Tian's bent head. He put his hands on the table and wearily pushed himself to his feet. 'You must rest first,' he said to Tian, taking him by the shoulders and gently raising him to his feet. 'Fu Cong always slept for two hours before a performance.' I noticed the ambassador's brows tighten at the mention of Fu

Cong, but then he too rose and took one of Tian's arms and the three of them shuffled from the room and disappeared into the stairwell, leaving me with the debris of their breakfast.

The week that followed was a disaster for Tian. He took no part in the competition, and hardly left his bed until it was time to leave. I performed my pieces – sonatas by Mozart and Brahms, and a Bach partita – over the course of several days, in the Romanian Athenaeum, and then, for the final performance, at the newly built Opera House in central Bucharest. While I played, the panel of judges seemed lost in their own reveries or in conversation with each other, but nevertheless I was awarded second prize, winning it jointly with a blonde American woman about my age who was shadowed throughout the competition by a teetering overstuffed sofa of a woman (her mother, I assumed, come to preserve her from the evils of world communism). My rival shook my hand politely during the presentation ceremony, and, when the time came for photographs, broke out the biggest and brightest set of teeth I had ever seen, and then shut them away again.

After the ceremony Director Ho seized my hand in both of his and would not let go. He made several attempts to speak, but his mind was racing so fast that it seemed unable to turn thoughts into words. When I eventually extracted my hand from his grasp to receive the congratulations of one of the judges, Director Ho stammered, 'I must cable Beijing immediately,' and disappeared into the crowd. I barely spoke to him for the rest of the evening, which was spent travelling in a limousine (the Vice-President's, I was told by our driver) to and from a succession of banquets and receptions.

We were due to leave for home at noon the following day; but at five in the morning there was a loud knock on my door. 'Comrade Xiao, Comrade Xiao, are you awake?' It was Director Ho. 'I must talk to you right now,' he said. Before I could get out of bed he had opened the door and entered. He turned on the light, and there was a moment of brightness before the bulb again failed. In that brief second of illumination I saw that his clothes and hair were dishevelled. He held a sheaf of papers in his hand.

'Don't get up,' he said, stumbling in the dark towards the chair and scraping it noisily across the floor to my bedside. 'I have been in constant communication with Beijing since last night,' he said. 'Yes, constant communication, including with the private secretary to Zhou Enlai himself. And I have told them that success can only breed more success.' He paused to lick a drop of spittle from the corner of his mouth. 'One must climb a mountain to see the plain beyond it. That is what I told them.'

In turn he held up each of his papers so that it caught the meagre window light. The first, he said, was an invitation to travel to Paris to prepare for another competition, a much larger one with more competitors and more famous judges. The second was a ticket for a train that left Bucharest in three hours. Visas had been arranged for the two of us, and letters of introduction. Tian would return home at noon as planned. The competition was two weeks away, he explained, and – of this he seemed immensely pleased – in the interim I would receive tuition from the head of violin performance at the Paris Conservatoire, whom Zhou Enlai knew personally from his time in Paris in the 1920s. 'And finally,' he said, laying down the last of his papers, 'to assure you that I have not forgotten how this all began, I have cabled your parents in Harbin with the news, and on our return I will arrange for you to return home to visit your father.'

We sat in silence for a minute, and I realised that other presences had slipped into the room behind Director Ho and waited in the darkness too: the ambassadors of honour and fear. I sensed my father and mother, and Kasimir, and, strangely, the rabbi's wife who had blessed me with a kiss. At that moment I wanted nothing more than to be left alone with these dark shapes in the coolness of the room.

'You must be tired,' I said. 'You have been working on my behalf all night.'

'You might say that,' Director Ho said.

'Perhaps you should get some sleep before we have to leave for the station,' I said. 'Please, just leave the papers on the table. I will meet you at the front gate.'

'Very well,' he said, his voice from the darkness suddenly edged with sadness. He stood and dragged the chair back towards the table by the window. I turned my face to the wall, and listened to the sound of his breathing as he lingered for a moment by the door.

'How is Tian?' I asked as he turned the handle.

'I don't know,' he said. 'I haven't seen him since the night before last. Don't worry about him, though; worry about other things, better things.' He closed the door softly and retreated down the stairs.

9. Cultural Labours

Director Ho and I did not board the train to Paris the next day. Something happened in Beijing overnight, some shift in polarity which one could guess at, but never hope to understand fully. The ambassador intercepted me at my door as I emerged with my suitcase and violin. He explained only that things had changed. Director Ho was nowhere to be found, and I dared not ask after him.

I spent the morning with Tian, who had recovered enough to sit at a refectory table, practicing scales along its near edge and quizzing me about the competition, the judges, the audience, and the other competitors. Only when we had exhausted the subject, and he was executing an extended trill with the right hand amongst some breadcrumbs, setting chopsticks rattling atop a bowl beside me, did he look up momentarily and say, '*Gongxi, gongxi*. Congratulations! You must be very proud.'

'Must I?'

'Of course you must. Pride is a duty too.'

Director Ho did not appear during the morning. I travelled to the airport with Tian beside me in the car wrapped in a blanket; although he assured me he felt much better, he succumbed to fits of shivering and muttered to himself several times that he was not looking forward to the flight. We waited for several hours in a draughty departure lounge. Our friends the soldiers arrived in the middle of the afternoon and greeted us warmly, asking us how the competition had gone. Tian seemed energised by their arrival: he produced a packet of cigarettes from his luggage and made a performance of staggering around the group clapping each soldier on the back and handing him a cigarette. They were a gift from me, he said, to celebrate my victory. The soldiers surrounded me and we shook hands merrily, filling the room with smoke and laughter.

An airport official announced that our plane was ready and we filed out onto the tarmac. It was not until we were seated on the plane that Director Ho arrived, accompanied by the commanding officer. He waved to Tian and me, but spent the journey wedged into the seat next to the commanding officer, speaking to him occasionally in low tones and not leaving the plane at all during its refuelling stops.

On our return to Shanghai we landed at the civilian airport. The plane pulled off the runway and, with its engines still running, deposited Director Ho, Tian and me, along with our luggage, on a grassy verge, and then turned around and roared back into the air, bound for the military airfield on the other side of the city. We trudged across the grass towards the terminal building, carrying suitcases and my violin in its case. A welcoming party of senior officials, faculty and students from the Conservatory rushed forward onto the tarmac to greet us. Three photographers and a camera crew moved around our flank and started pushing some of the bystanders back to allow them a better shot. A martial tune started up on the airport loudspeaker.

First to shake my hand was the Minister of Culture, a man with a face like a moon cake who beamed at me and crushed my hand in both of his. 'Comrades, look this way!' the photographers shouted. We looked, and in the resulting photograph we appear to be fighting over something I am holding in my hand. The bulbs flashed and burned my retinas so that I was blinded as the Minister attempted to present me with a medal and ribbon – 'Hero of Cultural Labour', it said – set in its own red velvet case. 'Comrades, once more!' Another flash. Another magnesium ghost harrowing the surface of my eyes.

And so it went on. The Mayor of Shanghai gave a speech. Flash! A gentle hug from Comrade Meretrenko and a more manly one from his wife. Flash! Two little girls loaded bunches of flowers into my arms. Flash! Flash! Professor Yu approached me, and his hand wriggled like a snake amongst the mound of foliage I was holding, until our fingers touched; he clasped my hand warmly as his eyes searched out mine, and he announced, with a catch in his throat, that I had brought honour to China. Flash!

The crowd encircled me as we moved towards the gate. My suitcase and violin had been seized by a woman in uniform. I called out for Tian, and was told that Director Ho had already taken him to the infirmary. A car door stood open and I was pushed into the back seat with my burden of flowers. The opposite door opened and Professor Yu slid into the seat. 'Now,' he said, as we pulled away, 'there are things we must discuss.' He apologised for the confusion over the competition in Paris. Director Ho had been misled about the dates, he explained. The competition was several months away. In the meantime, there were urgent matters he needed me to deal with. The Conservatory needed to prove itself worthy of China and its people, he said, and I would be in the vanguard. If we failed all could be lost. We all needed to play our part. That was all he could say at that moment. More would be known in a few days.

We spent the rest of the journey in silence. I turned away from him to hide the tears that welled up in my eyes. For I was certain that, whatever else this meant, I would not be allowed to return home to visit my parents.

The following day was a Sunday, so I slept late. Ling Ling took me to the Zhujiaojiao Gardens and we strolled arm in arm along the canals, and sat upstairs in the Moon Pavilion. She fed me sweets and oolong tea and, encased in an aromatic haze, I answered her questions about Bucharest, the finer points of powered flight, and Tian's illness. In the afternoon I returned to my room and as I wearily ascended the stairs I received the greetings of several of my Russian neighbours, among them Pavel and Raya who pressed a small parcel of dried fruit into my hand. On the top floor I flung myself at my bed and did not wake until the following morning.

Ling Ling had disappeared from our room before dawn, and I only met up with her at the gate of the Conservatory. She was bent under the weight of a large item in a canvas cover strapped to her back. 'A piano accordion,' she explained. 'They won't have any pianos where we are going.'

'Where are we going?' I asked. 'I have only just arrived back.'

'No idea,' she said. 'But read that, and you may have some idea what is going on.'

She nodded towards the main door of the Conservatory upon which was pinned the revised text of Mao's article, 'On the Correct Handling of Contradictions Among the People'. I read the document, as usual straining to pierce the familiar recitations of Marxist principle and reach through to some shadowy truth beyond.

What would become apparent was that the words of Mao's original article, after some clarification, were now revealed as censuring the untethered thoughts of intellectuals rather than encouraging public criticism and debate. How absurd that anyone had thought otherwise! In the weeks that followed we came to understand that the Hundred Flowers Movement was over, the scent of the new blooms having proved too pungent for the Party, and the criticisms of its cadres so trenchant and irrefutable as to be unpatriotic. Those who had spoken out were clearly Rightists in temperament, regardless of the sacrifices they may have made during the revolution or the Long March. In Shanghai, intellectuals were publicly shamed: some publishing retractions and self-criticisms, others, we would learn in the months and years to come, simply disappearing. There was whispered speculation that from the start the purpose of the exercise had been to entice 'bad elements' to declare themselves publicly. Perhaps I am fooling myself, but I recall somehow knowing all of this – not its detail, of course, but its essence – as sunlight struck the paper nailed to the Conservatory door and the characters started to swim in a pool of brightness: a surface luminous and painful to behold, but with depths of meaning refracted and elusive, shooting this way and that like tiny fish under the surface of a pond.

Ling Ling was at my shoulder. 'Tian was at the Director's house last night, so he may know more.'

'Tian is better?'

'Well enough, so it seems.' In a low voice, she related what she had been told the night before as I slept – that Director Ho was to be severely censured for praising Fu Cong and his father, Fu Lei; that the performance of Beethoven's Ninth was now postponed; that the whole Conservatory was under suspicion, and the faculty had decided that, to re-establish its revolutionary credentials, all students would be assigned to 'cultural labouring' tasks amongst the workers and peasants for the remainder of the summer. We were to pack up our instruments and a small bag of personal items and report to the Conservatory courtyard at midday.

'I want to stash this thing in the common room,' Ling Ling said, hoisting the piano accordion onto her back. 'Then let's go home and pack.'

*

We joined the crowd in the courtyard at midday. Tian and the Director arrived together, Tian with a bulging satchel over his shoulder, a cello case in one hand, and a locked metal case in the other. Director Ho greeted me warmly and handed me a copy of the *People's Daily*. The front page carried a report of the competition in Bucharest, referring to my 'victory'. I had fought bravely against great odds, it read. I had outsmarted my opponents, and had completed my prize-winning performance with the strains of 'The East is Red' ringing in my ears, a feat I found difficult to imagine. There was no mention of the American woman, and the winner of the violin section of the competition was identified only as 'a Ukrainian'. Nor was there any mention of Tian Mei Yun, the pianist who had spent the entire trip staring at the ceiling of his room.

The Director took me aside and laid his hand on my shoulder. 'Please accept my apologies,' he said, 'but for the time being I cannot arrange . . .'

'I understand,' I interjected.

He dropped his head. 'It is out of my hands, I am sorry.' With that he disappeared inside the main building.

Tian started to explain that the metal case was full of sheet music, and that he had spent the previous evening going through Director Ho's collection, selecting music that they thought would be fitted for the task of 'cultural labouring'. Ling Ling asked if he knew our destination, but we were immediately called to attention by Ding Shangde, the Deputy Director, who stood up on a chair and read out a list assigning each student to one of three teams. I was grouped with Ling Ling, Tian and a dozen other students, and Ding announced that we were to join the Hainan Autonomous Prefecture Cultural Work Team. A truck would carry us and our luggage to the station, where we would catch the train south to Guangzhou, and from there a ferry to the island of Hainan in the South China Sea, where we would help teach socialist principles to villagers from the Miao ethnic minority.

The train journey lasted twenty hours, and when our fellow passengers discovered that we were musicians on our way to join a cultural work team we felt obliged to put on an impromptu performance. Ling Ling strapped on her piano accordion, and we sang our way through the standard repertoire of revolutionary songs, finishing with the chorus from 'The Red Detachment of Women', which many of the passengers knew by heart. Afterwards, a young man from Guangzhou attached himself to us, insisting on singing for us, in a voice shaky with some deep infirmity in his chest, a traditional song from his home village complete with rather feminine hand gestures and a sad tilt of cheek and eyebrow. Then he shared around cigarettes, and told Tian what he knew about the Miao people while Ling

Ling and I dozed. 'Miao men share their wives with guests,' he said, bending his head towards Tian, 'especially those who bring a gift of rice wine.'

'And are Miao women worth a bottle of rice wine?' Tian asked.

'Definitely,' the young man said, 'in some cases, two bottles.' Ling Ling shuffled around on her hard seat, and I saw the shadow of a smile on her lips. I glanced discreetly at Tian, who was nodding earnestly to his informant.

Dropping his voice further, the man from Guangzhou went on. 'They stand to urinate,' he said, almost in a whisper. 'And they believe that regular sexual congress enables them to work as hard as men.'

'How regular?' Tian asked.

'Twice a day.'

'Twice a day. Indeed?'

'Yes, and more often in winter. Three or four times a day.'

'When do they get time to work as hard as men? And is all this sexual congress perhaps the reason why the men themselves have no more energy to work?'

The young man's face clouded, and he ignored Tian's questions and continued. 'But beware, because every five years the women form a hunting pack and castrate one of the men from a rival village – or a visitor who has offended the village headman – and then they cook up his testicles in a special soup that is fed to all girl infants under five years old.'

'I will be extra careful, then,' Tian said, looking around to wink at me. 'Are we approaching the five year mark?'

The young man could not say, but he passed on his last piece of wisdom: that each March, Miao youth who had come of age serenaded each other from opposite sides of the valley, young men facing east and young women facing west. Using only the sound of their voices, they paired off, and arranged to meet in the forest on the valley floor to make love. There were many stories of mistaken identity, he said, and while some spawned epics or farces, most of them ended as tragedies. Tian thanked the young man for his advice, and after he left the three of us fell into a prolonged fit of giggling.

The train rolled on into the night. I lapsed into a deep sleep, waking to find that I had slumped down onto Tian's shoulder. I saw Ling Ling on the seat opposite, looking at me with an expression I had never seen before – a sad, reflective look I would not have thought was part of her repertoire – and immediately went back to sleep. When I awoke next, Ling Ling was gone. I was still leaning against Tian, and discovered to my horror a wet patch on his jacket sleeve next to where my mouth had been. Tian looked down and noticed it too. *Dui bu qi*, I whispered. *Mei shi*, he whispered back. It's nothing.

The train stopped at a town near Canton, and the three of us got off for half an hour and bought some food at the station cafeteria. Tian complained of a sore neck, the result of a night spent pinned awkwardly against the side of the carriage. He said he had not wanted to wake me or to try to move me in my sleep. I told him he was too polite, and noticed that Ling Ling scowled at him when she thought I was not looking.

On the ferry to Hainan we slept on the deck, amongst soldiers returning home and peasants transporting breeding pigs to the island. What bunks there were below deck seemed to be occupied by officers, factory managers and Party officials. We were met at the dock by the leader of the Cultural Work Team, and transported by bus to bunker-like quarters on the edge of a village in the foothills of the main mountain range. There we were introduced to the rest of the team, an assortment of dancers, actors, and singers from every corner of China. We learned that our first task was to prepare for a celebration of Miao traditional culture (with references to sex and feudal values replaced with socialist messages). The dancers and singers were already rehearsed, but the team's musicians had been reassigned to another part of Hainan, so we were to fill the gap. We began our preparation immediately.

That night Tian Mei Yun showed us the contents of his locked case. The whole party gathered under a tree in the courtyard, and Tian released the lock using a key hung on a chain around his neck, and one by one placed before us his treasure of musical scores. None of the titles were in Chinese; instead, there were titles in languages Tian identified as French and English, as well as some in Russian (which I carefully avoided translating). For the most part, they were works by familiar composers; but there were some I had not heard of: Bartók, Kodály, Hindemith. There were also some scores from which the front cover had been ripped, along with the few centimetres at the top of the first page where the composer and title had been. I waited for someone to ask Tian to explain why these scores were damaged, but nobody seemed to want to know.

We practised Miao folk songs for the next two days, before being loaded into two buses again and heading up into the mountains. For the next two weeks we slept in empty storehouses, barns, school rooms and peasant huts, ate whatever food we were offered, travelled along narrow mountain roads by day, and every evening set up our stage in a new village and sent messengers to summon the Miao villagers to our show, which we performed in the light of hurricane lamps on poles. Our audiences were no doubt happy for some entertainment, but must have been irritated to find that attendance was compulsory, and amused or insulted to discover that the evening's fare was to watch Han Chinese dress up in Miao costumes and present sanitised versions of Miao songs and dances to the descendents of their authors, accompanied by traditional melodies, but with Western harmony and instrumentation.

On our return from the mountains, we were presented with a special challenge. We were to be sent to a district where villagers had destroyed a newly installed electrical system, believing it contained devils. A political team had already held mass meetings with the villagers and explained revisionism and its Maoist critique, but to no avail. The sabotage continued. Could we put together a performance about the advantages of electrification?

We had the performance worked out within three days. The dancers and singers would act out the story of how the peasants lamented having only oil-lamps for light; how the benefits of electrical power were recognised by Mao Zedong; how scientists discovered ways of capturing electrons; how they sent out messengers to the sky and the streams to convince them to lend their powers to assist the villagers to modernise, and then gathered in a harvest of electrons into their storehouse of transformers and wires; how electricity flowed down the wires and into houses and health clinics and factories, creating light and animating machines which milled grains, sewed sacks and warm clothing, and assembled guns with which to fight the enemies of socialism.

Tian assumed the role of musical director. We would break away from Mozart and Beethoven, he said, and instead use French, Russian and Hungarian composers. One of Bartók's *Rumanian Dances* represented the sufferings of the pre-electrified peasants. A march from Prokofiev's *Romeo and Juliet* accompanied the entrance of Chairman Mao and the scientists. Another Bartók dance and a movement from a string quartet by Ravel, played pizzicato, represented, in turn, the search for compliant electrons amongst the mysterious elemental powers of nature, and then the machines jumping into life. I was to be the soloist, accompanied by the rest of the ensemble or sometimes just by Ling Ling and her piano accordion.

To indicate the happy electrons leaving the generation plant and making their way along the wires, Tian chose a sprightly dance tune. It was one of the damaged scores, and so was without a name. This piece proved to be the crowd favourite when we visited the recalcitrant village itself and performed our 'electrification suite'. (I heard it again years later, in Paris, when a friend took me to a competition for young musicians in which her son was playing the violin. When the boy played the very piece that we had used to try to win over the hearts of suspicious Miao tribesmen, I asked my friend what music her son was playing. 'Tu ne le connais pas?' she said, taken aback in that Gallic way. 'Mais c'est le *Golliwog's Cake Walk* de Claude Debussy.')

The sabotage of the electrical system ceased, and, encouraged by the ineluctable power of scientific music, we turned out several more 'suites' over the next two months, some in support of 'goods' like family planning (a restful piece by Elgar played around the actors representing responsible parents who ensured adequate spacing between their children, while the stubbornly ignorant parents were dogged by an irregular march by Shostakovich), and others against a variety of 'bads', including gambling on cockfights (with music by Bartók), smoking opium (Hindemith) and consulting traditional healers (Kodály). By the time we were summoned back to Shanghai in September, every score in Tian's case had been copied, reordered, transcribed to a different key, slowed to a more useful pace or manipulated in other ways until it had found its true vocation as a means of promoting hygienic living and hard work among the Miao.

*

A few days before we were due to return to Shanghai, Tian called me out of a practice session and explained that we had a small task to attend to. He was carrying the case with Director Ho's scores and two straw hats. 'You'll need one of these,' he said, handing me a hat. 'It's hot today.'

He led me down to the waterfront past racks of drying fish, to a jetty where we boarded a flat-bottomed fishing boat. An old man sat at the helm beneath a flapping cloth awning, and once we were settled on the boards above the fish-hold he pushed the boat away from the dock with a pole and pulled the rip-cord on an outboard motor several times until it fired. Within minutes we had left the harbour behind and were skimming around the coast beyond the reef line.

Tian sat in the bow with the case by his feet. 'Where are we going?' I asked him.

'I am forbidden to tell you,' he said.

'What's the point of being secretive? I will find out very soon. Unless you plan to blindfold me.'

'We are going to a village along the coast. You can only get there by sea.'

'And why are you taking me?' I asked.

He refused to answer, and turned his face upwards to catch the breeze.

'Why are you taking me?'

He continued to ignore me. I pulled my hat firmly over my eyes to protect myself from the dazzle of the sunlight on the water, and settled into a drowse. After almost an hour the boatman throttled back the engine, manoeuvred past some rocks and tied up at the jetty of a small village whose dozen or so houses were built on stilts over the waters of a lagoon. The boatman helped us from the boat and led us along a rickety boardwalk, around drying nets and fish traps, patting local children affectionately on the shoulder, until he stopped at one of the houses, and rapped on its doorpost to announce our arrival. He introduced the village chief, and we were welcomed warmly and urged to sit and share a meal of fish and rice. This we ate in silence, and then our boatman spoke to the village chief in the local dialect and bade us farewell with smiles and bows and handshakes, assuring Tian he would return to collect us before nightfall.

The chief led us onshore and for half an hour we trailed behind his grass-sided shoes along a narrow path that wound through a mangrove swamp and up the side of a small bluff before descending into an adjacent bay. He took us to a solitary hut by the shore and pointed to a small adjacent jetty, speaking to Tian in his dialect.

'What's he saying?' I asked.

'I think he's saying that this is where our boatman will pick us up,' he answered. 'I hope that's what he meant.'

The chief beckoned us inside the hut. It was unfurnished and damp and smelled of rotting vegetation. The chief pulled back several of the fibrous mats that covered the wooden floor and then squatted down and showed us a trapdoor set into the floor. This he lifted and together we peered into a small cavity, around half a metre square and the same depth. I sat down on a mat for a rest.

Tian sniffed the air and ran his hand around the inside lip of the cavity. 'Too damp,' he said. 'Things will rot in here. I asked for somewhere dry.'

The chief shrugged his shoulders and turned his palms outwards in a gesture of misapprehension or indifference.

'Do you have nothing else? Nothing drier?' Tian said. The man shrugged again. 'Do you even speak Mandarin?' Tian asked, and looked to me appealingly.

'I thought I was just here for the ride,' I said, and Tian turned down his lower lip in a clownish gesture, so I huffed loudly, got to my feet and addressed myself to the chief: '*Vy govorite po-russki?*' The chief contracted his brows and gave a tilt of the head. 'Well, I tried my best,' I said to Tian. 'He doesn't speak Russian either.'

The chief turned and stood in the doorway in the mottled shade of the palm trees. He pointed towards the south, where the sun was now beating down on the surface of the bay. 'About a day's journey under sail,' he said, in perfectly adequate Mandarin, 'there is a small island where my uncle would spend the summer. There is an old mine on the island – nickel, I think. There are some concrete buildings there. It is away from the sea, very dry.'

Tian sighed. 'That's too far,' he said. 'We only have today. Is there nothing in your village?'

'Anything dry in our village?' the man laughed. 'We live on stilts over a swamp – or did you not notice that?'

'This will have to do then,' Tian huffed. 'Thank you, you may leave us.'

The chief remained motionless, until Tian, remembering himself, reached into his pocket and withdrew a small roll of bank notes. 'Thank you for your help,' he said, pressing them into the chief's palm. 'And for your silence.'

The chief nodded and withdrew.

As we secured the trapdoor and arranged the reed mats on top of it Tian explained to me that the scores were not safe in

Shanghai, and that he had promised Director Ho that he would conceal them in Hainan as soon as possible after we arrived, but that circumstances had intervened, and they were needed for our work here. This was our last opportunity to fulfil the Director's original instructions.

'Why did you need to bring me?' I repeated.

'I needed a second witness,' Tian said. 'In case anything happens to me, you will know where to come. I was going to bring Ling Ling, but I'm not sure I can trust her.'

'Her loyalty?'

'Her sense of direction.'

'Who else knows about this?'

'Only the Director,' Tian said. 'It is our little secret, yes?'

We sat on the jetty for several hours waiting for our boatman to arrive. The sun dipped towards the horizon. I suggested that we return to the village, as the boatman may have forgotten where he was to meet us; but Tian would have none of it. 'As soon as we do that, he will appear here, and then we will be lost,' he said. We did retrace our steps to the foot of the bluff, however, and he pointed out a tree he had spotted on our way in which was laden with red green globes. 'I think it's a kind of mango,' he said, and he hoisted me up onto a low branch from where I plucked several of the fleshy fruit and threw them down to him. They were under-ripe, but edible, and we returned to the jetty with twenty or so wrapped up in Tian's shirt, and consumed half of them as a cool wind sprang up off the sea, the waves sank into a dark grey shimmer and a half-moon emerged from over the bluff.

As the sun set we retreated to the hut, lay on the grass mats and talked quietly in the darkness. A family of small bats assembled under the eaves, firing angry glances at us from amidst their leathery folds. Tian told me about growing up amidst privilege in Suzhou and Shanghai, about his family's servants, and their holidays in California, and about the years he had spent during the Civil War with his sister and mother at his uncle's large French Provincial house in the outskirts of Hanoi. He told me how no matter where the family was they always carried his cello and arranged for a piano to be available for him, and in Hanoi even found him a tutor, a white-suited French paterfamilias who was married, it appeared, to two Vietnamese sisters. Tian asked me about my childhood, and I was only a few minutes into my story when I noticed his breathing soften and become regular. I continued speaking softly for a few minutes, finding that I was myself interested in listening to the sound of my own voice giving an account of my childhood, and stopping only when I started to explain my father's illness and realised how much I missed listening to him talk about how his latest symptoms had unmasked further curiosities of his body and his mind.

The sea breeze held up for several hours and then died away. I drifted in and out of sleep, unable to find comfort in the humid, salty air, lacking a pillow and in my dozing mind transfiguring the noises of the forest around us into a convocation of snakes and insects and rodents drawn to our hut by the scent of warm bodies. I told myself I would not be harmed if I lay perfectly still.

As the sky brightened towards dawn I half awoke and found Tian beside me, very close, leaning on his elbow and stroking my face with his right hand. His breath was warm on my face and he began kissing me – on the cheekbone, on the tip of my nose, and on my chin. I reached up my right hand and awkwardly held the back of his head. I grasped his skull through his wiry hair and pulled his face closer, so that his kisses were harder, so that they pressed through my skin and onto the muscle and tissue beneath. I pulled his head down towards my neck and my shoulders and my collarbone, and pressed it down again, further, onto the mound of my breast. We were tugging at our clothing, and then I felt the spidery warmth of his fingers moving down over my stomach, and soon I was holding him over me, grasping his narrow hips, welcoming him, claiming him. I closed my eyes and felt the movement of his bones, hard beneath his soft flesh, and suddenly I felt that I was holding some creature that was not Tian, or was only partly him, like the coiled snakes of happiness and grief, for he was letting out a sound like sobbing from somewhere deep within his chest. And then there was only wetness, mine and his. And he was saying, over and over, '*Dui bu qi, dui bu qi, dui bu qi.* I'm sorry, I'm sorry, I'm sorry.' Then he succumbed to the stillness of our hut, and I became suddenly aware of the harsh scent of our sweat and the damp gushing of the sea at our feet and nothing more.

For several minutes Tian's body hung over me, the heels of his hands pressing into the mat either side of my head, his torso sagging downwards, drips of sweat falling from his ribcage onto my stomach, and his head lolling from side to side so that his moist hair brushed my temple and his breath caressed my sternum with prickly gusts of heat. I thought suddenly of the scores in the case beneath us and of the need to protect their delicate dryness from this wet that would dampen and rot away the staves and the notes. So I rolled Tian onto his back beside me and he watched as I gathered my clothes. I walked down to the sea and edged my way forward into the gentle morning waves, clutching my arms across my chest, my toes testing each boulder on the seafloor as I progressed.

After I had immersed myself several times I picked my way back to the shore and sat on a large rock, naked, drawing my knees up under my chin and watching the sun rise out of the sea. Tian walked past me without speaking and made his fumbling way into the water. Rather than watch him wash, I dressed and returned to the hut. I pulled back the floor mats and opened the trapdoor. Director Ho's case sat snugly in the cavity. I closed the trapdoor and covered it with mats once more.

I heard Tian's voice calling out and, moving to the doorway of the hut, saw him dancing around on one foot as he tugged on a trouser leg, and then clutching his belt ends with one hand as he waved the other arm above his head. In the distance I saw that the little blue fishing boat had come around the point and was making its way through a gap in the breakers about half a kilometre offshore. Tian waved again after he had buttoned his shirt, and watched as the boatman approached our tumbledown jetty, gunned the engine for the last time and threw a rope around the largest upright. He beckoned to us, and I went to the back of the hut to gather up the remainder of our fruit from the night before. I found them covered with insects crawling happily amongst their gelatinous pulp, and left them where they were.

When I reached the shore, Tian was ahead of me, picking his way carefully along the uneven boards of the jetty. I followed him, steadying myself on the rotting posts, and soon we were in the boat and heading back out through the passage into the open sea. Tian sat in the bow of the boat, humming to himself and turning from time to time to give me a mischievous smile. I sat at the stern beside the boatman. He asked how we had passed the night. He seemed happy with my curt reply and left me to my own thoughts for the duration of the journey.

As Tian and I walked together through the fish market to the barracks where we were billeted, he whispered to me, 'You will keep our secret, won't you?'

'What secret is that?' I said. 'About Director Ho's scores, you mean?'

'Yes . . . and also about what happened,' Tian said.

'What did happen?' I asked. 'Tell me.'

'Nothing,' he said. 'It's a secret.' We walked on through the throng of townsfolk going about their morning business, and as we approached our lodgings he said, 'What I mean is: you won't tell Ling Ling. Will you?'

'Why should I?' I said. 'As long as the two of us know where the case is hidden, there is no need to tell anyone else. That was your plan, wasn't it? As you yourself said, these are things she cannot be trusted with.' I turned away from him and quickened my pace so that I reached the barracks several minutes before him.

*

Two days later we returned to the mainland and boarded the train to Shanghai. At the Conservatory little appeared to have changed. Classes continued as normal and Ho Luting remained the Director, although it was rumoured that only intervention from high up in the Party had saved him. Nevertheless, he was rarely seen around the Conservatory, and his duties were for the most part performed by Yu Huiyong, who now had the title of Adjunct Deputy Director of the Conservatory, in which capacity he led daily one-hour political instruction sessions.

'Western music is bound up in a system of social snobbery,' Yu explained at the first of these sessions I attended. 'Not only do Chinese listeners not understand it, but the working people of the West do not understand it, and a great many bourgeoisie only pretend to understand to show how civilised they are. So-called abstract music – music in which each section is simply identified by a technical description and a number (Symphony No. 4, Adagio in G, and so on) – is inseparably associated with the establishment of capitalist production relations and the rise of the bourgeoisie. Untitled music is the means by which bourgeois composers conceal the class content of their works.'

Yu's ideas severely threatened the teaching repertoire. What music could be taught in the Conservatory? the faculty asked, and in response Yu posted on the main door a list of music that passed the ideological tests: the *Yellow River Concerto*, the *Shajiabang Symphony*, the opera *A Storm on the Yangtze*, and a long list of choral works and songs: *The Red Lantern, Ambushed from All Sides, Chairman Mao Arrives at Tiananmen, Transfer to the Front-Lines after Graduation* and *Going up to Peach Peak Three Times*. There was immediate chaos. Were these the only pieces of music that could be taught or performed? Was the whole Western corpus to be discarded as bourgeois? What about Soviet or Eastern European music? And what of classical Chinese music? Of *Three Variations on a Plum Blossom*? Or Chinese folk music? Was the music composed after the Revolution of 1911 acceptable? Or was everything composed before the Communist victory of 1949 to be condemned as feudal as well? And what exactly were the principles that should be applied to distinguish socialist music from bourgeois music?

Some students made a bonfire of suspect sheet music on the front steps of the Conservatory, and refused to play anything that was not on Yu's list. A few members of the faculty, in mock zealotry, queried some of the items on Yu's list for having reactionary or revisionist tendencies. The Soviet advisors withdrew into an angry silence.

Director Ho remained silent throughout, having let it be known that he was busy composing an oratorio based on the Long March of 1934. Yu was forced to post revised lists on his door and entertain earnest delegations of students seeking clarification. Glinka and Haydn and Beethoven were rehabilitated, followed shortly after by Mozart and Chopin and (it was rumoured), at the playful instigation of the Soviet advisors, by their obscure compatriots Viktor Kosenko, Serafim Tulikov and Modest Tabachnikov. Rumour and counter-rumour circulated. Brahms and Strauss were sanctioned one morning, but banned again by evening. Schubert and Rimsky-Korsakov suffered the same fate on another day. Borodin came and went within the space of a few hours. The stock of each composer rose and fell at the prompting of an invisible hand, and outside the practice rooms in the evening we would listen nervously to what was being played within, lest anyone lapse into some reactionary arpeggios or bourgeois atonality.

One morning we found that all the lists on the main door had been torn down and replaced by a single-page manifesto entitled 'Four Principles towards a Socialist Theory of Music'. Professor Yu did not claim to be the author of the principles, although it was written in his own hand, but he later hinted that they had originated from a source high up in the Party. We were summoned to the refectory to hear him read them out and urge us to apply them to our work without any more bickering:

1. China's musicians must find a course independent of both Western bourgeois standards and native feudalism. The foreign tiger and the native tiger are both ferocious, and we must not be bound to them.

2. Western music is politically unhealthy. *Madame Butterfly* describes the shaming of Japanese women by American imperialism; and *La Traviata* dignifies prostitution. Capitalism's

music is headed for destruction, and you do not want to die along with it.

3. However, Chinese folk songs are not a satisfactory basis for creating a new musical culture. When the Ministry of Culture encouraged folk songs, no one sang revolutionary songs any more.

4. International musical competitions are capitalist at the core. Nevertheless, China does receive some benefit from the standpoint of international relations. China should establish an international festival of Asian, African and Latin American music, and then withdraw from Western competitions.

The principles were, I thought, from first to last extremely unhelpful; but to my amazement Yu's announcement fostered a kind of bemused euphoria. Faculty members resumed teaching Western music. 'First, master Mozart and Beethoven,' they said, 'and then surpass it. And as regards China's international standing, once we have carried home every trophy from the West, we will establish our own competitions.' Within days of Yu's announcement Beethoven and Brahms were again heard throughout the halls of the Conservatory, and as they entered the building each morning many students glanced ruefully at the scorch-marks left on the front steps by the bonfire of precious scores.

In the Foreign Teachers' Building the new plumbing system appeared to work no better than the old one had. There was dust everywhere, and for a few days we had to step over a pile of perfectly serviceable lead pipes that lay athwart the entrance way awaiting removal. Madame Huang took me to the roof of the building that backed onto mine, and showed me the small removable panel that had been installed by the fire escape on the third floor. She explained that a small cavity had been created in the internal wall of Raya and Pavel's apartment so that I would be able to climb down the fire escape, remove the panel, and crawl into the wall cavity to position myself at more or less the exact centre of the apartment: the bedroom would be to my right; the living room would be in front of me; and the bathroom, should I care to listen, would be to my left. The space had been equipped with a small shaded light to help me write down my notes.

Madame Huang explained that a reception for all the Soviet advisors had been organised for that evening to allow me to familiarise myself with my new listening post. Kirill was back in Shanghai, she said, and we were eagerly awaiting his next visit.

'Regarding your request to visit your parents,' she said, pursing her lips as if she had just swallowed something sour, 'I am afraid that is not convenient right now. You are too important to us here, and nobody else can do your work.' She placed her hand on mine and gave my fingers a squeeze. 'Be assured that the Party is looking after your father,' she said. 'I personally have spoken with the Party Secretary of the Shanghai Municipal Government. He is well connected in Beijing.'

That night I climbed from the window at the top of the stairwell onto the fire escape, where I stole a quick glance at the stars and the moon, stepped as quietly as I could down the steep metal staircase (ducking when it passed the window of an apartment), slid open the panel on the third floor, edged into the darkness, and settled myself into position. The workmen had installed a platform that I could lie on, about two metres above the floor, and ventilation grilles that circulated air and enabled me to see part of the living room and the bedroom.

Over the nights that followed, Pavel and Raya resumed their conjugal life, speaking to each other less, but with an odd courtesy. Every night they ate the meal Raya had prepared, and then Pavel cleaned up in the kitchen and they read books or newspapers and smoked cigarettes before going to bed. They rarely talked at length, and when they did they soon found themselves sliding towards an angry exchange and immediately pulled back. I wondered if they had some inkling that I was there listening to them; but then concluded that they had simply formed a truce, agreeing that arguments that could not be won were not worth starting.

The leaves were falling from the trees by the time Kirill returned to the building. I was returning from the Conservatory on my bicycle at dusk one day, and as I turned into our street my path was illuminated from behind by the headlights of a car. It tailed me for the last hundred metres, the street being too narrow to permit it to pass. I parked my bicycle and saw Kirill reversing out of the back seat onto the kerb, setting onto the sidewalk bottles of vodka and wine, a pile of new books tied up with string, and cartons of cigarettes which, later that evening, I would recognise as the same pungent-smelling ones I had watched Raya smoke at her door the night I had been trapped in the apartment. I offered to help him and he gave me a smile and thanked me as I picked up his stack of books and preceded him up to the third floor. I deliberately continued past Pavel and Raya's door, but he called me back. I put the books in the doorway as he knocked, and then, without waiting for any further acknowledgement, I ran up the remaining flights of stairs, throwing my violin onto my bed and climbing as fast as I could down the fire escape and into my listening post. The first thing I heard was the scraping of a chair.

'You will excuse me,' Kolya was saying as I put my ear to the grille. 'Some paperwork cries out for me upstairs.'

'How can you think of going, Kolya?' Raya said. 'Our guest has just arrived. How rude of you!'

'And see, I have brought the Moskovskaya,' Kirill said. 'Ten bottles, no less. If you go, Pavel will drink the lot and you will have none. Here, Raya, bring glasses.'

'Please, no,' Kolya said. 'I need to work. I can't drink and work. That is a skill I have never learned.'

'You have grown pale over the summer,' Kirill lamented. 'Are you working too hard? Have you been fasting? A single man like you needs some company. Stay a while.'

'I have been enjoying your company since we sucked at our mothers' breasts,' Kolya said. 'I am not short of your company.'

'Pavel will be back soon with some delicacies from across the river,' Raya said, and through the grille I saw her standing behind Kolya, wrapping her arms around his shoulders and pressing him back into a chair. She was mouthing words to Kirill, who sat across from Kolya, below my line of sight.

'What is Pavel doing over there? Is he playing provisioner now?' Kolya said as he squirmed beneath Raya's weight.

'Mitrofan has been taking him on his little excursions to show him the ropes,' Raya said. 'You knew that, surely. He needs to get the measure of our Jewish friends before Mitrofan leaves.'

'What measurements is he taking?' Kolya said, struggling free of Raya and pushing his chair back. 'This fraternisation with undesirables is . . . I will have a word with him, Kirill, I promise.'

'Don't fret, my friend,' said Kirill. 'Just stay with us and eat.'

At that moment a noise was heard on the stairs. 'Ah, Pavel! Pavel, is that you?' Kirill called.

'Kirill Mikhailovic! What a surprise!' Pavel called from the entrance. 'I didn't know you were back in Shanghai.'

'I really must go,' Kolya said. 'Once I have finished my report I will come back.'

'Promise me you will,' Raya said. 'Let me find your jacket.' Raya and Kolya left the room and I could hear them in the vestibule talking in hushed tones. Pavel, meanwhile, entered the room and placed a canvas bag on the table as Kirill rose from his chair.

'Welcome, Kirill Mikhailovic,' Pavel said, leaning across the table to embrace Kirill. 'It is good to have you back. How are things in Moscow? Does the spring continue?'

'The spring continues, yes,' said Kirill. 'This winter could be the best spring we have had in years.'

'Oh, how I love the way you diplomats talk. I love everything about you diplomats.'

'You should show some restraint,' said Kirill. 'Now, what is in the bag?'

'Not much. Some cod liver salad, a brace of roast pigeons, some chanterelles, and some more *knydl*, I particularly like their *knydl*.'

'And tell me about your work,' Kirill said, as he helped Pavel remove the food from his canvas bag.

'My work?'

'It's what you are here for. Isn't it?'

'My work proceeds as well as I can hope. We lost the repertoire last year, you may recall, but now it is mostly back in fashion.'

'But what are your students composing?'

'Shit mainly, if you must know,' Pavel said. 'Read Kolya's reports. I am teaching my students to write song cycles for the peasants on the collective farms. You know, titles like "Chickenshit is fine, but pigshit is the better manure" and "Chairman Mao says to eat greens is glorious".'

'Tell me more.'

'Read Kolya's reports.' Pavel folded the canvas bag and put it under the table.

'No, I want to hear it from you.'

'I am not in the mood. Now help me set this food out. Where is Raya? Where are you, Raya?'

'I am here.' Raya returned to the room, and she and Pavel busied themselves with plates and cutlery.

'Do we need knives?'

'Yes.'

In the darkness of my hideout I scrawled notes with a pencil on a small notepad and strained to hear every word. Does he know? I asked myself. Does Pavel know?

Over their meal Kirill asked about Raya's work (a study of similarities between the folk music of Sichuan and the Soviet Asian republics), and she in turn quizzed him about the illness of the Soviet Consul in Shanghai, which was rumoured to be life-threatening. They swapped details of their respective travels from the previous summer: Pavel in Moscow, Raya in Kiev with her sister, and Kirill in London, Washington, Paris and Kiev before returning to Moscow.

'You should have told me you were going to be in Kiev,' Raya said. 'My sister and her husband had a dacha by the river, about a half hour from the city.'

'I had only two days there, and barely left the Foreign Ministry. Do you know they have now installed an elevator in that beautiful stairwell? At the old building on Mykhailivska Square? It only has three storeys, for God's sake! An elevator for only three storeys! Kirichenko is behind it, Khrushchev's man. A monstrous thing, and I refused to use it. It is a gilded cage with clanking gates and sagging wires that drags you from the bowels of the building and deposits you at the door of Kirichenko's office.'

'Is it that you prefer to walk for your health?' Pavel asked, 'Or are you afraid someone will cut the wires and you will drop three storeys to your death?'

'Both; neither. What disturbs me is that it looks like a prison cell, and I have watched people as they ride up and down. They stop talking to each other and a look of vacancy comes into their eyes, as if their souls had taken the stairs while their bodies take the elevator. That is what scares me.'

'You are very amusing, Kirill,' Raya said. 'Here, drink.'

'To vacancy,' Pavel said. 'To elevation. *Bud'mo.*'

'*Bud'mo.*'

My knees and back started to ache. My small cavity filled with the smell of their cigarettes and I held my hand over my mouth and nose, closed my eyes to stop them watering, and lay in the darkness listening. Does he know? I asked myself again and again.

'Tell us more about your travels in the United States, Kirill' said Pavel. 'What news? Did they turn you into a capitalist?'

'Indeed, not. It is too hot there, too humid, at least in Washington. I do not understand how they get anything done. Who has the energy to engage in free enterprise when drenched in sweat? Give me London, where it rained without ceasing, or Berlin, where the leaves are falling everywhere,' Kirill replied. 'As for my mission, it is accomplished for the time being.'

'And my friend, Yudin, in Beijing? How is he?'

'Ah, that is a different matter altogether, I'm afraid,' Kirill said. 'Yudin is panicking, let me be frank. The ground slips away beneath him, and he fears he will be replaced and sent home in disgrace.'

'What has he done?'

Kirill lit a cigarette, and then, remembering himself, offered them to his hosts, lighting theirs with the glowing end of his.

'He has soured relationships with the leadership there,' he said. 'We have it on good intelligence that the PLA is planning to invade the channel islands off Taiwan. We don't know when, exactly. That's probably as far as they will go, since their purpose is merely to bring the US Seventh Fleet into play.'

'And who does that help?'

'Not us, anyway. It is well known that the Americans have Matador missiles in Taiwan. One of them is almost certainly trained on our little gathering here – on this table, on me, on this bottle of Moskovskaya. Invading Jinmen and Mazu is a ploy, of course. Mao wants to force Khrushchev to cancel the trip to Washington I have been so carefully preparing.'

'And what is our next move . . .' Pavel began.

'I will say nothing more,' Kirill said. 'Change the subject, please.'

'Why?' Pavel said. 'I know Yudin well. He and I have been friends for years. Call him; ask him; give him my regards.'

There was an extended silence in the room below me, and I imagined what wordless exchanges were going on, what narrowing of eyes and fingering of glass-rims, what staring at the colourless liquid in the vodka bottle.

'While you were in Kiev,' Raya began, 'nursing a phobia for elevators, I was visiting my uncle and aunt in Feodosia, where I witnessed a terrible sight: a large dog – a German Shepherd – that had been chained to a post at the side of the road, and had somehow twisted the chain around so that it cut into the flesh of its neck and started to draw blood. It was just off the town square, in broad daylight. The poor thing was writhing in pain, pulling and twisting and yelping, and making its situation worse.'

'I thought Kirill said to change the subject,' Pavel moaned.

'And nobody attempted to release it, or to find the owner,' Raya went on, 'but instead a group of people, ordinary people – housewives, young couples, old men – simply stood and watched as it slowly bled to death. Even as it started to spasm, nobody went to find a gun or a hammer to put the poor beast out of its misery.'

'And your point is, my dear?' Pavel asked.

'Perhaps the dog represents humanity,' Kirill said, 'and we witness its death throes, without a thought to take action to save it.'

'And what did you do, my dear?' Pavel asked. 'As an intelligent observer, as an intellectual, a *zhi-shi-fen-zi*. Did you, my one true love, did you release the dog from its suffering?'

Raya did not seem insulted by the question, and answered simply, 'I did nothing. I too did nothing.' The two men were silent. After a while Raya continued, 'I did nothing because I had been watching my nephews and nieces play in the river that day, and asking myself if they will ever be my age; if they will ever see their twentieth birthday, living as they do on a military base, their school-house no doubt in the cross-hairs of some missile waiting in a dark wood somewhere in Germany or Turkey.'

'I think I might have intervened, nevertheless,' Pavel said. 'I have no faith in our ability to build weapons and deny ourselves their use. But I would have found a rock and staved in the dog's skull. A rock is a fine weapon.'

'You are a good man, Pavel,' said Kirill, starting to laugh. 'Let me pour the next round, and let us drink to men such as Pavel, and hope that you survive the blast when it comes and that you have a large rock on hand to use on the rest of us. The last and greatest heroes of mankind, that is what such men will be, staggering from door to door, blood-stained rock in hand.'

'Do you deserve to die, Kirill?' Pavel said.

Kirill's laughter subsided quickly, and he sighed. 'I am implicated, my friend, like all diplomats,' he said. 'Just months ago I was in Beijing with our scientists and generals, handing over the first of the plans and specifications to their scientists and generals. My fingerprints are on the treaty. My image is in the commemorative photograph, third on the left, standing behind the Great Man himself. Soon the middle kingdom will be in the middle once again.'

'And my wife?' Pavel asked, dropping his voice. 'Tell me: does she deserve to have her skull staved in too?'

'No,' Kirill said, his voice lightening. 'Not at all. Like all women, she deserves to be spared any suffering.' There was a clink of glasses, then another and – after a pause – a third. Then the three of them laughed, first Raya, then Kirill, and finally Pavel.

'Drink up,' Raya said. 'Enough of this silly talk. I am going to bed, and you, Kirill, have a driver waiting outside in the cold.'

*

Madame Huang almost hugged me the following morning after I had relayed the conversation in detail. Was I sure that the word 'treaty' had been used? And that Kirill had clearly referred to an agreement between the Soviet Union and China? Which islands were we about to invade? And could I explain once more the story about the dying dog? In her view, it did not make any sense. The dog and its owner were both stupid. How could its death be a lesson?

As she rose to dismiss me I asked her once again when I might be able to return home to visit my father. 'Be patient,' she said. 'I had word yesterday that your father is responding well to treatment. But it is too soon for you to leave us; your work is too important.'

'You had word?' I said. 'A telegram? A letter? Can I see it?'

'Just word,' she said, sharply. 'Trust me.'

Throughout the winter I made my nightly pilgrimage down the fire escape, and observed the silent routines of Pavel and Raya. Although Kirill remained in the city, he did not return to the apartment on the third floor. Pavel and Raya had descended into their taciturn ways, and if Madame Huang had asked me to I could have written down their conversation verbatim on one small sheet of paper. I started to the read the *Shanghai Liberation Daily* every day, looking for reports of treaties and exchanges between China and the Soviet Union. As the months passed I read about how Tibet had been liberated from itself, how Taiwan was handed over to the Americans as an island fortress, and how India stubbornly resisted the great sweep of socialist history over the Xinjiang-Tibet Road through the Kunlun Mountains. As the year progressed, the newspaper also covered the successful testing of an intercontinental ballistic missile, the launching of the Sputnik satellite, and the journey of Laika the dog into orbit on a Soviet satellite. But there was no mention of any Sino-Soviet treaty. (Although my expectations of the Chinese press were misplaced, the treaty did exist, and its substance – the provision by the Soviet Union of plans for the construction of nuclear reactors and weapons, and the construction of a nuclear testing site in Lop Nur, Xinjiang, in exchange for the supply of Chinese uranium from new mines in Hunan and Jiangxi – became known only after it had been rescinded in 1960.)

One thing did catch my eye, though. While visiting Moscow, Mao delivered a speech in which he predicted that socialism would survive a nuclear war. 'If the worst came to the worst and half of mankind died,' Mao said, 'the other half would remain while imperialism would be razed to the ground and the whole world would become socialist. On the debris of a dead imperialism, the victorious socialist people would create very swiftly a civilisation a thousand times superior to the capitalist system and a truly beautiful future for themselves.' The speech struck the Communist world dumb. The Chinese press reported it without comment, as a self-evident truth.

10. The Year of Miracles

In January of 1958, the *Shanghai Liberation Daily* began to report the occurrence of miracles. 'The people have taken to organising themselves along military lines,' the paper said, 'working with militancy, and leading a collective life. This has raised the political consciousness of the five-hundred million peasants still further. The establishment of people's communes, where industry, agriculture, exchange, culture, education and military affairs merge into one, is the fundamental policy to guide the peasants to accelerate socialist construction, complete the building of socialism ahead of time, and carry out the gradual transition to communism.'

Eight million hectares of previously arid land had sprouted crops, and the flooding of the great rivers would soon be a thing of the past. Grain production doubled, then quadrupled and then increased tenfold. One million backyard steel furnaces were set to catapult China ahead of Britain in steel production within the course of the year. Peasants arose from their villages and set off to the deserts of Xinjiang and Gansu to prospect for oil and uranium. Was there any miracle that the peasants could not conjure from the good earth?

At the Conservatory, we felt keenly our duty to join in the *Da Yue Jin*, the Great Leap Forward. Director Ho was eager to apply socialist construction to composition and performance, as long as the quality of the work was not lessened. 'Our music must be one hundred percent music,' he said, 'just as steel must be one hundred percent steel and grain one hundred percent grain.' His first move was to revive the project to stage the first performance of Beethoven's Ninth Symphony with all Chinese performers. Immediately I was back in the orchestra, practicing in the grand salon on Bubbling Well Road; but this time I was sitting closer to the leader, because several of the players had unmasked themselves as Rightists during the Hundred Flowers Movement and were being re-educated.

One Monday we were summoned to hear Director Ho (flanked by Yu Huiyong, and Ding Shangde) address the Conservatory on the matter of production quotas. This was the first time he had been seen in public for weeks. Madame Huang, I noticed, now perched behind Yu's shoulder, whispering into his ear as she had once whispered into Ho's. 'Like every other work unit,' He began, 'the Conservatory must increase its production. We must strive for goals we have so far thought unattainable. For this reason, we are announcing today that the Conservatory will produce 600 new works during the next year, including symphonies, operas, instrumental pieces and songs. I invite all faculty and students to consider how they will contribute to this goal, and to notify Professor Yu of their personal production plans. I myself, in addition to my six days a week of administration work, will compose one symphony, one opera or oratorio, and ten instrumental works.'

Director Ho's announcement was met with enthusiastic applause. 'And now,' he continued, 'my comrades Professor Yu and Professor Ding will announce their personal plans for socialist musical construction.' He took his seat and there was a pause as the two Deputy Directors swapped glances. Ding moved first, clasping and unclasping his hands as he stood and took the podium, and in his squeaky voice committed himself to a personal production quota of ten learned articles on the class origins of the erhu and similar subjects, and five performances of socialist operas. He received polite applause. Professor Yu followed immediately, announcing that, in spite of his onerous

256

administrative burden he would compose twenty art songs, thirty songs for the masses, and thirty pieces for instructing children in the principles of Marxism. One by one the faculty, the senior composition students and then many junior students stood to make pledges to compose so many new works, or give so many performances in factories, or teach so many peasants to sing revolutionary songs.

Tian Mei Yun rose and told the story of the success of the 'electrification suite', and committed 'the Hainan Group' to composing ten more such works. At the end of the session, Madame Huang, who had been keeping a tally of the pledges, announced that the goal of 600 had been reached. 'Let the work of socialist musical construction begin!' Director Ho said, and dismissed us to begin our work. Professor Yu left the room quickly with Ding and Madame Huang, while Director Ho remained for several minutes, listening attentively as two students expounded the storyline of their new opera, a mischievous grin fixed to his face.

That evening I met with Ling Ling and Tian Mei Yun, and instead of practising we discussed our contribution to the Conservatory's quota. Tian produced his scores of the 'electrification suite' and its companions and dropped them on the table. 'Here are six works of socialist construction,' he said, settling himself onto the windowsill. 'Ten more should be easy.'

'I suggest we take a mathematical approach to the multiplication of music,' I said, picking up a piece of Brahms. I put it on the piano, and directed Ling Ling to play the first four bars. When she had finished I took the score and turned it upside down, and scrawled new treble and bass clefs on alternate lines. 'This is a technique pioneered by Johann Sebastian Bach,' I explained, as I drew in the flats to ensure that the inverted piece was still in B-minor. Ling Ling attempted the new piece, stumbling once or twice, but making it to the end. I was pleasantly surprised at the results. A few phrases sounded odd, and we had to change some notes to repair these. 'One journey up the mountain; a different journey down,' Tian commented from his perch on the windowsill. I got Ling Ling to play the next four bars back to front, rather than upside down. This was also a tolerable success. We gave the same treatment to the violin and cello lines and soon had several pages of a trio. Tian descended from the windowsill and we gave the piece a first run through.

A bell rang to announce that our practice time was over. There was a gentle rap on the door, and the handle turned. A bespectacled student stood in the doorway holding a handwritten score rolled up one hand and cradling a cornet in the other elbow. 'That sounded okay,' he said. 'A bit like Beethoven with Chinese characteristics.'

My scientific compositional technique – with its ability to multiply one great piece of music into an infinite number of passable derivative pieces – proved a very timely invention, for on Tuesday the newspaper announced the Conservatory's plans to contribute 600 new works, but also published the pledge by the Shanghai Musicians' Association to an initial goal of 1,000 songs to be composed during the next year. And on Wednesday, the Shanghai Writers' Association announced that they would produce 150 texts per week. On Thursday the Conservatory was reconvened and Director Ho informed us that, after consultation with the masses, he had concluded that we needed to set our sights higher. Another round of pledges followed and we increased our production goal to 1,734 new works. The news was carried in the paper on Friday; but the following Monday the Musicians' Association and the Writers' Association announced that they too had discussed their quotas with the masses, and agreed to raise them to 1,500 new works and 250 texts per week. For several more days the parties lobbed numerical grenades at each other, until there was a meeting somewhere over a meal and they agreed to an all-Shanghai music quota: exactly 5,873 new compositions for the year.

'The universe of music is vast,' Director Ho told us. 'That much should be obvious simply from the mathematics: so many notes, so many combinations of those notes, so many instruments, so many tempi, so many ways of arranging point and counterpoint. The number of possible compositions can barely be imagined, but it is not infinite. Over several hundred years the composers of capitalism have claimed vast territories. So too the classical composers of China. But these are still only a fraction of what is yet to be claimed by a diligent cadre of Chinese socialist composers. Music is a resource, like coal or oil. There may be twenty million compositions yet to be written, or a hundred million or a billion, but we have the capacity to train a million composers, to train ten million. We have the capacity, within a generation, if we meet and exceed our quotas, to claim for China a lion's share of all of the music that remains to be discovered.'

*

So during the spring and summer of 1958 the Shanghai Conservatory rang to the sound of hastily composed music. In corners of the refectory, on doorsteps of classrooms, in dormitories and corridors, alone or in small conclaves, students worried over rice-paper scores, arguing over half-tones, scratching in key-changes, humming to themselves in class, or grabbing whatever instrument was at hand to try out a new phrase. They uncovered music as my father uncovered mathematics, hidden in the clang of machinery or the ping of pebbles on bicycle spokes, in the laughter of old people or the scraping of a tin spoon along the bottom of an iron rice bowl. Throughout the night, from the windows of the practice rooms and dormitories, lights shone, voices contended, flowers of notes bloomed and faded and fell. The faculty tried to continue normal classes, but many students – encouraged, some said, by Professor Yu – openly defied their teachers, insisting that they knew enough already to devote themselves to composing and performing. Posters appeared encouraging 'barefoot composers' to go out and listen to the natural music of the masses, to the chaotic sounds of lathe and loom and furnace, of threshing and grinding, and give voice to their aspirations for the speedy arrival of communism. Some classes – in music history, piano and performance technique –

were abandoned in favour of premiere performances of the Pig Iron Sonata, the Rice Bowl Cantata, and Three Variations on a Donkey Cart.

At this time also I received several letters from my mother, telling me that my father's condition had worsened further. He was confined to a wheelchair, said the first letter. And in the second letter, which followed two weeks later, she admitted that he had caught a serious infection, spent several days in hospital and almost died. *He is better now*, she wrote, *and hopes to get back into his wheelchair and move around again. He spends a lot of time by the fishpond, and is visited every day by Zhu Shaozen, who brings him gifts of food. Zhu's nephew comes as well, and brings fresh live fish from the river and puts records on the gramophone for your father. Your father speaks of you often, and is very proud that you are serving your country with your talent.* The letter ended with an admonition to study hard, and a promise that, if my father's condition became very serious, she would send money for my train fare to Harbin.

I lay awake the night after her letter arrived, overcome by waves of cramp and nausea. What sleep I could find was no more than slipping into a shallow dream, which I found I could enter and leave at will: I was lying motionless in my parents' bed in our house in Harbin, feeling a ribbon of air slide around my face and my body, like a doctor's cold hand, and sensing that somewhere in the half-light a door or a window had been left open to whatever lay in the dark world outside.

The next morning I sent a telegram to my mother telling her that I would be back in Harbin as soon as I could. Tian Mei Yun happily supplied me with the money for my fare, but when I approached Madame Huang to seek permission to return to Harbin she told me that she had received a telegram from my mother telling her that under no circumstances was she to allow me to leave Shanghai. I should take my mother's advice, Madame Huang said, and wait until she summoned me home. 'You have work to do here,' she said, paying no attention to my tears. She hardened her tone as she explained that Pavel had been invited to

Beijing to give a series of lectures. 'We have guaranteed him an enthusiastic audience,' she said. 'We will make him the toast of the North China lecture circuit. He will have standing ovations wherever he goes. He will be away for two weeks this time, and we have plans to have him invited to Shenyang too, and Tianjin.' She gave me a wink. 'My mother was a matchmaker back in our home village,' she said, and giggled to herself.

Sure enough, the night of Pavel's departure Kirill returned and was pulled urgently into Raya's apartment, and I lay on my back a few metres from their lovemaking clutching a pencil stub and paper and waiting to record their conversation. The results were disappointing: whispers, a scattering of details about life at the consulate and events back in Moscow which Madame Huang told me afterwards had already been reported in *Pravda*. For the most part they lay on their backs and smoked quietly and then dozed until Kirill reached for his clothes, bestowed some final kisses on Raya's face and hair and breasts, and then slipped into the stairwell.

Meanwhile I made my contribution to the production quota, but I quickly lost my enthusiasm for surpassing Western music by mathematical means, and for travelling to the outskirts of the city, as we did almost daily, to give recitals of our new works of socialist construction to politely mystified workers. The one constant in my studies was my lessons with Comrade Meretrenko. He talked frequently about pieces I could play at international competitions. One night, however, he seemed unusually cool towards me, abrupt and cantankerous. At the end of the lesson, he placed his hand on my violin case as I began to put away my violin. 'I have received an interesting letter,' he said in Chinese, 'from a friend of mine who plays in the symphony orchestra in Odessa. She says she has heard of you, or at least, has heard of a young girl from Harbin who received a lesson from our great David Oistrakh some years ago. Oistrakh mentioned this girl to her. He was impressed by her playing.' Comrade Meretrenko looked me in the face, tilting his head like an inquisitive dog, watching for some sign of recognition.

'Apparently this girl was unusually tall for her age,' he went on. His eyebrows quivered, ready to pounce. 'And she spoke flawless Russian, because she had been taught by a couple of Russian Jews who, many years before, had been music teachers to the children of the last Tsar.' I looked away, seeking respite from his stare. He fell silent and I sensed he would remain so until our eyes met once more. When I turned back to him he said, 'You are that girl, aren't you?'

I was not inclined to lie to him. 'It was the Grand Duke's children they taught, and not the Tsar's,' I said. 'As for my Russian, he overpraises it. I am far short of being fluent, and that is why I don't try to speak it with you. And he overpraises my playing, too.'

'I suspect he does neither,' Comrade Meretrenko said, switching to Russian, 'but I accept your explanation. I am merely disappointed that you have required me to bumble along in a language whose subtleties I cannot grasp, when in fact your musical education has been in my mother tongue. This has been a lost opportunity, has it not? What is more, I have plans for you to compete in several competitions in Russia and to receive instruction from our finest teachers, and it would be very useful for you to be able to discuss music in Russian on these occasions; would it not?' I nodded my agreement. 'So from now on,' he said, 'we will speak in Russian.'

When I related this conversation to Madame Huang she seemed unperturbed. 'It does not matter,' she said. 'Now that you have your little compartment, we are not requiring you to lurk in the stairwell any more. I suggest you let it be known that you speak bad Russian. And make sure it is bad Russian.'

Two nights later Comrade Meretrenko and Ksenia ate with Pavel and Raya, and Sasha, the french horn teacher, in their apartment. 'Fyodor tells me our girl on the top floor, Comrade Xiao, the prize-winning violinist, understands Russian, and had a master-class from Oistrakh some years ago,' Pavel announced, as the meal commenced.

'She is a quiet, gawky thing,' Sasha said, 'and so physically awkward, like a large bat turned upright. I have met her a couple of times at the entrance hall. I am surprised she understands Russian, since I greeted her in Mandarin and she didn't seem even to understand that. I assumed she was a country girl speaking only one of those impossible dialects.'

'You probably insulted her mother without realising it,' Fyodor said, 'or invited her to share your meal, and she was too shocked or too polite to reply. Your Armenian and your Turkish are excellent, Sasha, but your Chinese pronunciation? Well, let us say it leaves something to be desired.'

Pavel said, 'There should be a medal for foreigners who can master these four tones. Did you know, I discovered the other day that with a minor error on one syllable – one solitary syllable – the question, "Do you have a religion?" can mean, "Would you like to have sex?"'

'So that is why religion is illegal in this country,' Sasha said, 'It distracts the masses from their procreative work!'

'And may I ask you, Pavel,' said Raya, 'exactly how you found out this fascinating piece of information?'

'In a church, perhaps?' Comrade Meretrenko said.

'From a book, of course,' said Pavel. 'Books provide me with all my most fascinating insights into life. Surely it is the same for you, my dear.'

'But she does play well, does she not?' Sasha said. 'Our lanky Russophile upstairs?'

'Indeed, she does,' said Fyodor. 'I grant that she does not look like a violinist; more like a basketball player, or – if you wish – like a large bat. Sometimes I think she will snap the poor thing in her hands without meaning to. But when she plays she has astounding tone and control, and her timing is like a Swiss watch. I swear she has swallowed a metronome at some time in her life, and it is still lodged in there, ticking away. She can draw emotion out of a piece too – Brahms, in particular, and Schubert too. I notice this in the slow movements especially. While my other students seem to think that the term *adagio* means to apply more vibrato and think of dinner, this girl's playing is like thick smoke from a smouldering fire. It is all unfolding muscles and sinews.'

'Smoke and muscles, Fyodor?' Ksenia said. 'You should not mix your metaphors, my dear. It is bad for you – it leads to unorthodox thinking.'

'Ah, yes,' Mitrofan said. 'One should keep one's metaphors in line, keep them marching in step like soldiers, goose-stepping like . . . well, like geese, rather than flying free and shitting on us like seagulls . . .'

'Do geese in fact do the goose-step?' Raya said.

'Or frogs frog-march?' Pavel said. 'But we digress!'

'Do we?' Sasha said, as she waggled the last fingers of vodka in the bottle, offering it around the table. 'Isn't that the point? Digressing, I mean?'

'You enter into the spirit of things very well, Sasha,' said Raya. 'The migraine has responded well to vodka, I see, just like I said it would.'

'Yes, my darling. I kiss you for your kind advice,' Sasha said.

'It is the sign of a life well-lived, is it not,' Mitrofan's voice rose above the others. 'Is it not a sign? To be at peace in one's dacha, children at one's feet, a plump and intelligent wife – forgive me, ladies – migraines and such troubles receding into the undergrowth at the smell of vodka, and with all of one's metaphors, every single damn one of the little bastards, neatly shot through the heart, ping!, stuffed and mounted on the walls, all in a line and completely unmixed.'

'Well spoken, Mitrofan,' Pavel said. 'We will miss you dearly, my friend. Don't leave us. Stay another month!'

'So, Fyodor, Fyodor!' Raya said, 'tell us more about your student! Are you initiating her into the Russian School of playing, Fyodor? Are you turning her into China's Jascha Heifetz?'

'Let her become what she will become,' said Fyodor. 'They have one prize from her, and they will have more, I am sure of it.'

The conversation turned to other matters, and then to 'our friend Kirill' whom Ksenia had heard was divorcing his wife, having lived apart from her for several years. 'It is not good,' she said, and there was silence in the room, as if to mark the occasion. 'I hear he will be back in Shanghai in April,' she added finally. 'We must be kind to him, since we know nothing of the circumstances.'

After the guests left, I listened to the clinking of plates being washed in the tiny kitchen. I was about to shuffle backwards from my listening post onto the fire escape when I heard another noise, a soft and rhythmic scraping sound, and my skin crawled – a wave of prickly coldness – as I realised that Pavel was sitting at the table quietly sobbing. Raya moved about the room tidying things, but ignored her husband. He was still sobbing when she announced that she was going to bed. I carefully manoeuvred my way onto the fire escape and up onto the roof. It was a clear night – a rarity for Shanghai – and the stars were laid out like cheap shiny trinkets on a street hawker's cloak. When I got back to my room I realised that my eyes were wet with tears too, and that my hands were shaking.

The following week Madame Huang told me that Pavel Gachev would be leaving the Conservatory for health reasons, and would return to Kiev for treatment. Raya Vishinsky would stay on and continue her musicological research.

In the months that followed, my lonely vigils were fruitless. For an hour each night I bore silent witness to Raya's new evening ritual: cooking for herself in a single pot, setting out a plate and a fork and glass of vodka, putting a record on the gramophone and smoking one cigarette – leaning back in her chair to exhale its smoke towards the ceiling – and then settling into the corner of the couch to read.

Raya left the city in July and was not due to return until September. Madame Huang told me she had given as her summer address a hotel in Sevastopol on the Black Sea, rather than her sister's home in Kiev as in previous summers. And it seemed that Kirill had been reassigned to Beijing to assist Ambassador Yudin. 'We are trying hard to bring him back to Shanghai,' she said. 'We are trying to convince the generals to hold some negotiations here, to which he will inevitably come. We just need to find something that needs to be negotiated.'

'So if I am not needed here may I return home to Harbin to visit my parents?' I said.

Madame Huang stared into the space between us, blinking and breathing softly. 'Let me be frank,' she said, seeking out my eyes with hers. 'I would advise strongly against it. You will be aware that your parents have had some . . . some difficulties.'

'You mean the Anti-Rightist Campaign?'

'It is hard to control local elements,' she said. 'Here in Shanghai we like to think we are genteel about our self-criticisms; but up in Heilongjiang . . . well, you know what it's like up there. For you to visit would complicate matters. I think it is better that you stay away from Harbin, at least until things have . . .'

'Have what?'

Madame Huang smiled at me with her mouth, but there was a flicker of desperation in her eyes.

'Don't tell me any more,' I said. 'I understand what you are saying.'

'We have a plan,' she said, and put her hand on mine. 'Be assured that Director Ho, Professor Yu and I, we have a plan.'

*

Madame Huang's plan saw me travel alone to Moscow in August, by plane, and then to Paris by train, accompanied by an embassy courier called Gao – Old Gao, he insisted I call him, although he looked no more than thirty. He was a squat man with a round, saggy face, unruly hair and watery, bovine eyes. His movements too were slow and ox-like, and after the slightest exertion – beginning with lifting my small suitcase onto the train – he released a long and deliberate breath and noisily cleared his throat as if he were about to speak. He rarely did. We had a compartment to ourselves, and it was no surprise to me that Old Gao positioned himself by the door, set his own cardboard case on the floor, raised his feet onto it one by one, and waited for the motion of the train to lull him to sleep. He stayed in that position for as much of the next three days as he could, raising himself only to accompany me to the dining car for meals, to show our papers to a succession of border guards, and, in Berlin, to gather all of our luggage except my violin and negotiate the series of dusty passages and passport checks necessary to transfer us onto a different train for our journey through to Paris.

I spent the hours conversing with my ghosts, studying my scores, and looking out of the window at landscapes veiled for the most part by rain or fog. During daylight there were glimpses of a real world: purple forests, grey-green farmland, fields full of wheat stalks sagging with ripe grain, rivers, villages and towns. And everywhere there were children playing in piles of rubble and calling out to our train in a succession of languages as we passed.

On one occasion the train came to a halt for several minutes and I watched a group of three railway children at play. Two boys connived together in the doorway of a shed, while a girl dressed in a thin cotton dress and a dun-brown cardigan rode about awkwardly on a bicycle that was too large for her. The boys seemed to have found some treasure; a wounded animal, perhaps, or some artefact of war. The girl would stop her bicycle and try to join in, but the boys closed ranks and pushed her away, laughing amongst themselves. The girl rode on, marking figure eights in the muddy yard and calling out to the boys. Our train jolted into motion once more. As the scene began to move out of my view, I saw one of the boys come running out of the doorway, yelling and carrying a brick above his head. The girl turned sharply away and rose on the pedals to make her escape; but the boy took aim and hurled the brick at her with both hands, hitting her square on the back. Although I could hear nothing I swear I felt the impact of brick against ribcage, and at that moment, with the girl throwing her head back in surprise and pain, our train entered a tunnel and the scene was lost from view.

We arrived in Paris at night, at the Gare de l'Est, where we were met by a slender man dressed in a belted coat and an astrakhan hat. He greeted Old Gao and handed him a small briefcase and another train ticket. 'I'm afraid you're on the 11.15,' he said to Gao. 'No time for a rest. It leaves from Platform Eight. I'm sorry; they want you back in Moscow by Monday.' Gao sighed, and took the ticket and briefcase. 'Here,' said the man, 'get some food in the café over there.' He nodded towards a dimly lit salon where two men dressed in whites lounged amongst empty tables, their chefs' aprons slung untidily over a chair back. 'And the briefcase never leaves your side, remember.' He patted Gao on the elbow, and without a word of farewell to me Gao walked briskly away. The slender man shrugged his shoulders and introduced himself to me as Ruan, a second secretary from the embassy. He explained that he was assigned to look after me during my stay. I guessed he was from somewhere in the West, from Sichuan Province perhaps, since he spoke a toneless Mandarin which was difficult to follow. He led me to the street where a car waited for us and, having installed me and my luggage in the back seat, climbed into the front and told the driver to move on.

'You will stay at the embassy tonight,' Ruan said, twisting around in his seat. 'But from tomorrow we have a delegation from Beijing arriving for a conference, so you will have to move out. Happily we have found a place for you at the Paris Conservatoire guest house. You will live there for the remainder of your stay.'

When we arrived at the embassy, Ruan excused himself, saying he still had many things to do to prepare for the delegation's arrival, and arranging to meet me the following morning to take me to the Conservatoire. The driver showed me to a small room in the basement and pointed the way to the communal kitchen where, he suggested, I might negotiate some food.

In the morning I met Ruan as agreed in the embassy courtyard, and we waited together for the car to take us to the Conservatoire. In the daylight I was able to study him more closely. He had a small slightly ovoid head, slick black hair with a low parting ruled unerringly straight, and a slightly upturned face which meant he always looked at you down his nose like a maitre d'hôtel greeting a party of guests. Nevertheless, he had a disarming, mirthful voice, and even as he spelled out the precise instructions I was to obey, his upper lip quivered and I felt he was inviting me to join him a quiet conspiracy against all things serious.

Ruan had a small suitcase with him, and it became clear to me as we spoke that he would be occupying an adjacent room at the Conservatoire, and that we would have an umbilical relationship for the duration of my stay. 'So long as I am with you, China is here,' he said, drawing a circle around us in the gravel with his umbrella. 'Here is the Middle Kingdom; out there beyond the circle it is France. When we move, the circle moves with us.'

'So it's like Blaise Pascal,' I said. 'The universe is an infinite sphere whose centre is everywhere and whose circumference is nowhere.' Ruan looked puzzled, but then pleased. 'What happens when I shake hands with the orchestra leader or the conductor?' I asked. 'Do I leave China, or do they enter China?'

Ruan thought for a moment, and then said, 'Diplomacy occurs when two spheres of interest intersect.' He seemed pleasantly surprised by the profundity of his words.

'And when the sound of my violin carries beyond this circle?' I said. 'What is that called?'

'Cultural exchange,' Ruan said, smiling.

'And when the audience throws roses at my feet?'

'Historical necessity,' he said, with a nervous laugh. 'When the socialist artist is honoured, socialism is advanced.'

The car arrived, and as if to reinforce Ruan's point it swung around us in a circle before it stopped and the driver got out to get our luggage.

The Paris Conservatoire was in the Faubourg Poissonnière, on the far side of the city from the embassy. During the drive through the streets I rolled down the car window and leaned out, letting the air caress my face and hair. It was a Sunday morning, and only a few people dotted the boulevards, standing dreamily in patches of sunlight, walking with hands clasped behind their backs, idly perusing the shop windows or watching falling leaves. They seemed to me like the figures in Chinese landscape paintings, going inscrutably about their lives, dimly aware that in doing so they were giving scale to all the grandeur that overshadowed them.

We first drove north to the Arc de Triomphe, and circled it before heading east along one of its axes. Some things were oddly familiar. I recognised from Harbin the tree-lined boulevards, the fan-shaped patterns of the cobblestones and the octagonal newspaper kiosks, and from the Shanghai Bund the mansard roofs and elegant stone façades of the buildings. But here those façades and cobblestones seemed to go on forever, street after street of them, palisades of reflected light and hard, carved shadows. It seemed to me we were indeed passing over the surface of a perfect sphere, a landscape of Euclidean lines and curves, every street or boulevard we crossed offering a long, receding perspective which drew my eye towards some distant monument – a church, a tower, an arch, or simply the bright and empty morning sky, infinite and unattainable. The city seemed me to be a piece of music set in stone – stately, fugal, decorated with trills and fanfares in the form of colonnades, gargoyles and wrought iron doorways.

We entered the Paris Conservatoire through a high portico like the prow of a ship, guarded on both sides by robed marble figures with hands raised in a disinterested wave. My eye was drawn upwards to the arrangement of wreaths and columns and carved flowers they balanced on their heads, which in turn held up a sturdy triangular pediment with a central porthole, through which poked another head, with a large square forehead, bent nose, blank eyes, an imposing coif of hair, and an expression of languid amusement. It reminded me most of all of a woodcut I had seen in a book about the French Revolution, and I thought all it lacked was the addition of a beefy stone forearm above holding the head up by the hair. Beneath this a wide panel announced, in stone, the 'Conservatoire National Supérieur de

Musique'. All in all it was the most ridiculous piece of artwork I had ever seen.

Our car came to a halt beneath the portico and a little man with slick black hair and a moustache roused himself from a table where he was playing cards and struggled into a blue jacket as he approached us. He straightened his collar, smoothed his moustache with a flick of thumb and forefinger, and leant forward to exchange a few words with Ruan before waving us on into the courtyard.

We stopped by a fountain shaped like an oversized flower, from whose central stamen water trickled softly at various points onto fleshy stone petals. I stumbled from the car and immediately found myself face to face with a young woman who had emerged from behind this flower, licking her lips as if she had been sucking its nectar. She was dressed in a tulip-shaped skirt of dove-grey broadcloth, a silver-buckled belt, and an open-necked blouse with a wide collar. A string of diminutive pearls lay along the ridge of her clavicle, and matching earrings peered out from beneath her light brown hair, which was tied neatly behind her head with a coloured scarf, leaving a fringe that hung lightly over her brows. Her jaw was long and tapered, and she seemed to be simultaneously sucking in her cheeks and pushing forward her lips, which were thickly painted a rich burgundy. She stood perfectly still, of a piece with the marble figures by the gate, cool and inwardly amused. She fixed me with an inquisitive stare, tilting her head and raising one eyebrow.

I felt a surge of terror before this beautiful and strange creature. '*Bonjour*,' she said, her lips lunging forward to make the sound, and then settling into a half-smile as she awaited my response. On her chin was a perfectly rounded spot, the same red as her lips.

'*Bonjour*,' I replied, extending my hand to her. It delighted me to reproduce the one word of French Ruan had taught me over breakfast, and to hear it echo around the courtyard. The woman took my hand and studied me with eyes like discs of metal, her irises flashing blue, then grey, then blue again, performing a little autopsy on my face, my figure and my clothing.

Before either of us spoke again, Ruan appeared at my side and began to talk rapidly to the woman in French. Indeed, as we walked to the main doors and climbed the staircase to the third floor, he poured forth a kind of verbal nose-bleed, an uninterrupted stream of words, as if he had started something he could barely stop. The woman listened intently, but several times stopped short on the stairs, narrowed her eyes, and asked him to repeat himself, sometimes two or three times until she nodded her head, said, '*Exactement*,' and walked on.

We were soon installed in adjacent rooms and told to wait until we were summoned to meet my violin tutor. I stowed my suitcase and violin at the bottom of a wardrobe and stood for a while in the centre of my room. The furniture consisted of a bed with an iron frame and a mattress tightly wrapped in sheets and coverlet, a matching wicker chair and table, a wardrobe and a heavy polished wooden music stand. Above the bed and table were small framed pictures, dreary watercolours of rain-fogged street scenes. There was a tall window, with a wide sill and thick damask curtains which were tied back with tasselled rope. The window was ajar and I leaned across the sill and looked out into a small courtyard, whose walls were covered in climbing plants. From below came the sound of crockery being stacked and of muffled laughter. Cool air rose, as from a damp well, carrying with it the earthy, sweet aroma of pleasant things gently rotting away.

Below and to my left was an iron-barred gate beneath a low arch, which gave onto a narrow alley and the untidy back end of an apartment building. It was not unlike something I might have seen in Shanghai – a jumble of slanting roofs like a pile of fallen books, a tiny elevated garden of ornamental shrubs perched on a wide ledge that seemed inaccessible except via the roof itself, and damp distempered walls with rectangular window cavities, dissected at this time of the morning by the slanting sunlight. That light, still golden in colour, illuminated random slices of the domestic scenes within: a bottle on the edge of a table, clothes being aired on a wooden frame, and in one window a girl, perhaps ten years old, her arms folded on the sill, gazing down into the empty alleyway and jerking her head forward repeatedly in an irregular rhythm. I realised after a moment that a woman was standing in the shadows behind her, drawing out the girl's long black hair with two silver combs which glinted occasionally like knives when the sunlight struck them. It brought to my mind something I had all but forgotten from the months before my father's stroke. After reuniting with my father, my mother had begun to wear her hair down, and in the early evenings, before he came home to eat, she and I would sit by the window and comb each other's hair, counting out one hundred strokes. This was the only time she ever spoke to me in Russian.

Lost in contemplation, I barely registered the knock on the door, and did not realise that someone had entered the room until a hand was placed on my arm. '*Mademoiselle.*' A voice that was gentle but firm, placing the stress on the *moi* and lingering over the *elle*. I turned to find a man standing close beside me. He had the whitest skin of anyone I had ever seen, his arm barely darker than the white of his rolled shirtsleeve and covered in fine hairs and a scattering of tiny pink spots, like paint spatters. He had large, green eyes with lashes that were almost transparent, and ginger hair in bristly waves. For a moment I thought he might be my new teacher, but he was barely ten years older than me – too young to have known Zhou Enlai during his stay in France thirty-five years before. He began speaking to me in French, and I must have given him a look of confusion and panic, for he paused and began again, speaking more slowly and in softly descending cadences which seemed so full of tender concern that I could not bring myself to reveal my complete incomprehension.

When he had finished he wrinkled his nose and widened his eyes, and waited for a response. At that moment Ruan appeared in the doorway behind him, and as he made to announce his presence with a rap on the door I drew a breath and said loudly to the young man, '*Exactement.*'

As it turned out, the man had come to fetch me for my first lesson with my teacher, which took place in a large airy room on the second floor. The young man was my teacher's assistant (his *homme de vendredi*, as he later told me), a role which so far as I could tell involved driving him around in a small snail-shaped car, carrying his large leather pouch, opening doors, helping with coats and hats, and running errands for glasses of water, sheets of paper and – towards the end of my first lesson – a small bunch of flowers for me tied up in brown string. My teacher certainly needed this attention. He was a long retired professor of violin, tall, stooped and flamingo-like in the slow articulation of his movements. His hair was thick and the purest white, descending in two curtains from a central parting, matched by a moustache of the same colour and then set off by a multicoloured silk cravat tucked neatly into his shirt collar, all of which gave him the look – from the chest upwards – of an ornithological specimen.

Most importantly he seemed delighted to have me as a student, to be liberated from his ordinary life, and he announced that I was to prepare the Saint-Saëns violin concerto for the competition. This we proceeded to do, running our respective fingers along the lines of the score his assistant had spread out along a high bench, the professor giving guidance in French with a scattering of Italian musical terms, Ruan attempting to render this into Chinese, and the young man, who lurked in the corner throughout, contributing his own suggestions when Ruan faltered, only to be silenced by an indulgent shake of the old man's head.

We were soon able to dispense with the services of our translator. The professor removed his jacket, with the help of his assistant, and stood by the window with his hands behind his back, listening to me play. Occasionally he would stop me and sing through a passage in a wavering falsetto, or play it on his own violin, whereupon I would repeat the phrase and he would say, '*Bon, bon; continuez,*' and return to his station by the window. As the lesson progressed the young man would produce from his jacket pockets a series of billowing handkerchiefs, one for the old man's nose, one to wipe his brow, and a third which was folded and refolded over the chin-rest of the professor's violin to protect it from his sweat.

Eventually, a nearby church bell struck one o'clock, and the professor straightened to attention and began to pack up his violin, the young man immediately fussing around him, shoving papers into his leather pouch and helping the professor on with his coat. When all was done they stood beside each other and simultaneously inclined their heads in a polite bow. '*A demain,*' the old man said, and his young friend mouthed the same words silently, took his charge by the arm and led him to the door.

So every day at ten Ruan and I would settle ourselves in the practice room and await the arrival of the small, snail-shaped car. Within minutes the professor and I would lose ourselves in the phrasing of some passage and our two companions would cease to exist for us until the clock struck one and the professor's assistant would step out of the shadows, holding out the coat into which the professor would meekly reverse his arms before bidding me farewell and making his way to the door. On the fourth or fifth day, the young man disappeared after an hour and returned shortly with hot water, tea cups and a small sealed paper bag which, from the aroma that shortly filled the room, I could tell contained Chinese tea. He offered a cup each to the professor and me, addressing to me a long discourse which, although I understood barely a word, seemed to explain how he had been pleasantly surprised to find, in a back street of the arrondisement where the professor lived, a shop owned by a diminutive Chinese couple of uncertain age which sold, among other exotic fare arrayed on sagging shelves in an unaired back room, small tins of oolong tea painted with Ming Dynasty scenes of lakeside pavilions and ladies with parasols standing atop arched bridges musing (although one could not be certain of this) on love and loss. Ruan had by this time succumbed to boredom and was outside by the fountain smoking a cigarette. The young man poured two more cups and, balancing them on saucers, left the room, appearing a minute later at the fountain where he offered one to Ruan, and began to drink from the other. Ruan stubbed out his cigarette on the underside of the fountain, and drank his tea, and the two remained there for the next hour, with the young man leaning his buttocks on the edge of the fountain and talking while Ruan held his fingers under the trickle of water and occasionally gave a response.

During our time at the Conservatoire, Ruan insisted that we remain apart from the other students and faculty. We ate at a table by ourselves in the refectory, talking only to the elegant woman with the gem-cut features and brown hair, who joined us from time to time, drank a plate of thin soup and sought assurances that our accommodations, the food, and my instruction were to our liking, greeting our repeated affirmations with a distrustful nod of her head. We walked briskly between our quarters and the classroom, faces turned down, aware dimly of the rush of students in the corridors and the scales, truncated phrases, rotations and repetitions that echoed from every window and doorway.

When I was not with the professor or practicing in my room, I convinced Ruan to accompany me on walks around the neighbourhood. Our normal route took us past the Place de la Bastille and south to the Seine, with Ruan maintaining a vigorous pace, as if we had something to prove to the locals by overtaking them on the sidewalk and showing them our heels. On the return he took things more leisurely, stopping at a row of green metal *bouquiniste* stalls by the Pont Marie to scan the titles and examine the contents page of a volume or two. Sometimes he would buy something, counting out the required number of francs and clutching them tightly as he watched the proprietor wrap a small plain-covered volume in a sheet of crisp brown paper and tie it up with string. He would also stop at a tailor's shop and study the group of headless mannequins in the window, meticulously turned out in pressed suits, collared shirts with matching cufflinks (changed every day, it seemed) and arrayed with hollow, handless arms raised, as if at a cocktail party, debating the leader from that day's *Figaro*: the establishment of the Fifth Republic, the death of the Pope, Pasternak's refusal of the Nobel Prize.

Towards the end of our walks we would stop at a café, and occupy one of the metal-hooped tables. The waiter would deliver our coffee and one of the selection of pastries from behind the counter, then retreat to the doorway, where he stood and sniffed the breeze, hands clasped behind his back, rocking backwards and forwards on the balls of his feet. Ruan would sit bolt upright in his wicker chair until the waiter's retreat; then he would remove his glasses, fold them and set them on the table, tug on his cuffs to straighten them, and address his cup and saucer: moving it to the midpoint of his gaze, turning the handle to the left and then the right, clearing his throat and bowing his head to the black-brown liquid as if paying homage to something foreign and perhaps forbidden. Once he had completed his little internal ceremony he would lift the tiny cup with his thumb and forefinger, as a philatelist lifts a stamp with a set of tweezers, and apply it softly to his lips. For myself I found the aroma exotic but the taste vile and abrasive on the tongue. While Ruan savoured his coffee and somehow managed to extend its thimbleful over a dozen or so delicate sips, I downed mine quickly like a dose of medicine and then tried discreetly to shift the bitter film it had attached to the back of my tongue.

When we had finished our coffee and picked up the last slivers of pastry with our fingertips, Ruan would produce a packet of Gauloises and a matchbook, and as he lit up he would ask me how my preparation was going, listening intently to my reply, questioning me about the challenges of Saint-Saëns and the professor's suggestions on how to play it as if the concerto were some vital matter of state and the professor a sympathetic foreigner whose advice should nevertheless be subjected to political analysis. I found his line of questioning slightly absurd, and turned the conversation onto other matters: news from

China or the vexed question of whether the professor's young assistant was working for French intelligence (Ruan assumed he must be; I thought it highly unlikely).

On one occasion a sparrow landed on our table as we were speaking, snatched up a crumb and ate it. We stopped talking. Ruan slowly lowered his cigarette and rested it in the ashtray to his right, cupping his hands over his knee. The bird stood its ground at first, eyeing another crumb under the edge of Ruan's plate. Then, in successive blinks of an eye, it turned to face three points of the compass, so quickly I swear I did not see any movement; and after the next blink it was gone, leaving the crumb untouched. Ruan picked up his cigarette again and summoned the waiter, indicating that he wanted to borrow a knife to cut the string on a volume he had just bought. The waiter produced the clasp I had seen him use to open wine bottles, extended a small blade and deftly released the string at the knot. Ruan thanked him, opened the parcel, and examined the small volume. 'Zola,' he explained, and he studied the handwritten inscription on the flyleaf. 'For Eugenie,' he translated, 'Noel 1955, with love.'

'Who is Noel?' I asked.

'Her husband, perhaps,' he replied. And, flipping the silk-ribbon page marker over the spine, he opened the book to the first page, lifted the volume to his face and began to read, stopping after a minute to light another Gauloise. I occupied myself with my own reverie for some minutes, barely aware of the customers at adjacent tables and the shoes and shopping bags of passers-by. Then I noticed that our little bird had returned, perching itself on the hooped edge of the table, hopping around the points of the compass once more, examining the empty cups, Ruan's spectacles, the discarded paper and string, and of course the solitary pastry crumb. Ruan once more lowered his cigarette onto the ashtray to his right, and then closed his book, placed it in his lap, and cupped his hands over his raised knee. The bird jumped to and fro, as instantaneously as before, and again, in an instant, disappeared. It was some moments before I realised that Ruan's cupped hands were now on the table by his plate. He released his thumbs a fraction and a beak poked out. I could hear the fluttering of wings under his hands.

'How did you do that?' I asked. 'I barely saw you move.' Ruan shrugged and smiled self-deprecatingly, but said nothing. The bird fluttered again, stopped and then was silent. 'How does the trick end?' I asked. 'Does the bird live or die?'

Ruan began to laugh softly, and then turned to watch a cylinder of ash fall from his Gauloise. I reached over and picked it up from the ashtray and held it towards his lips, but at the last moment, as he leaned forward, mouth open, to receive it, I pulled it away and held it over my shoulder. Out of the corner of my eye I saw the waiter start towards us, as if I had summoned him, and then step back to his post in the doorway.

'These cigarettes are very expensive, right?' I said. 'So you wouldn't want to waste one.'

'True, true,' he said. 'Be my guest and smoke it before it burns down.'

I held the cigarette up and examined it, allowing the smoke to tickle my nose and throat. 'I have never smoked,' I said. And immediately Ruan released the bird and held out his two fingers to receive the cigarette.

*

One afternoon, a week or so before the competition, Ruan appeared at my door with an unsealed envelope containing a letter from my mother. He apologised for having opened it himself and read it. He was instructed to do so, he said. He would return in an hour so that we could go for our walk. The letter was in my mother's hand, although the characters were loosely drawn. It read like one of the homilies she would give to me when I had performed well as a child. She wrote of her overwhelming joy and pride at my success in Bucharest, and her confidence in my ability to serve my country well in the upcoming competition in Paris. There the letter ended abruptly. There was no mention of my father's condition, or of her own life and work. It gave me some pleasure to imagine her writing it hurriedly between examining patients, scrawling the address on an envelope and passing it to an intern to run to the post office before it closed for the day.

I read the letter several times sitting on the window sill behind the damask curtain. When I had finished I found myself looking across at the apartment building beyond the gate, examining each window until I found what I was hoping to see: the young girl staring out at the world and in the shadows behind her the old woman combing her hair, counting down the strokes until they reached zero.

The day of the competition arrived. The concert hall was dark and cool, and a welcome respite from the heat. As I stood to play my first piece, my eye was caught by one of the name plates on the judges' table and prickly heat spread over my entire skin. *M. Shostakovich*, it read. A bespectacled figure sat behind it, chin on his hand, studying something on the table before him. Mitya?, I thought, could this truly be Mitya, the composer of the passacaglia, and author of the letter still sequestered in the lining of Vitja's violin case, somewhere in Harbin, or perhaps now somewhere in Moscow?

After my performance, and the ragged applause it inspired, the lunch-break was announced and I made my way to the judges' table.

'You are Mitya Shostakovich?' I said, in Russian, extending my hand to the young man.

'Mitya is my father, Dmitri,' he replied, as strands of blond hair fell forward onto the rims of his glasses. 'I am Maxim, his son.'

'I am sorry,' I said.

'Do not be sorry!' he replied. 'I am sorry I am not as famous as my father. And, indeed, I suspect I am here because some clerk in the Ministry of Culture misread the invitation. Or perhaps it is a joke. As you can see, my fellow judges are all old enough to be my father.' He flicked his eyes towards the three grey-haired elders sharing the judges' table.

Something in his manner made me trust him, or at least, made me think I could be reckless with him. I glanced over my shoulder, and spied Ruan some distance from me, stuck in the middle of a row of seats as the audience filled the aisle and shouldered their way towards the exit. He acknowledged me with a raised hand, half a wave and half an instruction to stop what I was doing. I turned back to Maxim and began to explain myself. He listened intently, nodding quietly as I related to him my link to his father via his grandmother's friends, Kasimir and Piroshka, and asked if he had any news of them since their return to Moscow. As I finished speaking I felt the air move slightly beside me and knew that Ruan must have arrived at my shoulder, because Maxim raised his hand to stop me talking, and picked up a sheet of paper from the table between us and turned it towards me. 'Perhaps it has not been explained to you sufficiently well,' he said. 'Sometimes the translators they use are barely competent. It says here you will be marked equally on all three of your performances: a concerto, a sonata and a solo piece. Judges are not at liberty to change this. I am sorry, that is all I can say.' And with that he walked away from us without another word.

I turned away from the judges' table, and found, not Ruan, but the professor's young assistant standing beside me, his silvery-white eyebrows raised in a gentle, mocking admonition. Ruan was still making his way towards the stage through a family group adoring one of the other contestants. The young man and I turned to watch Ruan struggle up the steps.

'What was that about?' Ruan asked. 'Do you know that man?' He indicated Maxim, who was already withdrawing, clutching a leather satchel to his chest.

'It was a mistake,' I said. 'A misunderstanding, that's all.'

Ruan took me firmly by the elbow and drew me down the steps. I felt the young man slip his hand quietly around my other forearm, and I descended to the stalls as if under arrest, with Ruan hissing at me under his breath and the young man mute and bemused. The latter steered us into the lobby, where my tutor was waiting for us. The old man seized me by the shoulders and planted kisses on each temple, and, pretending not to hear or understand Ruan's protestations that we must return to the embassy, drew me by the hand into the street and around the corner to a tiny bistro where a waiter showed us to a table set for four and produced, without our having to order, a light lunch accompanied by a bottle of white wine. This bottle, along with its two successors, was immediately commandeered by the young assistant, who filled Ruan's glass to the brim and cajoled him into a series of toasts – to France, to China, to the bonds of friendship, to enduring allegiances between nations and peoples – while my tutor and I pushed aside the plates before us and pored over the Saint-Saëns score for the last time.

We rose from our meal an hour later and returned to the concert hall. We sat together in the dark and cool awaiting my turn to perform, and Ruan quickly slumped backwards in his narrow seat and fell asleep. He did not awake until the middle of my performance, and when I arrived back at our seats I found him on the floor in the aisle with his head between his knees. 'Migraine,' he said, without looking up, and passed a shivering hand through the sweat-glistened hair on the back of his head.

In one swift movement the young man went down on his haunches, inserted his arms through Ruan's armpits, leant backwards and hoisted him upright, and the three of us marched him like a marionette out onto the street, stopping to let him dry-retch in the gutter before arranging his limp, damp limbs across the back seat of my tutor's tiny car. The young man jumped into the driver's seat and set off for the embassy, from whence he returned an hour later to inform me via a piece of mime that Ruan had taken a herbal infusion, was sleeping, and had entrusted me to his care.

The competition had by this time concluded, and the judges quietly passed notes amongst themselves and whispered to each other behind their hands before Maxim Shostakovich approached the microphone and, in what appeared to be passable French, announced the winners. I was awarded second prize once more, and my two companions leant clumsily from either side and kissed me firmly and wetly on both cheeks before releasing me to approach the stage, from where I returned richer by a large cone of flowers, a bronze statuette of a treble clef, and an envelope sealed with red wax which I later relinquished to an embassy official and never saw again.

We took my tutor home to his apartment, which was only a few blocks away, the young man helping his charge to the front door, and greeting the concierge with a kiss before placing the old man's hand onto her plump shoulder. He returned to the car, slipped behind the wheel and started the engine. '*Teplyye pozdravleniya!*' he said, smiling and turning towards me as much as his cramped seat would allow.

'Thank you,' I said. 'Your pronunciation is very good.'

'And . . .' he went on as we pulled away from the curb. 'Will you ask . . .'

'If you wish,' I said, clearing my throat: 'So where did you learn Russian?'

'In the Caucasus, and then I perfected it in Moscow. I was attached to a foreign embassy there for two years.'

'Attached?'

'Not surgically, you'll understand,' he beamed at me. 'I was their first customer on the consular side.'

'The French Embassy? In Moscow?'

'No. The New Zealand Legation – not strictly an embassy. The day after they opened the doors I was detained on the train from Tomsk for not having a passport. I was delivered into their custody and ended up staying there once they discovered I was the only one whose Russian was good enough to get sense out of an electrician or a greengrocer. The place was still full of boxes and crates, you see. The plumbing barely worked, and they were being charged exorbitant prices for food because they didn't understand the black market. The new ambassador didn't speak a word of Russian. And to fix it all they'd brought over a chap who'd been studying at Oxford. Nice fellow, wrote a dissertation on Pushkin or Zhukovsky – but no practical use as an interpreter, as you can imagine.'

'So you understood what I was saying to the judge today?'

'To Comrade Maxim Dmitreyevich Shostakovich, the composer's son? Every word. In fact, I bumped into him in the men's room and introduced myself, and I'm taking you to meet him right now.'

'Right now?'

'Indeed,' he said, 'at the Louvre. Have you been? Has your friend let you out of his sight?'

'No,' I said.

'No to which question?'

'To both. Why does he want to talk to me?'

'I suggest you let him speak for himself.'

The Louvre was emptying of visitors when we arrived, and my chaperone succeeded in getting us in without paying since it was so late in the day. He strode purposefully up one flight of steps and then slowed his pace and led me through several galleries of paintings before stopping before a large canvas of a battle scene. I watched his eyes scan the painting.

'Is this where he will meet us?' I said.

'Comrade Maxim? . . . Yes, yes. He said he'd be here.' He glanced into the adjacent gallery. It, like the one we were in, was empty. 'At the Blake exhibition.'

'So he wants to speak . . . in confidence?'

'I imagine so. Things aren't as bad in Russia as they were when the old man was alive; but they're still . . . well, bad. Maxim is a young man of considerable talent; famous father; the world before him. Can't afford to take risks, you know.'

Who can?, I thought, feeling suddenly chilled.

Loud clacking footsteps approached us from behind. I spun around. A security guard entered the gallery and, seeing us, stopped and started to smooth the worn blue serge of his jacket. He eyed us benevolently and, as if remembering an errand, wandered off.

When I turned back my companion was gone. 'Over here,' he beckoned to me from an adjoining gallery. 'William Blake,' he said, as I joined him, pointing to a series of woodcuts arrayed along a wall. 'I've only ever seen these in books. It's Blake's Job. Do you know about Job? About Blake? About God? I suspect not.'

I confirmed to him my ignorance. The naïve figures, the starry monochrome swirls, the winged creatures, the dumb, trance-like agonies, the eyes wide and lidless and blank, reminded me of Chinese folk art, none more so than a picture where Job lies on his bed and over him, smothering him like a lover, hovers a being, half-man half-snake, with hair like the rays of the sun.

'Who is that?'

'That is God, the Supreme Being, Ruler of the Universe, Almighty, Omnipotent Saviour, King of Kings, Lord of Lords, Good Shepherd, Consuming Fire and so on. Do you have gods in China?'

'We do indeed.' I looked more closely at the woodcut, at the figures beneath Job's bed, holding chains, reaching their arms up to try to pull him down into the flames which surrounded them.

'Well, you see, this figure here is Job, and he is God's most loyal servant,' my companion went on, 'and yet God has a wager with Satan the Accuser . . . see, this fellow here . . . and he sends all manner of plagues upon Job and has his family killed and his oxen poisoned in order to test his faith. And for forty chapters Job ruminates upon the nature of suffering while scraping his sores with broken pottery, and these chaps here . . . these are Job's friends who debate with him the question of why suffering occurs and conclude it is probably all Job's fault. But despite forty chapters of talk nothing is ever settled, and God tires of the whole thing and steps in and restores Job's riches . . . and leaves him richer and sadder, but no wiser.'

'When did Maxim say he would meet us?'

'Soon, I hope . . . But what Job discovers is that he is in fact morally superior to God; or at least that he is conscious and free in a way that God is unconscious and limited, and indeed amoral, even though he is all-powerful. You must read Jung on the subject, Carl Gustav Jung. He is very good. See how the snake and God are intertwined?'

285

I looked again at Job lying on his bed, with the God-Snake stretched out above him and the flame-licked figures beneath the bed clawing at him, and thought immediately of myself and Tian on our bed of reed-mats in the hut on Hainan, with Director Ho's forbidden scores in their case beneath us. I felt a shiver of remembered disgust.

'And when God finally fronts up to Job,' my companion went on, 'all he does is bluster about, saying how powerful he is, and how dare Job challenge him, and who made the monsters of the deep and so on. But the one thing God doesn't do is reprimand Satan. Why, you might ask? Because Satan is in fact that hidden face of God that God won't acknowledge. According to Jung, that is.'

'Did you really talk to Maxim?' I said. 'Or is this all a hoax?'

The young man turned down the corners of his mouth, clown-like, but did not look at me.

'No,' he said.

'No to which question?'

'To both,' he said. 'I didn't talk to Maxim; but it's not a hoax. I wouldn't call it a hoax. I just didn't want your time in Paris to end with such a whimper. You can't leave Paris without seeing the Louvre or the Tuileries or Sacré-Coeur. That wouldn't be right. Now that would be a hoax – to bring you to Paris and not let you see these things. So I have merely . . . stolen you.'

'Stolen me?'

'Yes. Is it your first time?'

'It is.'

'I will give you back, I promise,' he said. 'I told your Comrade Ruan I would bring you back after the Mayor's reception.'

'What Mayor's reception? I don't recall . . .'

'*Exactement*,' he said, taking my arm. 'So come with me now. We have maybe three hours at the most.'

We drove though the city as dusk fell and the streetlights sputtered into life. I contemplated jumping from the car and trying to make my way to the embassy, but realised that my violin was locked in the car boot, along with my trophy and flowers. Besides, this young man had awakened in me a new curiosity, a nest of new doubts, pecking their way out of their shells. From the corner of my eye I observed his face, illuminated in turn by streetlights, carlights, arc lights and then the glow of the cigarette he had lit. I saw in him a crazily shaped window with patchwork panes of coloured glass through which shone a chaotic, not entirely pleasing light.

'*Kak tebya zovut?*' I asked.

'Leon,' he said, without turning his head. 'After Trotsky.'

*

During my absence in France, Shanghai was becoming drunk on musical glory. As I was preparing to return home a wire came through from Leningrad announcing that Tian Mei Yun had won first prize in the César Cui Piano Competition playing Beethoven's *Emperor Concerto*. He was photographed shaking hands with Nikita Khrushchev, and when he arrived in Shanghai two days before I was due to return he celebrated by commandeering a large truck and transporting the Conservatory's grand piano to Huangpu Park by the river, where he gave an impromptu concert. The news magazines printed photographs: the piano shining like an enormous cockroach, surrounded by a crowd of dock-workers and porters, their mouths open in astonishment; Tian in his coat and tails, hunched intently over the keys playing Chopin and Liszt, and after his performance leaping atop the piano as if it were a tank and waving a red flag as he addressed the crowd. 'The piano has become a weapon for the proletariat,' the newspaper quoted him as saying, and he assured me when I asked him that these were his exact words.

Later that week an audience of factory workers, soldiers and party officials witnessed the first all-Chinese performance of Beethoven's Ninth Symphony. Between movements the Party Secretary read out accounts of peasants voluntarily reducing their already meagre rations so rural party secretaries could increase the quota of grain sent to the cities. Loudspeakers on street corners played newly minted songs from the Conservatory, sung by the Conservatory choir and orchestra; songs such as 'Marxism is one sentence: revolution is justified', 'To sail the ocean we depend on the Helmsman; to carry out a revolution we depend upon the Thought of Mao Zedong', and 'Mao Zedong Thought Glitters with Golden Light'.

The papers published a progress report on musical production for the whole country. The number of advanced music schools increased from four to eighteen, and the number of professional music associations from three to one hundred and forty-eight. Two thousand musical titles had been published in sixty million volumes. Thirty-two million records pressed, in 3,500 titles. Ninety-four Chinese accepted for entry into international competitions and seventy music groups touring abroad.

It was perhaps no surprise when I received a telegram from Professor Yu informing me that I was not to return to Shanghai immediately, but that I would remain in Paris to prepare for another international competition, which, for the time being, was not specified. Ruan and I moved back into the embassy compound and its four walls became, in effect, my prison. Leon would bring my elderly teacher to the embassy gate every morning and the two of us would help him up the stairs to the third-storey room beneath the mansard roof in which we would spend the next two hours practising. Ruan was reassigned to other duties, and I missed my walks with him. I also missed the busy corridors of the Conservatoire and the cacophony from the practice rooms.

The competition for which I had been kept in Paris turned out to be a small one, in a quiet, damp country town in Belgium which was shrouded in fog for the three days I was there. The other competitors were Flemish and Dutch schoolchildren, talented no doubt, but as I accepted first prize from the competition's wealthy benefactors and turned to acknowledge the applause of the small audience who had emerged from the foggy streets and half-filled the town hall, an audience comprising for the most part the families of the other competitors, I felt rather like a bully who has taken a liking to a small child's toy and dispatched its rightful owner with a slap of the hand. I realised that Madame Huang and Director Ho were detaining me in France to keep me safe, far away from China.

My monkish existence in Paris continued through the winter, and it was not until February 1959 that I was summoned back to Shanghai. Although Madame Huang's telegram to me said nothing of the sort, I thought I knew what its message was: she had succeeded in getting Kirill back to Shanghai.

I was met at the airport by Madame Huang, Ding Shangde, a girl carrying another medal of honour, and a photographer to record the occasion. I was soon installed in the back of a car with Madame Huang, and without a word she handed me a telegram dated a week before, placed a hand on my knee and turned her face to look out at the street scene passing by. It was from my mother informing me that my father had died. 'I am sorry that it turned out like this,' Madame Huang whispered to me. 'I had hoped it would turn out better.'

My father's final illness had been sudden, my mother wrote in the letter that arrived a week later. He had been immobile for some time and had developed pneumonia and bedsores that became infected. He had put up little resistance. I should be assured that his last thoughts were for me and for my future career, my mother wrote, and that this had made his suffering bearable. She promised to send money the following summer, so that I could visit during my holidays.

I sat in my room for three days and cried and slept. Ling Ling brought me tea, which I drank, and food, which I did not eat. Tian visited me and tried to talk to me for half an hour, and then gave up, leaving a small bunch of flowers. Comrade Meretrenko wrote me a kind note – in faltering Chinese characters (with a Russian translation) – and slipped it under my door. Strangely, it was Madame Huang who provided the most comfort. She bustled into the room and embraced me for what seemed like an hour, stroking my hair as if I was a child, and telling me about the deaths of her own parents and of the daughter she had lost to malaria. 'It is important to be alone,' she said, as she rose to leave. 'In China there are so few opportunities to be alone. We are always out serving the masses. In times to come you will look back on these days and be thankful.'

Every day I reopened my mother's letter and read it again, fresh tears tap-tapping onto the paper, blurring the words but not washing them away. When we met, some months later, she explained that she knew her letters were being read by the Party authorities, and did not want to jeopardise my position by reminding them of my past links to Rightist elements. She also apologised for lying to me about the circumstances of my father's death. She explained that they had both been detained as Rightists in the aftermath of the Hundred Flowers Movement. They had not taken any part in the Movement itself, she said; but the backlash that followed it gave a pretext for anyone who was out of favour to be arrested. My mother had been sent to a re-education camp in the countryside for four months, during which she heard nothing about my father's whereabouts or well-being, although she was permitted to send and receive letters from me.

Her release, and my father's, had coincided with my prize from Bucharest. My father had been in Xiangfeng Prison again, and this time shared a cell with Li Changching, with whom he had worked to restore order to Harbin after the defeat of the Japanese. His health had further deteriorated in prison, although Li had nursed him as best he could. When he was released my father could no longer walk, was occasionally incontinent and suffered from poor circulation in his legs. Mercifully, they were allowed to move back into their house. She had not lied about Zhu Shaozen and his nephew, however. And, unannounced, a doctor had arrived from Beijing to tend to my father, bringing drugs and an oxygen tent and other medical equipment. She recognised him as a fellow student from her medical training days in Beijing years before. He was a jovial fellow, for whom suffering and death were part of the universal comedy that also encompassed birth and food and play and the taking of modest pleasures. The doctor, my mother and Zhu were my father's companions during his final weeks, feeding and washing him, talking to him and noting without celebration his small responses, carrying him to and from a cot they had placed by the fish pond, cooling his brow with water, playing records and conversing with him as if he were fully present. Around and around they went, my mother told me, like children in a game, until the night fell.

11. The Liberation of Mudanjiang

One morning a week after I received news of my father's death I was woken by Madame Huang's hand on my shoulder. 'The Conservatory has a guest house in a fishing village on the coast,' Madame Huang said. 'I have arranged for you and your mother to use it for three days.' She handed me a telegram that read: 'Arrive Shanghai Monday.'

My mother had barely slept throughout the three-day train journey, and as she stepped down from the railway carriage she wilted onto my shoulder like a flower. 'Welcome to Shanghai,' I said, taking her suitcase. She smiled and said a few words in greeting, and I saw that her tiredness was not simply that of the journey. We emerged through the station doors into a greasy envelope of spring heat. Our cotton clothing plastered itself to our limbs as we waited to catch the bus to the small seaside town where the Conservatory had its guest house.

The house was one of several that were built amidst a copse of trees on the edge of a cliff. All were owned by large work units in the city – the ball bearing factory; the municipal power corporation; the Academy of Social Sciences – and were for use by senior cadres. The old couple who were employed as caretakers showed us to our room, a simple space with two cots under mosquito nets, a small chest of drawers, two chairs and a table, all painted white, and a washstand with an old porcelain water pitcher and a chipped white basin. A door led out onto the veranda from which there were views down to the fishing village below, and beyond it the sandy beach and the blue-grey mass of the sea, gently pitching and rolling at high tide. A steep staircase built into the rock gave access from the guest houses to the village and the beach.

It was the first time my mother had seen the sea. I myself had only seen the Black Sea from the window of an aeroplane. We stood side by side for several minutes on the cliff top watching its marbled surface, our capacity to think or speak muted by its immensity. I had never imagined that anything could be bigger than China; but from the viewpoint of those cliffs the sea seemed capable of welcoming China and all of her masses into its cool depths, swallowing our middle kingdom ten thousand times over.

Eventually I left my mother and went in search of some tea and something to eat. When I returned she was sitting sideways in a lounge chair on the veranda with her legs tucked under her and her torso turned towards the sea. Her eyes were closed, and she was tilting her face, first this way, then that, to catch the irregular flow of the breeze, and humming softly to herself. I put the tea and a plate of fruit on the low table by her chair, and she opened her eyes, turned to me and took my hand and wrote in my palm with her finger: 'Xie xie' – thank you. 'Bu keqi,' I wrote back – don't mention it. Then she turned back to the sea without touching the fruit or the tea. I went inside and lay on my cot and instantly fell asleep.

When I awoke it was dark. My mother was fast asleep on the bed next to me. Someone had unfurled our mosquito nets over us. I rose and found on the table two sets of chopsticks and three bowls covered with plates. Grilled fish with a hot chilli sauce, spring onions fried with egg, some steamed rice. I divided the meal in two, ate everything that was mine – even the last half-grain of rice – and locked the door to the veranda before undressing and returning to my bed.

The next morning at dawn my mother woke me and presented me with a small canvas bag. Inside was the notebook my father had kept, with his reflections on his illness. 'But he wanted this to be published in a medical journal,' I said. 'Don't give this to me. That's why he wrote it – as case notes for publication. Remember? Like Lu Xun.'

My mother leaned her head to one side and released a gentle harrumph along with a bitter smile. 'At this point in the nation's history I think to tell the masses about his symptoms would be . . . inconvenient,' she said. 'And I am sure his wish would be that if it couldn't be published, it would be given to you to keep.'

'Thank you,' I said. 'But you should keep it. Wait for a while and then send it to a medical journal. Why entrust it to me?'

She placed her hand firmly on my wrist, and drew my arm onto her lap. Her face suddenly lost its colour and went blank, her lower lip settling into an unnatural curl. 'It's all I have of him,' she whispered, not looking at me, but beyond me to the open door and the view of the sea. 'I gave his records away to Zhu, and the gramophone. Please understand, it's all I have of him now.'

She blinked several times.

'But . . . his books,' I said softly.

She blinked again, as if she had just woken with a start from a dream, and then exhaled a long harsh sigh. 'Come walk with me,' she said, and pulled me to my feet.

As we walked along the beach my mother explained to me the true circumstances of my father's death and her own imprisonment. She told the story matter-of-factly, itemising the location of my father's bedsores, the food the neighbours brought over, the arrangement of pillows she used on the *kang* to help him sleep in an upright position to stop his coughing, the patient she was treating when she received the news that he was dying, and precisely which records Zhu Shaozen continued to play to him after he had lost consciousness. These details and their randomness puzzled me at first; but I realised that they were simply those things that had lodged in her memory. For once she was leaving nothing out, and I sensed that this slow accretion of minute facts was to compensate for her inability to impose any order upon what she felt, even to know what it was she felt, during those days.

She told me more about the doctor from Beijing who was assigned to treat my father during his last illness – how he had arrived one day while she was at work, bringing with him a laryngoscope and canisters of oxygen and a canvas mask to help my father's breathing, asking Zhu, who was in attendance, to push aside the medicines my mother kept on her shelf, her mandrake root and her lunar caustic, her colloids and her extract of ipecacuanha, and stocking the shelf instead with vials of atropine and emetics and expectorants. He had introduced himself to my father when he next woke, receiving from him a confused smile. My mother had arrived home to find him attaching a jar of clear fluid to my father's forearm. He had explained that his orders were to stay for the duration, and then he sat at the table and made meticulous notes in a large black ledger.

She was surprised, she said, but relieved. My father's death would be sanctioned by the People's Republic. There was now a sense of necessity about it. To die in this way was another service to the masses, the final service he could perform. She was also convinced that his arrival had something to do with my success in Bucharest, although the doctor himself could not or would not confirm that.

On the night my father's breathing lapsed into agonal rasping, the doctor took my mother aside and told her the end could still be days away. His orders were not to leave his side, he told her, so that he could witness any last words, although he doubted there would be any more words.

That night the electricity failed, and my mother and the doctor lit candles and put them around the room, filling it slowly with the smell of pork grease and smoke. Zhu joined them, bringing firewood with which they stoked the *kang*. He started to play through all of my father's Brahms collection, starting with the four symphonies in order and the festival overture. My mother took each completed record from the gramophone and returned it to its brown paper sleeve as Zhu placed the next dark circle of shellac onto the platen and wound the handle.

Around ten p.m. the doctor sent Zhu to get some more oxygen from the hospital chemist, in case their supplies did not last out the night. As soon as Zhu left, the doctor took my mother by the arm into the courtyard. 'This could take days,' he said. 'Or I could give him a large dose of morphine now, and it will be a matter of hours. You know how it is. I assure you I would not record that in my notes, if you promise not to mention it to anyone.'

My mother agreed. They returned to the room where my father lay and she watched as he broke open the vial and filled the syringe. As he was about to administer it, she told me, she had to turn away. She could not witness that.

When Zhu arrived back with the oxygen my mother came to the gate to admit him. She was carrying the Brahms symphonies in their paper sleeves. 'I have put on the first of the sonatas,' she said, and took the first of the symphonies and brought it down heavily against the concrete side of the fish pond, breaking it. Her arm was descending with the second record when Zhu caught it. His eyes sought hers.

'Because . . .' she said, her eyes filling with angry tears.

'Please, not yet,' Zhu said, and pulled her back into the warmth.

The three of them sat by the *kang* through the small hours of the night, listening to the music from the gramophone – the sonatas, the trios, the quartets, the quintets, the sextets, the octets, and then the concertos – stoking the fire beneath the bed and relighting the candles when they went out. It was while the great second piano concerto was playing that the doctor put his ear to my father's chest and announced that his breath had faded into nothingness.

'There. See,' my mother said to the doctor, 'no last words.'

'I will record that,' the doctor smiled, and then he took a surgical needle and thread from his bag. My mother looked at him quizzically. 'You will understand that our instructions are always to sew up the lips of the dead,' he said. 'Especially for Party leaders. Just for appearances, in case they lie in state somewhere.'

'And have something they want to say?' asked my mother. 'Some message from beyond?'

He grinned quietly. After he had finished the stitching he made some final notes in his ledger, sighing in a workmanlike way over his calligraphy, and then bade my mother farewell with a warm hand on hers, telling her that he would cable Beijing in the morning and would come back during the day to pack up his instruments and the unused supplies.

She thanked him and after letting him out and sending Zhu on his way she wrapped her warmest coat around herself and sat in the dark courtyard by my father's well. She would have cried, she told me, she was intending to cry, except that she heard from somewhere close by the sound of another woman softly sobbing – probably the young woman on the next street, she thought, whose husband had taken to beating her after she had given birth to a stillborn son – and the rhythmic murmur of that other woman's distress, the way it echoed through the streets like footsteps, somehow sufficed for my mother. This too she told me matter-of-factly – that in the end she had not cried for my father. Instead, after the neighbour's sobbing had ceased she went and lay by her husband on the heated bed and slept soundly until the dawn woke her.

*

The days we spent at the coast had a dreamlike quality. We slept late, ate voraciously and went for long, meandering walks along the beach at low tide – two tall girls, loose-limbed silhouettes, carelessly scattering our footsteps, as the saying goes. On one occasion we were pursued by two barefoot young men from the village who ran after us calling out, '*Xiao jie, xiao jie*, Little sisters, little sisters,' and upon catching up with us were taken aback to find that we were mother and daughter. They retreated, embarrassed. On our return journey we saw

297

them sharing a cigarette in the shade of a tree, and they waved politely to us.

We did not speak much on our walks, although on several occasions my mother seemed on the brink of saying something, only to retreat into herself wearing a frown, dissatisfied with the words that had assembled in her mind. When I pressed her for her thoughts she would whisper a formula of gratitude, for the guest house, for the food which the caretaker brought to us several times a day, and for the honour I had brought upon her and myself by my playing and my international prize.

Often as we walked my mother would stop and look out to sea, as if she had heard a voice from amongst the restive waves. I would scan the horizon, searching for a lone swimmer or an injured seabird, but to no avail. I would speak softly to my mother, but she ignored me, and after a time she would turn and continue along the beach.

It occurred to me after a while that the sea itself was calling to her, inviting her to view its change of aspect: now rucked like a velvet curtain swaying in the onshore breeze, now hard and gelid as if it were a frozen mass marked by cracks and drifts, now an expanse of brocade flecked with silver threads thrown up by shuttles of air, now quivering in hard sunlight like mercury, throwing off sparks of reflected brilliance from its curved edges. 'Do you know that proverb, "*Nu ren xin, hai di zhen*"?' she said to me suddenly, on our last day. 'A woman's heart is like a needle at the bottom of the ocean. I have always liked that proverb, but until now I had never seen the ocean, so I could not understand it. I have always asked myself: what would it be like, for one's heart to be a needle, and for that needle to be buried in the depths of the ocean?'

'Now that you have seen the ocean, does it help you understand the proverb?'

She was silent for a long while, as we continued to walk along the shore. We came to the staircase and began our ascent to the cliff top and the guest house. I thought she had forgotten my question, or decided not to respond, but at the top of the stairs she turned to me and spoke: 'Yes, yes, it does help. How could it not?'

That night we ate together quietly in our room. Through the window I could see the silvery-white cheek of the moon turned three-quarters, and below it, on the surface of the ocean, a long silken scarf stretched before us, tightly woven and luminous in the far distance, but becoming more and more frayed the closer it came to the shore, its weft more and more interlaced with darkness. My mother had borrowed from me a sleeveless cotton top, and I remember observing the light from the moon and our two candles shaping the folds of skin on her neck and collarbones, which were tough and shiny like the buttresses of a tree. When she had finished eating she put her chopsticks down and began to speak, unprompted. 'I am so glad that you are now a child of our nation's history, that you can disown your parents if the need arises.'

'Now why would I do that?' I said. 'I am proud of my parents, just as proud as I am of anything else – my country, my playing, anything.'

'By all means be proud of these things,' she said. 'And of your father and me. What I said is that I am glad you do not need to be. You are not in my shadow or in your father's. Even when the sun shines, a shadow can be a cold place.' I looked away, not quite knowing what to say. I could see she was not in the mood to be contradicted, and I did not want to stop her talking. 'You remember the proverb,' she went on: 'Mountains stand far apart, so as not to touch each other with their shadows.'

She began to explain to me how it was my father's books and records that had brought about his arrest and imprisonment. It was the works of bourgeois composers and mathematicians in his possession that his accusers had pounced upon. He tried to argue with them ('How can mathematics be bourgeois?'), but was shouted down. It was their discovery of his copy of Lao Tzu that crowned his humiliation. They forced him to walk through the streets with a gag around his mouth on which they had written, 'The Way that can be spoken is not the true Way'.

'But did he ever betray the Communist Party?' I asked.

'Not with his heart,' she said. 'But I believe he may have with his mind. It began when he became sick, when he started getting confused about doors. Do you remember? I think at that time he began to doubt the reality of everything. He began to read Lao Tzu a great deal, although we never discussed it. So of course he must have asked himself whether the Party was right in everything it does and says.'

'But only to doubt,' I said. 'Does to doubt also mean to betray?'

'Yes it does,' she said, growing stern all of a sudden. 'In China, at this time, to doubt means to betray. If you do not understand that now then I am sure one day you will. Life will teach you that one day.' I opened my mouth to speak again, but she put a finger to my lips. 'There is something I have for you,' she said. 'It has been in my suitcase.' She walked to her cot, lifted her case onto the mattress and snapped open the locks. She took out a large box and set it in front of me on the table. I did not need to open the box, but I did. Inside, wrapped in its slip of blue silk, was the red wooden body of the violin that Jean-Baptiste Vuillaume had pieced together in his Paris workshop in 1860. I lifted it from the case and noticed again the bulges in the velvet lining. 'The letters are there too,' my mother said. 'They told me about the letters. It would have been unwise for them to take them back to the Soviet Union. I urged Piroshka to burn them, but she refused. The letters go wherever the violin goes, she said. The violin is not complete without the letters. Be careful with them.'

The next morning we took the bus back to the Shanghai Railway Station, and waited for an hour for the north-bound train. When the public address system announced its imminent departure we embraced on the platform, surrounded by swirls of steam and jostled by other passengers eager to get onto the train and claim their seats. My mother cupped my face in both her hands and examined my forehead, as if for signs of injury or illness. 'Look after yourself,' she said, and was gone from my life, leaving only the clammy imprint of her fingers on my cheeks.

In the letters we exchanged in the years that followed she never hinted at any of what we had talked about at the beach house, never mentioned my father, or Kasimir and Piroshka, never even implied by some omission or lacuna that they had existed. I told myself that she feared that her letters were intercepted by the authorities; but in my heart I knew that she would not have written any more if our correspondence had been secure. My mother's essential skill, her way of dealing with the world, was to allow things that were painful or troublesome to slip into non-existence and then to make a whole out of what remained. She used it with her patients, performing amputations as acts of mercy; and she also used it to survive the humiliations of the Anti-Rightist Campaign and, years later, my own defection. I remembered that when I was a child I would sometimes watch her deep in reflection, and would sense that she was scoring a hard line around something in her mind – some memory, some incident, some emotion – before applying the gentle acid of her intellect to erase it from her thoughts. When she was finished she would come to herself and look up. I would ask her what she had been thinking, and she would say, '*mei shi*, nothing,' and a smile of contentment would break across her face like a new day. And I knew that whatever it was that had troubled her it was now indeed . . . nothing.

*

When I got back to my room I placed the violin case on my bed and opened it. I sat on the small wooden stool and waited for something to happen, imagining perhaps that the instrument would somehow rise from its case and float around the room. After a while I picked it up and examined it carefully, as I would any new instrument I was about to play. I strummed the strings and corrected the tuning, and then put it under my chin and took the bow in my right hand, wondering to myself what I would play. But the hard surface of the instrument stung my left cheek, warm skin meeting cold lacquer, and this tiny shock awoke something in me, a fear or revulsion I could not name. I quickly put the violin back into its case, and left the room and sat in the stairwell for a minute, before making my way down the stairs.

It was mid-afternoon and the building was empty. I stopped by Raya's apartment and before I knew it I had knocked on the door twice, hoping to find her there, hoping to invite myself in, to ask to speak to her, to confess to her what I knew about her, what we were doing to her, what she meant to us, or even, I thought, censoring myself, just to ask her some inane question about her work, just to look her in the eye and have her look back. There was no reply, and I made my way back to my room, took up the violin and began to play through my repertoire. My Bach, my Mozart, my Kreisler, my Bartók dances, my Chausson, my Saint-Saëns: an endless stream of notes, white, cold, and precise – as precise, I realised, as the ten million planes which my father had shown me in the tiny sliver of light between his thumb and forefinger, those hard, strong, uncomplicated surfaces, one thing only and not another, which had the thickness of a single thought. Then, in the middle of a piece, between two notes in an arpeggio, I stopped and put down my bow. The light outside was fading and in the distance I could hear the bells of the Custom House telling me that the east was now red, even though it was towards the west that the sky had turned pink. There was a noise in the stairwell and Ling Ling entered the room and greeted me with kisses and took my arm and insisted we go for a walk before dark. We ate at the refectory, and although I partook of her happy conversation and told her about the guest house at the sea and answered in part her questions about my mother and let her rest her head on my shoulder as we walked through the darkness back to our building, I knew where I wanted to be. So I left her in the room, telling her I had to go and see Madame Huang, stepped noisily down the first flight of stairs before retracing my steps quietly, and, levering open the window, made my way down the fire escape to my listening post, where I lay on my back waiting for Raya to return.

Almost immediately I heard voices and smelt the sweet aroma of the flowers Kirill had brought and the musky trails of his cologne. What followed was a successful evening for all of us. Kirill and Raya ate and drank, tortured themselves with suppressed laughter, and made a breathy, urgent, muscular kind of love on the couch, without musical accompaniment. (They did, however, place Kirill's shirt over the stuffed bird, which Raya insisted was leering at her. 'It must be a young male,' she complained.) I averted my eyes from the ventilation grille, although all I could have seen was a tangle of feet and discarded clothing. Afterwards, lying naked on the couch, they shared a cigarette and began to speak softly. I took out a pencil stub and leant my ear into the striations of light that fell across my notebook from the grille, straining to pick up what they were saying.

'He has gone then?' Raya said. 'Is the rumour true?'

'Yudin?' Kirill said. 'Yes, he is gone. Where to, no one knows, except that he would be wise to avoid Moscow for a while.'

'What was his crime?'

'He lost the joint fleet. A terrible bungle.'

'Can one lose an entire fleet?'

'If it only ever existed on paper, yes. Militarily speaking, it was a fine idea. But it's stillborn now. Mao shouted at him, called him names, accused us of trying to seize the whole of the Chinese coastline as a naval base and to consign the PLA to the interior; and instead of taking it like a man and playing him along, Yudin summoned Khrushchev from Moscow, and what happened next . . . well, it is now history, and is known within diplomatic circles as the Battle of the Dumpling Baths.'

'Dumpling baths?' Raya said. 'Tell me more, or are these dumplings secret?'

'It is no secret,' Kirill laughed. 'Far from it. Khrushchev himself is telling everyone he meets, every troop of Georgian dancers, every African ambassador, every delegation of

American farmers. Clearly he thinks by telling the story himself he will avoid complete humiliation.'

'Do tell, then.'

'It is a simple story. On the second day of Khrushchev's visit we are told that Mao will meet us at his residence, and when we arrive we find him in his swimming pool. He invites Khrushchev to join him, and even has a pair of shorts ready for the purpose. So we have Khrushchev flopping around, toes barely touching the bottom, clutching onto a life-ring that somebody has thrown him, and getting water up his nose, while Mao calmly swims around him like a seal – backstroke, breaststroke, then the crawl, then backstroke again, blowing spumes of water into the air, turning somersaults under the water, and talking the whole time through an interpreter running up and down the side of the pool after him – talking about Marx and Lenin and collectivism in agriculture and the communes. It was a great performance, like an emperor baiting a visiting barbarian.'

'And where are you all this time, Kirill?' Raya asked. 'Stirring the dumplings?'

'I am guarding the First Secretary's clothes, until the two men end up chest to chest in the middle of the pool, arguing like a pair of rutting walruses, and Khrushchev signals to us to join him to explain the joint fleet proposal.'

'To join him in the pool?'

'Yes, because he did not trust Mao's interpreter, and so Yudin and I stripped down to our underwear and waded into the water and we bobbed about like corks, with Yudin translating for Khrushchev, who was still clutching his life-ring, and Mao floating on his back with only his face and his stomach above the surface, and the rest of us treading water and trying to save the joint fleet proposal, which, you can imagine . . .'

'. . . sank without trace,' Raya said, and the two bellowed with laughter.

'Indeed,' said Kirill.

'And what a tragedy,' Raya said. 'Like the Battle of Tsushima Strait all over again, only in miniature.'

'Don't say that.' Kirill's laughter collapsed into coughing. 'Don't say that, even though it's true. Our joint fleet lies wrecked at the bottom of that pool. It was all Yudin and I could do to tow the First Secretary out of the range of Mao's guns, get him back into his clothes and get out of there. And then in the car, Khrushchev turns to Yudin – water stains still on his shirt and his tie over his collar and one cuff-link missing – and he says, "How do you think that went?"'

'And Yudin says "swimmingly", does he?'

'Not exactly – before Yudin could respond the shouting began, and it didn't let up for three hours. You know how long our First Secretary can go on for.'

Raya rose from the couch and poured another round of drinks.

'Is this bad?' she said, as she stood over Kirill, balancing her glass on his upraised knee.

'Yes,' said Kirill. 'We are told they will start shelling Jinmen and Mazu any day, to soften it up for an invasion. The US fleet will be in the Taiwan Strait within a week, perhaps sooner. We will be obliged to come out in support of the Chinese. Thank God they haven't got a bomb ready yet, since I could never convince them that the bomb is something you have, but never use.'

'And your visit to Washington?'

'I believe Khrushchev's resolve will hold. He will go to Washington regardless. Besides, things are very fragile in Beijing. The leadership is a leaning tower; it must fall soon. The starvation in the countryside is horrific. There has been no harvest, none at all, because during planting time the peasants were at their village furnaces pretending to make steel. By God, it is bad. Today I spoke to one of our engineers newly returned from Sichuan. It is ghastly, he says, worse than what he witnessed in the Ukraine during the Holodomor: piles of corpses, whole villages wiped out by cholera, mobs rioting in the cities and towns, smoke swirling everywhere from half-burnt bodies, and no rats, he said, because whenever one pokes its head out of the sewer the people trap it and eat it.'

'Did they not fight a war to be free of that kind of thing? And didn't we fight the same war?' Raya said. 'Get dressed, Kirill. I cannot talk about famine to a naked man. Here is your shirt. Put it on quickly, the phoenix bird is staring at you.' She rose from the couch and began to retrieve her clothes.

'And, there are responsible people in Beijing whose hand we need to strengthen,' Kirill went on, reaching one arm into a sleeve. 'There is Zhou Enlai, of course, and Chen Yun and Peng De Huai, and Liu Shaoqi, perhaps, and there is Deng Xiao Ping, about whom we are less certain. So I have been arguing that the nuclear treaty should be quietly revoked, or at least delayed so long and so persistently that China will realise it is a dead letter. And I believe my view has won the day.'

'So I should conclude my research quickly and pack my bags?' Raya said. 'Or should I move into the basement immediately to escape the fallout?'

'Not yet, not yet,' Kirill said, watching her as she finished dressing.

'When will they be told that the treaty is a dead letter?'

'Khrushchev himself will tell them when he visits again in September,' he said, speaking more rapidly as he pulled on his trousers, buckled his belt and searched for his socks. 'He and Gromyko will come to Beijing for the Tenth Anniversary of the Liberation. The timing will be perfect, because they will be newly returned from Washington. They will have "peaceful coexistence" written all over their faces, and if they succeed the Americans will have agreed to withdraw their missiles from Taiwan and to support an Asian Nuclear Free Zone. There you have it.'

Raya lit a cigarette and leant back on the table edge. 'Very nice,' she said. 'Your plan is very nice. I see you have become an optimist all of a sudden, Kirill.'

'Diplomats are always optimists,' Kirill said. 'I am not dispirited. Yudin's failure is not a tragedy, but an opportunity. I see that very clearly. We are composers too, or conductors, perhaps, after a fashion. What is that term you use, when a piece of music draws you back to the key in which it started, makes you expect it, and long for it, even if you are only dimly aware of it?'

'The return to the tonic.'

'That's it,' said Kirill. He had finished dressing and he took Raya's cigarette from her raised hand, took a puff from it and slotted it carefully back between her fingers. 'That is the diplomat's art – to lead nations into harmony, without their knowing it. They think they are pursuing their own ends, but we shape their thoughts and actions, like an invisible hand, so that it will be the most natural thing in the world for Beijing to . . .'

'My God, Kirill,' Raya said. She turned away from him. 'Are you all innocents? Is this how you all think? You military planners and strategists?'

'No, my love,' Kirill said, turning his attention to his tie and flicking one end around the other twice to form a loose knot. 'Most of us don't think, you know that.'

'Don't mock me. You know what I have given up for you. I want to know it is all worthwhile.'

'I too have given things up. For you.'

'Oh yes, the wife you never told me about.'

'What would you have wanted to know?' he said, with a voice starting to fray. 'It is the same story of all young marriages, isn't it? Innocent deception on both sides.'

Raya was silent. I peered through the grille, but could only see her from behind. Her arms were half-folded and she was holding the cigarette, now burned down to a stub, next to her temple in one curled hand, dabbing at her hairline with her fingers. Kirill pulled sharply at his tie and moved to the window opposite, peering down into the dark street.

'It was during the war,' Kirill began, talking swiftly. 'I was a young officer fighting in the South. She was from my home village, one of a dozen or so sisters and friends who would let the boys tease them when we were home from the front on furlough. I could hardly remember which one she was. Anyway, she started to write me letters, simple, earnest ones to keep up my morale. I had a corporal in my unit who was from the same village, and he received them from another of the girls, letters which were almost identical to mine. We imagined them, those girls, sitting around a table in their sarafans after a morning of making bullets or rolling bandages, writing these letters to order, not knowing that at the front we would scour every word and the shape of each letter looking for some whiff of sex, and not finding it.'

Wordlessly, Raya pulled a chair out from the table and sat down, resting her elbow on the table and leaning her forehead on her hand.

'Smile if you want,' Kirill said. 'Laugh if you want. At the front that's what you do. So when the war was over I went back to the village to see my parents and she was with them at the station, arm in arm with my father, with a bold game-hen kind of look, and small eyes that pointed at me like fingers.'

'So you marry her.'

'I marry her,' he said. 'Within a year there are twins, boys; then another one, a girl; and another. I join the diplomatic corps and we move to Moscow. I travel every month, but that doesn't stop it. Two more boys, a girl who died within days of her birth, then another girl. My God it was like fucking the earth, it brought forth fruit in such abundance.'

'Why are you telling me this? Why are you ridiculing this poor woman and her children in front of me?'

Kirill turned from the window. 'I thought it would make you feel better.'

'I feel fine already. I don't need you to improve my mood.'

'Well, I'm sorry. I thought from what you said that you needed . . .'

'Needed what?'

'Nothing.'

'Well, tell me her name then.'

'Why? If you are not interested . . .'

'Tell me. What is it? Zinaida? Malanya? Galina?'

'No, it's Nadezhda.'

'God, no. Not that. Not "hope".'

308

'Everyone has to have a name.'

'*Lasciate ogni speranza*,' Raya said softly.

'What's that? What did you say?'

'Nothing. Just a line from an opera about China, Puccini's *Turandot*. A line about hope, after a fashion. Forget it. Nadezhda is a good name.'

'It's a name for a certain kind of goodness, I agree,' Kirill sighed. 'I must go now. I have work to do tonight. I must call the new ambassador in Beijing.' He took up his jacket and swung it over his shoulders. 'So, you are angry with me?'

'Not angry,' Raya said, 'I am just wondering how far this innocence will take you.'

'It has got me this far, and I had hoped it would take me a very long way.'

'Well, we shall give it a try, shall we?' She stubbed out her cigarette and drew a circle around the edge of his face with her finger, drawing from him a look of puzzlement and then a smile. 'Take me with you when you leave Shanghai. Will you do that? And will you kiss me?'

*

Madame Huang's jaw slackened, her eyes grew wide and for a moment I thought she was going to hug me again. 'Very interesting,' was all she said, and she got me to repeat what I had heard while she wrote it down. 'Yes, very interesting,' she said, 'I will deal with this immediately. And you must remember to tell no one what you have heard. I cannot believe he has been so misled about rioting in the provinces. I cannot believe he would repeat those malicious counter-revolutionary rumours. What starvation? What disease? What invisible hands?' She folded up her sheet of paper and put on her jacket. We walked together to the entrance of the building, where she squeezed my hand, hailed a bicycle rickshaw and disappeared down the street. Later that day I received a note from Madame Huang telling me that she and Director Ho were going to Beijing for 'discussions' and ordering me to report any further developments to Professor Yu.

A week later I read in the *Shanghai Liberation Daily* that Marshall Peng De Huai had stepped down as defence minister and had been replaced by Marshall Lin Biao. It emerged in the following months that at the Lushan Conference in Jiangxi Province Peng had boldly criticised the policies of the Great Leap Forward in a personal letter to Mao Zedong, predicting that they would result in mass starvation. Kirill had been right: the crops had not been planted, there was no harvest except the harvest of pig iron from backyard furnaces, some said that twenty million had died, and some said twice that many, and Peng De Huai was the first within the inner circle willing to say the unsayable. But Mao had reacted swiftly, circulating the letter to the other members of the Politburo, criticising Peng's continuing friendship towards the Soviet Union, and isolating him so that the other moderates, Zhou Enlai, Chen Yun and Liu Shaoqi, did not join in the criticism. Deng Xiao Ping stayed in Beijing and kept his head down.

*

Ten days later, I received a note instructing me to go immediately to Director Ho's office. When I entered he was at his piano. He waved me into a chair and as I crossed the room I noticed that he was working on a musical score, part of his personal production quota, I assumed. A breeze blew through the open casement window, rearranging papers on his desk, but Director Ho seemed to notice only the notes he was writing. 'There,' he said at last, leaning back in his chair with a satisfied look. 'An idea for a melody came to me while I was dreaming, and I have been humming it to myself since I got up this morning. Now it is captured forever on paper, like a little songbird in its cage.' He deposited the score on the table in front of me, and poured himself a cup of tea. Then, remembering himself, he offered me tea also. 'It will be a song for children,' he explained. 'I think I will call it *Behind Enemy Lines*. I have the words worked out too, and I will add them shortly. What do you think?'

I glanced along the lines of music. It was a simple melody,

strongly reminiscent of the opening theme of the third movement of Dvořák's New World Symphony. Before I could offer my opinion Director Ho settled himself in the chair opposite me and began to tell me about his visit to Beijing. It had been a very important visit, he said. The Party leaders were very grateful to the Conservatory and to me in particular for tracking down the 'bad elements' amongst the Russians. Indeed, Director Ho had mentioned me in person to Premier Zhou Enlai during a private audience, and Zhou – who had already heard of my prize in Bucharest – had asked Director Ho to pass on his personal thanks and commendations for my work.

'Zhou is very interested in the scientific approach to music,' Director Ho went on. 'We talked at great length about the value of music as a tool in diplomacy. And we both believe that it is time for music in China to stand up and demonstrate its role in the vanguard of the socialist enterprise.' He slurped his tea loudly. 'Premier Zhou has asked for the Shanghai Symphony Orchestra to play at a banquet in September in Beijing. It is to celebrate the visit of Premier Nikita Khrushchev and Foreign Minister Andrei Gromyko, which coincides with the Tenth Anniversary of the People's Republic. He asked me for advice on what music should be played on that occasion, and after some thought I recommended a recently discovered work by Xian Xinghai, called *The Liberation of Mudanjiang*. It concerns the uprising of the people of Mudanjiang during the rule of the Manchukuo puppet regime.'

'This is a great honour for the Shanghai Symphony Orchestra,' I said. 'Have you told Conductor Li about this?'

'No,' said Director Ho. 'I am telling you first, because you will be the soloist. This is Xian's lost violin concerto, and you will deliver the premiere performance. China has supreme confidence in your ability.'

'China does?'

'We do too.'

I tried without success to recall any mention of a lost violin concerto by Xian Xinghai. Meanwhile Ho went to his desk, and took a shallow cardboard file box from one of its drawers. 'Here is the score,' he said. 'You must learn it quickly and well.' He put the box in front of me. The characters of Xian Xinghai's name were stencilled on the top. 'What is more,' he said, dropping his voice and placing his hand on the box reverently, 'I must ask you not to show this to Comrade Meretrenko, or to tell him or anyone else about the performance in Beijing. This matter is highly confidential. I myself will talk to Conductor Li about finding an accompanist who can help you prepare. In the meantime, assume that only you and I and Madame Huang know about the performance, and even about the existence of this score.'

'Perhaps Tian Mei Yun could help me prepare,' I suggested.

'Perhaps,' Ho said, raising an eyebrow; and then he began to shake his head. 'Perhaps not.'

'When did Xian Xinghai compose the concerto?' I asked. 'I have never heard it mentioned.'

'In 1945, while he was in Moscow,' He explained, 'It was the last work he wrote before his death. It has recently come into my possession.'

I opened the box. The pages of the score were loose. Inscribed in neat hand-written characters at the top of the first page were the words: *The people suffer under the boot of foreign oppressors, but secretly plan their revenge.* Director Ho explained that the concerto was a programmatic work in four movements. The first was slow and brooding, as befitted its title. The second movement – faster and more difficult – was entitled: *The Party, the vanguard of the people, defeats the hapless occupiers and assembles their captives in the town square.* The mood becomes sombre in the third movement, he said: *The masses gather to try the crimes of their oppressors, offering them the opportunity to confess at the point of a gun, and receive lenient treatment.* He turned the pages to the final movement, which had the longest title of all: *The people celebrate their victory, dancing on the bones of those who refuse to confess their crimes and acknowledge the rightness of Mao Zedong thought and the historical inevitability of socialist victory.*

'I must leave you here for a while,' Director Ho said, 'I have some visitors to attend to. Please study the score here in my office. For the time being I cannot allow you to take it away. Once we have an accompanist I will give you exclusive use of one of the practice rooms. In due course you will have rehearsals with the orchestra too.'

I began to read the score to myself, taking it in one bar at a time, trying to meld together the violin solo with the multiple lines of accompanying music for the various parts of the orchestra. I found this impossible. I was used to reading scores for violin and piano, and perhaps a cello as well; but I lacked the capacity to hold five or six separate parts in my head at the same time, let alone the different timbres of strings, brass, woodwind and percussion. Eventually, I simply read through the violin part.

It was not at all like Xian Xinghai's other works. It was a melancholy work in a minor key, and I could not recall him ever composing something so emotionally charged. Of course, by 1945 he had been stranded in the Soviet Union for five years by the war, longing to return to his homeland and his family; he would also have been contemplating his own death in the dank Moscow hospital where he was receiving treatment, so it was easy for me to imagine the inspiration for the first movement – long, sleepless nights spent reflecting upon his own mortality, listening to footsteps echo down strange hallways, and, apart from the music in his head, hearing only the murmurings of nurses and doctors in a language he had not learned. If this was right, however, it seemed strange that he would choose to compose a programmatic work concerning Mudanjiang, a dusty city in my home province, and a liberation which had not to my knowledge acquired any degree of fame in recent Chinese military history.

By the time I came to the end of the second movement, I was certain that this work was not by Xian Xinghai, or any other Chinese composer. There were no echoes at all of traditional Chinese music, and none of the familiar homage to Beethoven and Mozart. I turned over the last page of the second movement and studied the opening bars of the third: *The masses gather to try the crimes of their oppressors, offering them the opportunity to confess at the point of a gun, and receive lenient treatment.* The booming kettle drum led off, with the bass strings and the brass section playing fortissimo, and I began to laugh out loud, not in the least surprised to find that I was reading the passacaglia from Shostakovich's violin concerto, whose premiere performance I had given in the parlour of a small house in Harbin nine years earlier. I suspect a part of my mind had already picked up the repeated pattern of notes throughout the first two movements, the D – E-flat – C – B sequence that spelt out the composer's name. I immediately looked down the margin of the page and, finding the word *cor ingles* at the end of a stave, ran my finger along the line that Shostakovich wrote for Piroshka's oboe.

Director Ho returned, bringing with him Madame Huang. I rose to my feet and poured both of them a cup of tea from the urn, being careful to hand them their cups using both hands – first, Director Ho, then, Madame Huang. My politeness put them on edge.

'I am honoured that Premier Zhou believes that I am the right person to play at the banquet in September,' I began. 'But my talent is as yet undeveloped. I feel I should refuse this assignment, and continue my studies for another five years. Perhaps then I will be ready to be a soloist for such an occasion.'

I could tell that my show of customary self-deprecation carried no weight. Director Ho sighed irritably and picked up his tea cup delicately between his thumb and index finger. 'It is out of the question,' he said. 'The matter is decided. You should not doubt yourself when China has no such doubts itself.'

'So what is it you really want to say?' Madame Huang eyed me.

'There is a question I want to ask,' I said. 'Is there a reason why you are attempting to pass off a work by Dmitri Shostakovich as if it were by Xian Xinghai? It may help me in my preparation if I know why. That's all.'

Director Ho's tea cup – which was describing an ascending arc towards his mouth – halted and performed two unsteady loops before continuing its journey. There was silence for a moment, and then both of them spoke at once: 'You must . . .' started Madame Huang; 'You see . . .' started Director Ho. And both fell silent again.

'I must . . . see,' I repeated. 'What must I see?'

'You must see,' said Madame Huang, glancing at Director Ho, 'that both truth and falsehood can serve the interests of socialism.'

'Well said,' Director Ho smiled and wagged his finger at me in excitement. 'And indeed, one might say that there is no falsehood intended. It is important that our guests recognise the true origins of the music as well; if not during the performance, then at least afterwards. You see, we trust their intelligence as much as we can obviously trust yours. Premier Zhou does not want them to be deceived, nor even to think that we are trying to deceive them. After all, what is the point, if they do not recognise that it is Soviet music we are playing for them, with Chinese characteristics added?'

'But this is a composer who is out of favour in the Soviet Union,' I said. 'His music has been criticised as reactionary and chaotic. It will be an insult to play it.'

'And in recognition of that we have renamed it as *The Liberation of Mudanjiang*, and attributed it to a Chinese composer, and given programmatic titles to each movement,' said Director Ho.

It must have registered on my face that the logic of this statement had escaped me. Madame Huang leaned towards me and said, 'Director Ho has discussed this matter with Premier Zhou, and' – she glanced towards Ho, who met her eyes and nodded to her – 'also with Chairman Mao Zedong. These are the instructions we have received, and indeed Mao himself helped to compose the titles for each movement.'

'And enjoyed himself immensely doing it,' Director Ho smiled.

'We need to trust the judgement of Chairman Mao and Premier Zhou,' Madame Huang said.

'I have arranged for you to have exclusive use of practice room number four,' Director Ho said, 'but you will need to come to my office first to collect the score and the key to the practice room, and you must return both to me once you have finished practicing for the day. You are excused from all other classes, including your lessons with Comrade Meretrenko.'

'And as for your other duties,' said Madame Huang, 'we have found another young woman who understands Russian. She will move into your room today and will take over your responsibilities. Her name is Fan Hong. You will move immediately to new lodgings close to the Conservatory. You see? We have thought of everything.'

12. A Child of History

We travelled by train to Beijing in September of 1959 – the sixty-five members of the Shanghai Symphony Orchestra, Conductor Li, Director Ho and me. We occupied two carriages of the train, and a third was piled high with our kettledrums, double basses, cellos and tubas. I kept Jean-Baptiste Vuillaume on the seat beside me. I had the score of the violin concerto in my suitcase, but hardly needed to consult it any more. It was everywhere I looked: on the ceiling of the sleeping compartment, suspended from the telephone lines along the side of the railway track, in the wet, glistening streets of passing villages and towns, and the low profile of distant, purple mountain ranges. I had played through the piece several times with the orchestra, after weeks of closeted practice with Fa Jilin, the head of the department of piano. The orchestra was excited by the music, and the prospect of a gala performance in Beijing and the premiere of a new work by Xian Xinghai, and if any of them had any doubt about its attribution to our great national composer none betrayed it.

In Beijing the streets were hung with banners proclaiming the tenth anniversary of the Liberation. There were open-air screenings of patriotic movies. The army had distributed extra rations of soybeans and rice and brought truckloads of pigs into the city to redden the cheeks of the locals for the big day. Every day, every hour, it seemed, there were parades through the

317

streets – of workers, of peasants from Hunan and Guizhou, of ethnic minorities from Sichuan and Xinjiang in their feathered costumes, of school children in white shirts – all of them converging on Tiananmen Square, in whose centre rose a cream plaster statue of Mao, three metres tall, guarded by a circle of unblinking Communist Youth League members in starched shirts and red scarves.

This is where we came too, on the morning after our arrival, to rehearse in the Great Hall of the People which had risen on the west side of the square, one of the Ten Great Constructions, completed in ten months, by ten thousand volunteers, to mark the Tenth Anniversary. From the stage where we unpacked our instruments we watched workmen moving around the vast, dark cavern of the auditorium like an infestation of ants: painting walls, installing seats, laying carpet, erecting decorative panels, or hanging spider-like from the ceiling amidst tangles of wires and lights.

Conductor Li came and stood beside me. He was a silver-haired man with an upright, chest out, military bearing, dressed in an immaculately pressed zhongshan suit. He had spent much of his life in France and England, and had returned to China after 1949 in response to the Communist Party's call for expatriate Chinese intellectuals to return to serve their nation. Together we looked into the gloom of the hall, and then up to the ceiling, from which hung a series of radiating rings of lights in the shape of the mayflower blossom, with the red star at the centre. He seemed at a loss for words, and I felt the same way. Surely, I thought to myself, in the presence of such a symbol of our race and nation, there were things that could be said, indeed should be said. But nothing came.

As the arrival of the foreign dignitaries drew near, the banners on the streets welcomed Premier Khrushchev and Foreign Minister Gromyko, and boxes of miniature Soviet flags were deposited at schools, hotels and factories and on street corners. Director Ho told me that I was to be part of the official welcoming party at the airport, along with Conductor Li, the

318

orchestra leader, Ho himself, representatives of China's ethnic minorities, and senior military personnel.

I could not sleep the night before their arrival, and I crept past the guard at our hostel before dawn and walked towards the Avenue of Heavenly Peace. 'Watch out!' a voice hissed from above me as I turned the corner. Something fell to the flagstone beside me with a loud metallic clank, and as I shrank backwards a white banner fluttered onto the pavement ahead of me. 'Sorry,' the voice said. A young man had shimmied up a power pole, and was clinging by his knees in the darkness several metres above me.

'What are you doing up there?' I asked.

'Following orders,' he replied, and descended rapidly to the pavement beside me. 'Orders from Zhongnanhai itself, from the leaders' compound.' He smiled and spun a small spanner around his index finger, threw it into the air and caught it. 'We are to take down the banners and retrieve the flags.' As we walked together to the next pole he told me that they had also rescinded the directive to the school children, factory workers and university students to assemble along the airport route. 'Just an ordinary day in Beijing today,' he said.

I continued on my way towards Tiananmen, walking under more of the banners bearing Premier Khrushchev's image. I watched the red ball of the sun rise above the Gate of Heavenly Peace, and recalled the newsreel my father had brought back to Harbin exactly ten years earlier showing Mao's speech from atop the gate. The immense square was empty except for a pair of street-sweepers and four soldiers standing to attention around Mao's statue, guarding the acres of cold flagstone. As I retraced my steps I met the young man again, hanging by his legs from the top of another pole, folding up one of the last of the red banners into a neat triangle.

An hour later I drove with Director Ho towards the airport against the centripetal flow of cyclists and buses. The welcoming party milled around on the tarmac as a team of workers set out rolls of red carpet in a line that led from a small podium out to the place where the Premier's plane would come to rest. An honour guard was forming up next to us, helmets held tight by their chin straps, rifles snapping around into various positions at the bark of an officer – across the chest, parallel with the torso, butt resting on the ground next to a polished brown boot, then back to the beginning again, and then again. It was hot in the sun, and I watched as Madame Sun Yat-sen, dressed in a thick woollen coat, produced a fan to cool herself, prompting several others to follow suit with whatever they could find in their pockets. I found myself positioned towards the end of the line, between Director Ho and the representative of the Miao people. To the latter I spoke a few words of greeting in the Miao language. We talked about my summer cultural labouring, and in the midst of our conversation he produced a Soviet flag, and started to fan his face with it. A military policeman tapped him on the shoulder and relieved him of the offending item.

The crowd suddenly grew silent. Someone had heard the noise of a plane and was making a shushing noise. When nothing appeared in the sky we started talking again. A man in uniform ran out from the terminal building and whispered into the ear of the officer in charge of the honour guard. 'You can't be serious!' the officer said loudly. 'Are you sure? Well, be it on your own head if you are mistaken.' He called the honour guard to attention, their dark shadows pooling around their feet, and with a few sharp commands had them marching back to the terminal, just as the Premier's jet plane arrived. It touched down with a loud whoosh and a long, low moan, and then slipped along the runway with pneumatic squeals and sprays of dust and disappeared from our view behind some hangars. We quickly formed into rows again along one side of the red carpet, clearing our throats, arranging our clothing and experimenting with different positions for our hands.

Eventually the plane nosed around the end of the terminal building and lumbered towards us, its engines emitting a high-pitched whine. It came to a stop at the end of the red carpet, and a team of soldiers pushed the metal staircase against its fuselage.

The engines died, and started to make ticking noises. We waited for several minutes. Nothing happened. Madame Sun Yat-sen fanned herself again. The Miao chief hummed to himself. Then a large black Volga emerged from behind the honour guard and drove at no more than walking pace to the foot of the staircase. Two men stepped from it onto the end of the red carpet. I recognised Premier Zhou Enlai, and Liu Shaoqi, the General Secretary of the Communist Party – both dressed in light blue zhongshan suits with four pockets on the front of the jacket. And then, in a darker blue suit, Mao Zedong emerged from the car.

The door of the plane opened and Nikita Khrushchev pushed his way out and almost bounced down the stairs. He was like a cartoon figure: short, with a shiny bald head, perfectly round like one of those wooden knobs on the end of a balustrade, and an enormous protruding chest and overhanging belly that were barely held in by one precarious button on his single-breasted jacket. I had the impression that if that button were to give way, the whole of the Union of Soviet Socialist Republics would burst forth with a roar and a clatter. He thrust his hand into Mao's and then clasped him in a bear hug. He greeted Zhou and Liu in the same way, both men grinning helplessly over Khrushchev's meaty shoulder. Andrei Gromyko followed him down the stairs, picking his way at a more sedate pace and politely shaking the hands that were offered to him. Even from a distance I recognised his trademark eyebrows, which were even more spectacular than Comrade Meretrenko's – woolly caterpillars bristling with antennae at their outer edges.

The delegation assembled at the foot of the stairs, and were surrounded by scurrying photographers and camera crews with microphones on poles. Mao led Khrushchev towards the welcoming party, clutching his elbow as if he were a blind man, and then stood aside to let Zhou Enlai perform the introductions. Khrushchev had by this time acquired a wide-brimmed fedora to shield his baldness from the sun. An interpreter clung to his side, taking tiny steps so as to keep his mouth by his master's ear. From a distance it looked as if they had agreed for some reason to share the hat between them.

When they reached me, Zhou calmly introduced me as Xiao Magou, the award-winning violinist, and as the interpreter whispered in Khrushchev's ear I said loudly, '*Dobro pozhalovat' v Kitay, tovarisch Khrushchev.*'

Khrushchev stopped and looked at me. 'You have diphthongs like my father did. Where did you learn to speak Russian like that?'

'In Harbin,' I said. 'My home town.'

'You learned it from the railway workers then?' he said.

'No,' I said, 'from White Russian exiles.'

Director Ho nudged me in the ankle with his foot.

'Did you hear that, Andrei Andreyevich?' Khrushchev said, turning to Gromyko. 'The ghosts of White Russia are lying in wait for us.' Zhou smiled at me, and, gently taking Khrushchev's elbow, propelled him forward and introduced him to Director Ho and Conductor Li.

We stood in the late morning heat while Mao and Khrushchev mounted the podium to speak. A cameraman, wielding a movie camera with a bellows lens and a film carrier on top shaped like large panda's ears, elbowed his way between me and Director Ho, took his stance and started to film. Mao congratulated Khrushchev on the success of his mission to the USA as an envoy of peace. We clapped politely. Khrushchev congratulated the people of China on their achievements during ten years of communist rule. While in the past it was said that 'Russia's present is China's future,' he reminded us, he was now convinced that both peoples walked side by side towards the achievement of communism. We clapped politely once more, and suddenly the formalities were over and we were shepherded back to the terminal building.

We were at the tail of the motorcade on the way into the city. It was turning into a hot autumn day. There were peasants resting in the shade of the birch and ash trees, a solitary roadside stall selling melons, and a line of wagons standing along the edge of the road, the drivers holding the bridles of their donkeys as a soldier on a motorcycle blocked their path to let us pass unhindered. Most people were going about their business, barely glancing at the procession of black Volgas. Our driver shook his head. 'I don't believe it,' he said. 'When their President was here for May Day in 1957, I could hardly see the road for all the people waving Soviet flags and cheering. But today it's like the plane arrived a day early and caught Beijing unprepared.'

We rehearsed the concerto again that afternoon in a hall attached to our hotel. As we were working on the last few difficult passages Director Ho arrived and called me out into the corridor. 'Which do you know best, Mozart, Beethoven or Mendelssohn? Which concerto, I mean?' Before I could answer he lowered his voice and went on, 'I have received a message from Premier Zhou asking us to be sure to have an alternative piece to perform, should the circumstances require it. We do have an alternative, don't we?'

'What circumstances?' I asked. 'You never asked for an alternative. Have you talked to the conductor? It's his orchestra, after all.'

'We may not get much notice,' he said, ignoring my question. 'But I suppose it's a matter of finding the sheet music. Surely there are sixty-five copies of another great violin concerto somewhere in Beijing. I will go looking.' And he was gone.

The next morning before breakfast, he knocked on the door of my room. 'It's Beethoven,' he said. 'I have talked to Comrade Li. He is sanguine about it. The scores will be flown up from Shanghai today. Can you believe it? By a jet fighter. What a country this is. Beethoven flies around by jet fighter.'

'So, to be clear,' I said, 'you want us to prepare Beethoven's violin concerto as an alternative?'

'Have I not been clear?' he said.

'In case relations between the parties improve,' I said, 'and *The Liberation of Mudanjiang* is no longer appropriate.'

'Yes,' he said, 'that is the plan. The second line of defence, you might say.'

'To be ready by tomorrow night to perform in the Great Hall of the People?'

'Yes,' he said, shaking his head from side to side impatiently. 'Yes, yes, yes,' and added, 'For China, of course.'

He produced from his jacket a crumpled copy of the *People's Daily* and handed it to me. It carried front-page stories on the arrival of Premier Khrushchev and Foreign Minister Gromyko, along with a page of photographs of the event. In one photograph Khrushchev was laughing at some joke with the representatives of the Uighurs and the Tibetans. My left foot had made it into the corner of the frame.

As Director Ho had predicted, the orchestra took the news that we were to prepare the Beethoven concerto as a backup with an air of mild irritation, and a condescending assurance that our audience would not be able to tell the difference between a rushed performance and one that had been rehearsed for weeks. 'Of course,' I said to the orchestra leader as she ate her rice congee at breakfast, 'none of you will be standing in the spotlight playing the solo.' She shrugged. 'I'll ask the bassoonist to play your part if you want,' she said.

We were told that the sheet music would arrive by midday. When it did not, there were hints of unease amongst the orchestra. 'Do they expect us to make it up from memory?' someone said. 'Let's do that,' someone else said, and a couple of cellists started playing one of the more famous themes from the concerto, and some horn players joined in. The timpanist added a drum-roll, the violas picked up the melody at the next bar, and things carried on for a while until somehow it turned into a rendition of 'The East is Red' in double-time. The performance ended in a blaring crescendo and scattered applause from the hotel staff who were setting up for dinner.

In the event it was early evening before a man dressed in a dusty uniform and thick leather gloves strode into the room. He handed over a large canvas bag to Conductor Li, saluting as he did so. Conductor Li looked nervously at the baton he was holding in his hand, and then put it down on a chair and returned the salute. He unzipped the bag and musical scores spilt out like the seed-pulp from fallen fruit.

As soon as we had the music arranged on our stands, Conductor Li tapped his baton on the lectern and called us to attention. 'Quiet please, comrades! And as we play just think of the Long March,' he said. 'I will be at the front, like Chairman Mao. I will beat the time. Try to keep up. If you get lost, skip a few pages. Hopefully, the rest us of will pass your way eventually, and you can rejoin us. If you fall too far behind I can arrange for you to be shot humanely.'

We set off, aided by our memories of Beethoven and by the swinging of Conductor Li's baton. The first movement sounded like nothing less than a full-scale military retreat. We were ambushed by missing pages of score, by an impulsive feint by the cellists and double basses, and by a flautist who turned two pages rather than one and played along happily in no man's land for a dozen or so bars until he was rapped on the head with the end of a clarinet. I tried to hold things together, but added to the confusion by drifting from a major to a minor key, before I was poked in the ribs by the orchestra leader with the end of her bow. The brass section meanwhile had missed an entrance and wandered off the track, and never quite returned. Thus ended the first movement.

'No time for an interval,' Conductor Li grumbled amongst the coughing and tuning noises. 'We have only just started. The next movement is slow, but don't fall asleep, especially you in the brass section.' In the event the brass section had to be slowed down several times. I glided through my solos, hoping to hit at least every third or fourth note, and we persevered, eyes on the road ahead, discarding muffed notes and jangling tempi as if they were the bodies of our dead and wounded.

Conductor Li rushed us onto the third movement, which started with solo violin and went passably well until I got caught in one of Beethoven's whirlpools, circling around and around while the orchestra watched helplessly. Eventually I found my way out, wet with perspiration, and we carried on, stubbing our orchestral toe on a key change and losing the second violins in a flurry of pointing and angry hissing. And in time we found ourselves turning the last few pages, and saw ahead the final tumble into a cool, safe valley, with the melody like a wind at our backs. At the last emphatic note we sagged into our seats and gave ourselves an exhausted round of applause. 'At least it's happier music than the other one,' the orchestra leader said to me, 'although you could hardly tell by the way we played it.'

Conductor Li called for quiet. 'We have survived our first ordeal,' he said, 'and climbed the first peak. And now, ladies and gentlemen, let us bury our dead and bind up our wounds and begin again.'

We played the concerto through again, avoiding our earlier mistakes and falling into a different set of errors. The room grew hot with sweaty bodies, and I excused myself and retired to my room for a while to practise some of the more difficult passages. We rehearsed until well after midnight, one run through per hour, until the hotel management asked that we consider taking to our beds before the other guests mutinied.

The following morning a work party arrived at the hotel and carried our instruments the kilometre or so to the Great Hall itself, where we recommenced, amidst paint fumes and the shouts of the workmen and the sounds of their tools. We rehearsed Beethoven throughout the morning, growing more confident and allowing ourselves an occasional smile, and laughing behind our hands at Conductor Li as he grew more irascible. 'It is not good enough,' he snapped at one mistake. 'We may be approaching the peak, but when we lose our footing we slip all the way to the bottom again.'

At half past three, in the middle of an extended solo, I noticed Director Ho striding down the centre aisle of the auditorium towards the stage. I stopped playing. The room fell silent, and Conductor Li glared at me angrily, but when I pointed out the approaching figure with my bow he put down his baton. Ho stepped up beside Conductor Li, took him by the elbow and whispered something in his ear. Conductor Li closed his eyes and took a long breath. Director Ho turned to us and said, 'I have just spoken to Premier Zhou Enlai. The performance he requires for tonight is the Xian Xinghai. He thanks you sincerely for your effort of the last twenty-four hours.'

There was the sound of a slow handclap from the woodwind section, and it was picked up by the cellists. Director Ho looked puzzled for a moment, fearing he was about to be jeered. Then the whole orchestra joined in the clapping and picked up the tempo and added syncopation. Ho himself began to clap, looking around nervously at first; and then he turned and seized my hand and presented me to the orchestra with a flourish. They roared with mock applause. He bowed to Conductor Li, who bowed back and allowed himself a smile, prompting another surge of applause; and then he pulled the orchestra leader from her seat and bowed with her; and then he raised his hands above his head to applaud the orchestra, and waved them vigorously to their feet to take a bow. 'The Long March is over,' Conductor Li shouted. 'Long live the Long Marchers!'

Director Ho took me aside as the orchestra members stretched themselves and began to talk loudly and excitedly about the performance to come. 'The talks have broken down,' he said. 'No communiqué and no agreement.'

*

That night – September 30th, 1959 – Premier Khrushchev and his party attended a banquet with Mao, Zhou, Liu and the others, and were then driven by limousine to the Great Hall of the People where they watched me, dressed in a tight-fitting *chi pao* the colour of the Chinese flag, as I performed Shostakovich's violin concerto, masquerading as Xian Xinghai's rediscovered programmatic work, *The Liberation of Mudanjiang*. Ho Luting, Director of the Shanghai Conservatory, announced the titles of each movement, declaiming them like an opera singer, and an interpreter relayed them into Khrushchev's ear.

Just before we went on stage, Ho had taken my arm firmly. 'I have every confidence in you. Tonight you bear all of China's ambitions and griefs.' Then his voice fell to a whisper: 'And remember, the future of the Conservatory, perhaps even the future of music itself in our nation, depends . . .' He was lost for words. 'If we can serve the masses well tonight . . .' I turned towards the stage and felt his hand push me gently forward.

I cannot be certain when it dawned on Premier Khrushchev that the music was not a piece composed by a Chinese composer about the liberation of a dusty railway junction from the Japanese occupiers. I was not watching him. I did not see if Andrei Gromyko or one of his aides tugged Khrushchev's sleeve and whispered to him words that darkened his countenance. I suspect the subtlety of the gesture escaped them at first. It was hardly a well-known piece of music, having only had a handful of performances. But I suspect that they were unsettled by it. It is unsettling music, after all; angry and despairing, resolute and mocking. And I am sure that they did not remain ignorant of its true provenance for long.

Although I had played with orchestras before, I had never before felt such a sense of animal comfort at knowing there were others around me. These were my fellow musicians, some friends, some strangers to me, all of them now moving as one, beside and behind me, apart from me, and yet creating with me and through me, for this half hour, a thing that had never before existed (not, at least, in this precise form) and would never exist again, an accumulation of tiny movements – the abrasion of horsehair on taut strings, the vibration of reeds, the reverberation of waves of sound within chambers of brass and wood, the collision of hammers against stretched skin or wooden key – facts which together made a world.

For myself I was aware of many things, but none of them had to do with my audience. I was aware of the warm body of Jean-Baptiste Vuillaume's violin balanced on my collarbone. I felt that I was now a part of its particular history, its cargo of humanity, the people who had touched it, handled it, suffered for it, played it and listened to it being played. I was aware of Shostakovich's hidden code; the repeated, niggling act of subterfuge buried deep within the music: D – E-flat – C – B, played straight through, played backwards, flipped upside down; a tattoo on the soul of the music. And as the drums and the brass and the basses – more deafening than I had ever experienced them, and faster, more urgent than in our rehearsals – launched us into the fanfare of the third movement, the passacaglia, I felt lifted off my feet and held aloft for a moment until it was my cue to begin to play, whereupon the long, flowing, angry notes that fell from my violin, that melody full of bile and disgust and triumph, returned me solidly to the stage. And I was aware – strangely aware – of my own physical being, of my muscles and bones and sinews and nerves, and of their connections and correspondences. I felt the ghost of a hand, Piroshka's hand, like a fulcrum pressed against the base of my spine, from where I was pushing, pushing, insistently pushing.

*

After the concert there was a reception in one of the adjoining rooms. We were introduced to Khrushchev and his party again, and we balanced shallow glasses of Hungarian champagne on our fingertips and participated in the familiar grinning competition that such occasions inspire. Khrushchev shook my hand heartily, and clung on to it, resisting my attempts to take it back. Then I realised that there were two photographers fumbling with their flashbulbs, and he was waiting for them to shoot. The flares popped, and he called for silence, and began to speak in Russian. 'You know, my dear comrades, that politicians love musicians most of all, for to a politician a musician is like a child. She is innocence itself. When she performs, when she bows to us, she becomes the child of everyone who listens to her. She becomes the living hope of Marxism, her talent owned collectively, owned by all of us.'

A young man stepped forward, buttoning his jacket and clearing his throat as if he was about to sing, but Khrushchev held him back. 'No, no, I will ask our young soloist – who was taught to speak Russian by the finest of teachers – to translate for me,' he said. With a lump in my throat, I obliged, and he continued: 'Now we can contrast musicians with writers.' He shook his jowls like a rooster's wattle and tutted under his breath. 'Writers are another matter,' he said. 'Not at all like children, but like stern parents, pointing out our faults and wagging their fat fingers at us. Even a writer who is a young man sets himself up as a father to the people. Translate that, my dear,' he said, and took small sips from his champagne as I did so.

'That is why politicians fear writers,' he continued, 'and why we try to keep them on their guard. But you musicians, you are blessed, because you remind old men like me of our lost innocence and our unrealised dreams.'

After I had translated his words, Khrushchev called for another glass and held it aloft towards the chandelier. 'A toast to the People's Republic of China,' he declared, 'and to undying friendship with the Soviet Union!' Around the room, from a hundred raised glasses of the swirling amber liquid, thousands of tiny points of light glistened.

*

We were to leave for Shanghai by train the next day. Beijing was swelling with officials, generals, performers, and members of the Communist Youth League in preparation for the Tenth Anniversary parades. In the morning Premier Zhou sent to our hotel brief letters of thanks, in his own hand, addressed to Conductor Li, Director Ho and me. At the train station we were delayed for hours as carriage after carriage brought in sailors in white suits, gymnasts for the synchronised mass performance, and ethnic dance troupes in their rattling costumes. I scoured the morning's newspaper looking for some mention of our performance, or some pained announcement of a split between China and its 'big brother'. Nothing. I mentioned this to Director Ho and he shrugged his shoulders and said something about 'doing our duty'.

'Was our performance a failure, then?' I persisted.

'Every performance is a failure,' he responded, with a gentle sneer. 'Performers always make mistakes, and can always find things to improve.'

'But what did we achieve?' I said. 'With our musical insult? Did we achieve anything?'

'Wait,' he said. 'Be patient. We all have to learn patience. It is the most useful of emotions.'

I let out a loud sigh.

'Don't sigh! What I say is true,' he said, taking me by the shoulder and fixing me with a gentle stare. 'Here we are waiting patiently for a train; but it will come. I have worked since 1949 for the opportunity to use the Conservatory's talents to serve the masses, and those opportunities have come. There is no end to the wisdom of patience. I am still being patient regarding things I did years ago, decades ago. I am being patient regarding things my father did, and his father before him.'

*

During my absence in Beijing the last of my belongings had been moved out of the Foreign Teachers' Building to make way for Fan Hong, the young woman from Beijing who was to take over my spying duties in the wall of Raya's apartment. I now had a room to myself in an apartment building nearby that housed mainly faculty members. It was a step up, but without Ling Ling and – I realised to my surprise – without my nightly encounter with Raya Vishinsky and her evening's selection of guests, I felt cut adrift, alone, incomplete. I spoke immediately to Madame Huang, asking to return to my old lodgings and my former duties. She ignored me, and told me that Kirill, the defence attaché, had not been in Shanghai since the last conversation I had overheard. I persisted and she held up a flat palm in front of my face. 'Be quiet!' she said. Her eyes flashed at me and for once she was not smiling. 'Do not challenge me! The decision is mine and it is made! Your work is done.'

Later that day I walked up to Comrade Meretrenko's apartment for my usual lesson. It had been more than a month since I had last been there. Ksenia let me in.

'*Dobro pozhalovat*,' she said. 'Welcome home. My husband says you have been away.'

Fyodor himself emerged from a bedroom. 'They told me you were sick,' he said, 'but I never believed them.' He smiled and kissed me on both cheeks. 'And then yesterday I met Comrade Guan from the orchestra and she let slip the secret.'

'The secret?'

'You have been in Beijing with the orchestra, no? Second violins, still? Or have they promoted you?'

'They have promoted me.'

'And the occasion? I expect it had to do with the Tenth Anniversary.'

'Yes, it did. We played a concert for Comrades Khrushchev and Gromyko.'

'Indeed!' Fyodor's beetle-brows began to undulate. 'Ksenia, did you hear that? A concert for our beloved Comrade from the Donetsk mines.'

Ksenia was twisting her hair into its bun, pushing clips into place and tucking in stray locks. 'I heard it,' she said, 'and I must go now, Fyodor. Sasha is waiting for me.'

'And did Comrade Khrushchev enjoy himself?' Fyodor went on.

'It was hard to tell.'

'Yes, I can imagine. I say good luck to anyone who plays music for that man! He has tried all his life to be a *hromadyanyn*, as we say in the Ukraine. Neither a Russian, nor a Jew, nor a Pole; but a Ukrainian, a miner and before that a peasant. He is proudly uncultured, shall we say. In Ukraine we love him, of course. A man of our soil – no, a man of the mines, so technically he is a man of the rocks beneath the soil, the rocks that continually work their way to the surface and break our ploughs. He is a great, a great . . . sack of Ukrainian rocks.'

Ksenia scowled at him, and Fyodor turned to me again. 'You won't repeat that, will you?' he said.

'Of course not,' I said. 'To whom would I repeat it?'

332

'I must go or I will be late,' Ksenia said, and she stared at her husband for a moment, rearranged his shirt front, tweaked his chin and then slipped out the door and clicked it shut behind her.

Fyodor set a glass on the table and poured out two untidy dashes of vodka from a bottle. I had never seen him drink before, and certainly not during a lesson.

'You might repeat it to your masters,' he said, looking down at his hands.

He swirled the drink in his glass several times and then threw his head back and emptied the contents into his mouth. He put the glass back on the table and placed his hands on the top rail of a chair, kneading it anxiously.

I turned away from him, towards the window. 'I'm not sure I know what you mean,' I said.

'Do you know the girl who has been in your room while you were away?' From behind my back I heard the clink of the vodka bottle once more, and then the rising metallic 'doy-eeng' as something hit the enamel water jug, two octaves in a split-second, prompting within me some involuntary mathematical speculation. 'Miss Fan is her name. She is a recent arrival at the Conservatory. I have been watching her play in the ensembles. She is a viola player, and is also in the second erhus, I believe, in the traditional Chinese orchestra. It's a travesty, don't you think? The "traditional" Chinese orchestra? Twenty-four erhu players, a dozen pipa players, a phalanx of zithers, the line of reed players, the gongs and cymbals, all sitting bolt upright on their chairs with their music stands, the men strangled by their collars and the women poured into those tiny dresses, all eyes fixed on the conductor in his tuxedo. Whose tradition is that? What are they going to play? Mahler's Ninth Symphony with Chinese characteristics? Now, that I would love to hear.' He made a high-pitched nasal hum, rehearsing several bars of something slow and majestic.

'Anyway,' he sighed, 'her playing is ordinary, talentless, and I think our efforts on her are wasted. It is a mystery why anyone thought she should be studying at a Conservatory.'

'I am sorry to hear that,' I said. 'That your efforts should be wasted.'

Fyodor came to stand with me at the window, and he pulled aside the net curtain so that we could see better the empty courtyard below and a protruding roof with a beard of grass growing in the gutter.

'She has had a cough, poor dear,' Fyodor said. 'We have all been hearing it up and down the stairs since she moved in. One of those asthmatic ones I suspect. Fluid in the lungs.'

'I am sorry to hear that, too,' I said, and I knew immediately what was coming next.

'We heard it at Raya's apartment the other night. Her cough, I mean. And it seemed so close it was like she was on the fire escape outside. Kolya poked his head out of the window and looked up and down the fire escape, but saw nothing. And then we heard the cough again.'

Fyodor released the net curtain and turned to face me.

'We found the panel and the little listening post,' he said. 'Do you have anything you want to say? I suspect not.'

I said nothing, and after a while Fyodor went on, 'For my part, I have something to say, and that is that it has been a pleasure teaching you, and I see no reason why we should not continue. However, I may not be the one making such decisions, you understand.'

'I understand,' I said. 'And I do have something I want to say, to ask, in fact.'

'What is that?'

'How is Pavel Gachev?'

'What a curious thing to ask,' he said. He took hold of the neck of the vodka bottle and made as if to pour another glass, but then stopped and placed it back on the table. There was a loaf of black bread on a plate, and he pressed one thumb into it, pulled off a corner piece and put it in his mouth. He chewed for a while, swallowed and licked his thumb. 'He is in hospital in Kiev,' Fyodor said. 'He tried to shoot himself.'

'Will he live?' I said.

Fyodor screwed his mouth to one side. 'He may, but I have nothing more to say about him,' he said. 'I have never respected him.'

'He seemed . . .'

'What?'

'Unlucky.'

'I know many things about him that you don't,' he said. 'And I assure you he has no reason to complain about his luck. But come now, tell me. What did you play in Beijing for our Great Leader?'

'We played Shostakovich.'

'Really! Shostakovich? Comrade Guan said it was a Chinese piece.'

'She was wrong. It was Shostakovich.'

'I can't imagine she would be confused. So clearly one of you is mistaken or lying.'

I gave him a shrug.

'Let's pass over that for today,' he went on. 'So what piece was it? A symphony, I imagine. That's what you need for that sort of occasion, something triumphant, the seventh, perhaps – the Leningrad Symphony? No, not that one,' and he pointed at me with his glass, propelling a spray of vodka onto the floor between us. 'Not the seventh, but the tenth, surely! The symphony they are already calling "the Great Tenth", the one . . . the one with the Ukrainian *hopak* dance in the finale . . .'

'No, it was the violin concerto.'

Fyodor made a sharp sniffing noise. 'The violin concerto? The Jewish one?'

'Yes,' I said.

'And, of course, you . . .'

'Yes,' I said.

'So, do you still want lessons from me? Now that you are both a modernist and a hero of socialism, is there any more I can teach you?'

'Yes,' I said. 'You can teach me to play like Jascha Heifetz.'

Fyodor snorted. 'I will try,' he said. 'So, play.' He sat down heavily on the chair and watched as I put my violin case on the table and opened it. I felt his eyes on me as I tightened my bow, placed the violin under my chin and strummed the strings lightly with one fingertip to make sure they were in tune.

'What is that?' he said, rising to his feet. 'Show me that.' He took the violin from my chin and held it up to the light from the window. 'Where did you get this?' he said. 'Where did you get it?'

'My mother gave it to me,' I said.

'Your mother! Rubbish! Where would a mother get a violin like this? It's a Guarneri, isn't it?'

'Are you saying I am lying?'

'You have lied before.'

'Everybody has to lie sometimes. My mother brought it with her on her last visit. It was given to us several years ago in Harbin by David Oistrakh, when he was touring China with Sviatoslav Richter.'

'You are mocking me.'

'And Oistrakh got it from Dmitri Shostakovich,' I said, raising my voice, 'and he got it from the Grand Duke!'

Fyodor handed the violin back to me. 'I don't want to hear any more.'

'What shall I play?' I asked, placing the violin under my chin again.

Fyodor shook his head. 'Nothing,' he said. 'I said I don't want to hear any more. I have lost my appetite for music today. Besides, I now see that when you play, there is so much more going on than just music, I no longer know what it is I am listening to.'

'Again, I don't know what you mean.'

'I mean these other things, these complications and histories and hidden codes and connections. This is what frightens me about modernism. Music is not just music when you play it. When you play, these other things come to life. That is what makes your playing so . . . full, so intimidating, so . . . magnificent, so intoxicating, so . . . toxic. Your playing is like vodka. Do you know that? Don't laugh. I am not being funny. It's like a good vodka. It has a land and a people behind it, whose lives and soil you can taste if you pay attention.'

'I still don't know what you mean.'

'Perhaps you don't. Perhaps you are too young still, but understand just this: that playing like yours does not arise in a vacuum, it is not tied to one place and time, as is that of your colleagues here. There are two or three people in this institution that play as well as you. And back in Moscow, at the Conservatory there, I could produce a dozen more. Many of them are better technicians than you, and for that reason may have more success than you, but you . . . you . . .'

He came very close to me, and I could smell the alcohol faintly on his breath, but I knew he was not drunk. It was not the vodka speaking. 'You are haunted,' he said, in a whisper, close to my face. 'I have felt it whenever you have played, and now I see it in my soul's eye. You, standing there on the stage with your violin, in front of a shimmering curtain, and behind that curtain there is a great darkness, and in that darkness, what shadows are there? What ghosts behind your back? A great orchestra of the dead and the half-dead, that's what I see, sitting to attention in a cavern of air that is cold, rich and damp, that is breathing you out into this world.'

'I don't know what you mean,' I found myself saying yet again; but I did know, I understood perfectly what he meant. I had felt that cold breath at my back. I felt it take shape, rouse itself, whenever I put Jean-Baptiste Vuillaume against my collarbone and tightened my bow. In Heilongjiang we called it the *Da Leng*, the Great Cold that always returns to claim us, that is our natural state.

'Perhaps it is best that you don't understand,' he said. 'Perhaps that way you will be able to free yourself. Do not become like Pavel, for whom you seem to care so much. He could not escape his ghosts, because he knew too much about them. That was his mistake. In Russia one must learn to look without seeing, to listen without hearing, to eat without tasting, to touch without feeling. Don't try to understand. For your own sake, don't try. Or you will end up like Pavel.'

There was a noise behind us and we turned to find Ksenia at the door.

'You are back early,' Fyodor said, resuming his normal kindly gruffness. Ksenia stood in the doorway and did not come into the room.

'I met Kolya on the street,' she said, flicking her eyes between me and her husband. 'There is a message. You must come to Kolya's apartment, you must come now.'

'We are not finished,' Fyodor said. 'Can't you see?'

'Now!'

'I am not finished!' He turned away from her, towards the table and the bottle of vodka and the bread on the plate.

She moved quickly to him, took his shoulder roughly in her hand and whispered loudly into his ear, almost kissing it, '*Pevchaya zhar-ptitsa.*'

Without another word or a glance they were both gone.

*

Late that night two trucks took all of the Russian advisors to the airport. The Soviet Consul himself was one of the drivers, and he deposited them and their luggage in the pitch dark by the runway and waited with them for several hours in silence until at first light an Ilyushin transport plane circled in from the ocean and dropped out of the sky. Ten minutes later it was airborne again.

Fan Hong heard nothing. As night fell she had crept up and down the stairwell a couple of times, as she had been instructed, and then descended the fire escape to her listening post. Raya did not seem to be home, and after half an hour paring her nails with a penknife and singing to herself Fan climbed back to the roof, and then made her way slowly to the ground floor, putting an ear to each door en route. There was not even a snore, and all the doors were shut. On the ground floor she spoke briefly to the concierge who lay in her tiny cot surrounded by mops and brooms, and then ascended the stairs and retired to bed. It was Ling Ling who heard the noises, the truck engines gurgling at the front door, the rush of stockinged feet on the stairs, Kolya's hushed voice calling to someone to hurry up. She came to my room in a panic, having run through the darkened streets in her night clothes. 'They're all gone,' she said, and began to cry. 'All the doors were open, and when I got down to the street they were loading the last suitcases into the trucks.'

We returned to the Foreign Teachers' Building and looked through the abandoned rooms. They had taken most of their clothes and their musical instruments and treasured possessions, but everything else was still there. We walked through each apartment, recalling whose it had been; each room seemed like a stage-set, sparsely but significantly furnished, waiting for the actors to enter. We found plates on wall racks, and cutlery in piles tied with string; there were heavy winter coats hung on hooks; record players with their lids open; ornaments hanging askance on nails, and beside them bare nails or chips in the plaster where nails had been; there were bookshelves with rejected volumes leaning against each other like victims after a firing squad; there were piles of letters weighted down with bottles of vodka or champagne, and pots and plates bearing the remnants of food hastily and half-eaten.

In Raya's apartment we found the samovar and the stuffed bird. The latter I examined closely for the first time, a long-legged specimen with marbled plumage on its slim back and a tapered, slightly upturned beak that was yellow around the nostrils but then black at the tip, as if it had been turned slowly over a flame. It was not my idea of what a mythical bird might look like. All of Raya's records were gone, although she had left a record player, and in an open drawer I saw a jumble of chess pieces, and amongst them a shotgun cartridge.

On the dresser was a shallow tin which had once contained some sort of potted meat, and inside it lay an assembly of twisted cigarette bodies, the results, I surmised, of Raya's normal manner of smoking, which I had often observed: taking two or three long puffs – during which all of her anxious or troubled thoughts would apparently flow into the cigarette, like passengers crowding onto a train – and then firmly pressing the body of the cigarette into an ashtray. Lying cheek by jowl in the tin, Raya's cigarettes, maybe eight or nine barely smoked items, reminded me of the images one sees of train wrecks, carriages buckled and twisted, jammed into a railway culvert.

In Kolya's apartment we found a small revolver in an open drawer. Why he had not taken it I could not imagine; perhaps it was an oversight. Ling Ling reached out her hand towards it, but I hissed at her not to touch it. And in the apartment Fyodor and Ksenia shared, the room where I had spent an hour the previous day, I found by the open door a small pile of seventy-eight records in brown paper sleeves. I picked them up and looked through them. There were five of them, recordings of Jascha Heifetz playing with Eugene Ormandy and the Philadelphia Orchestra. I told Ling Ling to go back to her room to rouse Fan Hong and get dressed, and then I tucked the records under my arm and descended alone to the street.

Madame Huang met me at the entrance. 'They are all gone,' I told her, and she nodded and smiled.

'We knew something was afoot late last night,' she told me. 'Our radio operators began to pick up a strange message going out from the Consulate to their people all around the country. Reports are coming in from all the provinces, and they all say the same thing, that overnight all five thousand Soviet technical advisors have packed their bags and are on their way home. It has been an impressive operation.'

'Is this what we wanted?'

'We should leave that question to others,' she said. 'I woke Director Ho to tell him and he seems satisfied, although I wouldn't say he was happy. He did laugh at one thing, though. Do you know what the message was? The code words they sent out to all the Soviet advisors, to tell them to prepare to leave immediately?'

'Tell me.'

She paused, took a breath and brought forth two words in Russian, and although she murdered them with her pronunciation, I could still make them out:

Pevchaya zhar-ptitsa.

The Phoenix is singing.

*

Three weeks later I was invited to return to Paris to study at the Conservatoire. I do not know who arranged it. Director Ho could not have done so by himself; not without Professor Yu's agreement or an instruction from further up. Tian refused to speak to me. Several weeks previously he had received an invitation to study at the Moscow Conservatory, but he did not expect to hear any more about it. Ling Ling accompanied me to the airport and clung to my arm, crying quietly, as I sat in the waiting room for my flight to Delhi to be announced.

I was ready to leave. There was nothing to keep me in Shanghai, and no one to teach me. I privately mused on the fact that fate was drawing Jean-Baptiste Vuillaume's violin back to its home town, with me as its passenger; that I would now be added to the cargo of souls it carried.

13. The Phoenix Sings

Memories of my childhood began to gather around me on the day before my fifty-fifth birthday, during the long drive home from the beach house at Castlepoint. They were tiny shards, enigmatic and unconnected – the clicking of my car indicator transformed into a song from my schooldays, a whiff of farm air bringing back to me the smell of newly pressed bean curd, tagging scrawled on a fence spelling out parts of my name in Cyrillic script on a concert poster, and the flanks of a certain hill becoming the gently curved gutter crown of the felt Homburg that Kasimir always wore. I had experienced this several times during the decades since I left China (in moments not claimed by my brood of children, or my husband's manic schemes), and I had learned simply to endure the hours during which the past rained upon my head like a meteor shower, fragments of my parents' lives, of my childhood, my youth, and my distant, abandoned career as a socialist musician and spy, the wandering jigsaw puzzle of something that was once a world, propelled through space by the inertia of its history.

In the course of my ascent of the Rimutaka Hill the muffler hose on my Toyota Crown came adrift, and as I turned off the motorway and climbed the final hill to Brooklyn my solid metal chariot was growling like a fat man gargling. The owner of the antique shop on the corner of my street looked up at me and waved as she brought in the wares she had arranged in front of her door. The lights changed to green, and the fat man roared as I leaned my weight against the steering wheel and gunned the engine long enough to pass the final rise, from where I could nurse the barge-like bulk of the vehicle around the last few corners with jerks and tugs on the tiller.

I arrived home, more weighed down by the silt of memory than by my small tightly packed suitcase, and began to climb the zig-zag path to my house on the Brooklyn ridge. During my month-long absence the wooden gate, whose white-painted slats had long ago become enmeshed in the adjacent hedge, had pulled away from the upright and now lay at an oblique angle, ancient screws dangling from rusted holes like little blackened larvae, revealing a pair of empty beer bottles, denuded of their labels, nestled amongst the twigs and leaf-litter beneath the hedge. The day was almost done and the path was dark and bosky, overhung by rhododendrons that had become ingrown and woody during years of self-rule. I emerged from their purple gloom into the evening light and stood between the two Canary Island palms that guard the entrance to my house, feeling protected by their squat symmetry, their tub-like trunks and explosion of sharp fronds. I turned to look out over the city that had been my home for a quarter of a century. It was the kind of evening that would have prompted my late husband to stand at our front door with his arms opened to the darkening sky and the spangle of city lights below it and pronounce theatrically, 'Has earth anything to show more fair?' He would repeat the question several times, changing where the stress fell, until satisfied he had subdued any contradictory voices that may have been lurking in the shrubbery.

I found myself admiring again the rounded belly of the inner harbour, the seemingly vertical stacks of houses on the western face of Mount Victoria, the sharp green edge of the ridgeline and then beyond it the layers of the distant mountains, their boundaries bleeding into one another like turquoise water stains, before merging eventually with the smooth lapis-coloured sky. I felt a surge of affection for the place in which the fragments of my life had settled and taken shape, like a nest of twigs deposited amongst rocks at the highest point of a now forgotten flood.

It had been a hot day, the hottest of the summer so far, and the evening air now pressed itself upon the city like a blanket of warm velvet, through which currents of cool air threaded like ribbons of liquid silk. Down the street a cluster of people sat around an open front door talking. I could hear the clink of a wine bottle, a man and a woman laughing, in turn and then in unison, *basso profundo* and *mezzo soprano*. A gust of wind arose from nowhere, like a sigh from the earth. It brushed the hillside, setting the treetops rustling like bridesmaids swirling their taffetas. The palm fronds above me clacked, bird-like, in response.

For a moment, in the sun's angled light, the scene became curiously still, as if fixed by some photographic chemistry. Then in the midst of this tableau a plane leapt heavenward from behind Mount Victoria, its fuselage seeming, from this distance, incongruously long, as if it were a stage prop, of necessity disproportionate in size to its surrounding scenery, being drawn steadily upwards by some hidden pulley and ropes. The plane turned over the city and roared off towards the west, and when I turned my gaze back to the harbour the light was there, the light of the sun concentrated on a shiny surface, a windowpane perhaps, amidst the foliage on the upper slopes of Mount Victoria. It flared like burning magnesium, nine million miles of light gathered into a point and reflecting a pencil of brightness, like a patriot's signal, across the vault of empty air above the city. I stood, my face and torso illuminated by this warm, yellow radiance, and my sense of distance, of perspective, was suspended momentarily. I saw the whole scene afresh as my father might have during one of his attacks: flat like a painted screen hanging from the sky just inches in front of my face, with the point of reflected light marking a tiny tear in the world's tapestry, a passage into a space beyond, from which someone was shining a searchlight.

The moment passed, but I was now thinking of my father's illness once more, and recalling our encounter with the front door, and the wetness of his blood on my hands after I had pulled him through, and the gloom that descended upon him in the weeks that followed. This is what memory can do, indeed it is what we most fervently want it to do: to flatten the perspective of time, bring distant mountains to our doorstep, so that every tiny detail of the past can become present to us once more, engraved as it were on a granite surface before our eyes, so that we can marvel at it, marvel that we were part of it, press our palms to its cool hardness, lean our weight against its mass, run our fingertips along its grooves, or, if we wish, rub its lines as a keepsake onto a sheet of thin paper.

I sat down on the bulging skirt of root-mat that ringed one of the Canary Island palms and leaned back against its trunk, feeling rather like a sage reclining under a sacred tree in some high mountain grove. The next day, I realised, it would be thirty-eight years since my father died. He died on my seventeenth birthday.

The light was fading as I turned back to the house. I stepped onto the veranda and into the patterned glow cast from within through the coloured glass panels of the door. Fumbling with the keys, I finally managed to open the door, to be greeted by a tall, slightly stooped woman who moved forward, one knuckle pressed wetly into her eye socket, to place some keys on the table below the large mirror. I am presented with this changing portrait of myself whenever I return home, slightly older, dressed in the emotions of the hour, captured for a moment in a heavy gilt frame. To place a mirror facing the front door of your house is good *feng shui*, they say, as it prevents the entry of bad spirits, who, unwilling to look at their own reflections, mill around the threshold disconsolately and eventually move on to the next house in search of shelter. I am always expecting to catch a glimpse of the grim face of some banished soul in the doorway behind my shoulder, but the only face I ever see is my own.

I turned towards the bathroom, and on the middle panel of the door found a rural scene painted in voluptuous oils: a country church, a field of lavender in curving rows, a peasant in clogs and yellow straw hat driving a cow towards a copse of trees where other beasts lay dozing in deep shadow. It was a pastiche of something Leon and I had seen in Paris, when we lived anonymously in a quiet corner of Saint-Denis and took the metro into the city on quiet afternoons when admission to some galleries was half price. On the door above the picture, in blue and yellow, were the words *Aix en Bains*.

Inside the bathroom I was surprised to find an intricate jungle gym of handrails around the shower and the toilet, in stainless steel etched with non-slip cross-hatching. How did this stuff get here? Then I remembered the workmen who had arrived, barely a week before the end, to install it. 'Tarzan of the Dunny', Leon had called himself. At least they had not touched Leon's decorations. The word *Aix* was still painted in a deep jungle green on the door of the medicine cabinet above the sink, and *Bains* in large orange letters on the wall above the bath.

Returning to the entrance I found a wad of letters on the table beneath the mirror, held together by a rubber band. I picked them up and began to thumb through them as I stepped towards the living room. And stopped. I rested my hand on the door frame and pulled myself through.

The photograph of Leon hung on the wall opposite, where my daughter had said she would put it before she returned to London. It was the one he liked best. A studio shot, head and shoulders, in monochrome to give it a timeless show-biz aristocracy look, chin resting upon his knuckles, an air of bemused self-confidence that everyone knows to be very far from the truth. He said his face reminded him of a large crumbling cheese; but as I approached it now, and as the light in the room began to dim, what I saw in it was a cliff by the seashore – loose, clay-like skin (in the original, tinged pinky red), fissures running diagonally across his forehead, nests of mossy hair perched on crags and ledges around the ears and neck, and fleshy buttresses beneath his chin separating gorges choked with a scree of distressed skin and tufts of looping grey hairs. On top of his head the hair retreated unevenly sideways and back into a wiry thicket, slanting upwards and to the right, like a juniper thrown about by windy blasts.

'Simultaneously the *eminence grise* and the *enfant terrible* of the theatre world,' the newspaper had said. Stepping nimbly from lighting director at the Opera in Paris to set designer at the Deutsches Theater in Berlin, and then returning home 'with his Chinese wife and growing family' to establish himself as a director, producer and eventually godfather to a theatrical generation, he was for the most part loved, but not without his rivals and detractors. Known for his generosity, especially to puckish young talent (from whom he selected Sascha, living with her for three years before returning to his wife as his health failed), but also for his temper, his irrationalities and his obsessions.

Yes, I thought when I read the piece: his irrationalities, his friable edges, and his inner core of hardness. The article concluded with the simple phrase, 'after a short illness'.

I passed by the photograph and went to the kitchen, where I made myself a pot of Yellow Mountain Famous Tea and set it on the coffee table, along with one ceramic cup. I sat down facing the window and the view of the darkening harbour. I turned on the lamp by the couch and its stained-glass shade coloured the ceiling above me with a soft patchwork quilt of reds and blues. Streams of vapour rose like a dancer's hands from the teapot.

Memory is a weight, but also an anchor. I recalled the puckish actresses, and also (discreetly omitted in the paper) the puckish actor, Perry, upon whom, for a period of several years, Leon bestowed roles he did not deserve and did not carry off. But these were also the years of our happiness – the children, the holidays camping by southern lakes, the opening night parties on our lawn, fuelled by 'cuvées' Leon created by pouring the contents of several half-full bottles into one, and by late night jazz standards played on the piano, with Leon producing our daughter's violin and scraping out a rendition of 'Oh, Shenandoah', to which our guests would all sing 'away, you rolling river', after which we would make our bed on cushions pulled from the couch, with a child or two beside us, and other sleeping forms around us like a colony of seals wrapped up in newspapers and blankets and coats, my back nuzzled into Leon's warmth, his arm over my side, lazily caressing my nipple between thumb and forefinger or, with his palm, cupping the new child within me.

A friend of Leon's in Paris, a curator's bagboy, had explained to me that sometimes a sculptor chips away incessantly at a piece of work until it slips beyond art and becomes unfinishable, and useless for anything except to instruct students. Such, I thought many times, was my husband.

He is everywhere; unfinished, and unfinishable.

*

I took up the pile of letters in order to break the spell of my reverie. The first was from my eldest daughter Miro, my dark jewel, now back in England with her fiancé and their children.

Are you all right now? she began. *Silly question, I know; as if you could be all right, this soon after, but you know what I mean. Here are the photographs of Bella I promised you. Isn't she fine? Rosa and Antonio are being very helpful with the children, and, as promised, we are keeping them on a short leash – only one rave per weekend! They are turning heads over here, you know – twins, hybrid vigour, androgynous good looks, and so on. I promise I will bundle them onto a plane soon and you will have them back before their term starts.*

I studied the photographs she had enclosed, lingering on the composition of my new granddaughter's face – a mat of dark hair, whispers of eyebrow, a tiny fluted nose, and wine-dark lips – and recognised, with a sudden moistening of my eyes, the outline of my own face from photographs more than fifty years old, photographs that I kept pressed between sheets of translucent paper in an album in my desk.

And now to the meat of this letter (although Miro is a vegetarian her letters always contain meat) . . . and she went on to explain the situation, aided by a clipping from a London newspaper. A dispute between Sotheby's and the Chinese government, no less, over a rare violin which the Chinese claimed had been stolen from their embassy in Paris in 1965, and which had resurfaced in the estate of a yachtsman in the Channel Islands. There was even some talk of the new Russian government claiming it, citing records that had it in the possession of the Romanovs. She had taken the liberty of registering my interest in it, she wrote. She knew I would not mind.

Colin thinks we should press our case. He's away from dawn until about 8pm most days, and he's travelling a lot, mostly to The Hague, so he thinks it will help me to have something to work on once the twins are back with you. He hates the thought of me vegetating around the flat with two children, doing coffee mornings and playgroups – he says that's the slippery slope towards macramé(!) and other such horrors. He says he'll help with the law if he can, but that I can handle the research side of things and the media. He even suggested you should fly over and be here in person! How things change!

Colin had put her in contact with one of the junior partners in his firm. And she had talked to a journalist friend, who thought it would make a great story, and was eager to interview me as soon as I returned from the beach house, in particular to ask me about the precise circumstances of the theft of the violin, and whether I had any insight into how it found its way to the Channel Islands. Sotheby's were being tight-lipped – the public interest might increase the price at auction, but they wanted to avoid a protracted legal battle over provenance.

I recalled a previous conversation with Miro about my failure to capitalise on my history. 'The whole field is opening up,' she had said. 'There are wild swans everywhere, calling out to each other from the mist, getting rich, being glorious.' Enmeshed in my satisfying, ordinary life, I had demurred.

'Who now remembers Khrushchev's visit to Beijing in 1959?' I replied. 'Or the performance he attended at the Great Hall of the People? Or the music played on that occasion? Or who played it? I don't even merit a footnote. Nowadays we think Chinese history started with the Cultural Revolution. Nothing that went before holds any interest. Has anyone even heard of the Sino-Soviet rift? No, and those that have probably think it's an earthquake fault or a mountain range in Siberia. And yet it was so important at the time: Russia and China screaming at each other, throwing plates, and half the world caught up in the dispute, the fist-shaking and table-thumping, and the troop trains heading north to the borders, and the bombers on standby. But now even that's just a footnote. No one remembers, and if they did, would they care? All they want to hear about is struggle sessions and Red Guards waving little red books – city kids, amateurs, thugs – not serious revolutionaries like my parents.'

'You care, don't you?' Miro had said.

'It's my duty to care, just as back then it was my duty to perform for communism's mother and father the last time they held hands and pretended everything was still all right. But that doesn't mean I have to write a book about it.'

'It must mean something more than just duty,' she said. 'What if they'd patched up their differences? Would that have made a difference to you?'

'I guess the moderates in China would have been strengthened and they might have acknowledged the disaster of the Great Leap Forward, and twenty million Chinese might have been saved by shipments of Soviet wheat.'

'That's worth caring about, isn't it?'

'Not entirely. With the Russians as friends, Mao and Lin Biao might have got the bomb sooner than they did. They might have had it during the Cultural Revolution, and I shudder to think what that would have meant.'

'There's the story then: "How my violin and I stopped Mao getting the Bomb".'

'On the other hand, perhaps my performance hastened the downfall of the moderates, of Liu Shaoqi and Deng Xiao Ping, leaving them out in the cold for the next twenty years. But on the other hand . . .'

'That's your third hand,' Miro had warned.

'On my third hand . . . perhaps my performance strengthened Zhou Enlai and helped him to survive the Cultural Revolution.'

'Which meant . . .'

'. . . that Madame Mao and the Gang of Four couldn't get the support they wanted from the military, so that, when Mao died in 1976 . . .' I stopped mid-sentence, my train of thought lost.

'Is there a fourth hand?'

'Yes, and a fifth too, and a sixth. You can read it all in MacFarquhar's three-volume history, there on the shelf behind you. I could have a thousand hands, like that statue of Guan Yin at Chongqing.'

'I think you've made your point,' Miro said. 'It's like what they say – the flapping of a butterfly's wings in the Amazon can alter the course of a hurricane thousands of miles away. But if you were to trudge through the jungle, braving the rapids and the crocodiles, and find that particular butterfly in its particular tree, there's still the question of what to do with it. Do you crush it? Catch it? Chase it off in a different direction? Pin it to a wall?'

'China has never had any doubts about what to do with butterflies,' I said.

*

I steeled myself for her telephone call. (She is a meticulous keeper of promises.) We would no doubt replay the argument, and I wondered if I would lose my patience and produce the final ace from my pack, my final reason for keeping the silence: *I don't want to tell the story because we had to kill a man to escape. Listen to me, Miranda, your father and I had to kill a man. That was what I had to do to slip through the Great Chinese Wall, through which death is the only door – if not one's own*

351

death, then the deaths of others. And if the latter, don't they deserve now to rest?

At eight o'clock precisely the telephone rang. I remained in my chair, letting it echo through the house.

*

I spent the early 1960s in Paris at the Conservatoire, living in two rooms in a building inhabited by Chinese diplomats and their families. For the first year I was under instruction to enter any competition I could find, and I duly brought honour to China by amassing awards and trophies which were handed over to my superiors and which, as far as I am aware, still lie, boxed and labelled, in some archive in Beijing. Only with difficulty did I convince the ambassador that my participation in small competitions in modest industrial towns in Belgium and Czechoslovakia and Northern Italy was doing no favours for China's reputation abroad. Besides, my schedule was starting to fill up with invitations to play with more prestigious orchestras and conductors, and to perform alongside the inevitable touring ensembles of Chinese musicians and dancers, the advance guard of cultural diplomacy. On all of my travels I had an embassy minder; sometimes Ruan, if his linguistic skills (which I began to realise were somewhat third rate) were not required on other duties, and at other times the bored wives of first and second secretaries.

In Sofia on one of these occasions I found myself on the same bill as Maxim Shostakovich. We had time to exchange a few sentences, and I asked Maxim once again if he knew anything about his father's old friends, Kasimir and Piroshka. He told me that they had been detained in Moscow for a month. He believed his father may have had something to do with their eventual release, but could not say for sure. (They returned eventually to Leningrad, I learned years later, and lived with Vitja until his death in 1970, following him within a matter of months.) Ruan was by this time breathing down my neck, tapping my ankle with his toe to try to get me to break off the conversation, but

I stood my ground. Maxim said that his father had heard news of the performance of his concerto at the Tenth Anniversary Celebrations, and that he had been 'distressed'. But the word Maxim used was carefully chosen, signifying an affected distress, a kind of theatrical swoon. I repeated his phrase back to him, and he smiled and said to me, 'Well, to be frank, he was highly amused. The first he heard about it was when he was in Dresden composing a string quartet. He was shown a statement that had been prepared for his signature, denouncing China's corruption of his violin concerto. He jokes that he can perform his signature upside down, so that they do not need to turn around the papers they bring to him to sign. This letter has not been used, however, as no word of your concert has reached the foreign media. But he was very amused.'

'I am glad to provide him with something to laugh about,' I had said, somewhat annoyed.

'You did just that,' Maxim said. 'It came at a time when he needed very much to laugh. He said the quartet he was composing would 'bring his life to an end', and we were beginning to worry about him; but after he heard of your interpretation of his concerto his mood became lighter. Nothing delights him more than a good musical joke, *Ein musikalischer Spass*.'

*

On my return to Paris I began rehearsals for a live recording at the Palais Garnier. (The dog-eared LP, whose liner notes refer to my 'recent tragic death', has pride of place in my collection.) During a pause in the proceedings I heard a voice calling to me in Russian from above my head, and looked up to find a young man dangling from a rope amidst the lights. It was Leon. He belayed down to the stage and shook my hand solemnly, and then began to laugh, as if he had spotted something amusing about me that had escaped my notice, some faux pas in my choice of clothes or some stray grains of rice lodged in my hair.

'I'm the *deus ex machina* around here,' he said, leaning on his rope, and when I angled a curious glance at him he explained:

'The ghost in the machine.' Then he took up Jean-Baptiste Vuillaume from the open case beside me, placed it under his chin and started to play a jig, tapping his foot and eyeing me mischievously, daring me to stop him. Heads turned towards us from amongst the orchestra, and the conductor, who was off stage conversing with the sound engineer, glowered at me. I noticed Ruan, who had been watching from his seat in the third row, immediately spring to his feet and make his way up the aisle towards us, but before he reached the stage Leon had lowered the violin like a sleeping child into its velvet snug, called to someone in the gloom above us, hooked his foot into a loop at the end of his rope and begun his ascension into the chaos of cables and lamps and brackets behind the proscenium arch.

After the rehearsal Ruan and I walked down to the Seine once more, and checked out the bouquinistes. He seemed uninterested in talking, even the obligatory questions about the rehearsal to provide him with material to report to his superiors, should they care to ask. He selected a book, in fact a set of three small volumes with a photograph of a dark, moustachioed man on the cover, and we retired to the nearest café. We drank our coffee and Ruan absorbed himself in the first of his volumes while I, for lack of anything better to do, took out my score and began to review the notes I had scribbled in its margins.

A shadow fell over our table, and I heard a familiar laugh and looked up to see Leon silhouetted against the afternoon sun. Behind his shoulder, clouds scurried like rats across the pale blue sky. Once more he had detected something indefinably amusing about us. 'Well, well, well, who do we have here?' he said, first to Ruan, in French, and then to me, in Russian. We said nothing, but without asking Leon sat down, examined one of Ruan's books and, laughing once more, explained, again first in French and then in Russian, that he had started to read it some years ago, that it was very good, but that he had not got beyond the first fifty pages. 'Nothing happens,' he said. 'And then his mother kisses him goodnight. And then nothing happens again. And again.'

The waiter approached and Leon ordered another round of coffees and started to tell us about his job at the Opera, and about my old teacher, who had settled once again into a despondent hibernation in a distant arrondissement. Every sentence was laboriously rendered in both languages. I told him that my comprehension of the French language had improved, even if my attempts to speak it were halting. However, he insisted upon this exhausting process, and I soon understood why, for the two strands of conversation began to part company, although Leon was careful to maintain the same tone of voice. And eventually, after telling Ruan something about French politics he turned to me, gave me a précis in Russian, and added, without skipping a beat, 'Come with me to Montmartre tomorrow, and I will paint your portrait.'

'You know I can't do that,' I replied. 'What you are asking me to do is not permitted.'

He 'interpreted' my response for Ruan, using the word '*socialisme*' twice, and then turned to me again. 'Surely you know you can trust me,' he said. 'Have you suffered at all from our last outing? Does your friend here even know about it? We already have one little secret – why not one more?'

At that moment our coffees arrived, along with three more pastries. Leon handed the waiter a banknote folded lengthwise into a V-shape, and, after a mutual round of eye contact – not unlike those I would share with Tian and Ling Ling the moment before we began to play the first note of a trio – we applied ourselves to drinking and eating. We barely spoke until we had finished and Leon had produced a book of matches and a packet of Gauloises. He tapped out three, handed them around, and lit them.

Leon turned to me, held his cigarette side-on and pointed to it as if he were about to explain its origin. 'Remember I am a Communist too. I am named after Trotsky.' He then turned to Ruan, once again holding up his cigarette for examination, and said something in French.

While Leon was talking, a pair of sparrows landed on the

adjacent table. One flew off immediately, but the other hopped across to our table and stood next to Ruan's cup. My eyes sought out Ruan's. He returned a gentle nod and his jaw settled to one side into a half smile as he lowered his cigarette to the ashtray and cupped his hands over his knee again, inches away from the bird. The sparrow took one crumb, then another, performing little jumps and jerkily rotating its head. I could see Ruan was watching it intently, although he continued to mutter polite acknowledgements to Leon. His breathing appeared to have slowed, as if he was clearing his mind. I waited for him to make his move.

Leon turned back to me, taking a drag on his cigarette. 'What is more, my father fought with the International Brigade in the Spanish Civil War,' he said. 'Under Colonel Belov at Albacete. You see? I have a pedigree you can trust.'

Ruan had still not moved. The sparrow jumped from side to side, eyeing the last crumb.

'What is the Spanish Civil War?' I said. 'And who is Trotsky?'

Ruan looked up at me and I saw his eyes widen a fraction. He turned back to the sparrow and then raised one hand and waved it away. In a feathery flash it was gone.

'If you wish, we can invite your friend here, as well,' Leon said, turning back to me. 'I see he is reading Proust. I can take you to see Proust's apartment, or if you wish to the restaurants he frequented in the Bois de Boulogne. He may enjoy that better.'

I placed my hand on Leon's and held up my palm to signal him to stop talking. I turned to Ruan and said, in Chinese, 'He wants to take us to a place called Montmartre, to a café he says is much better than this one, with live jazz music and exotic French delicacies we will not have tasted.'

Ruan raised his eyebrow.

'And he would like to paint your portrait, or perhaps he means he knows an artist there who will paint your portrait, as a memento of your time in Paris. I am not entirely sure which he means.'

Ruan looked at Leon, who smiled uncomprehendingly.

'He will tell nobody about this, and besides what harm could there be? He may even reveal something of use to you, if indeed he is spying on us, as you once believed. We could get him drunk and see what comes out. What do you think?'

*

The sky was darkening when we stepped from the metro into the heart of Montmartre. Leon grabbed my hand and I in turn took Ruan's and together we rushed through the narrow streets, weaving like a needle and thread between the lovers and the bohemians and the American tourists. As we arrived at the steps of the Basilica the sun, or at least its yellowish thumbprint, was smearing itself against the western skyline. 'Just in time,' Leon announced, as he drew us all into a line along the lip of the plaza, as if our next act would be to raise our clasped hands in triumph and to make a deep bow to acknowledge the silent applause from the retreating light. Instead Ruan and I released our hands and, as if to reestablish our separate identities, wandered apart a half a dozen steps and caught our breath.

'Let's go inside the Basilica,' Leon said, in my ear. 'Quick, before they close the doors.' He took my hand again and pulled me towards entrance of the sanctuary. I waited until we were halfway up the steps and then turned and called to Ruan to follow. He hurried after us, breaking into a light canter, as fast as he could go without breaching diplomatic decorum. This left me enough time to whisper to Leon that he should mollify Ruan with a few tidbits that would pass as state intelligence.

'Something about De Gaulle or Kim Philby,' I said. 'But nothing obviously fabricated.' Leon gave out a short grunt, which at first I thought indicated understanding and assent, until I noticed that a grey-haired woman of stern regard was firmly shutting the door to the Basilica, aided by a lanky youth in a button-up jacket with a long chain of keys drooping from his belt like a tinkling shirt-tail.

'*Merde*,' Leon muttered. And then louder, 'Damn! *Govno*! *Scheisse*!' The woman wagged a bony finger to and fro in front of us, like the wind-screen wiper on a car, and mouthed '*fermé*'. And that was that.

Ruan joined us, and we retired to a café where, with no more than a wave of his hand, Leon ordered a carafe of red wine and three glasses. Ruan watched the waiter fill each glass and then announced that neither of us would be drinking it, and ordered mineral waters. Leon poured two of the glasses back into the carafe, and smacking his lips, embarked upon the remaining glass. In the corner a pair of musicians, an accordionist and a violinist, tuned up wheezily and embarked upon a repertoire of slow reels. The accordionist was very fat, with stubby legs and a red face, and from our vantage point across the café I had the impression that the vigorous movements of his meaty hands were in fact intended to stop his sagging torso from collapsing onto the floor.

'That accordion player bears a slight resemblance to Nikolai Podgorny,' Leon said to Ruan, in French. Ruan glanced at me and I pretended I had not understood. 'I once met him, you know,' Leon went on. 'Podgorny, I mean. He was a great friend of the New Zealand legation in Moscow. Used to come for a drink or dinner every few months, and to ask us to act as go-betweens with the major powers. You know, to convey delicate messages to the Brits or the Yanks rather than lose face by saying it direct. Gentle regrets, apologies, offers to trade captured spies, that sort of thing.'

'Interesting work, I imagine,' Ruan said.

Leon nodded and said, 'Let's go somewhere else.' And throwing some francs onto the table he seized my hand again and we were off.

Somewhere else turned out to be a crowded bistro, where Leon ordered three *plats du jour* and as we ate he engaged Ruan in a conversation about the jazz greats each had heard over the years in Paris, a subject in which Ruan appeared surprisingly expert – Art Blakey at the Club Saint-Germain, Jimmy Smith at Le Caveau de la Huchette, Wes Montgomery, Lionel Hampton, Louis Armstrong . . .

'And Nikolai Podgorny?' Ruan said, folding up his napkin and placing it beside his empty plate.

Leon held a finger against his lips and glanced furtively around him. 'The walls have ears,' he said. 'Come with me, I have something to show you.'

We took the metro to the Latin Quarter, to a bar Leon said had just opened. We were shown to a table at the back, far from the stage, and Leon and Ruan each took turns at talking into the other's ear, with Ruan scratching notes with a pencil on the flyleaf of his volume of Proust. Presently the band made its way to the stage, accompanied by enthusiastic hooting and whistling from around the room. It was a quartet of black men in dark suits and thin ties, led by a pianist in a furry hat and a goat's beard. Ruan's jaw dropped and he placed his hand on top of Leon's to stop him talking. Their eyes met.

'Yes,' said Leon matter-of-factly. 'One night only.'

Ruan summoned a passing waiter and ordered red wine, ignoring my censorious glance. He closed the volume of Proust and placed his hands over it protectively, and then gave himself over to the music, barely acknowledging my presence for the next two hours as he breathlessly followed the movements of the hatted pianist. It was an odd performance. The man seemed not so much to play his instrument as to taunt it like a cat with a mouse. He would glare at the keyboard, stabbing at groups of keys with his fingers, rubbing his palms together as if to warm them, and waiting until the last moment to embark upon long phrases of melody which seemed then to be left hanging, whereupon he would feign a double-take as if to say to the piano, 'Is that all you can do?' From time to time he would get up from his seat and, repeatedly wiping his face with a cloth, would wander over to the drummer or the saxophone player and complement their solo turns with a shuffling dance to all points of the compass, jerking his arms up and down like a marionette. The audience hooted and clapped.

During the final set Leon announced that he had to leave us for a short while to use the telephone. 'So do you think our friend a fraud?' I asked Ruan. 'Has he told you anything useful or is he just making it up?'

'Why would he?' Ruan said.

'For the pleasure of our company, perhaps.'

'Perhaps. Is our company that pleasant for him?'

'It seems to be the case. What will you do next with this information?'

'You are not permitted to ask such questions,' Ruan said angrily, and then his face softened into a smile and he put his volume of Proust away in his pocket. 'Let's go. We owe this man nothing, and I have no authority to undertake espionage, other than a general obligation to keep my ears open.' He took out some bank notes and placed them under a tumbler on the table. 'If he has anything to offer us I'm sure he will be in touch.'

The next morning an envelope was delivered to my lodgings, and as I collected it from the concierge the telephone on her desk rang. It was Ruan. 'You'll be interested to know I have done some research,' he said. 'Our friend claims he was attached to the New Zealand legation in Moscow, but it was closed down in 1950. There is no New Zealand representative in Moscow.'

'That settles it then,' I said.

'Yes, I suppose it does,' Ruan said, and added, 'I have not felt it necessary to inform my superiors about this.'

I let the silence continue for ten or twenty seconds, listening to Ruan's breathing on the line. 'Very well,' I said at last. 'If that's your judgement then I won't inform my superiors either.'

Ruan laughed softly. I rang off, and opened the envelope. Inside was a sketch folded neatly into quarters.

*

I still have the portrait Leon drew of Ruan and me, on a sheet of thick paper using a wedge of charcoal clutched awkwardly between his fingers and thumb. We are seated outside a café on a cobblestoned street, with the monstrous blancmange of the Basilique du Sacré-Coeur looming over us. Ruan holds a book in one hand, upon whose spine one can just make out the word 'fugitive', and is coolly examining the cigarette in his other hand. I am leaning forward over a musical score, pencil stub in hand, but am gazing directly at the artist with an intensity that could be either anger or curiosity. Even after thirty years I cannot say which.

*

Winter arrived in Paris and, confined indoors at the embassy compound, I noticed how the talk amongst the diplomatic staff turned more to the strange political goings-on back home. It was clear that a split had developed amongst the Party leadership. The circle of comrades who traced their pedigree to the Long March and beyond, who had liberated China from the Japanese and fought off the Nationalists and their American backers, who had united the peasants and the military and the bourgeois and had summoned home a scattered generation of Chinese intellectuals from the four corners of the globe, that line of hardened revolutionaries my parents had seen atop Tiananmen in November 1949 had now split into several 'lines', like a piece of porcelain cracking under the strain of its years. Mao Zedong had disappeared from public view in November, shortly before his seventy-third birthday, and rumours abounded regarding his health and his whereabouts. In Beijing the Group of Five gained the ascendancy, led by Peng Zhen and Deng Xiao Ping, but their hold on power – in particular their power over the army – seemed tenuous, as if they were driving a truck whose steering column had come loose. Fissures appeared within our midst too, with a faction of incrementalists and a faction of revolutionaries contending within the embassy, shadowboxing in the corridors and doorways, trading insults and feints, concerning themselves not with the substance of any political argument, but with the nuances of each other's language, of whether by the choice of a word or a phrase one could unequivocally announce one's membership of one 'line' or another.

Mao's wife, Jiang Qing, appeared in Shanghai, refusing to be drawn upon her husband's whereabouts, and announcing

361

confidently that a struggle was brewing over culture, that art and form were now the battleground, rather than politics and economics. 'That sounds like a genteel form of combat,' I commented to Ruan. 'A war fought with pens and paper and musical instruments and calligraphy brushes.' Ruan looked at me askance. 'You of all people should know better than that,' he said. 'Snake poison may take days to kill you, but a poisonous ideology will do the job in minutes.' As if to illustrate his point, Ruan told me that Madame Mao had appointed Yu Huiyong as Chairman of the Shanghai Cultural Revolutionary Committee. It was also rumoured that the Shanghai Conservatory would soon be closed down. That was all he could say for certain. There were other rumours, but they had been contradicted, and Ruan did not want to perpetuate them. I asked him what else he had heard, about the Party leadership, about Liu Shaoqi and Deng Xiao Ping, but he shook his head and said, 'It is not for us to know, not yet, at least, and perhaps not ever. Surely you understand that by now.'

It was not until July that Mao reappeared, first in Shanghai and then famously in Wuhan, where he jumped into the Yangtse River and swam with the current for two hours, lecturing his entourage of supporters and peasants on the finer points of collectivisation. 'Just like in the Dumpling Baths incident,' I suggested to Ruan, but he claimed never to have heard of it.

Mao's swim in the Yangtse, like my father's in the Songhua, was a signal to those in the know that an elaborate series of traps was now primed and ready. In the weeks and months that followed, an old order was swept away. Ruan passed on to me the news from Shanghai as it came through. We learned that Ho Luting was humiliated by Yu Huiyong and imprisoned, that his wife and children were forced to criticise him, that one of his daughters committed suicide rather than take part. We learned that my friend Ling Ling had been exiled to a village in distant Gansu Province (where she would remain for more than a decade, forgotten, and forbidden from performing). We learned that the head of the department of piano, Fa Jilin, was beaten by her former students, and that the pianist Liu Shikun was sent to Taicheng Prison in Beijing. It would be years until all of the stories came out. Some never did, of course. I was pregnant with my twins before I learned what had happened to Tian Mei Yun, that he had gone home to Suzhou and gassed himself and his mother in their apartment.

Later that year I was in Turin performing a series of concerts, and had just finished a rehearsal of Beethoven's *Romances* in the concert hall when Ruan handed me a telegram from the embassy in Paris. I had been recalled to China, it said. Ruan told me that I was booked to travel that night from Turin to Vienna and then to Prague, where we would catch a plane.

'We?'

'I am to accompany you.'

'I need a bodyguard, do I?'

'I have been recalled too. No doubt Beijing has its reasons.'

I felt Ruan searching my face for some kind of clue, of what I wasn't sure. Nor was I sure what my face might be expressing. Apprehension? Resolution? Indifference? I found myself closing my eyes and saying, with a sense of vertigo, 'Can we not, for once, doubt Beijing's reasons?'

I kept my eyes closed, not wanting to see what Ruan's face might be registering. I wanted only to hear his words, sensing that they alone, stripped of all other impressions, would tell me whether I could trust him.

'It's true, one can always consider the alternative,' he said softly. 'But you know as well as I do that we are encouraged to behave as if we had no choice. At some point in the past, perhaps so long ago we cannot remember exactly when, we have made a decision not to have choice.'

'I don't recall doing that,' and I was about to add that, even if I had, I now wanted to reconsider. But I kept my thoughts to myself.

'Very few of us do recall,' Ruan said. 'But what is the alternative for you, anyway? Surely you recognise your situation. You are not simply a musician. You are in very deep. You know things, you carry secrets, you have . . . intelligence that may be of interest to the West.'

'What things?' I opened my eyes and looked sharply at him. 'What are you talking about?'

'I have read your file in full,' he said. 'I know what it was you were doing in Shanghai, and it is safe to assume that our hosts here know something of it too, and also our friends at the Soviet embassy. So if you throw yourself onto the mercy of the West they will want to know everything you know. And the Soviets will want to stop that happening, to shut you up.'

'Why would they . . .' I began, but certain truths about my life in Paris had begun to fall into place, like the tumblers in a lock.

'Imagine that China – the China for which we struggle – is not so much a country,' he said, 'as a game played on a vast chess board, and that it is not limited to sixty-four squares and thirty-two pieces, but involves a hundred million squares – two hundred million . . . so many they can hardly be counted – and millions upon millions of pieces, spread across every province, every corner of the Motherland and also across all of the continents: a chess game without borders. Here, as in Beijing or Shanghai or Harbin, there are games within larger games, in which the placement of each piece has its purpose and its significance, gives comfort to some and causes alarm to others. The players themselves are numerous and ever-changing, deploying their pieces for attack, for defence, for posturing, for threatening, and of course for sacrificing, and all for reasons that may become apparent immediately, or after another five moves, or ten, or a hundred, or remain hidden forever.'

'And I am a pawn?' I sighed. 'Is that all you are telling me? What a cliché! As if I didn't know that.'

'No, no, you are not a pawn; it is me that is the pawn,' Ruan said, tapping his chest. 'You are something more powerful; you, I would say, are a knight, since you can do things no other piece can. You are uniquely gifted, but that makes you uniquely troublesome and uniquely vulnerable. Your abilities make you a magnet for others – they make you valuable, and also dangerous.'

'And who are these players?' I asked.

'There are many players,' he said. 'Their number and identity changes all of the time. I don't know who placed you here or who has permitted you to stay so long in Paris. Perhaps it was the work of several people, perhaps unknown to each other, or even enemies to each other, but sharing a common interest in placing you here.'

'And now in recalling me.'

'Perhaps, but remember you have been here six years; the game has changed and the players have changed. You don't know who will be aided by your return, and who will be threatened, and what that will mean for you. You will have to find that out for yourself, if you can.'

'And you too? You will find out why you have been recalled?'

'That also is true. But let me say just one more thing, the only thing that one can say for sure about the players: that each of them is also a chess piece, is also in the game, is a part in the stratagems of others, knowingly or unknowingly. No one is outside of the game. That is the important thing to remember. Bring to mind the faces of our leaders, the members of the politburo. Do you not realise that each of them also stands alone upon his single foot of jade or bone, on a single square of black or white, vulnerable to attack from all points of the compass, and in particular from the blind-side attack of a knight?'

'Of a knight such as me?'

'A knight such as you.'

'I find that hard to imagine.'

'In that case it will not happen,' Ruan said. 'Those who survive do so by imagining. That is what I have always believed, but perhaps what I am telling you no longer applies. The reports from the Motherland make me fear that the rules have changed. Perhaps no stratagem can survive this new revolution that Madame Mao has called. All I can say is that if you fail to imagine yourself as having power, then you will be certain not to have it.'

'So what should I do?' I said. 'What will you do?'

I studied the glassy surface of Ruan's eyes, searching for a passage through them into his thoughts, trying to make him betray himself. I could see nothing.

'I will think,' he said. 'Think and strategise. My parents and my younger brother live in Chongqing, and because I am in the game it means they are too. So my advice to you is to think about your family, about your mother and what your actions may mean for her, your mother' – and here he hesitated for a fraction of a second – 'whose health is not good.'

'What do you know about my mother's health? Who told you? What have you heard?'

Ruan held up his palm towards me to calm me. 'Let me be completely frank,' he said. 'I was advised that, if you resisted the idea of returning home, I should tell you that your mother is unwell and needs you. That is all I know.'

'So this may be a lie, a ruse to entice me back?'

Ruan was silent for a while, and then pulled his face into his sweet half-smile and said, with a note of triumph, 'See, you are already strategising. You are thinking like a player rather than a chess piece. You are already playing the game.'

In that moment I sensed that the world had changed, although I did not know quite how. I became aware of the space around us, the noise of people moving in the auditorium, the currents of cool air, the dark vault above us. 'I will think about my mother, then,' I said.

'Do,' he said. 'Our train leaves for Vienna at midnight, so we will go to the station immediately after the performance.'

*

My mind remained curiously restful in the hours before the concert. I thought briefly of my mother, but she soon faded from my mind. I returned to my hotel and packed my suitcase, and when we returned to the concert hall several hours later I stashed it alongside Ruan's in my dressing room. The curtain rose and I watched from the wings as the orchestra marched its way through a Bruckner symphony. Ruan was waiting with me, as he always did, to see me safely onto the stage before taking his seat in the auditorium.

'I've been thinking about what you said this afternoon,' I said to him, without facing him.

'You have? That's good.'

'And I have a proposal to make.'

'A proposal?'

'Quite literally.'

'Go ahead.'

'My proposal is that when we get to Prague we ask the ambassador there to marry us, before we set out for home.'

'To marry us? You and me?'

'Why not? There are times when a knight comes to realise that she needs a close ally, even if he is only a pawn. A knight and a pawn working together can be a strong combination.'

'I'm not sure I quite understand you.'

'You surprise me. I thought you would understand perfectly.'

'That a knight needs a pawn? Yes, I can understand that – although the pawn might seem to have the greater need.'

'Be that as it may,' I said, 'the important thing is . . . it counts as a move in the game, an act of imagining, a way of taking the initiative.'

'I see. You are thinking that if we arrive home and announce that we are married then it would, at the very least, put some people off their stride.'

'I'm sorry if this all seems . . . dispassionate and cold.'

'You don't need to apologise for that. If only more marriages began that way.'

'So you'll consider it?' I said. I turned to face him and took hold of the sleeve of his jacket, turning the buttons on his cuffs with my fingertips. His face was half in shadow, but I could see that he was blinking rapidly, making his own calculations, the nature of which was hidden from me, although frankly they were of no importance to me. 'Don't answer me now. I've got a performance to give. Wait until we're on the train to Vienna. We can discuss it then.' Very slowly I raised my hand to his cheek and touched his cool, damp skin. He took my fingers and drew them into his hands, and held them gently, but firmly, as I imagined he had held the sparrow.

'When did this idea occur to you?' he asked.

'I just thought of it.' I said. 'This very moment, as I was putting my suitcase in the dressing room alongside yours.'

'Well, I will consider your proposal,' he said. 'Very seriously, as it deserves.'

'While I'm playing you can think it through,' I said, and I opened the violin case on the table before me and lifted Jean-Baptiste Vuillaume into the half-light. 'And now let me be alone for a while. I have a performance to think about. We'll talk again on the train.'

I turned away from him, and heard his footsteps withdraw into the corridor behind me. Bruckner rolled onward like a heavy sea, and I allowed it to carry my thoughts in its swell for another half hour, whereupon, after the business of applauding and bowing and standing and sitting was concluded, I was summoned to the stage. I looked out into the auditorium. It was a full house, I had been told, but the footlights illuminated only the front few rows, where Ruan sat in his customary seat surrounded by the Piedmontese intelligentsia, glistening in their tuxedos and furs like a fringe of foamy breakers tumbling onto the filigreed carpet from out of the dark sea of humanity behind them. I nodded to the conductor and raised my bow; Beethoven's first *Romance* flowed steadily from my violin. After I had finished I bowed my head and felt the applause falling like a shower of rain upon my head, a light shower, it seemed to me, for some in the audience were clearly unsure if it was the done thing to applaud between two works that were, perhaps, of one piece.

When it had ceased I caught the conductor's eye once more and struck the first note of the second *Romance*. And although my audience heard me play Beethoven, in the key of F major, in some other part of my mind I had slipped through a wall, and was again playing Bach's double violin concerto, in the key of D minor. I felt once again the snaking presence of David Oistrakh's violin around mine, and then as the melody unfolded I stepped through a curtain into a timeless world where I was standing on a high ridge, and music was flowing past me and through me, pressing around my form like a cold wind rising up from a vast dark plain behind me, from a great abyss of feeling – my own, and that of my parents, and Kasimir and Piroshka and Dmitri Dmitrievich, and so many others with them – and the only outlet for that feeling was the curved soundbox of my violin, of Jean-Baptiste Vuillaume. I sensed that it was inexhaustible, that I could keep playing for my whole lifetime and it would never be spent. The music carried me forward, bar by bar, theme by theme, and I felt that I was playing something more than what either composer had written, something universal: the music of the turning world. But it was not endless, indeed, as Director Ho had said, music is not endless or infinite, but instead carries within itself the promise that once it has played itself out, no matter if it takes decades or centuries or millennia, it will resolve itself once more into silence. In that moment it occurred to me that if I ever spoke again with Director Ho I would tell him that I had fulfilled his wish for music and China, that I had played out in its fullness that vast but ultimately finite domain of melody and harmony. I would tell him that I had heard the song that the Emperor Huangdi had tuned his lyre to centuries ago in that high mountain glade, and that now I could, if he wished, restore the yellow bell pitch to China. For as my performance in Turin came to its end, I realised that I had heard the song of the phoenix as a young child without knowing what it was, that I had learned it by heart and carried it within me all these years. It was the simple note sounded by the bell on my father's bicycle, the new bell that he bought after his stroke, the key into which he would transpose all of his favourite tunes as he rode to work: the key of D, or D minor.

I lowered my arms and bowed my head, bathed in yellow light, holding Jean-Baptiste Vuillaume by its neck in one hand and my bow, sprouting several loose strands of horsehair, in the other. There was silence, and for a moment I thought that some miracle had occurred – that I would look up to find that my audience had aged thirty years during the quarter hour of my performance and were now staring, dumbstruck, at the wizened skin of their hands and faces. But in the next moment I was enveloped by a waterfall of noise, a roaring column of bright light and sound that weighed down upon my head and shoulders and obliterated all sense. I felt the air compress me from all sides, forcibly emptying my lungs, and, finding myself unable to breathe, I ran from the stage and leaned against a wall, gasping. Then I felt a cool breeze behind me, and turning around saw an open fire-door at the end of a short corridor. It led out onto the adjacent alleyway, and I saw through a stone arch onto an empty piazza whose cobblestones were carpeted in a luminous blue moonlight. I ran to my dressing room, laid my violin in its case, and put on my coat. I threw open Ruan's suitcase and was relieved to find two diplomatic passports, mine and his, lying on top of his folded clothes. I stuffed my passport into the pocket of my coat and picked up my violin and my suitcase. Then I turned back and seized Ruan's passport as well and made my way along the corridor towards the door.

The audience was getting restless. They had been clapping for several minutes, and yet I had not reappeared. It would surely be only a few more seconds before someone came looking for me. I turned and walked out into the alley.

*

I did not sleep during the journey to Marseille, nor on the train I caught from there to Paris. I did think of my mother, as Ruan had suggested, although no picture of her came into my mind, nor any of the emotions that I expected to feel. What came to my mind was a disembodied voice (I was not even certain it was hers) repeating to me the proverb she had recited at the beach house near Shanghai the last time I had seen her:

Nu ren xin, hai di zhen.

A woman's heart, a needle at the bottom of the ocean.

*

I was the last passenger to disembark at the Gare de Lyon. I walked along the corridors from carriage to carriage, looking out of the windows at the people on the platform, trying to spot an official from the embassy or a member of the gendarmerie. I could see none, and no one tried to stop me as I descended from the train. I found myself on the steps of the station and realised I had nowhere to go. Clearly I could not go to the Conservatory. I had a few friends in the Paris music scene, but I had only ever visited them in the company of Ruan; he had their names and addresses, and since they had been sanctioned by the embassy I could not be sure they would protect me.

I decided it was best to lie low for a few days; so I checked into a small hotel on the Left Bank – not knowing how I was going to pay my bill, since Ruan allowed me very little money of my own, most of which I had spent on my train tickets – and stayed in my room all day, dreading every footstep on the stairs. I only ventured out at night to find food. I knew that Leon worked at the Opera at nights, so after a few days I thought I would find a vantage point nearby, and wait there until the evening's performance was finished and try to spot him leaving for home, wherever that was. I found a place behind a pillar on the building opposite the staff entrance, wrapped a coat around myself and waited. I don't know what happened on the first night. Perhaps he wasn't working, or perhaps I fell asleep at the wrong moment. But he was there on the second night, and left with a friend at around eleven o'clock. I checked to see that no one was following them, and then shadowed them to a tiny bistro a couple of blocks away.

I stood outside in the cold for a while, wondering if I should go in. Would they know I was missing? What were their loyalties? I felt sure Leon would help me, but who was the other man? I decided to go in. I decided not to have any choice. The place was dimly lit, and almost empty. Leon noticed me immediately, and he waved to me and beckoned me to his table. He introduced his friend as Thierry, the stage manager, and invited me to dine with them. We ate together and for an hour neither of them said a word about what I was doing there. We talked about Paris and New Zealand and China, with Leon translating my Russian into French for Thierry, and I learned a great deal about Leon: that his first job in Paris had been as an electrician at the Moulin Rouge; that his father was a noted artist in his home country; and that, despite being a Protestant, he attended Mass every week at Notre Dame de Paris. (I remember Thierry objecting strongly to this. 'Ach, to waste the body of Christ on heretics who presume to drink his blood!' he proclaimed with a snort. I asked for an explanation and both of them looked at my puzzled expression and then at each other. Leon began to explain to me the doctrine of transubstantiation, how the wafer and wine were transformed into Christ's flesh and blood by the prayer of the celebrant, but he had not got very far when Thierry leaned over and drunkenly kissed him on both cheeks, saying, '*Je vous salue, mon frère, pleine de grâce.*' And Leon patted his stomach and said, '*Pleine de grasse*, you mean.')

Then Leon ordered some brandy, and as he poured some into a glass for me he said, 'You're running away, aren't you?' Without waiting for a response, he turned immediately to Thierry and poured him a glass, whispering, '*Elle veut echapper.*' And Thierry said '*En effet?*' and looked at me with eyes wide in excitement.

'Yes, I'm trying to,' I said, 'but I need some help.' So the three of us discussed my situation right there in the bistro, as the staff closed up the kitchen and set the tables for the next day's lunch, and started to turn out the lights. Thierry wrote down the name of an uncle and aunt in Brittany who he was sure would harbour me for as long as I wanted. They had been in the resistance during the war, he explained, and could not turn away anyone who was hiding from authority. I don't know how serious the plan was, but Leon took down the directions to their farm and assured me he would get me there within twenty-four hours.

Then we walked to my hotel. Thierry lived in a street just beyond it, so he accompanied us most of the way. The concierge was not very happy to see me bringing a man up to my room at one-thirty in the morning, but Leon waved a small white name card in front of her face and muttered, '*Sécurité diplomatique*' and she let us pass. I asked him why he did that, and he said he had seen it in a movie. I looked at the card in his hand. On it was printed the name of my violin teacher with the crest of the Paris Conservatoire. When we got to my room, I started packing my things. I asked Leon if he trusted Thierry not to call the police, and he said, 'I don't think it matters now.' I looked up to find him at the window, looking down onto the street below. 'I think our friend from the embassy has been following us.' And sure enough, there was Ruan standing under a lamp-post looking up at the hotel. As we watched, he crossed the street towards us. 'Keep the chain on the door,' Leon said, and he slipped out of the room.

I waited for a few minutes, listening for the noise of some kind of fracas downstairs. But nothing happened. Then there was a gentle knock on the door, and, thinking it was Leon, I opened it, leaving the chain on. It was Ruan.

'Welcome back to China,' he said, pressing his weight against the door.

'But there's still a chain between us,' I said, pushing back, 'and I have decided to go away.'

'Where to?' he said.

'Anywhere that isn't the centre of the universe,' I said.

I could see only half of Ruan's face. His cheek was flushed and his eye was watery, and for a moment I thought he might offer to help me escape. He had come alone, after all, and would not by himself have been able to manhandle me back to the embassy.

'But you are in danger, Comrade,' he said. 'Don't you realise who' – and at that his eyes turned up into his head and he slumped against the door, his face sliding down the crack until he was jerked away from behind, and I heard a series of thumps as he fell onto the carpet of the landing.

When I opened the door Leon was down on his knees beside Ruan. In one hand he held a Parisian cobblestone. 'I got him! I got him!' he was saying excitedly. Then he appeared to embrace him, putting his ear to Ruan's chest to make sure he was breathing. 'He's alive, thank God,' Leon said, 'but he's out cold. It'll be at least an hour before he wakes up.' I didn't ask Leon how he knew that. I guess he had seen it in a movie too.

We left Ruan in the hallway and made our escape, walking briskly down towards the Seine, arguing about which station the trains for Brittany left from. I could tell from the spring in his step that Leon was delighted to be running away with an exotic woman, and, I have to say, a part of me was delighted to be the exotic woman he was running away with. The other part of me felt guilty, because I was running away from my responsibility to the masses, to my people, to my mother, and yet, like Xian Xinghai in the movie, my body felt lighter, as if I had somehow stepped through into a world where gravity was lessened. The burden that had weighed on me like a cloak of lead since I was a child had been removed, and now I was able to float unencumbered into the air.

Then, as we were starting to cross the Pont Neuf, there were some footsteps behind us and Leon went sprawling forward onto the road. It was Ruan again. He pounced onto Leon's back and began hitting him (like a diplomat rather than a spy, I suppose, because Leon easily managed to shake him off), and the two of them struggled and punched while I, to my shame, picked up my suitcase and my violin and stood there watching. They rolled across the flagstone footpath, more like overgrown schoolboys playing rough than a representative of the East wrestling with a representative of the West for the privilege of walking away with me. I stood over them as they fought wordlessly, and I remember vignettes from amidst the blurry soup of their bodies and coats: Ruan's fingers splayed out across Leon's cheek; Leon seizing Ruan's belt buckle and hoisting him off the ground; and one of Ruan's shoes skittering into the gutter and coming to rest upside down in a puddle, from which I immediately rescued it. A taxi swung its headlights around a nearby corner and paused momentarily, casting onto the bridge's solid handrail the flickering shadows of the two men, which then merged into a single shadow flighting with itself. I waited for the sound of car doors opening, of shouts, of offers of help, but nothing came. The taxi turned away. I remember thinking to myself, 'Maybe I should try to stop them; maybe Ruan actually wants to help; maybe he believes Leon wants to harm me.' And before I did anything with my thoughts the two men struggled to their feet and split asunder. I rushed forward and interposed myself and we became a six-legged animal – pushing against each other, hip grinding on hip, arms and fists swinging, fingers clutching, swaying together, slamming against the stone rail of the Pont Neuf – and then . . . I was falling through space, with Ruan beside me, the air rushing past my face and reaching its cold fingers into the crevices of my clothing like a pickpocket. I landed with my hips on something soft and my shoulder on something hard and flinty, and rolled face first into the river. The cold was shocking. The water enveloped my legs and torso, pulling me into the flow. My hands closed around a large flat rock which wobbled under my weight, and I looked up to the riverbank. Leon was racing down the steps towards me, carrying my violin and suitcase. He put them down on the tow-path, stepped into the water and clasped my right hand. As he pulled me up onto dry land a pain shot through my arm and into my shoulder and my chest. I collapsed onto the embankment unable to breathe until I rolled onto my left side. Leon was standing above me. 'Oh, Christ!' I heard him say.

Ruan had fallen face-down. His legs were in the water, but his upper half was on a broken slab of concrete that sloped down into the river. I couldn't see any movement. Then, as his clothes became waterlogged, the river started to tug Ruan into its flow. Fraying ropes of water wrapped themselves around his limbs and torso; I saw the water turn him over, open his raincoat and pull at his shirt, then one arm went under and he slipped sideways and disappeared. Leon jumped into the river, plunged his hands into the water and caught hold of Ruan by the armpits, but he had no footing and the effort of pulling Ruan upwards simply drew both of them in deeper. Leon fell backwards and released his hold, and as the river pulled them both towards the faster water in the centre of the channel I saw Leon's arms flailing – whether to save himself or to reach Ruan I could not tell. Moments later they were both gone.

I got to my feet, seized my case and, with great difficulty and pain, positioned my violin under my left arm and began to run along the tow-path, scanning the surface of the dark river, calling out to Leon and Ruan. After a hundred metres or so I found Leon sitting on the riverbank with his head in his hands, moaning to himself repeatedly, 'Oh Jesus, oh shit.' I knelt down beside him. 'Oh Jesus, oh shit,' he said again.

I knelt beside Leon for several minutes, listening to him shivering and muttering his pointless little mantra under his breath. Then suddenly I was possessed by an idea. I opened my suitcase and took from it only my father's notebook and my pouch of letters, leaving the two diplomatic passports tucked amongst my clothes. I closed it again, swung my left arm back and threw the suitcase into the river. I pulled off my coat and my shoes and threw them in too. And I was about to throw Jean-Baptiste Vuillaume in, except Leon arose from his stupor and grabbed it from my hands.

'What are you doing?' he said.

'I'm faking my own death,' I said. 'I'm drowning myself in the Seine.'

I wrenched the violin case from his grasp, stepped into the river and released it into the flow, standing back and watching it float away, as one watches a child riding free for the first time on a bicycle. I watched it catch the water's first ridge, ride into a shallow trough, turn on its axis and spin gaily through one eddy and into another, and then finally skate out onto the powerful thrust of the river's core, where it wobbled and straightened and righted itself, and then gathered speed until it was lost from sight.

*

So my years of happiness began on a train bound for Nantes, sitting in wet clothes between two provincial matrons, fashioning for myself a makeshift sling for my sore arm, wondering if, like Kasimir's, it might be permanently damaged, and indeed embracing the notion of a wound that would end my playing days. (As it turned out I had suffered only severe bruising, and it was other circumstances that kept me from playing the violin for several years.) Leon sat opposite me in the train carriage, grinning from time to time. As for Ruan, they fished his body from the river the following morning, and found my empty suitcase and my coat and one shoe half a kilometre further downstream. We read about it in the papers once we were safely in Nantes with Thierry's uncle and aunt: 'Body identified as Chinese diplomat'. And then, the next day, 'Chinese violinist missing, feared drowned in Seine'. One paper speculated on some kind of crime of passion, a doomed affair between Ruan and me. Another had it on good authority that we were both trying to defect.

For the next year Leon and I lived as fugitives in the French provinces, working in small towns and on farms, moving frequently, enjoying the very act of surviving. We had our secret codes and emergency meeting places and our stashes of emergency cash. We rehearsed our alibis, invented histories and tragedies and comedies, and as our circumstances required that we pose as man and wife we became just that. I wish I could say that we uncovered some depth of emotion, but in the end it was only our shared knowledge that held us together.

I was pregnant with Miro when we gave ourselves up to a police chief in Lyon, who held us in the cells while he placed phone calls to Paris, then took our statements and, eyeing the lump at my belly censoriously, escorted us around the corner to the office of his cousin, a notaire, who duly married us. Somehow it emerged through discussions in Paris amongst diplomats and officials of various departments – discussions in which we took no part – that the obvious place for our child to be born was Berlin.

*

The clock said eight-forty. Miro would call again at nine o'clock. This has been our arrangement for years, to call every hour on the hour until a connection is made. I rose from my chair and took an LP from the shelf, Shostakovich's second piano concerto (too gushy, too beautiful to be by Shostakovich, one would think, unless there is some hidden code or purpose or message within it; even so I confess to liking it). I laid it on the turntable and lifted the needle arm carefully to position it in the shiny groove between the first and second tracks. As the music began to play I walked to the window and looked out over the city.

In the darkness the fronds of the Canary Island palms rattled for a moment and then fell silent. A ship was nosing its way silently into the inner folds of the harbour, lights hanging like magnesium flares from its dark flanks, and as the fronds shifted in the breeze they hid the ship for a while and then revealed it again, each time slightly closer to its destination.

Another plane sprang from behind Mount Victoria, and I found it strange that, despite all the power and fury of its engines, I could hear nothing other than the music in the room, the plane seeming to float through the air, propelled by the power of a piano and an orchestra. My thoughts floated with it. Music, I reflected, is indeed the language of doubt and of doubters. At least that was so during my era in China, when no other language was available to us.

I thought now of mythical birds, of the phoenix and the phoenix song. Of the phantoms that entrance us, that we try to grasp and to make our own, the elusive things that we must go to the mountain to find, that are passed from generation to generation through characters written with a fingertip on the palm of a hand. I thought of the ten thousand planes between my father's finger and thumb, and of poor, sweet Ruan, sliding into the cold embrace of the Seine, and then, in turn, of my family and my friends, of the living and the dead. And as the hand of the clock moved towards the hour, I tried what I suspect most of us try to do on occasion: to assemble the life we have so far lived, and all the people we have known, into one harmonious sequence, a song unfolding in time – lost, found, and once again lost.

Acknowledgements

The Asia Foundation of New Zealand unwittingly planted the seed that grew into this book by awarding me a fellowship to study Mandarin in China in 1995. The Foundation's chief executive at the time, Peter Harris, arranged for me to be a visiting scholar at the Heilongjiang Academy of Social Sciences in the city of Harbin, where, he assured me, the dialect is pure, the people friendly and if any language other than Chinese is heard it is most likely to be Russian.

Although the main characters in the book are fictional, I have sought to create an accurate historical setting for them. Kyleigh Hodgson at Victoria University Press has worked assiduously to ensure that, although the central events in the plot did not happen, they could have happened more or less as described.

Readers are urged to explore the historical records for themselves. For those with time on their hands, Roderick MacFarquhar's three-volume work, *The Origins of the Cultural Revolution* (Oxford University Press, 1973–1997) is unparalleled, filling out the detail of the larger story told in works such as Jonathon Spence's *The Search for Modern China* (Norton, 1990), a copy of which came with me to Harbin. My major source for the fascinating story of classical music in China was *Rhapsody in Red: How Western Classical Music became Chinese*, by Sheila Melvin and Jindong Cai (Algora Publishing, 2004).

The life of Dmitri Shostakovich, and in particular his attitude towards the Stalinist regime and its cultural policies, has sparked vigorous debate, especially since the publication in

1979 of Solomon Volkov's *Testimony*, which purported to be Shostakovich's memoirs 'as related to and edited by' Volkov. My Shostakovich clearly owes a great deal to Volkov, and to other writers who have portrayed a composer at odds with the state apparatus that ruled his life. For those who want the facts without the polemic, I would recommend Ian MacDonald's *The New Shostakovich* (Pimlico, 2006).

Finally I am immensely grateful for the advice and encouragement provided by Bill Manhire and Kathryn Walls of Victoria University, the late Nigel Cox, and my classmates in the International Institute of Modern Letters Masters in Creative Writing at Victoria University in 2002.

A note on the pronunciation
of Chinese words

Throughout the text I have used the Pinyin system of romanisation to render Chinese words into English. This is the system used in mainland China, and while it is generally easy for English speakers to use, some of its more difficult renderings come up frequently in the novel and merit some explanation.

- The letter 'X' is pronounced as a very light 'sh' sound. Thus, the protagonist's surname, Xiao, is pronounced 'Shee-ow', and the name of the Chinese composer Xian Xinghai is pronounced 'Shee-an Shee-ing-high'.
- The letters 'Zh' – as in Zhou Enlai and Zhu Shaozen – signify a soft 'j' sound, as in the French 'je', but with the tongue resting on the roof of the mouth.
- The letter 'Z' by itself (as in Mao Zedong) is pronounced 'dz'.
- The letter 'C' (as in Feng Cean) is pronounced 'ts'.
- Finally, in case the reader needs to be reminded, Chinese names begin with the surname, followed by one or more given names, which are sometimes run together as a single word in English.

The Director of the Shanghai Conservatory, Ho Luting, is a special case. Pinyin would normally render his surname as He, pronounced 'her'. However, to avoid confusion with the English pronoun 'he' I have opted to use Ho instead, following in this one instance the Wade-Giles romanisation system commonly used in Hong Kong, Taiwan and Singapore.